MW00331520

THE SHADOW RIDER

A CROOKED PIECE OF TIME

Dave Dragon

Copyright © 2010-2014 – One Asterisk Publishing

All rights reserved. Without limiting rights under the copyright reserved above, no part of this publication may be reproduced, stored, introduced into a retrieval system, distributed or transmitted in any form or by any means, including without limitation photocopying, recording, or other electronic or mechanical methods, without the prior written permission of the publisher, except in the case of brief quotations embodied in critical reviews and certain other noncommercial uses permitted by copyright law. The scanning, uploading, and/or distribution of this document via the Internet or via any other means without the permission of the publisher are illegal and are punishable by law. Please purchase only authorized editions and do not participate in or encourage electronic piracy of copyrightable materials. Thank you for your support of the author's rights.
For permission requests, email One.Asterisk.Publishing@gmail.com or write to the publisher at the address below.

One Asterisk Publishing
35595 U.S. 19 N., #3335
Palm Harbor, FL 34684

ISBN: 0615980333
ISBN 13: 9780615980331

DEDICATION

For my family, friends and loved ones.
- Dave Dragon, The Shadow Rider – A Crooked Piece of Time

ACKNOWLEDGMENTS

The author expresses his heartfelt gratitude for the help he received in the creation of this book. The following individuals all contributed their time and energies in numerous ways, allowing the author to remain focused and move forward with this project:

Linda & Phil Stokes, Suzy Holsomback, James Langley, Jori Golden, Raffy Kouyoumdjian, Cheryl Plaza, Steve Rowe, Chris Steffens, Rita Deringer, John Steffens, Sue Molennor and Durango.

A special thank you, to Dr. Diego Feldmann Hernandez, Psy.D, for releasing me from the frozen grip of P.T.S.D., using the breakthrough A.R.T. (Accelerated Resolution Therapy), and The Camaraderie Foundation for their unwavering support of America's Veterans.

Thank you all.

1

Standing stone-like in the shadow of the darkened doorway at five a.m., Louis Parker embraces the silenced Walther P-22 with his right hand, concealed behind his leg. He scans the quiet street, ensuring there will be no witness in the still darkness.

His next victim is alone, out for his early morning stroll, now in range, but unaware of the menacing presence of one of Death's most effective agents.

The Walther is perfect for a head shot at close range, a specialty of Louis', honed to perfection since the days when he acquired his tradecraft.

Louis silently steps out from the shadows raising the pistol, taking precise aim at his target, instinctively placing his right thumb against the back of the slide to prevent the shell casing from being ejected.

Willfully drawing a slow, deep breath while taking one step closer, he relaxes, closes his left eye, stopping all motion except for his trigger finger, and ever so gently squeezes off the round.

With a muffled hiss, the bullet pierces its target's body at the top of the spine, just below the base of his skull.

In an instant, his victim falls motionless to the ground, his motor control abruptly switched off by the impact and penetration of the high velocity hollow point.

Louis immediately draws the pistol down behind his leg and again scans the street for witnesses before taking another step closer to his mark.

Towering over his conquered victim, he places his left hand over the ejection port of the Walther and jacks a new round into the chamber, capturing the warm spent shell casing, along with the essence of burnt gunpowder.

Once more, Louis takes precise aim at the back of the motionless skull lying at his feet, and taps him a second time, to be sure–always the professional.

Tripping the safety, Louis slides the pistol into his belt below his shirt and squats next to the blood-oozing corpse, lying prostrate in the front yard of the quiet suburban home.

A calmness settles over him in the afterglow of the close-in kill, seasoned by the years of practice, growing the body count, now too numerous for Louis to recall.

There is no adrenalin rush, no flight response to suppress, just the quiet confidence that accompanies a seasoned mechanic with Louis' training and experience.

With a satisfied grin, he lifts the dead armadillo by the tail and carries it across the moonlit street. As he swings the carcass into the retention pond, he's thinking, *Alligators have to eat too, and that's one less possum on the half-shell that'll be digging in my yard.* While meandering back across the street to his garage, the realization sets in. *I need to spray the yard with pesticide or the armor-plated bug plows will be back.*

Once inside the garage, Louis pulls the Walther from his belt and drops the magazine into his hand, ejects the second empty shell casing from the chamber, drops the hammer and replaces the magazine. *That leaves eight in the clip*, he thinks. *More than enough*, he assures himself while he places the two spent shell casings inside an empty Mountain Dew bottle sitting on the shelf above the trashcans, then flips the switch for the overhead light.

Louis continues packing his motorcycle for the road trip. The right side case of the BMW R1200GS Adventure stands open, ready to be filled. He reaches inside, trips the two levers that secure the false back, and opens the backing plate. This simple hiding place for his Walther and a few other choice weapons is lined with foam and separated into compartments to prevent vibration or damage to his expensive tools. He stashes the Walther with its silencer still attached and secures the hide, then loads the side case with raingear, a bike cover, an extra pair of sneakers and a box of burn gloves.

Louis carries his electronics in the bike's top case. The Netbook, Nikon digital camera and toiletries bag all fit here neatly, and he stashes his radar detector and GPS here when he is away from the bike for any length of time. In the left side case is his mesh riding jacket, extra riding gloves, basic toolkit, tire plugs and a 12V air-compressor for fixing flats that happen when you are in the middle of "a-freaking-nowhere", as Louis says. He lifts the waterproof duffel bag, packed with clothing, sitting it on the rear seat of the bike and strapping it down with bungee cords.

The duffel bag doubles as a backrest while riding, making the miles go by a little easier. Louis takes a small infrared detector from his workbench before turning the ignition switch to the accessory position, which powers up all the lights around the bike. He walks behind the motorcycle and flips the detector to the on position to verify the high output array of infrared LEDs embedded in the frame around the tag are operational. These extremely high output LEDs flood the area behind the motorcycle with infrared light, virtually blinding traffic and red light cameras that use infrared to photograph vehicles.

When the bike's tag was new, he sprayed it with several coats of clear film containing highly reflective, microscopic glass beads that defeat the cameras which use high intensity flashes to photograph vehicles passing through intersections. The microscopic beads are more reflective than the tag's surface, causing the tag to be completely washed out in any photograph by the reflected light of the strobe flash, shielding the tag number from detection.

Standing back, he looks the bike over, paging through his mental checklist as he rubs his clean-shaven head, ensuring he's forgotten nothing for the trip. *Okay, that looks about right,* he thinks. *Diane should be getting up shortly, and I'll hit the road.* On his road trips, Louis misses Diane every time he thinks about her, and that occurs several times daily. She is the warmth of his heart, the keeper of his soul, and he could not live without her–and would not want to.

• • •

It's 5:30 a.m. and Diane's alarm clock pierces the pleasant silence of the bedroom. She taps the kill switch and sits up in the bed, gently stretching away the comfort of the warm sleep interrupted. Glancing over her shoulder, she sees Louis' pillow lying there empty. *He's already up? I hope he got some sleep last night,* she thinks, although he seldom does. She ponders it while heading into the kitchen to put her tea-kettle on to boil.

Louis bounds into the kitchen from the garage. "Hey baby, how'd you sleep?"

"Like a log; did you get any?"

"Not much, as usual–night before a road trip and all."

Yawning and stretching she asks, "You want a cup of hot tea before you go?"

"No thanks; I've got a Dew on the bike."

The kettle whistles off-key, signaling she can make her breakfast tea, their normal fare.

"How long will it take you to get to Memphis?"

"Should be there by 10 p.m. Eastern if I'm outta here shortly."

"Remember, it's my gym night–won't make it home till eight. Be sure to call me."

"I'll call you from Rendezvous; I'm having dry-rubbed ribs for dinner," Louis says with a teasing grin.

"Just make sure you call me."

Louis kisses Diane then hugs her so tightly her back pops, and whispers a gentle, "I love you, baby." She follows him to the garage, tea-cup in hand, while he wraps his high-visibility riding jacket around his barrel-shaped chest, then dons helmet and gloves. Backing the bike out of the garage, he fires up the engine of the big BMW that settles into a gentle rumble of quiet bass notes. Diane leans in and gently kisses him, and in a few seconds, he is riding toward the corner, turns and disappears, leaving only the cool, quiet morning for her to enjoy before dressing for work. She misses Louis when he's gone riding. She tries not to worry and knows he's a great rider, but still prefers they were together daily. Being a Motorcycle Travel Blogger means riding and traveling to get the stories and photos, although at times, she wishes he would just phone it in from the house. Riding is in his blood; it gives expression to his wanderlust, and he always returns home more peaceful and content than when he left.

• • •

Out on US 19, Louis is heading north through the traffic of New Port Richey and beyond. He activates the bike's GPS, not for guidance, just to listen to the built-in satellite radio. Within a few seconds the screen comes to life and the audio flows into his headset. It helps with the boredom of a long familiar route. One hundred-fifty miles up the road, it's getting dark and the weather radar on the GPS shows a huge mass of rain and thunderstorms coming off the Gulf from the west, Louis pulls to the side of the road to put on some additional raingear.

Climbing back on the bike, he heads into the darkness, hoping the lightning stays far away from him. The lightning is all that concerns him, and out on this stretch of US 19, along the Nature Coast, there is no cover to be found for the next 50 miles.

As he penetrates the wall of water, visibility drops to a few car lengths. He switches on all of the lighting and flashers while slowing his pace, just to be able to see the road a short distance ahead of him through the downpour. Louis cracks open his visor to get a little airflow to clear the fog that's building on the inside, when a massive lightning bolt strikes the ground across the highway and momentarily blinds him with its atomic flash. The enormous explosion and thunderous out-rush of air reminds him of a B-52 strike, causing his butt to take a bite out of the seat.

If I stop here, without any cover, I'll be an even bigger target for the lightning, so I'll just keep moving, he's thinking. *If you don't ride in the rain, you just don't ride. Isn't that what they say?* he thought. *Yeah, but sometimes "they" are idiots.* The radar shows this to be one of those elongated summer storm fronts that extends from the Gulf well into South Georgia and Alabama. *It's just going be one of those days. Hell, I needed to wash the bike anyway, but I can do without the damned lightning.*

Louis hears the stuttered crackling of the sky splitting open above him as another strike explodes just up the road ahead of him. He thinks of the old adage, 'If you can't get out of it, you might as well get into it', and he cranks up the volume of the radio to drown out the roaring staccato rain blasting against his helmet. *This is going to be a long day, and my first gas stop is still 50 miles up the road through this electrified car wash and shooting gallery,* he thinks as another lightning strike detonates behind him.

The shockwaves and noise from these nearby strikes momentarily take him back in time to when he was on the receiving end of SWAPO mortar fire, where all you could do was haul ass out of the area or become fertilizer for next year's plants. Louis continued north in the driving rain that seemed to be stalled over US 19 while the front marched eastward on giant legs of lightning, stomping out violent thunder with every step.

Now a few miles up the road from where he entered the wall of water, most of the lightning strikes seem to be occurring on the east side of US 19, but still close enough to him to cause his motorcycle to shudder violently. With each unpredictable strike his neck felt shorter, as if he were a turtle withdrawing his head into the protective cover of the shell. He wiped the water from the screen of the GPS, hoping to find a break in the downpour ahead, and saw the indicators of the lightning strikes superimposed on the screen, surrounding his position and extending another 10 miles north of him.

Louis continued with his head down and an eye on the sky, searching for the Valkyries he was sure were coming for him, when just as quickly as it started, he rode out of the rain and could see the sky above him surrounded by tall dark thunderheads. Even though the road was wet and lightning was still crackling around him, for a moment he felt protected from the furies, before again piercing the opposite wall of water and getting pushed sideways by the violent down blasts of wind from the enormous storm above him.

He resumed his left-leaning tack into the wind to maintain his straight-line course up US 19. The bike would veer suddenly toward the edges of the road every time the wind changed directions, requiring the opposite tack to stay on the pavement.

A lightning strike directly ahead of him caused the surface of the concrete roadway to explode, sending small bits of vaporized concrete into the air, bouncing off the bike's forward surfaces, as well as Louis's feet and the top of his helmet as he passed over the spot of the strike. Time itself became elongated, as seconds stretched into minutes during this indefensible assault of blasting water, rapidly changing winds and explosive electrical discharges.

Louis finally stopped thinking his way through the gauntlet and began instinctively reacting to the motorcycle's veering directional changes caused by the unpredictable wind gusts, loosening his grip on the handlebars to prevent over-steering that was making it worse. After a month-long 45 minutes of this abuse, the rain began to let up, as did the wind and the lightning as the gust front of the storms passed to the east of US 19.

The rain continued but was much lighter, and visibility ahead of him increased to more than a mile, revealing vehicles on the road ahead of him he had not been able to see until this point. Louis continued north, heading toward his first gas stop, now a pleasant 10 miles ahead of him.

2

Sitting at his desk in the hidden study of his Huntsville, Alabama home, Nathan Malone is busy accessing one of the many highly restricted websites that members of the intelligence communities use to relay information of a sensitive nature to one another.

These sites are maintained in out-of-the-way locations, away from the prying eyes of congressional oversight committees, agency watchdogs and NSA monitors. For years, Nathan has worked as a part-time contractor to the FBI, Department of Defense and NSA, and continues to do so. The US government invested millions in his training and he uses his skills as a consultant for these entities when they are in need of expertise not readily available to them on staff, or sometimes they use him instead of their staff, strictly as a contractor, outside of oversight. Nathan was granted access at a very high level in order to perform the tasks required of him as a consultant and contractor.

These agencies call on him every few months to handle projects or to do research that aids the government's cyber warfare initiatives. He has a very specific set of credentials he uses in the multitude of systems he accesses. Through these credentials, the various agencies and entities track what Nathan accesses and the data he adds to their systems, as well as the data he updates as he contributes to their enormous knowledge base of systems, techniques, exploits, best practices and dirty tricks.

On occasion, they request that he work in-house at various government installations; other times he works from home or remotely from other locations, depending on the need of the project and the parameters of the operation he's supporting. Nathan created ghost accounts on virtually all of the systems he had access to in order to perform intrusion and penetration testing to harden the systems from such attacks.

Some of these ghost accounts granted root level access to the systems and were compiled into the source code from which the systems were built, virtually guaranteeing they would never be discovered or removed. These backdoors were only known to and used by Nathan. Even though every one of the systems underwent a high level of scrutiny and security audits on a recurring basis, none of these ghost accounts or backdoors had ever been detected.

Actions performed using these ghost account credentials left no entries in the system logs and preserved the date timestamps of all files that they accessed, updated or removed, again leaving no tracks that could be detected during audits or security reviews; they truly were as if a ghost accessed the system, leaving no footprints or fingerprints behind.

Some of the more mundane systems in which Nathan worked included NCIC, or National Criminal Information Center, part of the FBI information system that all police agencies have access to and in return, the FBI has access to every system that accesses the NCIC.

This gives Nathan access to every city, county and state law enforcement agency's computer systems, enabling him to search and cross-reference data using the ghost accounts. Nathan helped to improve the NSA's Echelon Systems capabilities for successfully monitoring and tracking all telephone communications, hard-line and wireless, as well as all Internet traffic in and out of the United States.

Echelon allows the NSA to capture and record in real time every telephone conversation as well as every e-mail, fax and telex and all website traffic in the United States. These capabilities were extended to every continent through satellite and ground station facilities strategically located around the globe. These resources are shared with friendly governments and they in turn share their resources with the US government.

Nathan works closely with New Zealand's GCSB, or Government Communications Security Bureau, their equivalent to the NSA, to spy on countries located around the Pacific Rim. Needless to say, Nathan has extraordinary access to intelligence information and capabilities of the US government, as well as several foreign governments who share their information with the US.

Through these systems, Nathan can search the massive haystacks of intelligence data harvested by the systems every day, every hour and every minute. Nathan also has access to FedWire, the central banks funds transfer system managed by the Federal Reserve; RTGS, or Real Time Gross Settlements; and CHIPS, or Clearing House Interbank Payment System.

Virtually all financial traffic occurs on these networks and all banks around the world have access to and use one or more of these networks to carry out wire transfers of monies between banks and accounts. The computers Nathan uses are bunkered behind multiple 128-bit encrypted firewalls, using secure IP address proxies that rotate the addresses several times a minute, and Mac address clones of several thousand free Wi-Fi hotspots located all over the United States.

The 16 separate carrier dispersed firewalls he uses are configured in a matrix that allows only one accessible route out of two to the 16th number of routes, which change every two seconds. To say Nathan's systems are secure would be a drastic understatement and underestimate of his technological prowess. Nathan checks the sites daily, looking for business opportunities.

A contact will post a message with a brief description of the work contained within the contract, along with electronic contact information for more specific details. Nathan searches the descriptions for the keywords "wet", "mechanic", "terminate" and "assassinate", and when he finds a match, he saves the message. Also in the message descriptions will be the location indicators where the contract work is to be carried out, if possible. If it's in the continental United States or Canada he continues with the message; if not, he deletes the message.

Once he has located a message that indicates wet work to do in the continental United States or Canada, he accesses the electronic contact information embedded in the message. Contact can be made using several means, such as secure or encrypted e-mail or an encrypted post on a public bulletin board with an encrypted image, etc.

There are literally hundreds of ways to accomplish this securely. Nathan prefers using encrypted image files because of their simplicity and elegance: "hiding in plain sight" is always the best camouflage, he would say. Encrypted image files can be created on any PC by selecting a JPEG image and creating a zip file with the same name as a JPEG image, and then adding the original image, along with whatever encrypted documents you wanted it to carry, called its payload.

When the encrypted image is displayed using an image viewer or on a website or in a digital camera, all you see is the image. If anyone actually figured out the 128-bit key that unzipped the encrypted image file, then he could see the image plus the still-encrypted payload. They still need to decipher another 128-bit key to decrypt the payload—or documents, as it were.

The requester posts a message containing an image and then transmits the encryption key to the contact by other secure means. In this case Nathan then grabs the image off the net and copies it to his local computer. Using the encryption key, he opens the encrypted image, and then calculates the next encryption key using the original encryption key and the second encryption key to decrypt the payload. It's all very complicated and cumbersome, which is the point.

The payload documents contain only basic information about the work to be performed, the value of the contract, any key or critical timing information and some basic, nondescript information about the target, along with the payment methods. If Nathan accepts the contract, he notifies the requestor by the same means and receives in turn the specifics of the contract, along with an agreed-upon partial payment, usually to an offshore bank account, or as a funds transfer to a personal account at a casino, where the funds can be taken out in chips and converted to cash, or transferred to another account.

The layers and techniques of laundering this money are virtually countless, and tracking it back to its origin is almost impossible. Once Nathan has the specifics of the contract, he transmits them to his partner for action, and once completed, he relays the confirmation to the requester and receives the final payment.

The symbiotic relationship between Nathan and his partner has been reinforced repeatedly through the years, forging the bonds of a blood brotherhood that far exceeds the loyalty one could expect between mere siblings. Louis only accepts contracts from Nathan, and they split the proceeds equitably.

Nathan and Louis have known each other for many years; they grew up in the same city and knew many of the same people. They first met at the farm in Virginia where they were introduced to their tradecraft and then individually trained in the specific skills for which they were chosen.

Louis was nearing the end of his tour in the Army when he was recruited; Nathan was fresh out of college when the recruiter approached him. Nathan's first assignment out of training was as a controller of covert operators on the ground in Africa; he was a natural and never exposed his operators to undue risks, always ensuring there was an escape route to be had when an op went bad–and they did.

Louis became one of his operators after he completed a covert deployment in Rhodesia in the mid-70s. The operation in Rhodesia developed his cover that led to his recruitment by Executive Outcomes, a private army for hire out of South Africa that had contracts for operations up and down the west coast of Africa.

While Louis was on the payroll of Executive Outcomes, and getting plenty of trigger time, he was also a mole that reported all actions and operations up through Nathan, who in turn reported up to his handlers at Langley. There was a Chinese Wall constructed between Langley and their "kites" in the field; the handlers didn't know who the kites were and the kites didn't know who controlled them.

This provided an insulator called Plausible Deniability, to protect them from the international firestorms that would flare up on occasion when an Op went bad or an operator was captured or killed. When operations in Africa came to a close in the early 1980s, Louis was reassigned to Central America, the latest hotspot.

Wherever drugs and/or guns were, there too was much money, and worthy of the agency's attention. Again Nathan was the controller and Louis the kite, flying under the radar, doing the bidding of the guy at the other end of the string. The gig paid well but you can be cut loose at any time if you get tangled up. Nathan also rides motorcycles and shares Louis's wanderlust.

Together, they have ridden all over the United States on trips that took weeks and even months to complete. Touring through 10 or 15 states by motorcycle can be like heaven when you're riding with your best friend. They held conversations that lasted hours, and sometimes days, on the same topic. The conversation might start at a gas pump, and then continue during a lunch stop and continue at each subsequent stop until the subject was exhausted and completely wrung out.

To look at Nathan, you wouldn't realize the physical strength he possesses. His grip with either hand is vise-like and comes from many years of working in his shop building furniture and just about anything else that he put his mind to. At about five-foot-eight with a stocky build, you wouldn't want to engage him in a fist fight. Nathan lived his childhood in rural Tennessee, spending countless days in his grandfather's backyard wood shop, learning the craft and techniques of a master woodsmith while still a child.

After his family moved to Birmingham, he would still spend summers with his grandparents in Tennessee, memories he's treasured his entire life. Nathan parted with Central Intelligence many years earlier and now officially earns his living as a local electronics plant's engineering manager. He enjoys the work because he is constantly building something new for the facility.

He made his unofficial money with Louis and enjoyed a seemingly quiet existence in North Alabama. On this day, a message found its way out onto the cloud, like the others that have found their way before it. It possessed the key words that Nathan searched for, so he opened the message.

The Huntsville, Alabama location piqued Nathan's interest. He decrypted the payload of the message and found that this was a single hit on a white male named Nathan Malone. He sat back in his chair, staring at the screen, while a single bead of sweat trickled down his brow.

Seeing his name in this context, knowing others could as well, froze his spine with a quite unfamiliar sensation of terror that almost paralyzed him.

His mind raced with questions: *Who wants me dead? Why me? What did I do? Who else has read this message? Has anyone accepted this contract?*

I have to get ahead of this, think this through, get this stopped before someone else accepts this hit.

Nathan quickly composed a response requesting more information, encrypted the message and sent it to the contact. He grabbed his cell phone and gave Louis a call that went directly to voicemail. In a scared and shaky voice, he left a single word message. "Emergency".

While up pacing the floor, trying to figure out what his next step would be, an answer came through to his reply from the contact. His hands, trembling from the adrenaline, had difficulty steering the mouse pointer to the message. He closed his eyes, took a deep breath and exhaled to the count of eight to slow his heart rate. He opened the message and decrypted its payload.

The message body confirmed his worst nightmare: he was indeed the target, and there was no mistaking it. At this point, he had no way of knowing the identity of the contact requesting this hit. He also knew the contact had no way of knowing he had intercepted this message. Nathan called Louis' cell phone and again going straight to voicemail, he repeated his message, "Emergency".

Knowing he might only have minutes to lock in this contract to prevent someone else from taking it, he composed a reply, encrypted the message and sent it to the contact.

This was truly a first, accepting a contract on yourself, but with very good reason to do so. He anxiously awaited the acknowledgment indicating he had locked in the contract, thereby preventing someone else from taking it.

In the two minutes it took to get a reply, Nathan aged two years. *Where the hell is Louis? Why hasn't he called me back? Who the hell wants me dead?*

3

Louis, now well up the road, is behind the storm's gust front. It's now just gentle rain as far as the eye can see, and the radar shows the lightning is far to the east. The thunderstorms he has been riding in for the past hour and a half have cleansed the air. Riding in a gentle fall rain like this is a pleasure known by the few motorcyclists who are actually willing to ride in the rain, to get wet and little cold at times–this is the payoff.

Up the road a ways, on the right side, is an old gas station where Louis always stops for fuel while heading north, up US 19. It has a large canopy, big enough for 18 wheelers to pull under, though he's never seen one there. It's a shady spot, well in the center of nowhere, to stop for gas and a cold drink if you want one. He pulls in next to the pump, extends the side stand of the bike with his left foot, and leans the bike over gently. Louis slides off the bike, dragging his right leg across the seat. Now with both feet on the ground, he stretches out his back and extends his legs to improve circulation. He removes his helmet and gloves, laying them on the seat, unlocks the gas cap and tops off the 9-gallon tank with regular.

Louis yanks the key out of the bike's ignition and heads toward the side of the building where the restrooms are located. He walks past a curiously parked Chevy that's backed in next to the air pump. Leaving the restroom, he notices the tag on the rusted out Chevy is bent in half. *What a jackass,* he thinks as he walks by. As he enters the front door of the store, he's greeted by the little lady behind the counter, who is probably somebody's great-grandmother, shaped like a four–foot-eight refrigerator with thick glasses on her well-wrinkled face. "It's a little wet out there to be riding a motorcycle isn't it?"

"No ma'am, it's a nice Florida morning for a ride," he says and gives her a grin, proceeding toward the back wall for cold diet Dew. As he opens the door of the cooler, he sees a young man standing in front of the beer cooler at the end of the row, walking back and forth, looking in the cooler as if he can't make up his mind about what he wants. Louis grabs a 16-ounce Dew and heads back to the cashier. He sits the bottle on the counter then reaches into his left front pocket for his cash.

"That's $19.50 for the gas and soft drink."

"Here you go." He hands her a twenty.

As the guy from the beer cooler is approaching from the right, she opens the cash register drawer to make change for the twenty. Before she can close the drawer, the guy produces a pistol in his left hand, places the muzzle against Louis' right ear and yells at the lady, "Leave the drawer open or I'll shoot him in the head!" and then begins thumb-cocking the hammer.

Without hesitating, Louis sharply raises his right hand from his side and jams his open hand under the gun, wrapping his fingers around the punk's hand while wedging a finger between the hammer and the frame, raising the gun above his head.

The woman begins screaming and ducks down behind the counter.

Louis turns toward the punk with his right foot so they're face-to-face and grabs him by the throat with his left hand, which instinctively wants to choke the life out of him.

The punk reeks of burnt Styrofoam. "A damned crack-head," Louis growls at him as he lifts him by the throat and slams him to the tiled floor with a thud, cracking his head, while controlling the pistol still in his right hand.

Louis releases his death grip and places his left knee on the crack-head's throat, keeping him pinned down while he takes the pistol out of his hand.

Once Louis has full control of the pistol, he punches the crack-head's solar plexus hard, to take the fight out of him, then uncocks the hammer and shoves the pistol in his own back pocket.

The woman, still screaming like a Stuka Dive Bomber and hiding behind the counter, never stood a chance against the armed crack-head–probably why he chose this remote store to rob.

Louis hollers over the counter to the woman, "Ma'am, you can stop screaming now. I've got the situation under control and he can't hurt you."

The woman's hysterical scream winds down like an old-time weather siren that is switched off. Louis tells the frightened woman, "Try to calm down; everything is under control. Just catch your breath while I deal with this."

"Are you sure it's safe?" she yells from behind the counter.

"Yes ma'am, he's down and I have his pistol in my pocket. Ma'am, if you would, how about locking the front door to keep anyone from wandering in here."

"Don't you want me to call the police?"

"Not just yet, ma'am. Give me a few minutes to handle this before you do."

The woman fumbles in her purse to find her keys and then locks the front door, before she turns around to watch what Louis is going to do.

Louis still has his left knee on the crack-head's throat when he looks him square in the eyes. "If you want to live through this exercise in stupidity, you're going to do exactly what I say, you understand me?"

The crack-head attempts to nod his head in compliance, indicating he understands. Louis releases his knee from his throat, replacing it with his left hand, and tells him, "Slowly, roll over on your stomach."

Now with him face-down, he puts his left knee across his neck to keep him there while he goes through his pockets. Louis finds his car keys and a wallet and tosses them up on the counter.

Louis tells him, "If you wiggle without me telling you to, I'll snap your neck like a chicken bone and feed you to the alligators out back! You got me?"

"I got you, I got you, I'll be cool. Mister, I wasn't going to shoot you, I swear."

"I haven't decided whether I'm going to shoot you or not. Slowly move your arms down to your belt and remove it."

The crack-head slid his hands under his belly and unfastened the buckle, then slowly pulled the belt through the loops and out from under him to the right.

"Now put your arms behind your back and cross them."

Louis grabs the belt and wraps it tightly around his arms, passing it through the buckle like a noose, then wraps it between his arms and around the buckle like an over-tightened bow tie.

"When I tell you, we're going to get up off the floor together, and you're not going to move until I tell you how. Don't even twitch or I'll slam your ass back down on the floor and we'll start all over. Got it?"

"I got it, mister. I ain't gonna give you any more trouble. I swear."

Louis removes his knee from the crack-head's neck, replacing it with his left hand.

"Now we're going to slowly stand up, one move at a time."

Louis tells him, "I'm gonna raise you up till you're on your knees." He has his hand firmly on the belt securing his arms behind him, and with his left hand still on the crack-head's neck, he lifts him to his knees.

"Now raise your left leg and put your foot flat on the floor. Now stand up."

"Ma'am, you can unlock the door now, please," Louis said.

"Ok, just a second."

"Are there any customers outside?"

"No, the lot is empty, except for us."

"That's just fine. If you could just stand behind the counter while I take the trash outside."

The woman moves behind the counter, keeping a watchful eye on what is happening in front of her.

Louis grabs the car keys from the counter and spins the crack-head around, pushing him toward the door and through it. He leads him to the car waiting at the edge of the building, and slams his face down on the trunk. Louis locates the key to the trunk and opens it.

"Man, you're not going to lock me in the trunk, are you?"

"It's either that, or I can shoot you in the head; which one would you prefer?"

Louis scans the open trunk, checking for weapons, then shoves the crack-head in face first and lifts his legs, stuffing them in. There's a gallon jug of Clorox in the trunk in a basket of laundry. Louis opens the jug using a t-shirt to touch it and pours the Clorox all over the belt wrapped around the crack-head's arms, soaking it thoroughly, while the crack-head loudly protests, and closes the trunk, tossing the jug in the trash barrel next the store.

Louis wipes his prints from the keys, takes the pistol out of his back pocket, and wipes it down using the t-shirt as he's walking back inside the store.

"Have you got a small paper sack under the counter?"

"I've got a bunch of them," she says, handing one over the counter to him.

"Do you mind if I wash my hands? I want to get this grime off me; there's no telling where that crack-head's been."

"Oh, not at all, it's through that door back there on the right; there's hand soap on the sink as well."

He sits the crack-head's keys on the counter. "Thanks, I'll be right back."

Louis heads to the back room, drops the pistol in the bag, washes his hands and walks up front to the counter.

He asks, "Ma'am, I don't see any cameras in the store. Is there a hidden one I just can't see?" while he casually wipes down the punk's wallet with the t-shirt and sits it back on the counter.

"No, I think the owners are too cheap to install them!"

"Well, I hope they will after this. Anyway, the crack-head is locked in his trunk outside and you have the keys and his wallet. Don't open the trunk. I'll leave the pistol in the paper sack sitting under the rear of the car. I need to head on down the road; I'm late for an appointment. If you would do me a favor, give me a few minutes before you call the police to report this. I really don't have time to deal with them right now, and I'll call them later to explain what happened and give them my details. Can you do that for me?"

"Honey, I'd cook you Sunday dinner right now if you wanted me to! I'll give them a call in a little while then; I guess he's going nowhere. Thank you so much for being here and doing what you did. There's no telling what he would've done if I'd been by myself."

"You're welcome, and I appreciate it, ma'am. I need to go now."

"Don't forget your Mountain Dew; it's probably still cold."

"I think I'll get a new one from the cooler, if you don't mind," he said to her as he grabbed the drink from the counter and walked back to the cooler to wipe down the door handle, keeping the Dew. Louis walked out the front door and over to the trash barrel. He grabbed the jug and poured Clorox all over the pistol in the sack, soaking it thoroughly, and dropped the sack on the ground under the rear bumper before heading to his bike. He slid the diet Dew into his bottle holder on the handlebars and wiped down the pump handle he used to fill the bike. Tossing the t-shirt in the trash can, he put on his helmet and gloves.

The little woman walked out to his bike before he left and asked, "What should I tell the police?"

While putting on his sunglasses, Louis says, "Just tell them the crack-head tried to rob you and a customer in the store stopped him. Tell them the crack-head's locked in the trunk of his car, with his arms tied behind his back, and that the pistol he used is in the paper sack under the bumper, on the ground."

"What if they ask me to describe you?"

"Just tell them what you remember, if you feel you need to remember it. It happened so fast, and was so scary that you may not remember too much detail," Louis said with a friendly smile. "Just be safe, and tell the owners they need to install security cameras in the store."

"I'll do just that." She smiled, then turned and walked back inside the store.

Louis heard the tone from his cell phone that was still in the tank bag of the bike; he knew he missed a call but didn't have time to take it now. He fired up the bike and glanced at the GPS. He'd been stopped at the gas station for 14 minutes; it was still raining and the air smelled fresh on the otherwise beautiful Florida morning.

4

Thirty minutes on up the road, near the Georgia line, Louis pulled into the parking lot of the dog track and parked in the shade of the tall pines to take a break. Climbing off the bike, he removed his helmet and jacket and retrieved his cell phone from the tank bag to see who called. It was Nathan; he called twice. Louis checked his voicemail and heard the message, "Emergency." He then listened to the second message, which was the same. Louis returned Nathan's call and after one ring, Nathan answered.

"Where have you been, Bro? I left a message forty-five minutes ago and have been climbing out of my skin ever since."

"Sorry man, I didn't hear the phone. I was riding up 19 in the rain. What's up?"

"We need to talk ASAP. Where are you?"

"I'm sitting at the Florida-Georgia line in the parking lot of the dog track."

"Where are you headed?"

"I'm headed to Rendezvous for some ribs; you want to meet me there?"

"I can't, I'm up to my eyeballs in it at the moment and need your help."

"I'm only going be in Memphis for a few hours, so I can meet you tomorrow morning somewhere. If you feel like taking a ride, we can meet out on the Trace, at the campgrounds on the Lake."

"I can get away from the house for a few hours, I guess; I'll meet you there tomorrow morning, then."

"All right, Bro, I'll see you there and we can talk about it, later man."

"Later."

Louis never knew Nathan to panic, so this was major, and something they couldn't discuss over the phone. He'd get the details when they meet on Natchez Trace tomorrow morning. Climbing back on the bike he heads north toward Albany, Georgia. Louis enjoys this route because it connects to Highway 280 and passes through Fort Benning, his old stomping grounds when he was just another grunt pounding the Georgia red clay while going through training. Fort Benning changed dramatically over the years and was no longer an open post that anyone could drive on. The 'War on Terror' called for it to be locked down tight, with concrete barricades and guard towers at all the small post roads that crossed the highway.

Rolling on through Columbus, Georgia, crossing the Chattahoochee River that separates Columbus from Phenix City, Alabama, he takes it slow and easy going across this bridge, knowing Alabama State Troopers sit in the median on the western end of the bridge, running radar to catch the unsuspecting drivers. On up the road, Highway 280 passes through Opelika, Alabama, the home of Auburn University and way too much traffic to deal with. He turns west on US 80, a cutoff that leads to Interstate 85 toward Montgomery and bypasses Auburn. Once in Montgomery, he turns north on Interstate 65 for the uphill run to Birmingham.

Having ridden this route numerous times, Louis does it on autopilot. Riding through Birmingham is a dangerous pain the ass, with legions of distracted drivers hell-bent on running you over. The intersection of Interstates 65 and 20, built in the 1970s, is a minefield of potholes and cracks in the uneven rain-grooved concrete. Louis made his way to Highway 78 and late in the afternoon arrived in Tupelo, Mississippi, where he pulled into a rest stop that had concrete picnic tables. He parked close to one of the tables, retrieved his laptop from the top case, and took a seat.

He takes the memory card that's been inside his Casio digital camera in the tank bag and puts it in the card reader of the netbook. He opens the image of the Bell Tower, sent to him by Nathan, and saves it to his desktop, decrypting the archive file and its payload documents hidden within. It's time to review all the intel he has available concerning Marcus Gray; the real reason he's bound for Memphis.

Five years earlier, Marcus Gray was a priest at a small parish located in Brandon, Florida. 'The Church' moved Gray from place to place around the world after he finished seminary in Leeds, England, where he was raised. Gray did missionary work in Africa before being moved to the archdiocese of Chicago. He was in Chicago less than a year when he was moved to Brandon, Florida. He was in Brandon for a year and a half and was in charge of the youth outreach program there. No one in the community knew Gray's history, or why he was moved around so often by the church, but events unfolded that left little doubt.

April, a close friend and a former teammate of Louis' when he was still managing IT departments, made her home in Brandon with her husband Mike and their two children, Michael, now 13, and Sarah, now 11. They moved to Brandon from Port Canaveral, Florida when Michael was three. April and family attended the church in Brandon where Gray was assigned. He appeared, on the surface, like so many other priests they encountered over their lives in the church, dedicated and in the service of the church. However, Gray was overly enthusiastic about his job working with the children of the parish. Michael and Sarah were both in after-school care at the church while in elementary school. Gray had constant access to them and all the other children, as well. After a few months around Gray, Michael's behavior began to change. He became sullen at times and hostile at other times, not at all characteristic of Michael's normally gregarious behavior and demeanor. April, being sensitive to changes in her children, tried to talk to Michael about what was going on with him. Michael wouldn't say–or couldn't say–what was bothering him. His acting out was from fear and his lack of understanding of what was happening to him. A man his parents said he could trust was treating him like no other man in his life did, and he was scared. While April tried to talk to Michael about what was bothering him, she mentioned the upcoming overnight camping trip, arranged by Gray, and asked Michael if he was excited about the trip. Michael's face turned pale as he told his mother he didn't want to go on the trip, where just two weeks prior he was excited and looking forward to it.

April's husband Mike, who was at the time stationed at McDill Air Force Base in Tampa, was preparing for deployment to Afghanistan. April and Mike discussed Michael's behavior and mood swings, trying to understand and determine what to do. They decided to schedule an appointment with one of the counselors at the health services building at McDill. Mike made the call and was able to get an appointment for the following day. April picked Michael and Sarah up from school and drove from Brandon into Tampa and on post at McDill, where she met Mike at the health services building. They all went inside and took seats in the waiting area while April and Mike filled out the paperwork for the counselor. The counselor spent a few minutes with April and Mike in his office discussing the situation and what they perceived were the changes in Michael's behavior. Was it his father's upcoming deployment that was bothering him? Or was it something else entirely? April mentioned the camping trip which Michael had been so excited about, but lost interest in and wanted nothing to do with now.

Mike went back to the waiting room and sat with Sarah, while Michael went into the counselor's office with his mother. April introduced the counselor and Michael, and spent a few minutes with them both so they could get comfortable with each other. The counselor struck up a conversation with Michael, asking him about school and what he thought about baseball and football and what he thought about his father's deployment to Afghanistan. Michael was having no problem with these questions and answered them enthusiastically. When the counselor asked about school, Michael talked about his teachers and his classes and how much fun they had on the playground catching lizards and playing soccer. When the counselor asked about the after-school time at church, Michael became solemn and quiet, almost sinking into his chair, and stopped making eye contact with the counselor. April could see the red flags going off in the counselor's mind as she read his facial expressions while he made a few notes.

The counselor asked Michael if it would be okay if his mother went outside to the waiting room so he and Michael could talk alone for a few minutes. You could tell Michael was uncomfortable but he agreed with a nod of his head. After all, this man was wearing an Air Force uniform, just like his father's, so he felt he could trust him. As April got up to leave the office, the counselor turned on his tape recorder, got up from his desk and sat in the middle of his office floor, facing Michael, still sitting in a chair. They were more or less sitting on the same level now, an attempt by the counselor to help Michael relax and trust him, so he could open up about what was bothering him. The counselor asked him if there were any problems with the other kids at the after-school care and Michael just shook his head no.

"Is there someone else there that bothers you?"

Michael's eyes gazed down at the floor with his forehead wrinkled and mumbled, "Yes sir."

"Can you tell me about it?"

"He said I'd get in a lot of trouble if I told anybody."

"Well Michael, I'll tell you something, buddy; you can't get into any trouble at all by talking to me. It's my job to help people, and that's what I want to do for you. Whatever the trouble is, we can fix it, I promise you."

Michael's posture relaxed as he studied the counselor's face.

"Who told you that you would get in trouble, Michael?"

"Father Gray," he mumbled in a shaky and scared voice, on the verge of crying.

"Michael, do you think you did anything wrong?"

"No sir, I was just cleaning the chalkboards, and Father Gray grabbed me and wouldn't let go."

"How did Father Gray grab you?"

"He put his arms around me and reached inside my pants and wouldn't let go. When I tried to get away he told me I was gonna get in trouble if I didn't behave. He said if I told anybody, my mom and dad and sister and me would get kicked out of church," Michael said with tears streaming down his face.

"Michael, I think you're a brave little boy. You don't have to worry anymore, because Father Gray is not going to bother you ever again, I promise. Do you mind if I talk to your parents now?"

"No sir, I'm kinda tired of talking," Michael said with a more relaxed expression, still sobbing and wiping away his tears.

The counselor got up from the floor and walked around behind his desk, picked up his telephone receiver and pressed the intercom button; it was answered by his nurse/receptionist.

"Linda, would you step into my office for a moment and bring Michael's parents with you, please?"

"Yes sir, I'll be there in one moment."

Shortly, the door to the office opened and April, Mike and Linda stepped inside.

"Linda, would you get Michael and his sister something good to drink and show them to the playroom for a few minutes?"

"I'd be happy to do that. Come along with me, Michael, and let's look in the refrigerator."

Linda shut the door behind her as the counselor walked around from behind his desk. "Let's sit down and talk for a few minutes."

April and Mike sat on the couch next to each other while the counselor pulled up a chair directly in front of them. "I believe I understand what's going on with Michael," he said with a somber, matter-of-fact expression. "Michael told me that Father Gray, at his after-school care, touched him inappropriately."

They were both in shock. How could this have happened to their little boy? *What do we do now?* they thought to themselves.

"What do we do? Is he okay? What can we do?" April asked with tears building in her eyes. Mike sat there for a moment with his mouth hanging open with a look of pale disbelief on his face.

Handing a box of tissues to April the counselor said, "We're going to take Michael over to the base pediatrician for a complete examination, right now. Our first priority is Michael's health and safety. I'm going to call the pediatrician's office and get you in there immediately. While you're over there, I'll be filling out some paperwork that I'll need when we report this to the police."

April and Mike were both streaming tears and grasping each other's hands tightly.

"I can't emphasize this enough; you both need to remain calm and composed. I believe, from Michael's description, that he was only touched inappropriately and nothing more. However, let's get him a full physical just to be sure. Again, you both must remain calm and composed. After the physical, you all need to go home, try to have a normal non-stressful evening–no questions, don't interrogate him–and if he wants to talk to you about it, just listen to him. I'll be notifying the authorities for you; they will get in contact with you. We also need to schedule some sessions with Michael, to get him past this and get him back to his normal self."

April and Mike both nodded in agreement, wiping away the tears and sniffing.

"I have one other thing to say to you before you leave my office. Neither one of you is to contact the church or Father Gray or anyone else about this. This will soon be in the hands of the police, and they are the ones trained to deal with it."

"If you think that's best, that's what we'll do," Mike said while looking at April.

The counselor continued, "Unfortunately, I have some experience in this area. I know your first instinct is to protect your son, and that's exactly what you should do. However, after this sinks in, you may be tempted to take matters into your own hands. You absolutely cannot do that. You have to let the police handle this."

Mike looked the counselor square in the eye and said, "I'll let the police handle it."

"The children are down the hall in the playroom with Linda. Just hang out there with them and send Linda back my office, please."

April and Mike left the counselor's office and walked down the hall toward the playroom, where they found the children entertaining themselves with Legos. "Thanks for watching them, Linda," April said with a warm smile. Linda left, and then returned to the playroom a few minutes later with an appointment slip for the base pediatrician's office. "Here you go, they're waiting for you now. It's located in building 31 around the corner to the right, and two blocks down on the right."

They left the building and piled into April's car for the short trip to the pediatrician's office. The nurse took Michael right into the examination room with the doctor, along with his dad, and completed his thorough physical including blood tests, looking everywhere for signs of trauma. Within the hour, they were on their way home to Brandon.

April shared all this with Louis while at lunch one day. She told him that Gray was questioned at the church by police, and then questioned at the police station for several more hours before being released on bond. Two days later, Gray disappeared, moved in the middle of the night to another parish in another archdiocese with more unsuspecting parents and children.

While Michael got over this event with the help of the counselor, it continued to haunt April and Mike and added an almost unbearable level of stress on top of the anxiety during Mike's deployment to Afghanistan.

• • •

The air horn of an 18-wheeler out on Highway 78 snapped Louis back to the present from his thousand yard stare, sitting alone on the roadside picnic table with his laptop open in front of him. He again focused on the information in front of him and the service he would perform in the coming hours.

Louis alone decided to deal with Gray, retribution for what was done, and to prevent him from doing it again. The Church had centuries of experience hiding their pedophiles from prosecution, and Louis knew the police could never handle it the way he would. The internal dialog of the right or wrong of killing had ceased to exist years ago within Louis' mind, his conscience sacrificed over time in order to cope with the post-traumatic stress.

It took Nathan two years to track down Gray, as he moved from place to place with no paper trail to follow. Nathan found him by having the telephone of Gray's elderly parents in Leeds, England bugged, in the hope that one would call the other at some point. Gray called his parents at home in Leeds on their 60th wedding anniversary. He made the call from a church in Collierville, Tennessee less than a week ago, Louis wasn't going to let him disappear again. He had been anticipating this for two years, and the opportunity now presented itself.

This became personal for Louis; he was involved, and Gray was living his last hours.

5

ouis planned his route to the church in Collierville, studying the location on Google maps to become familiar with the area. He also planned his egress from the area, ensuring he had several options, should he need them. He removed the memory card from his laptop and put it back in the small digital camera, then wiped the data he copied from the memory card off his laptop. He put the laptop back in the top case and turned off his cell phone, placing it and his wallet in the top case of the bike. Louis removed his riding pants and slipped into some blue jeans and sneakers. He reached inside his toiletries bag in the top case and took a beta-blocker to control his adrenaline over the coming hours. Securing everything on the bike, Louis climbed on and pulled back out on Highway 78 heading toward Memphis. The sun was still above the horizon but sinking fast over the Mississippi Delta to the southwest. He turned north off Highway 78 onto 309 at Byhalia, Mississippi, heading due north to Collierville, Tennessee, now just 20 miles away.

Once in Collierville, Louis pulled into the parking lot of the Hampton Inn located near the church and parked his bike next to a long line of motorcycles that were already there, a fortunate coincidence that provided some camouflage. Louis locked the handlebars, opened the left side case, stuffed his riding jacket and helmet in, and took a ball cap out to cover his head. Now in his t-shirt, jeans and sneakers, he casually walked through the Hampton Inn before exiting through the front door and across the parking lot, crossing the street to the ball field located on the church grounds.

It's 5:30 in the evening local time, and the lights are on at the ball field while a girls' softball team is practicing as parents watch from the stands. Observing for a couple minutes and scanning around the lot and at the church to check for security cameras, he walks away from the ball field across the lot toward the back of the church and past the rectory, a simple row of small apartments with individual doors. Louis walks around to the front of the church and scans the message board by the street, looking for the name of the priest, then walks up the steps to the open front door and looks inside. A parishioner seated by the front door says, "Welcome, may I help you?"

"Yes, are confessions available tonight?"

"Yes, Father Marcus is in the confessional to the right and will be available until 8:00 pm; have a seat anywhere with the others for your turn."

"Thank you, friend, I'll do that."

Louis scanned the interior of the church for security cameras as he removed his hat and took a seat near the confessional. After a few parishioners completed their confessions, the priest receiving them left the confessional to take a break. It was Gray; Louis recognized his face from the photos he received from Nathan. Louis got up and left the church, walking back to the ball field and then returning to the parking lot of the Hampton Inn. He knew confessions would continue for several more hours so he had time to kill before the kill.

He decided to ride west to Memphis and eat dinner at his favorite rib joint, a few blocks off Beale Street. The ride west on 72, heading through Germantown and into Memphis, was a little crowded with traffic, but it moved well. In forty-five minutes he was on Beale Street, a place he truly enjoyed in the past, but no place to park a motorcycle unless you wanted it to disappear. Louis decided to park at the Peabody Hotel and walk over to Rendezvous for dinner. He parked the bike near the front entrance and grabbed his cell phone and wallet from the top case. He spoke to the valet as he handed him a 20. "I need to grab a bite to eat; will you keep an eye on the bike?"

"Yes sir, that shouldn't be a problem."

"Thanks man, I appreciate it; I'll hit you again on the way out."

"Enjoy your dinner, sir."

Walking in the front door of the Peabody as if he owned the place, he headed to the side exit to cut across the street and up the block for dinner. There's always a line at the front door of this world-famous barbecue joint. It's a big place and can seat a lot of people. While waiting in line he turned on his cell phone and called home to speak to Diane. She had just returned from the gym and was about to get in the shower when the phone rang.

"Hello."

"Hey baby, guess where I'm standing?"

"If I know you, you're about to eat some dry-rubbed ribs for dinner you lucky dog."

"You got me; how was your workout?"

"It was great; the Pilates instructor killed us tonight. You made good time, didn't you?"

"Yeah, the traffic was light most of the way and I didn't fiddle-fart around too much."

"How long will you be in Memphis?"

"Just long enough to eat dinner, then I'm going to head back to meet with Nathan in the morning."

"Just be safe and enjoy the ride. Take lots of pictures. I love you."

"I love you too, baby. See you in a day or two; bye-bye."

About the time he finished the call, the maître d' asked him, "How many in your party, sir?"

"Just one. I'm by myself, so you can stick me in a corner if you want," Louis said with a grin.

Louis followed the man to the small two-seater table in the middle of the main dining room, adjacent to the open kitchen area. He asked for a large glass of unsweetened iced tea as he scanned the menu for any new items since the last time he was here. When the waiter brought the iced tea, Louis ordered a full slab of dry-rubbed ribs, coleslaw, baked beans and bread. Everywhere he looked around the room, he saw smiling faces eagerly devouring the various barbecue offerings, while wiping the sauce from their cheeks and chins after every bite. For Louis, this was barbecue Mecca, and worth the ride to Memphis just for this. Within minutes, the waiter sat his food in front of him, and he dove in face first, enjoying every exquisite morsel with pleasure. When the waiter came back by the table to check on him, Louis asked him to go ahead and bring the check. Reaching inside his apron pocket, he produced his check already prepared, and said cordially, "Thank you, and we hope to see you again."

"I make a point of eating here every time I'm in Memphis, so you will definitely see me again."

Louis left cash on the table with the ticket and a generous tip for the waiter, finished his iced tea, got up and left the restaurant, walking back to the Peabody and out the front door to the valet. Handing him another 20, he said, "Thanks for watching my bike."

"You're very welcome, sir. Enjoy your ride."

Louis turned off his cell phone and placed it and his wallet in the top case before he pulled out of the parking lot of the Peabody and headed over to Beale Street for one more pass before leaving the area. When he arrived back in Collierville, he again parked among the other motorcycles at the Hampton Inn. He stowed his helmet and jacket in the side case and removed a long-sleeve button-down shirt to put over his t-shirt and a ball cap for his head. Louis opened the right side case of the bike, unloaded a few objects to the ground and opened the hiding place. He put on his shoulder holster and quickly put on the long-sleeve shirt to cover it. Louis looked around the lot carefully before removing the Walther with the silencer and sliding it into the vertical holster under his left arm. He then removed the stun gun from the hiding place and slipped it into his right rear pocket. Louis picked up the items on the ground, put them back in the side case and stuffed a pair of flesh colored burn gloves into his left rear pocket, then locked the bike and walked around the end of the building to the front parking lot.

He walked across the street to the ball field, where the lights were now on, and there was now a game in progress. The parking lot was full, as were the stands around the ball field. Casually walking around to the front of the church, he looked inside. There were still a few people waiting for confession so Louis walked back to the ball field for a few minutes before positioning himself close to the rectory to watch for Gray.

Leaning against the left-field fence, observing the game while keeping an eye on the rectory, he crossed his arms, slid his left hand onto the grip of the pistol, clicked the safety to the off position, and cocked the hammer.

He slipped on his gloves while taking long slow deep breaths, waiting for his prey to arrive. Twenty minutes crawled past before Gray appeared around the end of the building, heading toward the rectory.

Louis pulled the stun gun from his back pocket and flipped the switch to 'On' to let it charge to full capacity. He held the stun gun behind his right leg as he walked on an intercept course across the parking lot, toward the rectory.

He slowed his pace to allow Gray to reach the darkened front door of his apartment just ahead of him.

Louis slipped in quietly behind Gray as he opened the door, thrusting the stun gun into the back of Gray's neck and releasing the 5 million volts of energy into his body, hurling him to the floor inside.

Louis looked around to ensure no one had seen him, stepped inside the apartment, and closed and locked the door.

The apartment was almost dark, but the light from the ball field gently illuminated the room through the curtained windows.

While Gray lay twitching and convulsing face-down on the floor, Louis switched off the stun gun and returned it to his pocket.

Lifting Gray by his hair and belt, he dragged him into the bathroom, dumping him face first into the large bathtub, then shoved his arms and legs inside the tub.

Drawing the Walther from his shoulder holster, he ensured the silencer was snug as he placed his thumb against the back of the slide while taking aim at the back of Gray's head.

He spoke in a calm tone of voice, "This is for Michael," and squeezed off a round that entered at the base of Gray's skull, stopping his still-violent convulsions.

Jacking a new round into the chamber of the Walther while capturing the spent shell, again he locked the slide with his thumb, putting a second round into Gray's head just above the first.

Louis chambered another round, capturing the second spent casing, and returned the Walther to its holster as he flipped on the exhaust fan to remove the smoke and heavy smell of gunpowder from the room.

Pushing the lever that closed the drain on the tub, he cranked open the hot and cold water, letting it fill the tub until it covered the body, then stopped the water and closed the shower curtain and bathroom door, returning to the front room.

Sliding the two spent brass casings into the watch pocket of his blue jeans, he glanced out the front window of the apartment before making his exit.

Locking the door behind him, he stepped off the porch toward the ball field, when a priest appeared around the end of the rectory, walking toward him at a clip.

The priest, noticing the lights were off in the apartment, asked Louis, "Is Father Marcus not in?"

Louis walked past the priest and turned his back toward the ball field lights to conceal his face in the shadows.

He crossed his arms, placing his left hand on the grip of the pistol under his shirt. "No Father, I just knocked to ask if he wanted to watch the ballgame with us, but there was no answer."

Thinking, *Don't make me kill you, priest,* he turned to walk away, when the priest spoke again. "That's curious, he left the church just minutes ago after confessions. I'm wondering where he could've gone so quickly?"

To pedophile hell if there's any justice in the universe, Louis thought.

"I couldn't tell you, Father; perhaps he went for a walk," he said while turning and walking away calmly toward the ball field, glancing back over his shoulder to keep an eye on the priest, who then disappeared around the end of the building from where he came.

After a minute of pretending to watch the ballgame from the left-field fence, Louis turned and walked through the parking lot and across the street around the Hampton Inn to his bike.

With calm purpose, Louis put on his helmet and dark jacket and pulled out of the parking lot, heading southeast toward Mississippi on Highway 72, under the speed limit and taking his time, keeping a watchful eye out for LEOs.

Once in Mississippi he turned south on 311, heading toward Holly Springs and back to Highway 78.

Pulling into a Subway sandwich shop at the intersection of State Road 4 and Highway 78, he rode to the end of the parking lot, where there was no overhead light, and parked the bike.

Being careful to conceal his actions, Louis put the Walther and the stun gun back into the hiding place in the right side case, storing the holster in the bottom of the case. He removed the flesh colored burn gloves as he walked toward the dumpster to dispose of them.

Putting on his riding pants and high visibility riding jacket and gloves, Louis left the parking lot and headed southeast on Highway 78. He switched on the GPS to listen to the news as he rode toward Tupelo.

It was a cool and cloudless night in northern Mississippi. The chimney smoke from the homes in this rural area flavored the air with oak and pine; the clock on the GPS screen indicated it was now 10 pm eastern. Continuing southeast in the dark, enjoying the multitude of stars overhead, Louis thought about his actions, reviewing each step in detail. He was calm and at peace with it, knowing there was one pedophile that would never again harm a child. A mile up the road, Louis spotted a truck stop near the Natchez Trace exit and pulled into the lot next to the payphone with an overhead light. He removed his helmet, took the netbook from the top case of the bike, and closed the case, using it as a table for the laptop. Snagging a Wi-Fi connection from the truck stop, he composed an e-mail to Nathan, asking him if anything interesting was happening in the Memphis/Collierville area. A few minutes later, he got a reply that said, "Nothing newsworthy." Louis replied with, "See you in the morning, Bro."

He put the laptop away and locked the bike before walking into the truck stop for a bio break and to get some stuff for the night: a six-pack of bottled water, a couple of cold sandwiches and a diet

Dew for in the morning. Before leaving the store, Louis stood watching the overhead television that was tuned to CNN. The talking heads were discussing the latest Hollywood celebrity crisis, which interested him about as much as a toothache. He placed the goodies in the side case and again headed southeast on 78, exiting at the Natchez Trace Parkway. Louis turned left, heading north at an easy pace. He was in no hurry to get where he was going; he had all night if he wanted it. Louis exited the trace near Bay Springs Lake and slowly entered the public campgrounds on the gravel road. Parking the bike near the picnic tables by the lake, he chose a spot far away from everyone else. Louis slipped out of his riding gear and put on some warm clothes in the crisp night air. He set up the laptop on the picnic table and established a broadband connection through Verizon.

Logging onto CNN headline news, he checked for any news out of Collierville. All was quiet on that front. Gray's body probably wouldn't be found until tomorrow, and Louis left nothing behind to be found. It was a clean hit and brought him no more anxiety than killing an armadillo, but a greater sense of satisfaction. Shutting down the laptop, he prepared his 'Iron Butt Motel'. He retrieved a bike cover from the side case and laid it out like a sleeping bag on top of the picnic table. It was now midnight, and he knew he wouldn't get any sleep.

Stretching out and relaxing would be enough; Louis long ago learned to deal with lack of sleep, after a lifetime of insomnia that started when he was just a kid.

Using a rolled up towel as a pillow, he lay there looking up at the stars, listening to the breeze as it moved through the pine trees all around him, and enjoying the smell of campfires. Louis couldn't tell April what he did, or anyone else for that matter. Knowing she would eventually see it on the news, he hoped she would find comfort in the closure. April's husband Mike died during his tour in Afghanistan, and she was raising Michael and Sarah on her own.

Louis relaxed on and off during the night, checking the news online periodically to satisfy his curiosity. He drank several bottles of water to rehydrate after his long day of riding, causing him to make a few trips to the edge of the lake for relief. This was a peaceful place, where he had stopped a few times before while riding the Natchez Trace. Cocooned inside the bike cover, with only his face exposed to the cooler night air, he thought about Diane, alone, asleep.

Nathan would arrive early in the morning, sometime after sunrise. Louis was still curious as to the nature of his emergency. Whatever it was, they would figure out how to handle it.

6

Louis managed to sleep for a few hours during the night; like many nights before, a catnap would be all he got. The sky was getting lighter to the east as sunrise was imminent. He climbed off the picnic table and put the bike cover back in the side case. Louis fired up the laptop to check the news for any tidbits. There was nothing on the Internet that he could find; Nathan might know more as he had access to the police blotters. He retrieved the sandwiches and the Mountain Dew from the side case and ate his breakfast while surfing the web, checking his e-mail and listening to a little music. It was a cool, crisp morning and the thermometer on the bike indicated 52°.

This time of the morning in Florida, it was in the mid-70s with humidity somewhere in the 90s. It was that time in the morning when the call of the outhouse could not be ignored so Louis closed the laptop, put it in the top case, and walked with purpose the 50 yards to the nearest facilities. There's nothing like the sting of the cold toilet seat on your warm butt to motivate you to a speedy completion. As he walked back toward his bike, the sun beamed through the trees. From across the lake he heard a rooster salute the sun. Tree squirrels and chipmunks were out foraging and there was already a John boat out on the lake with a couple of guys drowning worms.

Just then, he hears the sound of gravel popping under tires and turns to see Nathan riding up on his Goldwing in his familiar red riding jacket. Nathan pulls his bike up next to the BMW and kills the motor. As he swings his leg over the seat, he says, "How's it going, Bro?"

"Not bad at all; just finished my breakfast and my business and watching the squirrels. What time did you leave the house?"

"Maybe two hours ago, if that; left Huntsville well before the sun came up."

As they shook hands, Louis asked, "Anything on the net that I should be aware of?"

"I searched around for about 20 minutes checking the blotters before I left this morning and didn't find a thing about it."

"That's good, but it won't be long until someone finds him."

"How did it go?"

"Smooth as fresh paved asphalt!"

"That's good, that's good."

"Did you have good ride this morning?"

"Yeah, it was warmer over in Huntsville and got downright nippy once I got on the Trace!"

"So tell me about your emergency," Louis said as he sat down at the picnic table.

Nathan sat on the other side table, folded his hands in front of him, and said, "While checking the secure boards yesterday I found a message from a principal contracting a hit."

"Well there's nothing unusual about that, is there?"

"The unusual part happened when I decrypted the message; the contract is on me!"

"You're shitting me!"

"I shit you not!" Nathan replied. "I couldn't believe it when I read the message; it was surreal seeing my name in that context. I never expected it."

"Is that when you called and left the message?"

"Yeah man, I kind of panicked; it took me a few minutes to get my thoughts in order. I went ahead and replied to the message, accepting the contract before someone else did!"

"Who the hell would put a contract on you, Bro?"

"I don't know yet, but I'm working on it. The requestor is sending a partial payment; perhaps I can back-track the transaction and figure out who it is."

"Don't count on it. There's no telling how many hops it will make before it lands in your account."

"Well, I think I may know who's behind it. I've been hearing some scuttlebutt from the community. It seems that good old Senator Richland of Wyoming has his eye on a run for the White House."

"Well, there you go; I bet he's looking to get rid of the skeletons still cluttering his closet. I'm surprised there's not a hit out on me, as well!"

"I truly believe your tracks were covered way back in the day with the Chinese walls that were set up by the agency and us. Even though I reported to him at Langley, he never possessed access or means to discover your identity," Nathan told Louis.

"I hope that's still the case, but in any event, we have to deal with Richland if he's behind this. You bought us a little time by accepting the contract, but you'll have to stall him while you track down and verify that he initiated the contract."

"I can stall them while I backtrack the transaction, but I doubt it was him directly; he'd use a third party to stay out of it."

"We may have to kill you to buy the time to track it down," Louis says, "on paper, anyway. I'm assuming they're asking for verification?"

"Yep, they want hard verification. They want to see a body in the morgue."

"Then that's what we'll have to give them. You need to find a body roughly your size and weight and height that we can burn beyond recognition, destroying any DNA! Looks like it's gonna have to be a car bomb. I hope you're not too attached to your pickup truck," Louis says with a sideways grin.

"Damn, I'm gonna miss that truck," Nathan says with a smirk.

"Well, you need to get back home and start bird-dogging that transaction. Keep me in the loop, and if they contact you again, let him know you assigned it for action," Louis said as he retrieved the laptop from the bike to check the news.

On another topic, Nathan asked, "You remember Paul Seltzer from Montgomery?"

"I remember him but have no idea what he's up to; it's been a few years."

"I just heard from a contact of mine at the Bureau that he graduated from the Academy and is now working in the Memphis field office."

"Well, isn't that just too perfect. He always wanted to be a G-man. I guess he's done it."

"My contact said he's not real happy there. The AIC is riding his ass pretty hard, like they do all the newbies."

"Poor little G-man–should have been careful what he wished for. Who knows, perhaps the time will come when we can use him, or help him along."

Nathan walked over to his motorcycle and removed the memory card from his digital camera. "Are you in a hurry to get back home?"

"Not really, what you got in mind?"

"I have a bit of business down on the Rio Grande that needs to be dealt with if you have time."

"Well, if you got the money, honey, I got the time!" Louis sang with a laugh, quoting Willie Nelson.

"You remember the company I worked for in Madison? One of their subcontractors in Juarez has started moving cocaine across the border in their shipping containers. The warehouse manager in El Paso found a pallet that should have contained radios packed with coke."

"Well, that's one way to boost the bottom line," Louis said.

"The problem is, if he gets busted doing this, it could cause the company to lose the contracts they're still holding, and that would put them and their 120 employees out of business and on the street."

"Who's paying the fee?" Louis asked.

"The fees already been paid; this is kind of a favor for an old friend."

"Are you sure you can trust that old friend?"

"I can trust him, and he has no idea how I'm going to handle it. I told him, 'I know a guy' that can handle it if the money is right, and all I'm going to do is hand it off to him."

Louis reached for the memory card and stuck it in the laptop to look at the data.

"Which image is it?"

"The one with the Welcome to Texas sign."

Louis decrypted the image archive and opened the payload documents. He gave them a quick read. "I'll handle it for you. Well, since I'm going to Texas I may as well drop in on the BMW gang in Houston that's having a service party this Saturday."

"You do realize that's tomorrow, don't you?"

"Yeah, I know today's Friday but didn't think about it until you mentioned it. I can be in Houston in 10 or 12 hours from here without breaking a sweat."

"I better head back to the house and get to work; I've got a body to find and need to track the source of that message and transaction, ASAP."

"You ride safe, Bro. I'm gonna plot a route and head out myself after I send Diane an e-mail."

"Tell her I said hello!"

They shook hands once more and Nathan climbed on his bike for the ride back to Huntsville. Louis took a seat at the picnic table in front of the laptop and banged out a "Good Morning" e-mail to Diane. He told her that he received an invitation to the service party in Houston, and since he was in the neighborhood, it was only polite that he stopped by. Diane responded to the e-mail within a few minutes and told Louis to ride safe and have a good trip, and that she missed him. He responded, "I miss you too, baby. It will only be a couple more days before I'm home, and I'll have a lot to write about when I do. Have a great day and I'll call you later."

Louis shuts down the laptop and stores it in the top case, and fires up the GPS to plot a route to Houston. He decides to follow Natchez Trace Parkway as far south as it goes, then due south to Louisiana, where he'll pick up Interstate 10 west to Houston. He cleans up around the picnic table, and takes another bio break before gearing up for the ride. It's 8:30 am on a beautiful Friday morning in northeast Mississippi.

Louis fired up the bike and headed back out to the Parkway, where he turned south for the downhill run to Louisiana. Riding south on the Natchez Trace Parkway, passing through Tupelo and on to

Jackson, he stopped for fuel before continuing south. Crossing the famous Highway 61, he knew he was getting close to Natchez, where the parkway ends at Liberty Road, and with a short quarter-mile hop, he was on Highway 61 heading south. In another half-hour he was at the Louisiana line, and a half hour after that in Baton Rouge, where he took the 110 south to Interstate 10 west, and on through Port Allen and Lake Charles before crossing the border, just northeast of Orange, Texas, then through Beaumont to Winnie for the night.

The ride down the Natchez Trace Parkway passes through some of the most beautiful scenery in Mississippi. The easy pace of the Parkway gives you plenty of time to think. Louis passed hours thinking about Nathan's problem, and how best to handle it, if Senator Richland was the one responsible for the contract on Nathan's life. They would have to make it look like Nathan was killed, probably a horrific one car accident on a remote road. That meant Nathan had to stay out of sight until Richland was handled, and that Nathan's friends and family would have to believe he was dead, which had to include a funeral that Louis and Diane would have to attend.

Finding a body can be tricky, a problem made a lot easier when you throw cash at it. Staging the wreck would take some planning and coordination; that was after planting a bomb under the gas tank and detonating it in a suitable location, where it would take a long time for emergency services to respond, allowing the vehicle to burn out and destroy the body inside. The whole scenario would get messy and cumbersome, and painful for the many people involved. There had to be a cleaner way, with fewer civilians involved, Louis thought.

Louis found a room at the Winnie Inn, located in lovely Winnie, Texas; it was on the ground floor, where he could park the bike directly outside of the room. He took the duffel bag and the top box contents into the room and switched on the air conditioner. Stripping down, he climbed into the hot shower to drain the road tension from his muscles and wash away the funk he had accumulated over the past couple of days. After the shower, he dressed in clean jeans, some fresh socks, sneakers and a t-shirt before taking a walk up the block to the Mobile station with the Subway sandwich shop he passed on the way in. After enjoying a big Philly Cheesesteak, he refilled his large unsweetened tea and walked back down the street to the motel.

Louis opened his laptop and plugged it in to charge while he checked his e-mail and located the address in Houston where the BMW group was holding their tech session the following day. He shot a message to the host and asked if they minded him dropping in for a few hours, as he was passing through Houston.

It was 7 pm local time, and the sun was still above the horizon in the western sky when he walked out to the bike with a damp towel from the shower, cleaning the layer of bugs that he accumulated over the past two days of riding off the windshield and headlights. He also cleaned the face shield of his helmet and the mirrors on the bike; it was a winding down exercise, which also prepared his gear for the ride the following morning. Louis went back inside the room and turned the television to CNN, listening to the news while he answered his e-mail and relaxed. The message came back from Winston on the BMW board telling him they would be starting around eight in the morning, with lunch around noon. Louis responded that he would be there in the morning. He went back out to the bike, fired up the GPS, and entered the address in Houston, saving it as a waypoint, and then shut down the GPS, locked the bike up and put a cover over it for the night.

At about 7:30 pm, he called home to speak to Diane and catch up on what was happening. They spoke for about 15 minutes, bouncing around from topic to topic as they usually did; they exchanged "I love yous" and said good night. He set the alarm for 6 am and stretched out in the bed, in hopes of getting a night's sleep. There was still nothing on the news out of Collierville about Gray, so he shot an e-mail to Nathan asking if the thing had made it to the blotters. A few minutes later Nathan responded, indicating there was nothing reported. Louis wasn't going to worry about it now that he was out of the area, but he knew it wouldn't be long before Gray's body is discovered. He turned the air conditioner down to sub-Arctic, turned off the TV and the lights and climbed under the covers, waiting for sleep to take him.

● ● ●

The unfamiliar alarm went off at 6 am, jolting Louis awake in the strange room. After a few seconds, he realized he had managed to get some sleep. Perhaps it was the 1600 miles he ridden in the previous two days, but he had done that several times before. Climbing out of bed, he felt alive and refreshed. Within a few minutes he was dressed and repacking the duffel bag. Walking out of the motel room, he noticed the heavy, overcast sky and the smell of rain in the air. He removed the bike cover and strapped the duffel bag to the rear seat, then placed the laptop and other goodies in the top case in preparation for the ride. After making one more pass through the motel room, to ensure he'd forgotten nothing, he cranked the bike and put on his riding gear. Louis pulled out of the motel lot and hung a left, slowly cruising toward the corner, to the Mobile station for fuel and his morning diet Dew, his only caffeine source. Rolling in under the canopy, he stopped in front of an empty pump and climbed off the bike, removed his helmet, sitting it on the seat and walked into the building to prepay for gas. Leaving the attendant $25, he returned to the bike to fuel it.

A half minute after he started pumping gas, the station was suddenly swarming with police cars that blocked all the exits but didn't have their sirens or lights on.

The cops came out of the cars with their guns drawn, taking cover behind open doors and the fenders of their cruisers.

Remaining calm, Louis continued to fuel the motorcycle until the pump shut off at $25. He returned the nozzle to the pump and closed the gas cap on the bike.

There were now six police cars in the lot, two on the side of the store and four blocking exits. *I guess they found the body, but how the hell did they find me?* He thought while trying to remain calm.

Casually looking around at all the cops, he noticed their eyes were on the store, not on him.

Louis donned his helmet and gloves and was mounting the bike when an officer ran up alongside him.

"What's going on, officer?" he asked, while trying to portray the curiosity of the civilian.

"You need to leave, now!" the officer barked.

"Okay, what's going on?"

"There's a man in the store with a gun; now get out of here like I told you."

Louis fired up the bike, did a U-turn around the pump, and left the lot through a small space left open between the front bumper of the cop's car and the curb.

He turned in the direction of the Interstate 10 west on ramp and looked back over his shoulder thinking, *I didn't see anyone with a gun in the store; guess the Dew will have to wait.*

As he rolled up the on-ramp to the interstate, he switched on the GPS to navigate to the address of the tech session he would be attending. The adrenaline rush was subsiding and the tension release sent a tingling sensation throughout his body with a giant sigh of relief.

With 50 miles to go before he hit the Houston traffic, he settled into an easy cruise to his destination. Completely focused and alert, Lewis was thinking, *A Mountain Dew is nothing compared to a shot of adrenaline to get you going first thing in the morning.*

7

A s Louis approached the outer loop around Houston, the traffic was already getting heavy, and the crazies were out early on this dreary Saturday morning. The sky was dark and overcast, but the radar on the GPS showed no rain in the area. The GPS routed him into the heart of Houston traffic, from Interstate 10 to 59 heading southwest, which carried him all the way to Sugar Land, and the Riverbend Country Club, where the tech session was being hosted, just off of Sugar Creek Boulevard, in one of the cul-de-sacs that backed up to the golf course.

Arriving in the circle at 10 minutes after eight, he found a small parking lot of BMW motorcycles ridden by the attendees. Members of the BMW Luxury Touring Community hold these events on a regular basis. The riders get together to kick tires, share riding stories and pitch in to do maintenance on each other's motorcycles. At these events, new owners can learn to do the standard maintenance on the bike, without paying the exorbitant rates for maintenance at the dealerships. Typically, the host of the event has all the tools you would need, and possibly, sometimes a motorcycle lift everyone can use. They also provide lunch, along with water and sodas throughout the day. Everyone makes a donation to cover the costs, and usually, whatever is left over is donated to the online community to support the website that brings everyone together.

Louis parked his bike on the edge of the cul-de-sac, near the driveway, and climbed out of his riding gear as a small contingent of riders gathered around to greet him. They all shook hands and introduced themselves, although Louis already knew a few of them. They stood around the bike and talked for a few minutes, asking questions and commenting on the big R1200GS-Adventure Louis rode, as was customary. They all walked up the driveway toward the garage, where there was a K1200LT on the lift, with a couple of guys busily changing the oil and filter, transmission oil and differential lube.

Louis spoke up. "Hello everybody! The Florida delegation has arrived."

He spent a few more minutes shaking hands and catching up with old friends. Mark Williams, the host of the event, handed Louis a cold diet Dew, saying, "Since I knew you were coming, I stocked up," throwing a big Texas grin at him.

"Thanks Mark, I appreciate the invitation and the cold drink."

"Where did you stay last night?"

"In the giant metropolis of Winnie, Texas."

"Did you hit rain on the way over?"

"No, it was just the same heavy, overcast clouds that you have here."

Throughout the morning, Louis took a ton of photos, as bikes rolled in and out of the garage and up and down on the lift, while busy hands performed maintenance and installed farkles on the variety of BMW motorcycles. Somewhere around noon, Mark's wife Tammy appeared in the garage and announced, "Lunch is served on the patio," where she was busy grilling burgers and dogs for the crew. The crowd moved to the patio, where everyone grabbed a plate and a seat, enjoying the food while a cacophony of conversations occurred around them–the male equivalent of a hen party. Mark announced to the crowd, "It looks like Louis takes the long-rider award for the day, having ridden in from the Tampa Bay area." Then he asked Louis, "How many miles is that, anyway?"

"Somewhere between 1500 and 1600, I guess. I made a little detour to Memphis for some ribs, then back to Tupelo to ride the Natchez Trace down to Natchez, then south to Baton Rouge before heading west."

Floyd, another one of the riders, chimed in, "How long will it be before we can read about it and see the pictures online?"

"That kind of depends on how long I'm out on the road this trip. When I leave here, I'm heading to Albuquerque to visit my sister, before turning around and heading home. That is, if I don't add any additional destinations, which I tend to do," Louis said while shrugging his shoulders and moving his eyebrows up and down.

Tammy asked, "So where did you go for ribs in Memphis? I just adore Rendezvous."

"That's exactly where I went; I rode all the way from Florida for their dry rubbed delicacies."

Tammy spoke again, "Did you hear? There was a story on the news, about an hour ago, about some priest outside of Memphis; he was found murdered in his bathtub."

"No, I haven't watched the news in a few days now; what happened?" Louis said, feigning curiosity.

"They didn't say much more than that. I guess the story is still developing."

To change the subject, Louis stood up and spoke. "I'd like to thank our hosts, Tammy and Mark, for opening their home to us today, and for the delicious lunch, and their gracious hospitality." Everyone applauded in agreement before cleaning up the mess and heading back to the garage.

The happenings in the garage continued as riders slowly trickled away, heading back from where they came around the area. Louis topped off the engine oil of his bike, checked the pressure in the tires, and added some octane booster to the fuel tank before gearing up for the ride west to El Paso. Shaking everyone's hand and exchanging cordial goodbyes, he left the cul-de-sac and Sugar Land at 2 pm, heading north to intersect Interstate 10, to head west. This was a fun day, hanging out with friends, swapping stories while working on bikes, but there was work to do ahead of him, and it was time to get to it.

El Paso was 700 miles and 11 hours away, the GPS indicated. Louis remembered the old adage about Texas being 'miles and miles of more miles and miles' but that had never deterred him from riding across the beautifully expansive state. The route took him around

San Antonio, through Boerne, north of Kerrville, and northwest to Junction, where the cities and towns get sparse in the still somewhat wide-open west Texas. Louis stopped in Ft. Stockton for dinner, as the sun was going down; the scent of sage was in the air. The live oaks gave way to scrub brush and cactus, and the buttes were topped with wind farms, harnessing the almost constant wind that sweeps unimpeded out of the desert southwest this time of year.

Louis enjoyed a steak and salad and called Diane to catch up before refueling the bike and again heading west, into the darkness on Interstate 10. An hour and a half later, as he passed through Van Horn, he recalled the last time he was here, searching around for a deputy sheriff to sign his witness form for the Iron Butt 50CC challenge he was riding. Van Horn is 1500 miles from the beach at Jacksonville Florida, where he started the Iron Butt ride a few years earlier. If you can find a witness to sign the form, and you make it in less than 24 hours, you qualify for an additional certificate from the Iron Butt Association. Louis completed the 50CC ride, which is coast-to-coast in less than 50 hours. He made it from Jacksonville to San Diego in 39 hours and 3 minutes; an accomplishment that only a small percentage of motorcycle riders would ever attempt and even fewer would complete.

Another 50 miles up the road, and he was riding parallel to the Mexican border. This stretch of highway was lit up like daylight, and you see Border Patrol vehicles every few minutes, some parked while doing surveillance and some moving quickly from place to place. Louis remembered the last time he passed through here. It was dark then as well, and a group of about eight Mexicans darted across the highway in front of him, causing him to lock down on his brakes to prevent becoming a bowling ball to their pins. Louis watched carefully, hoping it wouldn't repeat, as he rolled on toward his destination in the cool night air. It was 2 am local time as Louis exited Interstate 10 at Hawkins Blvd. in east El Paso and rode through the empty parking lot of the Cielo Vista Mall and into the parking lot of the 24-hour Wal-Mart next door. He parked near the corner of the building, next to some picnic tables, and climbed off the bike. After walking around and stretching his legs and back for a few minutes, he retrieved the laptop from the top case and took a seat on one of the benches.

When the laptop came alive, he located a free Wi-Fi signal from Hooters across the street. He checked his e-mail and found several messages from Nathan, indicating the parish priests, who opened Gray's front door and looked in the apartment for him when he failed to show up at mass Saturday morning, found the body. Nathan copied Louis on the blotter information from the Collierville Police Department that indicated an adult male, assumed to be Marcus Richard Gray, was found dead in his bathtub, face-down, with what appeared to be two bullet holes in the back of the head. The remains were floating in water and the body was bloated, requiring dental confirmation for positive identification. It further indicated the body was in the possession of the Shelby County Coroner's Office.

Louis fired off an e-mail to Nathan. "Thanks for the info, looks interesting. I'm now close to next." He then opened the CNN website to see what they were reporting. They had an interview with one of the parishioners, who was expounding on the shock and surprise of such a senseless killing of their priest. There was a video, with one of the talking heads commenting on what they knew about Gray–how long he had been at the church in Collierville, etc. The news anchor mentioned that not much was known, at this point about where Gray was located in the years since his ordination, but they were sure to look into it, as this was a juicy story gaining attention nationally.

A deputy Sheriff pulled up behind Louis' motorcycle, parked at the curb. Louis continued to stare at the laptop screen while he watched the deputy speak into his microphone. *Probably running the plates,* Louis thought. The light from the screen of the deputy's laptop illuminated his young, clean-shaven face. A minute or so later he stepped out of the cruiser and left his door open as he approached Louis.

"What are you doing out here this time in the morning?" the deputy asked.

"I just stopped to take a break and check my e-mail; I'm passing through on the way to Albuquerque," Louis replied with a smile.

"I need to see your license and registration."

Louis replied, "My wallet's in the top case on the back of the bike; it's unlocked if you want to get it yourself," knowing the deputy wouldn't want Louis to open it, in case there was a weapon inside.

The deputy switched on his Mag-light and opened the lid on the top case, glancing around a few seconds before grabbing the wallet and handing it to Louis.

Louis retrieved his driver's license and registration from the wallet and handed them to the deputy, who looked them over for a few seconds before handing them back.

"It's kind of late at night to be riding, don't you think?"

"I prefer riding in the desert at night. There's a lot less traffic and cooler temperatures," Louis said, as he closed his laptop before asking the deputy, "Is there an IHOP nearby? I need a bite to eat," knowing he rode past one when he left the highway.

"There's one on the other side of the mall across Hawkins Boulevard." He pointed in the general direction.

Louis said, "I'm gonna grab some breakfast before heading out. Would you like a cup of coffee?"

"I appreciate the offer, but I'm on patrol and need to get back to it."

"Well, be safe and have a good night," Louis said as he placed the laptop and his wallet in the top case and locked it before sliding into his riding jacket and helmet for the short ride across the parking lot to the IHOP. As he rode out of the Wal-Mart parking lot and across the mall's empty parking lot, the deputy followed at a distance. When Louis crossed the boulevard into the IHOP parking lot, the deputy turned north and disappeared around the corner at the next light. Louis parked the bike by the front door, carried his laptop inside with him and took a seat in the booth near the entrance.

A redheaded forty-something waitress, who walked as if she'd been on her feet for two weeks, took his order and returned to the table with a large glass of orange juice and a friendly, "Your pancakes will be out in a few, honey; can I get you anything else?"

Louis smiled and replied, "No thank you; that should just about do it for me."

He continued reading the article on CNN and then searched other news outlets to see what they had to say as he relaxed and ate the blueberry pancakes the waitress delivered. Reviewing the dossier Nathan provided him on Esteban Morales, his next bit of work, he studied the background information, the photos and the locations of the Morales home and business in Juarez, the receiving warehouse in El Paso where shipments from across the border arrive, as well as the location of a small apartment he kept in south El Paso. The dossier included his family life, his education at Universidad Benito Juarez, where he received a bachelor's degree in business administration in 1996, and a list of his known associates in the drug trade on both sides of the border.

Morales owned a small electronics company in Juarez where they built subassemblies of radios and engine controllers that were then shipped to Huntsville for final assembly and delivery to the auto manufacturers scattered around the nation. When the bottom fell out of the US auto industry, the contracts dried up and so did the money that was flowing across the border into Morales' business. Apparently, in an effort to keep his business afloat until the US auto industry got back on its feet, Morales fell back on what he knew about drug trafficking and began moving cocaine across the border, packed in airtight sterilized bags hidden inside pallets of radio assemblies. The special antistatic shipping containers would hold 25 radio assemblies per tray, with five trays per pallet; that was before Morales hollowed out the center of the trays to conceal the bags of cocaine, with one row of radio assemblies on the outside, all the way around. They then plastic-wrapped the stack of trays onto the pallet, and labeled it for shipment to the El Paso holding area warehouse.

Someone at the El Paso warehouse was intercepting the pallets carrying the cocaine and removing them, but somehow missed one pallet, leaving it in the shipping container. The warehouse manager found it. When he looked up the order number labeled on the pallet, he found no such order existed. He cut away the plastic wrap to examine the contents, and when he lifted off the top tray, he saw the black rubberized bags hidden in the center of the stack. The four bags contained 25 kilos of cocaine each.

The warehouse manager called the business owner in Huntsville and told him what he found. They decided to rewrap the pallet in plastic, replace the shipping label and put the pallet back in the shipping container where he found it. Eventually someone would come looking for it; its owner would definitely miss 100 kilos of cocaine. A video camera on top of the warehouse, pointing toward the container, recorded around the clock. Two days later, a small moving truck backed up to the container and four men loaded the pallet into the moving truck and drove away. The driver of the truck was Esteban Morales. There was no doubt he was responsible. Morales kept a low profile, with no security guards around him while on the north side of the border; projecting the image of a minor businessman was his aim.

Louis decided to check out his place at the Father Pinto apartments on south Ochoa Street, located near the warehouse. If he found him here, on this side of the border, it would make his task a lot easier to accomplish. Morales owned a 98 Mercedes SLK hardtop convertible; it would be an easy car spot in that neighborhood. Morales' apartment was on the eighth floor facing south, toward the Mexican border, less than a quarter of a mile from the apartment.

He punched the address into the GPS for the fastest route and put on his dark-colored mesh riding jacket. Sunrise was only a half hour away when he pulled out of the IHOP parking lot and back on Interstate 10 heading west. The apartment was just 15 minutes away, and there should be little traffic this time of the morning. Arriving at the apartment building on south Ochoa St., Louis parked the bike at the end of the building, locking the handlebars before walking down the sidewalk to check for security cameras. Seeing none, he scanned the parking lot for the silver Mercedes convertible. He was in luck, finding it parked in front of the building.

Returning to the bike, he sat his helmet on the seat and stuffed his riding gloves in the tank bag of the bike, then opened the right side case to remove the Walther from its hiding place, shoving it in the left sleeve of his mesh jacket, at the armpit. He grabbed his baseball cap and a pair of burn gloves and walked around the end of the building, over to the Mercedes.

Louis looked around to ensure no one was watching. He stomped the bumper with his foot, hard enough to set off the car alarm, and then quickly moved to the entrance of the building, past the elevator door, while the car alarm was blaring.

Putting on his gloves, he reached for the Walther, cocked the hammer and tripped the safety as the elevator started down from the eighth floor.

When the doors opened a dark-haired man in a blue bathrobe with car keys in hand headed out the front door. It was Morales, in a rush to check on his high value car.

Louis stepped inside the elevator and pressed the eighth floor button; the doors closed and he ascended.

When the doors opened, Louis noted that you exit the elevator turning right to proceed down the hall.

On the left, outside the elevator doors, were some artificial plants with the corridor wall behind them, some four feet back from the elevator door.

Louis stepped out, looked around and backed into the corner, waiting for Morales to return when he heard the elevator begin to move.

The enclosed area around the elevator had no windows or doors, and at the end of the corridor, you turn left or right to access the apartment doors.

The elevator returned to the first floor; then seconds later started back to the eighth. Louis drew the Walther from the jacket sleeve.

With his back in the corner and the Walther behind his right leg, he waited in ambush, slowing his breathing, focusing his mind.

The doors opened, Morales exited the elevator heading toward his apartment, as he must have done a thousand times.

Louis stepped out from the corner, raising the pistol toward Morales' head, when a young woman turned the corner, heading toward the elevator with her head down, digging in her purse.

Louis quickly concealed the Walther inside his jacket, and as she passed him, turned to follow her into the elevator. *Damn, that was close,* Louis thought.

He stood next to the attractive young woman, dressed in hospital scrubs, as the elevator descended to the ground floor and the door opened.

She walked straight to the parking lot while Louis hung back until she was in her car and rolling out of the lot.

Once again, Louis walked over to the Mercedes and booted the bumper, again tripping the car alarm that wailed in the pre-dawn silence.

Louis moved quickly, past the elevator entrance, waiting and hoping that Morales would fall for it again.

The elevator went to the eighth floor and came back to the ground level with Morales heading toward the lot, this time with an automatic pistol in his hand.

Slipping inside the elevator, Louis pressed the eighth floor button, ascended once more, and got in place in the corner behind the elevator.

While awaiting the mark's arrival in his kill zone, Louis again slowed his breathing and heart rate, in preparation for the money shot.

A minute later, the doors opened and Morales quickly exited the elevator, walking the hallway toward his apartment.

Louis raised the Walther and took aim with the slide locked by his thumb and released a round that struck Morales in the back of the head, and he instantly collapsed to the carpeted floor.

He quickly walked the fifteen feet up beside him while chambering a new round, then tapped him a second time.

Turning, he walked directly to the elevator while the doors remained open, and pressed the first floor button.

Inside the elevator, he chambered a new round, put the Walther in his belt under his jacket, and slid the two empty brass casings into his pocket.

The elevator doors opened at the first floor and Louis, with his head down and his hands in his jacket pockets, quickly walked around the end of the building to his bike.

He put on his helmet, started the bike and did a quick U-turn, heading north on Ochoa St.

Several blocks up the quiet street, he pulled into the empty parking lot of a warehouse, stopping the bike and leaning it on its kickstand, leaving the engine running.

Louis moved around to the right side case, stashing the Walther in its hiding place.

Removing the grey mesh jacket he was wearing, he put on the yellow high-visibility jacket, climbed back on the bike and continued north on Ochoa St.

Turning left on San Antonio Ave., then right on N. Campbell St., up the on-ramp to Interstate 10 heading east and moving at the same pace as the Sunday morning traffic.

Within 20 minutes, he was calmly heading southeast out of El Paso on Interstate 10, parallel to the Mexican border, with the warmth of the blazing sunrise in his eyes.

Louis noticed a fast moving dark sedan, weaving through traffic, coming up behind him. The car was still a hundred yards back when he saw the rail of lights across the top.

Holy shit, He thought, *where did he come from?* The Texas Highway Patrol car was in the same lane as Louis and stayed back, following at a distance, no longer weaving through traffic once it was behind the bike.

Louis quickly identified his options. He could haul ass down the road through traffic and try evading the cop, or pull to the side of the road, as if there was an issue with the bike.

Perhaps dive into the median, make a quick U-turn heading back toward town, and get lost in the traffic.

The patrol car started moving closer, closing the distance between them. *This can't be happening,* Louis thought. *Stay calm and let's see what happens next.*

Louis moved one lane to the right and backed off the throttle a little. The cop stayed in the center lane, creeping up beside him.

He watched the cop in his left mirror and could see his face clearly. The cop reached for his microphone and then replaced it before hitting his lights.

The cop slid over into the left lane and entered the median before making a U-turn and heading away.

Louis stood up on the pegs of the bike, un-wedging the seat from his ass, and continued toward Sierra Blanca, 80 miles away, where he stopped for fuel, a cold diet Dew and a bio break. In the parking lot of the truck stop, he fired up the laptop on the back of the bike and checked his e-mail. Louis composed a brief note to Nathan. "Request completed; see what you can find for me."

While he waited for a response, he dumped the burn gloves in the trash receptacle at one of the pumps, and sipped his Dew, watching the traffic coming in and out of the truck stop. He powered up the GPS and deleted the waypoints he no longer needed and erased the track logs that showed where he had been. He checked the news online to find out the latest on Gray. No new facts had surfaced, but the story had made national headlines, and was on BBC News as well. One of the 20 or so e-mails he received overnight was from April, still living in Brandon, Florida.

"Hi Louis, how have you been? I've been watching the news and wondered if you remembered that long conversation we shared at lunch, maybe two years back when we still worked together. I told you about the incident with my son Michael, and the priest that disappeared before they could prosecute him. It's all over the news that he was found dead at a church in Tennessee. Apparently, someone shot him in the head. I knew karma would catch up to him eventually. Anyway, I just wanted to make sure you saw the story, take care. –April"

Louis responded, "Hi April, good to hear from you, been a long time. I'm at a truck stop way over in west Texas, just out for a leisurely ride on the motorcycle. I haven't watched the news in several days; been too busy enjoying the fine weather in the desert southwest. It sounds like karma ran over his dogma and paid him back with a vengeance. We'll have to get together for lunch at some point, when I'm back in Florida. I hope you and the kids are doing well. Diane and I are great. Later –Louis"

He was thinking, *I hope that closes the book on that episode in their lives,* when he noticed that Nathan responded.

"That didn't take long. Nothing on the news there but the blotter shows officers were called to the scene a few minutes ago. It seems I owe you some coin; how would you like that?"

Louis replied, "In my account at the Beau Rivage in Biloxi; I want to play some cards before heading home."

Louis closed the laptop, placing it in the top case before walking into the truck stop to hit the head once more and get another diet Dew before heading east. The truck stop had overhead monitors with the weather and the national news. Louis purchased the Dew and watched the news for a few minutes, and walked back out to the bike. He again opened the laptop and received another reply from Nathan. "Good luck with the cards, Bro. The casino acknowledged the transfer. The blotter now indicates detectives are en route to the scene, as well as the corner. By the way, I enjoyed some luck with that other transaction; they didn't cover their tracks the way a professional would. Check back later. I'll stay on top of the events still unfolding."

Shutting down the laptop, he stored it away and climbed back into his gear. Within a few minutes, he was heading east on Interstate 10, listening to the radio and enjoying the sunny west Texas morning.

8

Louis continued east on Interstate 10, again passing through Van Horn and across the arid expanse of west Texas. He found himself thinking about what the counselors at the Veteran's Administration told him about his PTS, years earlier. After returning from Africa and Central America, he noticed changes in his personality, an almost constant irritability that could become explosive, and a sense of dread and paranoia that would overtake him when he spent any time in crowds. He found that he became impatient and intolerant of average people; the civilians, around whom he would spend the rest of his life, seemed to be a well of ignorance and apathy of which there was no bottom. Even though he realized it was he who had changed, not humankind, he found it difficult at times to just carry on a civil conversation. In the seemingly month-long nights without sleep, as his mind darted from thought to thought, and from bad memory to worse memory, he often considered suicide to stop the constant pain and mental anguish his life had become.

The VA shrinks categorized him as a Combat Related, 10% disabled vet and prescribed a battery of antidepressants, antipsychotics and sleeping pills that left him feeling intellectually and emotionally numb, as well as impotent, but somewhat able to cope with the daily emotional roller coaster he experienced, between boredom and extreme anxiety, while developing a career in the IT industry. Finding it almost impossible to remain with a company in one position, he was constantly looking for promotion or his next job. He rose quickly through the ranks, and easily distinguished himself as a detail-oriented, hard worker who always ended up managing others, and that's where things would start to fall apart. When working alone, or in a team, his focus was on the task, that when completed, provided a sense of satisfaction. However, once he began managing others, dealing with the daily minutia of personality conflicts and petty emotions made him feel like he worked at the offices of Auto-du-fé Inc., and the grand inquisitor, Torquemada, was personally sandpapering his ass with an industrial grinder.

Soon he would be looking for another job in yet another company and the process would start all over again. Louis developed an employment shelf life of four years or less, and while this, in and of itself, was not unusual in the IT field, the process was emotionally traumatic for Louis, who suffered social defeat each time it happened.

During this long lifecycle-loop of job after job, Louis slowly developed some coping skills that helped him deal with the stresses that burdened his mind. Riding a motorcycle daily, and enjoying the freedom of it, along with the risks, released a lot of stress. Taking long multi-day trips around the country by motorcycle a couple of times a year did wonders for his mindset and attitude. And throughout it all, there was the constant friendship and support of Nathan, who suffered through Louis' raw-nerved tirades and extended bouts of depression that hung like a storm cloud over his head for years. Nathan accepted Louis, and the trainload of emotional baggage he drug around, without complaint or judgment, hoping his friend would one day emerge from his lifelong death sentence.

After a pair of failed marriages, spanning 13 years, Louis moved to Florida, where the daily bombardment of almost constant sunshine considerably improved his outlook on life and proved to be an effective ally in fighting the depression that the load of medications did little to improve. It was in Florida where he first met his angel, Diane. Louis met Diane when she interviewed him for a position in the IT department of a national drugstore retail chain. During the employee orientation that she was leading, he annoyed the living hell out of her with questions about topics that would be covered in a later orientation. It wasn't his intention to annoy her, but he did a fine job of it nonetheless. In the weeks that followed, he made a point to apologize to her for being such a pain during the orientation. He began to send her Dilbert cartoons by e-mail in the mornings, when he found one on the topic of human resources or clueless management. It was a friendly, self-deprecating way to continue extending the olive branch to her. After a couple of years, and several life situational changes later, they began to date, and fell in love, something that scared the hell out of both of them, given their experiences with relationships. Within a year they purchased a home and were living together. Moreover, for the first time, they both enjoyed a peaceful and happy home life, where stress was something only pertaining to work.

Following a few more job changes, Louis realized that working in corporate America was incompatible with his mental health, because the PTS permanently altered his mental processes, and no amount of medication could break the cycle chiseled on the headstone of his life. Many years earlier, Louis began journaling as a therapeutic means to deal with stress and in an effort to get the thoughts out of his head and down on paper, where possibly they could be discarded. The journaling turned into blogging as the technology came about, and provided a forum for his thoughts, opinions and photography. However, he still needed a source of income to support his lifestyle and it couldn't be in the minefield of stress that is cube-world in corporate America. Knowing Nathan was still active in the intelligence community, he decided to return to his training and apply the skills the government invested so much in providing him. In this world, he answered only to himself, and found no emotional stress or remorse in it. The PTS had long since burned out the wiring in that part of his brain. He was a Mechanic, and he was good at it.

Diane supports his blogging and writing, and even accepts their time apart while he is on the road, collecting stories and photographing his rides, as she sees the beautiful change it brings about in him. In her mind, the money flowing in comes from the blogging and the advertisers; this is the only secret Louis keeps from her.

• • •

Louis stopped in Junction for fuel, and was now approaching San Antonio and decided to pass on through town before stopping on the east side for lunch. Traffic was heavy on Interstate 10 through San Antonio, even for Sunday afternoon. He continued east to Schulenburg before stopping at the Dairy Queen on Kessler Avenue, just south of the interstate. The Dairy Queen was packed, and the parking lot was full of Honda Goldwings. The local Goldwing riding club was out on this fine Sunday afternoon, making the rounds, and chose this Dairy Queen as their place to meet. Everywhere you looked, there were Goldwings of every color, year and variation, along with the riders and pillion passengers dressed like twins, sporting the same shirts and vests and hats–a common theme among the older Goldwing riders. Louis parked the BMW in the only open space he could find, between two Goldwings next to the street. As he was removing his jacket and helmet, one of the geezers sitting on his trike spoke up. "You're in the wrong place aren't you?"

"Not unless they've run out of food inside."

"Did you ride that thing all the way from Florida?"

"Nope, it was in my pocket while I rode the Greyhound out here," Louis said with a grin, before heading toward the front door.

After waiting in line for 20 minutes, Louis received the burger and chocolate shake he ordered and headed back out to his bike to eat his lunch and watch the goings-on in the parking lot. He sat the shake and the burger on the top case and grabbed the small Casio digital camera from the tank bag to snap a few photos of the crowd and bikes, before inhaling the burger. The geezers moved in waves, two by two, around the lot, in and out of the Dairy Queen, the pins on their vests sparkling in the bright sunshine.

Louis finished the burger and took a walk around the lot, sipping on the shake and taking in the sight of all these Wings, sporting every piece of chrome known to man, and every variation of accessory, from giant windscreens called Sails to wood-grained appliqué covering everything in the cockpit to leopard skin seat covers and custom tow-behind trailers, painted to match the bike. These people were clearly proud of their rigs, with many a retirement check invested in them.

Across the parking lot, in front of the Dairy Queen, the sound of a police whistle interrupted all the conversations. The geezers quickly moved, two by two, toward their Goldwings, mounting their rides and forming an orderly line out of the parking lot, turning south toward downtown Schulenburg, and on to their next destination on this Sunday club ride. Within five minutes, Louis was alone in the parking lot, with just his BMW and the cars belonging to the workers inside the Dairy Queen. He walked inside, where there was now no line for the men's room, a welcome sight at that particular moment. Heading back out to the bike, he geared up and rolled out of the lot, returning to the highway and his eastbound trek across the state.

● ● ●

It was now 4:30 pm, and the sun was well behind him while he covered the remaining 100 miles to Houston, passing straight through toward Beaumont, where he again stopped for fuel.

The GPS indicated that he was just 400 miles away from the Beau Rivage in Biloxi, where he planned to exchange his chips for cash and spend the night, getting some rest. Louis continued across southern Louisiana, where the smell of creosote was so thick you could pave the highway with it. The long bridges across Lake Bigeux and Des Ourses Swamp created a rhythmic double tap as the tires bounced over the expansion joints between the bridge sections that repeated every hundred feet or so. At Baton Rouge he exited Interstate 10 for 12, passing north of Lake Pontchartrain, and then back on 10 in north Slidell, before crossing into Mississippi, just north of Pearlington, then a few miles on down the road turning south on 110 for the short downhill slide to Biloxi.

The Beau Rivage was just off 110 on the south side of 90. Louis rolled up to the valet parking area and climbed off the bike, near the curb, away from cars. He removed his helmet, jacket and riding gloves, locked the bike and walked over to the valet window to tell them he was headed to the VIP check-in and would be back to move the bike to the parking deck shortly. Entering the lobby, he headed straight for the men's room to freshen up a bit before continuing. It was 10:30 pm local time, and there was little going on at the VIP check-in. He took a seat at one of the tables and handed his credit card, driver's license and player's club card to the attractive thirty-something blonde, whose perfume doubled as mosquito repellant, prepared to help him.

"Welcome back, Mr. Parker," she said with a wide smile. "How can we help you today?"

"I don't have a reservation this time, but you should've received a wire transfer into my account here this morning. I'd like a small non-smoking room for the night, after I have some fun in the casino."

"Yes, I see your transfer of $25,000, but unfortunately, we have no rooms available at the moment."

"That's okay, just put me on your list for next available and give me a parking pass so I can pull my motorcycle into the secure parking area in the deck."

"I can do that for you; it'll just take a minute to print the pass."

"I'm in no hurry; this chair is kind of comfortable," Louis said as he leaned back.

The blonde's fingernails sounded like castanets as they flew over the keyboard when she put Louis on the waiting list, then she asked, "What type of motorcycle is it?"

"A silver BMW with a Florida plate, DBLTAP," he replied.

"Thank you Mr. Parker, I'll have that permit for you in just a moment."

She stood up from the table, turned and walked into the small hallway to get the permit from the special printer. "Here you go, when you pull into the parking deck, turn to the right and slide this card into the reader. It will open the security gate for you. You have to swipe it again to get back out."

"Thank you very much. I'll be right back in to play some cards."

"When a room comes open, I'll send you a message on the floor. Have fun," she said, smiling warmly.

Louis headed back to the valet parking area and rode his bike around the circle to the parking deck, to the secure parking area. As he swiped the card, the 10-foot tall gates slid open, and he rode inside, parking the bike at the first available slot. He opened the duffel bag and retrieved a clean polo shirt and jeans, stuffing his t-shirt back in the bag. Standing against the wall at the end of his parking slot, he removed his riding pants and slipped into the blue jeans, and put on the sneakers that were in the side case.

It was now time to convert chip to coin and enjoy some time off the bike.

9

Locking the handlebars and the cases, Louis exited the secure parking area with a swipe of the card. He walked across the parking deck and into the double doors that led toward the check-in area, and again stopped in the men's room to get comfortable before heading into the casino. Louis took a seat in the high-stakes card room at an empty $50 per hand blackjack table. Handing his player's card and driver's license to the dealer, he said, "I'd like $25,000 from my account, please."

The dealer turned and handed the cards to the pit boss, passing along the request. The pit boss slid his card through the reader of the terminal and stared at the screen. He quickly made a few entries and turned to the dealer with a nod to okay the chip request. As the dealer stacked out the twenty-four $1000 chips, five $100 and ten $50 chips in front of him, the pit boss looked on to approve the count. "Here you go, sir, good luck," said the dealer, as he sat the deck of cards into the Shuffle Master, waiting for them to reappear ready for play.

Just then, a cocktail waitress touched Louis on the shoulder and asked, "Cocktails, sir?"

"Yes please, I'll have a vodka sour, made with Absolut, please."

She sat a cocktail napkin down and said, "I'll be right back," with a smile.

Louis bet a $50 chip and the dealer started dealing. Louis held a seven and a four, the dealer was showing seven. Louis slid out another $50 chip and said, "Double down." The dealer dealt him a Jack, and Louis said, "That's 21 for me," as the dealer turned over his down card to reveal a 10. The dealer said, "You're a winner," and sat a $100 chip next to the two $50s Louis played.

The cocktail waitress returned with the drink, placing it on the napkin, Louis handed her a $10 for her tip and asked her to come back by in a few minutes with another one. The vodka sour tasted like sweet lemonade with a kick, just what Louis needed to relax after a very long day of riding. Louis played heads-up blackjack for three hours straight, as the dealers rotated through his table. He was on a rush, winning three times as many hands as he lost, while maximizing his bet at every opportunity. After three vodka sours over a three hour period, Louis needed a bio break.

Returning to the table he found his rush was still on, as the cards favored him for a few more hours and his original $25,000 in chips grew to over $37,500. When the worm turned, and he started losing, he told the dealer, "Color me up, please. I think I'm done." The dealer exchanged his chips for thirty-six $1000 chips, while the pit boss watched the exchange.

Louis walked to a cage and cashed in $4000 worth of chips, slipping the cash into the front pocket of his jeans, and walked around the different games on the casino floor for a while, walking up to a different cage and exchanging another $4000 in chips for cash, adding it to the bankroll his front pocket. Still waiting to hear if he was going to get a room for the night, Louis cashed in another $4000 in chips, and then more at the different cages in increments of $4000, until all he held in chips was $4000, and he took them to a craps table. Louis stood there for a while, with his chips in his hand, watching the dealers rake in everything from both ends of the table. *Only the house is winning here,* he thought, so he cashed in his remaining $4000 in chips and headed to the buffet to strap on the feedbag.

After enjoying a plate of fresh fruit, along with some blueberry crêpes, a glass of orange juice and a hot cup of English breakfast tea, he was ready to return to the casino with his batteries fully charged. He glanced at his watch to discover it was approaching 7 am and thought for a few moments before he headed toward the door, stopping at the nearest restroom before he left the casino. Louis stood in the handicapped stall, counting the cash he had stashed in his front pockets. He was up just over $11,000 without having to pay taxes or sign any of the forms. Cashing it out a little at a time does that for you. Luck at blackjack had turned his $25,000 into $36,000 in just a few hours, with a minimum of risk and the application of good money management skill. He stuffed his wallet with all the $100 bills it would hold and folded the rest back into his pockets before using the facilities and heading over to the VIP check-in office to cancel his room request; then Louis headed out the door to his bike.

It had been a good night and Louis was feeling fine as he entered the secure parking area. He quickly slipped into his riding pants and a t-shirt, stuffing his blue jeans and the polo shirt in the duffel bag. He slipped on his riding boots and put the sneakers away in the side case. Louis decided he should check his e-mail before heading home, so he fired up the laptop and after a few seconds found that there was no Wi-Fi connection available, probably blocked by the hotel or casino.

He closed the laptop, placed his wallet in the top case, and locked it. He climbed into his jacket and helmet, fired up the bike and left the secure parking area, pulling back out on 90 and turning to the right to locate a free Wi-Fi signal at a coffee shop, or restaurant or bookstore; they are pretty much everywhere. A couple of thousand feet down the road, he saw a Starbucks sign, below the Hard Rock Casino sign, so he pulled into the parking lot and stopped. He opened the top case and the laptop and there was the Wi-Fi he was looking for, so he checked his e-mail.

There were a few messages waiting from Nathan, so he scanned them all. The blotter showed the full story on Morales, who was now in the morgue. The blotter indicated that there were no fingerprints, gunshot residue or empty shell casings left at the scene. The detective's notes attached to the blotter indicated a possible connection with a known drug dealer, an associate of Morales, or one of his crew, any of whom could be responsible for the early morning 187.

Nathan's last e-mail also included a link to a story on the BBC website that indicated Gray was previously a person of interest in three separate child molestation investigations in different parts of the United

States, but disappeared when the Catholic Church moved him around, refusing to cooperate with the authorities. Louis fired off an e-mail to Nathan indicating that he was in Biloxi playing cards all night and enjoyed some luck at the tables. He asked him if he made any progress tracking down the source of the transaction.

While he waited for Nathan to respond, he turned on his cell phone and called Diane on her cell phone. It was 9 am, Monday morning in Tampa, and Diane was already at work when she answered the phone. "Hey baby, I was starting to worry about you. Where are you?"

"I'm standing in the parking lot of the Hard Rock Casino in Biloxi, waiting on Nathan to get back to me by e-mail before I decide what to do next."

"Well, how did the tech session go in Houston?"

"It was busy as hell, with tons of bikes, lasting all day. I took a lot of photos and spent the night before meandering back this way."

"Are you coming home today?" she asked.

"Probably, just waiting to see what Nathan has on his plate before heading out."

"Well, I should be home around 6:30 tonight; call me and let me know what you're going to do, okay?"

"I'll call you back before I leave here, I promise. I love you!"

"I love you too and miss you; bye-bye."

When they hung up, Louis felt like an ass. He hated lying to Diane but there were some things he just couldn't tell her.

Louis again checked his e-mail and found that Nathan replied.

"Hey Bro, check out this weird photo I found," which was code for download the image and decrypt it.

Louis clicked on the image and saved it to his computer. With the image on his desktop, he decrypted the archive, as well as its payload document containing what Nathan wanted to tell him.

Nathan backtracked the partial payment he received to a bank in Barbados, then back to a bank in Morocco, and then back to its source, a bank in Panama. He found all the routing numbers and individual bank accounts, as well as the names and contact information of most of the account holders. Louis thought, *Nathan has been a busy boy.* Sen.

Richland had become quite sloppy, considering his background with the agency back in the day. However, back then, the Internet didn't exist, and Richland had aged past the point where developing computer skills and knowledge of the net and its capabilities were of any interest to him.

One of his techno flunkies, a former lackey of his at the agency, was on his staff as an aide, and handling security issues well beyond his knowledge and capabilities. This dust mite of brilliance posted the message for the hit, which Nathan intercepted. The aforementioned dust mite then initiated a wire transfer, using his cell phone, from Richland's offshore account in Panama to an existing account of a known shell company in Morocco. He then initiated a wire transfer from the shell company to the bank in Barbados, from his personal laptop with only the most basic of security software installed and configured, not at all a challenge for someone of Nathan's capabilities.

Nathan searched the phone records of everyone on Richland's staff and located the call to the bank in Panama. Once he collected all the pertinent numbers, he made contact with a former coworker, now working for the NSA, who made a simple digital recording of the actual call from their monitoring systems. With the recording of the call, he harvested the information that Nathan was looking for and sent it to him by encrypted e-mail from an Internet café. Not only did Nathan have the account numbers, he also held the passwords; it was worth the $10,000 it cost him; now having the information to save his own life. The rest of the account tracking, along with the transfers, was a piece of cake. Nathan responded to the original message, indicating the partial payment was received and completion of the contract would happen within a week, buying Louis the time to handle it their way, with extreme prejudice.

Louis composed another e-mail to Nathan. "See if you can track down a copy of the Senator's medical records for me; at his age, there's probably something we can use. I'm heading home to get some rest and a home-cooked meal and see what I can cook up in the shop."

After sending the e-mail, Louis called Diane back on her cell phone and after a few rings went to voicemail, left her a message. "Hey baby,

I'm heading home now and should arrive about the same time you do. See you tonight. I love you, bye."

As he was about to close the laptop a reply from Nathan came back. "I'll see what I can find, ride safe."

Louis closed the laptop and turned off his cell phone before locking the top box and firing up the bike. Pulling out of the parking lot of the Hard Rock Casino, he turned left on 90 for the short hop to 110 north, then on to Interstate 10 East. 30 miles later, he crossed into Alabama, and within the hour, he was approaching Mobile and the tunnel under the head of Mobile Bay. A few miles later, he was riding past the USS Alabama on a five mile-long stretch of bridges over the northern backwaters of Mobile Bay, and 30 miles after that, he crossed the Florida line. Ten years earlier, Florida became his home, and he always felt a sense of relief as he crossed the state line heading for the house, now only 460 miles away. The GPS indicated it would take eight hours, at his present speed. The sun was shining brilliantly, without a cloud to be seen. Louis was tired, but he felt good. Any time he left a casino with more money than he arrived with tended to have that effect on him.

As he reached for the GPS to turn on some tunes, the radar detector went nuts. The Valentine One indicated it was receiving a very strong laser signal from directly ahead. With several large cars in front of him, he rolled off the throttle and landed on the speed limit, as the Florida Highway Patrol car came into view. The Trooper was standing next to his car, in the median of Interstate 10, just waiting to ruin someone's morning. Louis maintained his pace, dead on the speed limit, as he approached, then passed the Trooper, who continued to shoot West at oncoming traffic. The Valentine One once again paid for itself, and Louis, now painfully alert, continued his trek east as he approached Pensacola Bay. FHP was notorious for prowling this stretch of Interstate 10, which passed north of what was euphemistically called the Redneck Riviera. This part of the Panhandle of Florida sits directly south of Alabama. Vacationing Alabamians pour south across the line to the beautiful white sand beaches of Pensacola, Fort Walton, Destin and Panama City every chance they get; for the FHP, it is like hunting in a baited field.

• • •

Nathan was at home in Huntsville, remotely hacking around in the laptop belonging to Richland's aide. Through the laptop, Nathan was able to access the local area network in the Senator's office and located the Senator's appointment calendar. He scanned backward several months before locating a doctor's appointment for a physical exam nine months earlier. After creating an eFax account with a 202 area code that automatically forwarded incoming faxes to an e-mail address, Nathan composed an e-mail from the Senator to the nurse receptionist contact he found in the Senator's calendar, asking her to fax over the results from his last physical, as he needed them to update his life insurance policy. He included the new fax number and watched the Senator's e-mail account for any response from the doctor's office. The nurse replied to the e-mail, "The Doctor is out of the office at this time, but I can fax you those results within the hour." Nathan immediately deleted the reply.

While Nathan waited for the fax of the physical to come through to the bogus Hotmail account he created, he copied the calendar and all the Senator's e-mail and contacts, sucking them down to his local computer. Twenty-five minutes later, an e-mail landed in the Hotmail account containing a tiff image attachment, which was the result of the physical. He then altered the eFax account, replacing the Hotmail address with the e-mail address of the Senator's aide. Still connected to the laptop belonging to the aide, he cloned the laptop's Mac and IP addresses and slid in a Trojan horse that replaced the virus scanner on the laptop. So now, wherever that laptop went, it would phone home to one of Nathan's servers every time it connected to a network anywhere. This provided Nathan with a back door into the Senator's life, through his office's network and every computer and device connected to it. On the hard drive of the aide's laptop, he found a password-protected folder, the only one on the hard drive, so he ran a cracking program to determine the password while he inventoried all the computers on the Senator's office network. Within a few minutes, the cracker discovered the password, so Nathan opened the folder and found that it was shared over the network with a folder of the same name, located on the Senator's laptop, and contained a single Excel spreadsheet.

The spreadsheet was a historical ledger, detailing all of the Senator's bank accounts, both in the US and overseas, along with the account numbers, passwords and bank contact information. The spreadsheet contained dates that went as far back in time as 1970, long before such electronic spreadsheets ever existed, so at some point, all of this data was entered in the spreadsheet from its original sources. Nathan thought, *I now hold in one hand the key to Solomon's mine, and the Senator's balls in the other.*

Nathan spent the next few hours combing through the data he harvested via the aide's laptop, and compiled a comprehensive inventory of the data, which he then compressed and encrypted into a hidden archive behind the photo of a "Welcome to Wyoming" road sign. He then composed an e-mail to Louis with the photo archive as an attachment and said, "You remember the last time we rode around the Big Horn Mountains? Let's get together and plan another trip as soon as we can," then sent the e-mail.

10

Now four hours later, Louis passed through Tallahassee and exited Interstate 10, heading south on US 19, stopping for fuel and to stretch his legs before continuing home. Last Thursday, when he came through here, it was raining sideways with massive thunderstorm clouds walking east on legs of lightning; there would be no repeat of that today. As he continued his downhill run along the Nature Coast of Florida, he remembered the crack-head at the gas station that stuck a gun in his ear, and wondered what he told the police when they pulled him out of his locked trunk. He also wondered what the little lady who worked at the gas station told the police about the incident. It really didn't matter to Louis, as he would have nothing to say to the cops about it.

A hundred miles farther South, while traveling a stretch of US 19 through the Waccasassa Conservation Area, a 50 mile stretch of highway between towns, the rear end of the motorcycle started to get wobbly as the noise from the rear tire became uncharacteristically loud. The tire was going flat and Louis was still traveling at 60 miles an hour when he rolled off the throttle and pulled in the clutch.

Louis eased on the front brakes, knowing that if the ABS kicked in, he could end up tumbling across US 19. Within a few seconds, he stopped the bike on the edge of the pavement. With only rocky sand at the edges of the road, he knew trying to ride it through the sand with a completely flat rear tire was asking for trouble. Therefore, he climbed off the bike with the engine running, still in first gear, and eased the clutch out with a little throttle, to coax the bike a safe distance away from the road, where he could address the flat. He popped the transmission into neutral and killed the engine before attempting to hall the big bike up and onto the center stand while it stood in sand. He took off his helmet, jacket and riding gloves and laid them across the seat, walking around in circles for a few minutes to allow his frustration to subside.

Louis opened the side case, and unloaded its contents to the ground to get to the air compressor and tire plugging kit in the bottom of the case. He sat down behind the bike, facing the rear tire, in an effort to locate the hole. Slowly rotating the tire by hand, the head of a Philips-head screw came into view. Using pliers to grab the head of the screw to extract it from the tire carcass, he twisted it to allow the threads to back it out, instead of ripping open the rubber. Louis cleaned the hole up a bit with the small rasp that came with the plugging kit. He inserted the mushroom-shaped plug into the head of the plugging gun before putting a few drops of oil on the tip of the gun so that it would be easier to push through the small hole in the tire. After five minutes of wrestling with the plug gun, it finally slid into place and Louis pumped the handle of the plug gun to push the mushroom-shaped plug into the hole.

Louis grabbed the stem of the plug, now sticking out of the tire, with his pliers and wiggled it vigorously up and down and side to side, to seat the mushroom head against the inside wall of the tire. Then, clipping the air hose of the small compressor to the valve stem of the tire, he removed the motorcycle's seat to attach the compressor battery clamps to the battery.

He had learned the hard way to crank the bike and let it idle when using this compressor to air up a tire; if you didn't, your next problem was starting a bike with a drained battery. When the bike settled into an idle, he flipped the switch on the compressor and it rattled to life as air flowed into the tire. A few minutes later, the tire was again rigid with pressurized air. Turning off the compressor, he removed the clamp from the valve stem of the tire and checked the air pressure with the gauge he kept in the side case. It was a few pounds high, so he bled off a little air before placing the cap on the valve stem. After repacking the side case, he walked to the edge of the woods to take a short break in the shade before continuing the ride south. Not a single car or truck passed by in the 20 minutes it took him to repair the rear tire. After relieving himself on a Palmetto, he returned to the bike and geared up for the ride.

Mounting the bike before attempting to remove it from the center stand, which was buried in the sand, he cranked the bike, put it in first gear, added some throttle and let out the clutch to move forward and bring the center stand up on under its own power. He slowly steered the bike through the sand and back to the edge of the pavement as an 18-wheeler went blasting by. Once back up on the pavement, he quickly moved through the gears, getting up speed, and taking it easy until his confidence returned in the rear tire.

An hour and a half later, around 6:45 pm, he was rolling into his driveway and into the garage door, which Diane had opened for him when she arrived, a few minutes earlier. He climbed off the bike and out of the gear as Diane came through the door with a large glass of ice-cold tea and a beautiful smile to welcome Louis home. They hugged and kissed each other a few times before walking into the house.

"Well, how was the trip?" Diane asked, wanting all the details.

"It was a good time, and I got in a lot of miles, with just a flat tire for my only trouble."

"Where did that happen?"

"On 19 north of Crystal River, in the middle of one of those long isolated stretches. It didn't take too long to fix."

"So you've been riding around on a plugged tire all this time."

"It happened on the way home, this afternoon, so I'm gonna take the wheels to the bike shop in the morning for a fresh set of rubber; the tread on the tires is getting thin anyway."

"What do you want to do for dinner tonight?" Diane asked, while changing out of her work clothes.

"It really doesn't matter to me, but I need some Motrin and a long hot shower before I do anything else."

Diane joined him in the shower as they reacquainted themselves with each other, as was their custom, washing each other's back, legs, and arms before getting to the fun parts. The intimacy in the shower would last until the hot water ran out, when they would step out into the steam-laden bathroom to towel off.

Louis slipped into his knee long shorts, t-shirt and sandals, headed back to the garage, and unpacked the bike, while Diane slid a pan of lasagna into the oven. Louis unstrapped the duffel bag and sat it on top of the dryer before unpacking the top case and carrying the contents into the house. He removed the Walther from the side case, walked over to his workbench, and disassembled it on a clean rag. He poured a mixture of kerosene and bore solvent into the ultrasonic cleaner and placed all the pieces of the Walther into the mixture and switched on the cleaner. This was just the first stage of the cleaning process that would liberate the lead and gunpowder residue from the expensive automatic.

Louis returned to the dryer and dumped the contents of the duffel bag on the floor, removing the cash in the pockets of the blue jeans, along with the empty shell casings he accumulated, before loading the washing machine. He placed the cash in his safe and then walked back into the kitchen. Wetting a microfiber towel, he wrung it out, grabbed his spray bottle of hydrogen peroxide, and misted the windscreen, headlights, fog lights and hand guards of the motorcycle, which was covered with dehydrated bug goo. The peroxide rehydrated the dried out bugs, turning them into a soapy consistency that wiped off easily, without scratching the windscreen.

He enjoyed his glass of cold peach tea while wiping down the bike and waiting for the timer to go off on the ultrasonic cleaner. Louis then carefully removed all the pieces from the cleaner and laid them out on the clean towel, and dumped his cleaning fluid into a motor oil drain pan under the bench. He then sprayed each component of the weapon with WD-40, to remove all the kerosene and solvent residue, placing these parts one at a time on another clean rag. Putting a cork in one end of the silencer, he mixed and poured in equal parts of mineral spirits, acetone, kerosene, and automatic transmission fluid, a homemade recipe known as 'Ed's Red', sat the silencer aside, and wiped down and oiled all of the components of the Walther while reassembling them. He would leave the mixture inside the silencer overnight, before dumping it into the oil pan. Then, wiping down the silencer with a clean rag, he would sling the remains of the mixture out of the silencer and screw it back onto the Walther before storing it in his gun safe.

Louis headed back into the house to check his e-mail before eating dinner. The aroma of the lasagna in the oven that was nearing completion made his mouth respond like one of Pavlov's dogs. He found a message from Nathan waiting in his inbox, so he opened the e-mail, downloaded the photo to his desktop, and decrypted the payload, revealing the comprehensive document of data Nathan collected. Scanning through this huge document, Louis couldn't believe his eyes, given the scope and depth of the information that Nathan provided. He held the actual doctor's report from the Senator's last physical, and the details of all the banking transactions and all the accounts belonging to the Senator, going back to the 1970s. Along with this was a chronological history of the Senator's personal e-mail, going back two years, and his appointment calendar, with entries that were six months into the future.

Louis had been consistently amazed over the years at Nathan's ability to harvest the atomic level details that he could use to plan and execute the mechanics of the assassination of his targets. Together, they were an unstoppable team that left nothing to chance while in play. However, the next target was to be handled differently from the others. Killing senators was the tradition in ancient Rome, but nothing like this has happened in the US since California Congressman Leo Ryan was executed during the Jonestown massacre in Guyana. Richland made himself a target, the moment he contracted a hit on Nathan, no longer untouchable. And while it would be easy enough to take him out with a bullet at any number of locations, the full weight of the Justice Department would come to bear with the extensive and exhausting investigation that would follow. It's never wise to wake a sleeping giant; just ask post-Pearl Harbor Japan. No, this operation must be carefully handled, with finesse, and made to look like anything but an assassination. A car accident or heart attack, or maybe a stroke that resulted in death would be the way to go; in any event, it should look natural, or every investigative and intelligence agency in the US would be on the clock until it was resolved.

Louis was tired; the miles on the road and sleepless nights since the previous Thursday caught up to him. When the hot lasagna Diane prepared for dinner landed in his belly, it was all he could do to keep his eyes open. He got up from the couch where he planned to watch the news and closed the garage door for the night. Walking through the house, he checked the locks on the front door and the sliding glass doors that led out to the lanai before shutting off the lights in the house. Louis climbed into bed, lying on his stomach, as Diane gently scratched his back with her freshly manicured nails. He lasted two minutes before he succumbed to exhaustion-induced sleep.

• • •

Louis awoke to the smell of hot tea drifting in from the kitchen as Diane passed through the master bedroom with her cup, heading into the bathroom to put on her face for work. Louis threw his legs over the side of the bed and stood up, stretching away the sleep clinging to his muscles. Diane had already prepared him a cup of hot breakfast tea that awaited him on the kitchen counter. Within thirty minutes, Diane was dressed and ready to leave for work. Louis was sipping his tea while scanning the news online.

Gray's history of pedophilia and the Church's complicity in moving him around to avoid prosecution was now a matter of record, oozing from every news outlet on the web and becoming the recurring theme of the talking heads every thirty minutes on the headline news channels. The consensus was that a parent or family member of one of his victims discovered his location and performed the vigilante service, which was not far from the truth.

The news reports on Morales were much fewer in number, as it was all but written off as the action of a drug gang's internal rivalries– a somewhat common occurrence in the border towns of the desert southwest, though few of those victims were found in such sterile conditions. Most were blown apart by a shotgun blast or riddled with bullets from submachine guns; some were just found with their throats cut, but all were left lying in the open as a reminder and example to those who would cross them.

Diane leaned in and kissed Louis. "How did you sleep?"

"Did I sleep? I thought I'd died and you revived me this morning," Louis said with a grin.

"I'm ready to head out. I'll see you this evening, after my workout; I should be home by eight."

"Have a great day, baby, and be safe. Enjoy your workout, and don't hurt yourself," Louis replied as he followed her to the garage, carrying her gym bag to the car for her. Louis watched as she backed out of the garage and driveway to the street and soon disappeared, heading to Tampa. He rolled the trashcan out to the curb and glanced up at the dolphin weathervane on the gable of the house, to see which way the wind was blowing this morning.

Returning to his computer, he continued reading Richland's dossier, provided by Nathan. In there, he would find the key to completing his next mission in a way that would raise little suspicion, while getting the job done cleanly. While reading the results of the physical examination Richland previously underwent, he found the doctor's handwritten notes, indicating an increase in Coumadin, a blood thinner/anticoagulant the doctor had Richland taking to reduce the chances of recurring blood clots in his legs, which he became prone to from the many hours a day spent sitting in meetings. Making a mental note of that, he thought it could be very useful when the time came, and he continued reading page after page of information as he pieced together the possibilities, techniques and approaches to this challenge.

While taking a break, he decided to take the wheels off the bike and go to the shop for the new tires. He went out to the garage, positioned his floor jack under the skid plate below the engine of his motorcycle, and slowly lifted the bike off its wheels. After removing the wheels, he loaded them in the back of his car and went into the house to wash his hands before heading out to complete his chores. He gathered up the checks he received from the advertisers on his blog and stuffed them into his wallet, to deposit them while he was out and about. Just a few miles away from his home was an independent sport bike shop that he had used for the last couple of years to swap out the tires on the rims of the bike that he would bring in from home. The guy did a great job and charged a fair price for it. Louis would always rather support an independent businessman in a small shop than a corporate dealership where attention to detail was often lacking and the rates they charged were way too high, with most of it going to the dealer instead of the mechanic who did the work.

He dropped off the wheels at the bike shop and paid the guy in cash for the set of tires he always kept in stock for him, and his nominal fee for mounting and balancing them. Louis told him he would be back in a while to pick them up and left to make a run to the bank. While driving the five miles to the nearest branch, he began thinking about the spreadsheet that detailed all of the Senator's accounts and how he entrusted this information with his aide. A plan began to percolate in the back of Louis's mind as he free-associated the data from the dossier. *We can always make it look like the aide killed him, using greed and his access to the Senator's funds as motive,* he thought, *but that's too clear-cut and easy; yet it may end up being the best way to proceed.*

As Louis stood inside the bank, filling out a deposit slip, the free association kicked in again. The Senator was scheduled to head home to Wyoming in a few days, for a week of vacation and a hunting trip. *I wonder what he'll hunt,* Louis thought. *What's in season this time of the year in Wyoming?* Completing the deposit, he returned to his car and drove to the bike shop to pick up his wheels. After arriving home, he quickly reinstalled the wheels on the bike and put it back on the center stand. He grabbed his jacket and his helmet and gently rode his bike to the nearest gravel and sand road he knew of, a couple of miles from his house. He rode the bike up and down the gravel road several times, as the sand and gravel scuffed away the mold release that covered the surface of new tires, and made them slick as ice until it was gone.

Returning his bike to the garage, he went inside and got back online to figure out what Richland could be hunting in Wyoming this time of year. After searching the Wyoming Department of Wildlife website, he determined it could be elk, antelope or bighorn sheep. He decided the best means to find this out was to go to an inside source–the aide. Louis snagged a free proxy server address from the web, downloaded a copy of Skype to his desktop, and created a bogus account for this one-time use. He then looked up the number for the Senator's office in Washington and placed a call, pretending to be a writer for *Outdoor Magazine.* He gave the receptionist the name of one of the writers he knew of and asked to speak to the Senator's aide concerning the upcoming hunting trip in Wyoming. The aide answered the call, "Hello, this is Thomas Blunt, Senator Richland's personal aide. How can I help you?"

"Good morning, this is Dennis Thomas; I'm a Writer with *Outdoor Magazine.* Just doing some fact checking on the Senator's upcoming hunting trip to Wyoming. Perhaps you can help me with the few questions I have?"

"Good morning Mr. Thomas, I suppose I can help you if it doesn't take too long."

"Thank you Mr. Blunt, I won't take up too much of your time. I just have a few short questions to round out my piece on the Senator's hunting trip. Can you tell me what type of game Senator Richland will be hunting this time around?"

"I believe that would be Bighorn sheep on this trip."

"Thank you, would you happen to know the type of weapon he'll be hunting with?"

"The senator only hunts using a compound bow; he gave up gun hunting years ago, though he is still a member of the NRA."

"Thank you, that's an interesting angle. Would you happen to know what ranch or hunting area the Senator will be using during this trip?"

"He usually hunts sheep in Ten Sleep Canyon, near his home outside of Buffalo."

"Thank you. Do you think the Senator would consider having me along, for a few photos and an easy interview, limited to hunting?"

"No, this is his alone time, to get away from the press and relax. Plus, he always hunts alone, and has done so since he was in his 20s."

"Thank you, that's all the questions I have, and I appreciate your time. Have a nice day."

"Goodbye."

Louis then deleted the Skype account and removed the software from his desktop before releasing the proxy server address that hid his actual location and IP address. He now possessed the information he was looking for, thanks to Mr. Blunt's willingness to talk to a writer on behalf of the Senator. This dust mite truly was clueless where security and confidentiality were concerned. Louis found it amazing that the Senator trusted him and probably only did so because of the years he had worked for him.

"So he's going to be bow hunting alone in Ten Sleep Canyon for bighorn sheep. That's just the kind of location where accidents happen," Louis spoke aloud to himself, to fix it in his mind as he continued to free-associate. Louis and Nathan had ridden through Ten Sleep Canyon a couple of times, on different motorcycle trips that passed through Wyoming. It was a beautiful place with a long Native American history. Louis recalled reading a large sign on the side of the road in the Canyon that detailed a hunting trip by a British Member of Parliament, the Hon. Gilbert H.C. Leigh, in 1884, where Leigh was staying with his host, a local rancher named Moreton Frewen and hunting bighorn sheep in the Canyon. Leigh went off alone one day to hunt on the canyon walls where the bighorn sheep are found, but failed to return. He was found dead on a ledge, five days later. It was speculated that Leigh mistook the tops of the trees rooted well below him on the canyon walls as shrubs and ventured into them, falling to his death.

The plan was coming together nicely in Louis' mind, but he was going to need the help of modern chemistry to pull this one off. If the Senator was going to take a nose dive into the canyon, where he hunted many times over his life, it was going to have to look like an accident or possibly a medical condition that caused it. Louis also bow hunted years ago, but his prey had been Whitetail deer in the woods of Alabama and Georgia. He used a Whitetail Hunter recurve bow and a

Ben Pearson Mirage compound bow back in the day. The newer bows were much more powerful and accurate, and modern arrows flew straighter and farther to deliver their deadly punch.

Back in the days when he was bow hunting, he used a concoction they would put on the razor Broadheads of the arrows, which caused the animal to quickly bleed out and die before running too far away. The enhanced bleeding would leave a clear blood trail directly to the animal. The anticoagulant was based on trisodium citrate, an anticlotting agent commonly used in the meatpacking industry. It was mixed with distilled water, glycerin and xanthan gum, common thickeners used in food products like salad dressing and other condiments. The mixture was either brushed on the Broadhead, or it was dipped in it, and the thickeners caused it to stick to the Broadhead. Pulling these relatively common ingredients together was easy enough, if there was time to do it, but it would be a lot faster to pick up a premade bottle of it at a hunting outfitter's store, if you could find one. Louis hopped on Google and tracked down the outdoor stores in the area and those located along US 19 N. in the large hunting areas of the Nature Coast.

After making unsuccessful calls to local stores who didn't carry it, he started calling the outfitters located north of him in the hunting areas. One gentleman, who owned a store near Chiefland, Florida, said he still had some in the back room that he would sell him in person but couldn't ship it anywhere. It was only 90 miles up the road so Louis hopped in the car and headed north. About two hours later Louis was at the outfitter's location.

"Hi, I called you a couple of hours ago about some anticoagulant for bow hunting."

"Yes, I remember the call. You never hear it mentioned anymore since it was outlawed here. I still have a full carton in the backroom, just sitting there."

"Can I take a look at the package? I'd like to read the ingredients before deciding."

"I don't mind at all; let me go grab it from the back room. I'll be right back."

Less than a minute later he returned with the box and sat it on the counter. "This stuff is great for deer hunting; they don't make it very far before they collapse."

"What about much bigger game, like yearling elk and bigger?"

"This stuff would hardly faze an animal that size. You would need what we use for hunting wild boar that can grow to 300 pounds or larger. I've got some of that in the back, as well."

"What's the difference between the two?"

"The only difference is a much higher percentage of the anticoagulant; instead of 10% it's more like 50%, and it's dangerous stuff. You don't want to scratch yourself with a Broadhead with this stuff on it; you'll need a tourniquet and a fast ride to the nearest emergency room."

"Sounds like just the stuff to use while hunting elk."

"Yeah, it'll do the trick. Where will you be hunting?"

"Northern Colorado; heading there this weekend."

"Man, I wish I was going with you. I never killed an elk!"

"How much you asking for the stuff? I'll pay cash and don't need a receipt."

"I'll take $20 bucks for the 12 ounce bottle of the big game stuff."

"How much for the spray bottles, for deer hunting?"

"Five bucks a bottle."

"I'll take two of those as well," Louis said as he reached into his pocket and handed the man $30.

"If you get caught with that stuff, how about forgetting where you got it?"

"What stuff?" Louis replied with a wink.

While in the store, he took the opportunity to try on a pair of one-piece mossy oak insulated coveralls. After a few tries he found a pair that were roomy enough for his six-foot body and carried them to the counter.

"If you give me a $50 they're yours."

Louis handed the man two $20s and a $10 and headed back toward home with his purchases. Stopping by the Dakota winery in Chiefland, he picked up a couple bottles to add to the wine rack. Diane enjoyed sweet wines and the Dakota had several from which to choose. When he arrived home, he shot an e-mail off to Nathan indicating, "After reading your proposal thoroughly, have come up with a few ideas to resolve the problem. It's been a while since I toured Wyoming so we need to talk about an expedition. I'll take a ride north to your location as soon as I can get away, possibly Wednesday. –Later"

Later that evening when Diane arrived home from the gym, Louis was busy at his workbench in the garage, making his usual modifications to the hollow point rounds he used in the Walther.

"Hey baby, did you enjoy your workout?" Louis asked as he walked over to give Diana a kiss.

"Yes, it was wonderful, and I needed it after a particularly stressful day at work."

"Well, I left something on the island in the kitchen for you. I hope it brightens your day. And there's a cold one in the refrigerator door."

With a somewhat puzzled look on her face, Diane walked into the kitchen from the garage and found several varieties of the wine she enjoyed from the Dakota. Louis already opened a bottle that was in the refrigerator, and now thoroughly chilled. Diane poured herself a glass and walked back out into the garage.

"Thanks for the wine, sweetie. I appreciate you getting that for me."

"You're welcome, baby. Something told me you needed a pick-me-up today."

"It must be the telepathic link again," Diane said as she smiled. "What you working on?"

"Just making some more of my armadillo killers. I've already used up the last batch I made," Louis said.

"Do you mind if we have leftover lasagna for dinner?"

"Not at all; I love the stuff. I should be ready to eat in about 30 minutes, if that's okay?"

"Then I'll heat it up in the oven instead of using the microwave; it just tastes better that way," Diane said before she walked back into the kitchen.

Louis went back to working on the hollow points he used. He purchased subsonic, long rifle hollow points at local gun shows, where he could pay cash for them without the paperwork. He never handled the rounds without wearing gloves. He used a small drill bit to enlarge the hollow point tip, making the cavity a little wider and deeper. He would then fill the cavity with rat shot from 410 shotgun shells, placing up to 10 of the tiny pellets inside the hollow point before gently crimping the tip of the bullets closed. This made the rounds hit like an anvil and explode like tiny grenades as they penetrated their targets. The rounds were no longer accurate at longer ranges, but were dead on out to about 30 feet; all the kills with the Walther were well inside that range. At times, he would use mercury to fill the hollow points instead of rat shot, but that required him to pull the rounds out of the casings before soldering the tips closed using lead. Then he gently squeezed the rounds in a hand mold to accurately reform the tip and reinserted the bullets into the casings; a lot of work, but those rounds were vastly more accurate and devastating at longer ranges, especially when shot from a rifle.

After completing the modification to the rounds, Louis reloaded both clips for the Walther, 10 rounds in each and placed the clips in the gun safe where he kept the Walther. There were many other guns in the house, most in the gun safe, but a few in hidden locations well out of the reach of the grandchildren; just in case some unfortunate soul decided to break into the house and donate their life to the cause.

During dinner with Diane, he told her he needed to take another road trip up to Huntsville and visit Nathan. From there he would most likely be heading west again, as he wanted to visit the crash site in Iowa where Buddy Holly, Richie Valens and the Big Bopper perished in the small plane crash. She knew he had always wanted to do a piece on that topic and was a fan of Buddy Holly and Richie Valens.

"How long do you think you'll be gone this time?"

"I'm thinking about a week at most. Nathan will probably go along for the ride, as he wants to visit the site as well."

"It's going to be getting cold out in the Midwest shortly; you'll need to pack your cold-weather gear and your heated liner."

"You're right; I'll probably need those things. And this is going to be my last trip for a while, I promise."

Diane took that last comment with the appropriate grain of salt, knowing that while he meant it when he said it, the road had a way of calling Louis out of the house.

"So when will you be leaving?"

"Tomorrow or Thursday. I still need to get a few things done before I go, but I did get the new tires on the bike today, and I'll probably change the oil in the morning."

Diane and Louis watched a little TV before climbing in the shower and then into bed. Within an hour of intimacy, they were both exhausted and drifted off to sleep together, although Louis would only get a couple of hours' sleep before his eyes came open and remained that way.

11

Louis finally gave up, climbing out of bed around 4 am Wednesday morning, and quietly slipped into his blue jeans, tennis shoes and an old sweatshirt. He walked out to the garage, put on a riding jacket and helmet, and then backed the motorcycle out of the garage before starting it. He rode the bike around the neighborhood, up and down the different streets for several minutes, to get the engine nice and warm before returning to the garage to change the oil. Sliding the oil pan out from under the workbench and under the motorcycle engine, he removed the oil filler cap before he removed the drain plug, and the expensive synthetic oil, now black as crude, flowed easily into the drain pan. Removing the old filter, he laid it gently into the drain pan before retrieving a new one from the shelf, along with four quarts of new synthetic lubricant. He laid there on the floor mat and watched as the oil dripped from the engine into the pan. The familiar smell of the warm used motor oil was a touchstone in his life, which always brought with it the memories from his youth, when he and his father would work on the old man's car in the driveway.

Changing the oil, cleaning the plugs and setting the points were his old man's ways of spending quality time with Louis. It instilled in him the simple pleasures of maintaining his vehicles that had stayed with him throughout his life. His old man didn't teach him about money or work ethic, the importance of education or things of character; those things meant little to his dad. Getting his load on in the morning and maintaining a steady drunken state throughout the day appeared to

Louis to be the important things in his father's life, the only consistent pursuits he'd seen.

After replacing the drain plug, Louis filled the new filter with oil before installing it, and then poured the new oil in the engine and watched the sight glass as the oil rose to the center, indicating it was enough. As his old man taught him, fresh oil in the filter protects the bearings from a dry start up. His old man knew engines, inside and out, better than he would ever know his son. Louis pulled the spark plugs one by one, methodically cleaning them and checking the gap, while the childhood memories of his parent's divorce drifted through his mind like a cold, ancient fog.

Louis wiped down and put away his tools and returned the drain pan to its location under the workbench before again backing the bike out of the garage and firing it up to ensure it ran smoothly. While the engine idled and warmed up to operating temperature, Louis stared off toward the East, transfixed by the brilliant shafts of red, orange and yellow light that shone through the clouds ahead of the sunrise. The gentle morning breeze made the tops of the palm trees sway, as echelons of migrating Warblers and Water thrushes passed over, heading to points South. The staccato calls of the Sand Hill Cranes echoed through the neighborhood, as Flatland came alive on this beautiful fall morning.

Louis turned the key to silence the motor and pushed the bike back into the garage as Diane appeared in the doorway. "So there you are," she said as she walked toward him with a warm cup of tea in each hand.

"How long have you been out here?"

"I got up around four–couldn't sleep, got tired of staring at the ceiling and doing the rotisserie."

"Where did you go?" Diane asked, looking over the rim of the cup, taking a sip.

"Nowhere, changed the oil, cleaned the plugs and let the engine warm up in the driveway."

"I need to finish getting ready for work," Diane said. "What you got planned for today?"

"I need to pack for this trip, plan my route and head North to Nathan's."

"Make sure you call me when you get there. I worry when I don't hear from you."

"I'll call you, baby, as soon as I get there," Louis replied while they walked into the kitchen.

Diane headed to the master bedroom, while Louis removed his clothes from the dryer and folded them prior to shoving them in his duffel bag. He went to the closet where he kept his cold weather riding gear and removed his heated jacket liner and a pair of winter gloves and socks. He took them and the duffel bag out to the garage and sat it down next to the bike and headed back inside to check the weather along his route to North Alabama.

Louis composed an e-mail to Nathan. "I'll be heading your way shortly and should be there this afternoon. I'm packed for the trip out West."

Diane reappeared from the bedroom, dressed and ready for work. Louis got up from the desk and wrapped his arms around her, telling her, "I miss you already, baby."

"You be safe, and try to have some fun with Nathan on your trip. I'll miss you too. I love you," Diane told Louis "And don't forget your heated jacket liner."

"I've already sat it out next to the bike, but thanks for reminding me."

Diane picked up her purse from the kitchen table and dug around for her car keys while she walked toward the garage. Louis followed her out and hit her garage door button as she climbed into the driver's seat of her small SUV. Louis leaned into the open door, and they kissed for a few moments and exchanged "I love yous" before he shut the car door and watched as she backed out of the garage and into the street. They both waved as she pulled away on her 30-mile commute to the office.

Louis walked back into the garage and shut the garage door as he passed through, heading toward the kitchen and then into the giant walk-in closet where the gun safe was located. Opening the safe, he removed the Walther with its silencer, along with both clips loaded with his modified hollow points. He counted out $10,000 just–in–case cash for the trip before closing and spinning the lock on the safe and heading out to the bike. He opened the hiding place in the right side case and placed the Walther and the cash inside before removing the stun gun to install fresh batteries and returning it to the side case. He went over to his workbench and removed the two small spray bottles of deer hunting anticoagulant from their plastic packaging. He dumped the contents of both bottles into the oil drain pan and refilled them from the large bottle that contained the more potent anticoagulant, meant for larger game hunting. He placed both bottles in the side case and continued to pack the bike for the trip.

Louis went back inside to his desktop computer and deleted the dossier on Senator Richland. Then he kicked off the program that Nathan provided him that sanitized the computer by deleting all the temporary files, cookies and anything in the recycle bin before defragmenting the hard drive and overwriting all the white space on the drive multiple times, ensuring everything he deleted was unrecoverable. The same program was on his netbook.

Retrieving his toiletries bag from the bathroom, he returned to his desk and removed the netbook from the charger, along with his digital camera, and headed to the kitchen, grabbing his wallet from the counter, and stored them in the top case of the bike. Louis went to the cabinet above the workbench and removed a pair of OD green binoculars and a pair of third-generation night vision goggles, thinking *It's better to have them and not need them than need them and not have them.* He opened the battery compartment on the night vision goggles and inserted fresh batteries; he never stored them with batteries inside.

Louis then retrieved a small black box about half the size of a cigar box from the cabinet. Inside was a tracking device with a magnetic mount that contained an internal GPS, capable of tracking 16 satellites simultaneously. The unit also contained a GPRS transmitter, as well as a receiver that captured and stored a vehicle's lock and unlock signals from the key fob. The second component inside the little black box was a GPRS receiver that he would plug in between the GPS antenna and the GPS itself. The transmitter and receiver pair worked in unison to track the movements and location of a vehicle or package and transmit the exact location to the receiver, which was then displayed on the host GPS. The transmitter would activate automatically once it sensed motion, and when motion ceased, it transmitted its location and shut down to conserve the batteries. Using GPRS, the transmitter could communicate with the receiver all the way across the country or practically anywhere the core network existed. Nathan took an off-the-shelf GPS tracking device, modified it, and repackaged it specifically for Louis' personal use.

Louis put the field glasses and the night vision goggles inside their protective cases and stored them, along with the tracking device, inside the right side case of the bike, wrapped up in a heavy blue towel, before loading in his raingear and sneakers. Louis grabbed a fresh bottle of octane booster from the shelf and stuck it in the left side case, along with his heated jacket liner, winter gloves and the insulated cover-alls. He made a pass through his mental checklist as he went back inside to ensure the doors and windows were locked before he left. Louis strapped the duffel bag across the rear seat of the bike and climbed into his riding pants and boots before putting on his jacket, helmet and gloves. He backed the bike out of the garage and cranked the motor while he shut the garage door. Rolling out of the driveway, he turned to look over his shoulder at his home, hoping the next time he saw it, he could stay longer than a day.

Once out on US 19, Louis again headed North, up the Nature Coast of Florida, although this time around, he didn't stop for fuel at his favorite location, as he did the previous Thursday. This time he would stop farther up the road for fuel in Perry, Florida, before continuing North and crossing into South Georgia. Following his previous route, he passed through Albany, Georgia, then on to Columbus before crossing into Alabama at Phenix City. Once in Montgomery he turned north on Interstate 65 and stopped for fuel in Clanton before continuing North, passing through Birmingham and beyond. Well North of Cullman, Alabama, he crossed the Tennessee River just East of Decatur and turned East on 565, headed toward Nathan's home in Huntsville.

Nathan's house is on top of Monte Sano, the highest point in the area. The view from Nathan's backyard looks West over Huntsville and beyond to the horizon. It is a beautiful location, and probably why Werner von Braun and his crew of German rocket scientists chose Monte Sano for their homes when they were relocated to Redstone Arsenal.

Louis rolled up to the keypad in front of the gates and entered his access code, triggering the gates to swing open; they closed behind him as he rode down the driveway and parked outside the garage.

Nathan had cameras everywhere; there were the obvious ones on top of the house that pointed toward the gate, the front yard, the backyard and either side of the house. Then there were the ones you couldn't see, the night vision cameras and the one across the street from the house, in the waterproof enclosure, hidden in the trees. Nathan wasn't paranoid; he was prepared. Louis was climbing off the bike and removing his riding gear when one of the garage doors opened, and Nathan stepped out into the late afternoon sunlight to welcome Louis to his home. They shook hands as they always did, and Nathan asked, "How was your ride, Bro?"

"Not bad at all, clear weather all the way and it only took 11 hours to get here."

"Go ahead and roll your bike inside the garage. I got some things to show you," Nathan said before heading into the house.

Louis stood the bike up off the side stand and pushed it in the open garage bay. Opening the top case, he located his cell phone, switched it on and walked to the edge of the backyard while giving Diana a call.

"Hey sweetie, I've been waiting for your call. Have you made it there yet?"

"I just rolled into his garage and decided to call you before walking in the house."

"You have good ride?"

"It was fine, and the new tires were smooth and quiet, to boot. How was your day at work?"

"Busy-busy, as always, it seems. I stopped at the mall after work and I'm still on the way home."

"Be careful heading home, and try to relax a little. I'll call you later tonight. I love you baby."

"I love you too; have fun; bye."

Louis stepped out of his riding boots and pants while still in the garage and dug a pair of jeans out of the duffel bag, and his sneakers from the side case before walking in the house. The door from the garage led to a hallway, with the laundry room on one side and a restroom on the other. A little farther down the hallway, the dining room was on the left, on the back of the house, with a formal living room to the right on the front side. At the end of the hall was a small den with a wall-to-wall bookcase that extended from floor to ceiling, opposite the door leading into the den. At the left end of the bookcase, the hidden door was open for Louis to enter what Nathan called his study, a hidden safe room of the house with no windows and only the one door that Louis knew of.

The walls are trimmed with flat screen monitors, with the exterior camera views presented across the top of one wall. Against another wall is a large workbench where Nathan tinkers with electronics or cracks open one of his computers when it's time to make an upgrade. Behind the bench is a sliding glass door that serves as the access point to a large walk-in style closet that is actually a server room, complete with cooling, humidity control and racks filled with computers and networking equipment. There is an L-shaped couch in one of the corners and a refrigerator in the corner below the workbench. Nathan was standing at the workbench fiddling with a laptop, with a pile of cardboard boxes and packing styrofoam on the floor behind him.

"Come on in, Bro, I've got us some new toys," he said without ever turning around.

"What you got there, man?" Louis said as he walked up to the workbench.

"I picked us up a pair of high-performance laptops, which were specially designed for secure communications," Nathan replied. "These little jewels have two distinct modes of operation, the first one being, just like any other laptop, you can surf the web, use e-mail–all the standard stuff. The second is a hardened security mode. It only connects to my servers here and exchanges a different encryption token every few seconds, making them virtually impossible to hack." Nathan was grinning from ear to ear, beaming with pride in his new toys, the tools of the trade.

"How do you change between modes?"

"You simply type in the passphrase 'go secure now' and no matter what you're doing, or what app you're running, it deletes the passphrase from the keyboard buffer and the document or browser you're using, then you have five seconds to place your right thumb on the little biometric scanner next to the touchpad. If you do, then it goes into secure mode, automatically connecting to my servers. You'll also notice the LED on the power button will flash rapidly while in secure mode."

"That's just too cool, man; can we then exchange messages without having to encrypt them?"

"Yes, as long as you're in secure mode it's safe, and after three minutes of no activity they return to normal mode automatically and you're right back where you were when you left. You can also touch both shift keys simultaneously to jump out of secure mode, as well."

"Where do you find cool toys like these?" Louis asked, knowing Nathan would be tickled to tell him.

"They fell off a truck on the way to the NSA," Nathan said, rolling his eyes upward and to the left, "but they've been modified even beyond what the NSA does to them. If you look here on the left side, you'll see there are two memory card slots. The one toward the top of the keyboard, you can use any time you want, but the second one, the one with the memory card already in it–if you eject that memory card, five seconds later, it will destroy the security encryption cards and the motherboard inside the laptop and fry the hard drive with primer cord. It's kind of a failsafe device that only you and I know about."

"What's on that memory card?"

"A particularly nasty virus, which completely bypasses virus scanners and implants itself in the operating system of whatever computer tries to read it, then it phones home to let me know it's in the hands of someone else. So never remove that card unless you've been compromised and need the laptop rendered unusable."

"I got it, but what do I do with the other netbook?"

"If you got it with you, then bring it in and I'll clone your laptop over to this one, so you have all the stuff you're used to using."

"I will get it off the bike and be right back," Louis said before exiting the room and heading out to the garage.

"Bring your old cell phone back with you," Nathan shouted. When Louis returned he handed his netbook over to Nathan, who connected a USB cable between the old and the new laptops and said, "It'll take a little while to move your stuff over, but when it's done it'll feel like your old laptop in a new case, and more than just a little faster than the old one."

"Well, that's just too cool. It looks like you've been busy in here–almost didn't recognize the joint when I walked in. You've finally hung all the monitors on the walls and your little server room is built out. It looks nice.

What you going to do with my old cell phone?"

"I'm going to clone it to your new one, so no one can tell the difference between them."

"What do you mean my new one?"

"I procured us a pair of incredibly smart phones, which also fell off a truck before arriving at the Cookie Factory," Nathan said as he toggled his eyebrows up and down. "These phones are dual mode like the laptops: they behave just like regular smart phones in one mode and will provide us with secure voice and data communications while in secure mode. To activate secure mode, press both the up and down volume buttons on the side while the camera is pointed at your face; if it recognizes you, it will vibrate and go into secure mode and will stay there until you again press both the up and down volume buttons at the same time. In secure mode, it displays a small key next to the signal strength meter."

"Well, James-freaking-Bond," Louis said. "We're shittin' in high cotton now!"

Nathan then plugged Louis' old cell phone into a USB cable hanging from another laptop, to copy over his contacts and to clone the internal numbers. He then removed the SIM from the old cell phone and inserted it in the new one before attaching it to the USB cable of the laptop. A few seconds later, the new cell phone rebooted and Nathan unplugged it from the USB cable.

"You're good to go now," he said as he handed the new cell phone to Louis.

"All this new technology is going to make our communications a lot easier and faster." Louis said while playing with his new Android-based phone.

"We were due for an update; by the way, did you get a chance to study the dossier I sent you on Richland?"

"Oh yeah, I think I located just what I needed to seal the deal, and while we're at it, we may as well drain his bank accounts in our direction–at least some of it, anyway."

"What you got in mind?" Nathan asked, as he grabbed a printout of the dossier and took a seat on the couch.

"Do you still have access to the laptop belonging to the Senator's aide?"

"Of course I do, and the dumbass leaves it on at the office when he goes home at the end of the day. He's mighty accommodating. What are you thinking?"

"We might as well lay this at the feet of somebody when it's done, and the dust mite fits the bill, wouldn't you say?"

Over the next hour, Louis and Nathan discussed everything they knew about the Senator and the aide, along with the upcoming trip to Wyoming to deal with the Senator and put down any ambitions he might have for the future. Nathan grabbed a couple of beers from the refrigerator; they left the study and walked out the sliding glass door of the den to the deck that opened up to the backyard. They walked the 20 yards across the well-manicured grass to the back edge of the property that slipped away steeply down the side of the mountain. They stood there drinking the beer and looking out over the lights of Huntsville, talking about whatever came to mind. The view was amazing to Louis, who was used to living at sea level.

"Hey Bro, I discovered we have some hills down in Flatland."

While drawing a long slow sip from his beer, Nathan glanced over at Louis and raised his eyebrows as if to ask, "What?"

"Yep, they're building overpasses on US 19," Louis said with what could only be called a "shit-eating" grin, causing Nathan to jettison beer from his nostrils. They stood there laughing for several minutes as they shook off the tensions of the day. They decided to head into town to grab some dinner, and climbed into Nathan's truck for the ride down the mountain. They rode over to the restaurant on Jordan Lane, where the Redstone Riders were holding their monthly meeting. Nathan had been riding with this club for many years and at one time was the road captain, who planned the trips they would take a couple times a year. This wasn't the first time Louis attended one of these meetings with Nathan, and many of the group knew and greeted Louis as they entered the restaurant. They both enjoyed barbecue sandwiches and fries, along with the appropriate amount of ice-cold tea, as the meeting continued around them. When the meeting broke up for the evening, Nathan and Louis hung out with a few of their friends in the club before heading back up the mountain for the evening. Once back in Nathan's driveway, Louis called Diane, as she was getting ready for bed.

"Hey baby, what you doing?"

"I'm getting dressed for bed. I'm worn out; it was a long day. What have you two been doing?"

"We drove down into Huntsville for dinner during Nathan's club meeting but we're back at his house now."

"When will you to be heading out to Iowa, to visit the crash site?"

"Tomorrow or the next day. We're leaving as soon as Nathan is ready to go. I'll let you know before we do."

"Well, you all have fun and ride safe, and stay warm out there."

"We will. I love you baby; sleep well and I'll call you sometime in the morning."

"I love you too, sweetie. Good night."

12

Louis grabbed his duffel off the bike and headed into the guest room, where he normally slept, to drop off the bag, then walked back into the study were Nathan was online, connected to the laptop belonging to the Senator's aide.

"What you doing?"

"I'm using the aide's laptop to surf around to different websites of some overseas banks that let you open accounts via the web, just building some history on his laptop before executing the plan."

"If you don't mind, man, I'm going to hit the shower before hitting the rack; I've got a long ride ahead of me tomorrow."

"Go ahead, man; it's only 10 o'clock and I got some work to do before turning in."

Louis located the little box that the new smart phone came in and took it with him to the bedroom where he would try to get some sleep. After a hot shower, he toweled off and slipped back into his jeans and T-shirt before reclining on the bed to browse through the manuals that came with phone. In the box, he found a small pair of stereo headphones with a microphone located on the wire for the right ear-piece. After a few minutes of familiarizing himself with the manual and learning to navigate the screens on the phone, he downloaded an app that connected to the satellite radio service. Within a minute, he was listening to E Street Radio, one of his favorites, when the phone vibrated and the screen showed an incoming call from Nathan.

Louis noticed the key flashing in the corner of the screen before he tapped the touchscreen button labeled "answer the call" and he connected to Nathan, still in the study.

"Hey," Louis said, "I'm listening to the radio over the new phone and the earphones make …"

Nathan interrupted.

"Louis, get your pistol; we've got prowlers in the yard, two of them and they're armed," Nathan said in an excited voice.

Louis jumped up from the bed and quickly moved down the hallway to the unlit garage, and while retrieving his Walther, he told Nathan, "Kill the lights now. Where are they? Describe the weapons you see."

"One is coming around the north end of the house with a pistol and silencer; the other is standing at the back of the driveway near the gate to the backyard with an SMG and silencer, the size of an Uzi."

The house went dark when Nathan hit the kill switch in his study. Louis said, "Lock the door, stay on the line and don't leave that room," while he quickly dug out the night vision goggles and put them on.

"Where are you?"

"I'm in the garage; where are they now?"

"The one with the pistol is approaching the sliding glass door of the den; the other is walking back up the driveway toward the front of the house."

Louis cycled the slide of the Walther to chamber a round as he quickly moved from the garage and up the darkened hallway just outside the door to the den, quickly peeking at the sliding glass door and pulling his head back.

"Where are they now?"

"The one on the patio is standing to the side of the sliding glass door, with his hand on the handle of the door; the other one is looking through the garage door windows."

Louis heard the sliding door slowly opening and peeked around the doorframe with one eyepiece of the goggles. The lights from Huntsville momentarily made the view in the eyepiece quite bright before it automatically adjusted.

Louis raised the Walther, aiming at the shadow in the opening of the doorway, when Nathan said, "He's sticking his head in the door now," as Louis squeezed off two rounds in rapid succession, directly at the head of the shadow.

"He's lying on his back on the patio, but he's still moving," Louis heard in his earpiece.

"Where is the other one?"

"He's headed toward the backyard."

Louis quickly moved to the sliding glass door and released another round into the head of the man lying on the patio and moved back into the den, asking Nathan, "Where is he?"

"He's walking backwards up the driveway toward the gate, pointing his gun toward the back of the house, but he's still beside the house."

Louis moved out of the sliding glass door and ran around the opposite end of the house to the front yard and toward the privacy wall next to the street, while looking to the right, watching for the gunman in case he appeared around the house. Climbing over the wall, he discovered a third man exiting a Chevy Tahoe, parked along the wall between him and the gates.

When Louis landed on his bare feet, a few yards behind the Chevy, the third man turned his head to look over his shoulder in the direction of the rustling leaves, received a bullet in his right ear and collapsed to the ground.

Louis scanned inside the Chevy to check for more, before putting a second round in the same ear.

"Where is he now?"

"He's halfway up the driveway heading toward the gate, maybe 20 yards from it."

Louis slid up next to the large brick columns that supported the gates and took a kneeling position between the column and the hedges in front of them. Nathan could see him from the camera across the street.

The gates were still closed and locked when Louis heard them rattling.

"He's climbing the gate now."

Louis stood up and stepped around the edge of the brick column, aiming his Walther at his next victim's head.

When the fence-climbing dead man spotted Louis, his eyes and mouth opened wide in horror, just milliseconds before Louis put a bullet in his mouth and his body collapsed across the top of the gate.

Louis stepped closer to him and extended the tip of the silencer to within a foot of his head and fired again, causing a death rattle that shook the gate.

"Open the gates," Louis said into the microphone before turning and scanning the street, then returning to the Tahoe to ensure there was no one else inside.

"Leave the lights off and come out to the gate and help me with these bodies."

"Bodies, as in more than one?"

"Yep, there's a Tahoe parked close to your wall with another one lying next to it. We need to get them out of sight ASAP."

Louis opened the doors on the rear of the Chevy, dragged the body around to the back and heaved the dead weight into the rear of the vehicle before quietly closing the doors. As he was walking back toward the gates, Nathan said, "I'm coming out the front gate, please don't shoot me."

Louis laughed into the microphone and disconnected the call. The clock on his phone indicated it was 10:44 pm, as Nathan appeared at the gates and walked toward the front of the Chevy.

"I think you need an additional camera just up the road a bit."

"You're right; I never saw this behemoth on my monitors. When did you see it?"

"Not until I jumped off the wall behind it and shot number three while he was climbing out of it. I've already put him in the back, see if you can find the keys and back this thing into the driveway, while I get number two off the top of the gate."

Nathan found the keys still in the ignition and pulled it past the driveway before backing in and stopping between the gates. Louis climbed on top of the Chevy and grabbed the body around the neck, lifting it up and over the gate, and it fell to the ground. Climbing down, he opened the rear doors again, so they could stuff in body number two before backing it down the driveway next to the house and collecting body number one.

Louis spent the next 10 minutes locating and picking up the seven spent brass casings from Nathan's den, the grass strip between the road and the privacy wall and the area in front of the gates, as well as the weapons the gunmen were carrying. He then returned the night vision goggles to the side case of the bike and swapped the used clip in the Walther for the new one. He slid on a pair of burn gloves, and reloaded the used clip before stashing it and the Walther in its hiding place. Louis headed inside to dress, while Nathan grabbed a scanner from his study and swept the Tahoe, looking for any tracking transmitters, which he discovered didn't exist. Louis reemerged in the garage and said, "Let's find out who these assholes are" while opening the doors on the rear the Chevy and removing all of the personal effects from the three bodies inside, collecting them into a trash bag.

Nathan went inside the house and came back with his digital camera, an inkpad and a piece of white poster board. Over the next 25 minutes, he methodically fingerprinted the three bodies and photographed their faces. Louis noticed that all three men were wearing Army-issue desert boots. He thought for a few moments, and then removed the size 13 pair he found on the oldest of the three, adding them to the collection. He then wrote down the tag number, as well as the VIN number from the plate inside the windshield, and dug through the consoles and glove box of the vehicle, collecting every scrap of paper and object he found into the trash bag.

"We need to get rid of this vehicle and its occupants, like right now."

"Let me make a call, I'll be right back."

All the lights came on after a few minutes, and Nathan arrived in the garage. "A buddy is gonna meet us up the road in about 30 minutes. You drive the Chevy and follow me to his place."

"How do you know this guy?"

"He's good at getting rid of large things and doesn't ask any questions. I've used him before."

"Then lock up the house and let's get out of here."

Nathan pulled out of the driveway and onto the road, turning left as Louis followed. They headed down the mountain and across town. Louis' phone rang; it was Nathan. "I owe you big-time, Bro; I'd be dead if you hadn't been there."

"Don't sweat it, man; just stay focused until we're done," Louis replied, before terminating the call. At the intersection of University Drive and Highway 53, they turned north, a short time later arriving at an auto salvage yard. They pulled up to the gates. In less than a minute, the gates swung open and they pulled inside; the gates closed behind them. They drove through the scrap yard, stopping near a large crane, and climbed out of the vehicles. The acquaintance of Nathan's powered up the crane and swung the boom around, stopping above the Chevy and lowering the giant pinchers to the roof. They bit down on the body and lifted it off the ground, before swinging it over and dropping it into a giant crusher.

The crane operator shut it down and climbed down from the cab, and walked over to the controls of the crusher. After he turned a key and pressed a few buttons, the whine of high-pressure hydraulics and the sound of glass and metal being crushed filled the air. After several minutes of this, the door on the end of the compactor swung open to reveal a ton and a half cube of metal and strips of rubber, bedazzled with thousands of small fragments of safety glass and oozing blood, diesel and oil. The operator then picked up the cube of metal with the crane and sat it into an open fire pit, where the diesel fuel immediately started burning. The crane operator then climbed into a small bulldozer and started pushing all manner of flammable scrap around and on top of the burning cube before he parked the dozer and walked up to Nathan, saying, "I'll keep that burning for a couple of days before I send it for recycling on our next truckload."

Nathan handed him an envelope, thick with cash, and they shook hands before Nathan and Louis climbed into the truck to leave the junkyard. Nathan's mind began to race; in all the years that Nathan and Louis had known each other, this is the first time that Nathan came face-to-face with the bloody reality, the business end of the world in which Louis thrived.

A few minutes after leaving the junkyard, Nathan's hands were visibly trembling as his heart pounded so hard in his chest he was certain Louis could hear it.

"That's your body responding to the adrenaline," Louis said in a calm voice. "Why don't you pull over and let me drive?" he added, knowing Nathan might spew at any moment.

Nathan immediately pulled off to the side of Highway 53 and climbed out of the driver's door to walk around to the other side. As he passed by the tailgate of his truck, the gut-wrenching volcano within him exploded, and it was all over a few heaves later, except for the shakes.

Louis drove south about a quarter of a mile and pulled into a 24-hour Shell station. He left Nathan in the truck as he went inside and purchased a couple of bottles of orange juice. Nathan was standing outside the truck, leaning against the door, when Louis handed him a bottle.

"Here, drink this; you'll start feeling better almost immediately. All of that adrenaline you're not used to burned through all your available blood sugar. The hypoglycemia is what made you sick."

Nathan downed the bottle of juice, and Louis handed him the second one, saying, "Just sip this one; the worst of it is behind you."

As they got back into the truck, and started across the parking lot, Nathan asked, "Does that ever happen to you?"

"Nope, I've learned to manage the adrenaline. I've got a touch more experience at this than you do, Bro," he said with a matter-of-fact glance toward him.

Within half an hour, they were back in Nathan's driveway, and although he felt better, Nathan was still rattling with a mild case of the shakes and went directly into his study to track the VIN number and license plate of the SUV that no longer existed. Louis took a seat in the lawn chair at the back of the property, overlooking the lights of Huntsville. He leaned his head back and stared up at the stars above him through the clean, unpolluted air of North Alabama, thinking about Nathan, and what would've happened to his only friend had he been alone when the three killers came for him. It was now obvious that someone else took the contract on Nathan, but who was it? Nathan had to figure this one out as well. He had the vehicle information and the wallets and weapons of the three gunmen, along with their fingerprints and photos. It would keep him busy throughout the night, allowing him to work through the stress. *He'll get past this,* Louis thought while watching the stars.

Louis got up, walked into the house and to the study, where Nathan was analyzing three screens of data on the wall. Louis grabbed a beer from the refrigerator and headed back outside to the lawn chair, without interrupting his friend's concentration.

He kicked back in the chair and reinserted the ear buds before kicking off the app and once again tuning in E Street Radio. He closed his eyes and listened to the live recording of one of Springsteen's concerts while he drank his beer and relaxed, before he nodded off some time later.

13

Inside his study, Nathan emptied out the contents of the trash bag containing all the personal effects of the three and everything they found inside the Tahoe. It was all laid out in an orderly fashion on one end of the workbench. He was wearing gloves and meticulously scanned each item found. He also scanned both sides of each weapon, including serial numbers and manufacturer's data on the weapons and the suppressors.

There was a small Acer Aspire One notebook with a USB wireless modem attached, along with a power adapter to keep it charged while in the Tahoe.

Nathan powered up and inventoried the hard drive and found that the USB modem connected automatically to the Verizon network. He shut it down and continued his task of identifying the killers.

The Tahoe's VIN was registered to the owner of Opses Limited, a small private security firm located in Fayetteville, North Carolina. The Tennessee plate belonging to a dark blue Chevy Tahoe was registered to a man with a Chattanooga address. The company's website expounded on their professionalism and experience, and while it looked professionally built, Nathan hacked it in less than six minutes.

The Web server's link to the Internet was over an ISDN line, with a lightweight firewall embedded in a Cisco router, whose default password was never changed from "administrator". The router contained a four-port hub with only three ports that were active, connected to PCs; one of those was the Web server. The who-is information from Network Solutions listed the contacts as well as an address in Fayetteville. The domain name Opses-Limited.com was registered two years earlier.

Nathan opened a terminal services connection to the first PC, and the remote desktop looked like it belonged to a 20-something female social media addict. The prominent icons on the desktop were Facebook, Twitter, MySpace, Chiq, Glam, Teamsugar, AOL Women and others. Isolated on the left side of the desktop were the standard Office icons. Nathan opened Outlook to find this user was the e-mail administrator. He selected all the e-mail accounts and generated a .pst file and copied it over the net to his local computer.

Nathan removed all of his tracks, closed the session and connected to the other PC on the network. When Nathan opened the remote desktop, he found a videoconference session still running, with a view of the top of an empty chair sitting in front of a wall covered in picture frames. The logs showed the address of the other participant, which was disconnected. Nathan cloned the PC's IP and Mac address and copied the videoconference software down to his local computer. After digging around in the hard drive of this PC, he located software to interface to the docking station of a satellite telephone and a copy of the configuration files, which contained the account information and passwords that would unlock the phone. The software had a paging feature with texting capabilities.

Curiosity got the best of Nathan and he clicked on the paging button. About 15 seconds later, one of the phones from the trash bag that was laid out on the end of the workbench started beeping. Nathan had already placed each satellite phone in a Ziploc freezer bag to preserve the fingerprints left on them, while still handling them. He picked up the phone and entered the security code. The beeping stopped and a dark screen lit up, showing the date and time of the page. Nathan erased the page from the logs on the remote PC and continued scanning the hard drive.

He copied over all the office documents before erasing his tracks and closing the remote session. He next connected to the Web server and found it to be just another PC that also had a satellite phone docking station attached. He again copied over the logs and configuration files for the docking station software, and again pressed the page button to find that another one of the phones they harvested from the bodies went active. Nathan entered the password to silence the phone and again cleared the logs that detailed the page. There was a simple text file located on the root of the C drive of this PC; it contained a string of five numbers: 04 23 58 20 10.

He next dug through the log files of the Web server and its contact page and copied them to his local PC. Feeling he had located all there was to find, he removed his tracks and disconnected the remote session. Nathan next focused his attention on the identities of the three killers. Two held North Carolina driver's licenses, and one a Tennessee license. None of the three matched the owner's name of Opses Limited. He did a simple public records search and verified that all three driver's licenses were in fact genuine and state issued.

A public records search on the name of the company owner showed no driver's license but did show a Social Security card that matched the Social Security number of one of the men. Over the next hour, Nathan put together a dossier on all three killers, containing their IDs, places of residence, vehicles registered to them, weapons registered to them and to the company, the IDs of their family members that shared their home addresses, as well as their bank account numbers he harvested from direct deposit information found in their e-mail. He also tracked down the ID of a female who worked at the first PC he connected to, who was apparently the receptionist and bookkeeper of the small company.

The gunman from Chattanooga, William C. Pritchet, was the youngest of the three at 29, and lived alone in a small apartment, at the base of Lookout Mountain. The next oldest, Theodore N. Marcum, was 32 and lived with his wife Kelly in Fayetteville; she worked as a nurse at the base hospital on Ft. Bragg. The oldest of the three, Walter L. Barkley, was 41. He was divorced from his wife of 10 years and lived in a condominium in Fayetteville; the ex-wife, Sharon, lived in Atlanta with Taylor, their eight-year-old son.

All three of the men were prior military, with Gulf War experience. Two were airborne, all three were infantry, but only one of the three was Special Ops trained.

The oldest of the three, Barkley, lost his Green Beret status due to substance abuse while still in Iraq. Once he returned home after his tour in the desert, he legally changed his name and created the small subchapter S Corp., Opses Limited. When the other two returned from Iraq, they were employed by him doing private security work. It was now 4 am; Nathan left the study and stepped out on the patio through the door of the den.

Louis, still seated in the lawn chair near the far edge of the backyard, sat up and looked over his shoulder when he heard the sliding glass door open. Nathan saw him and walked across the yard, taking a seat in the other lawn chair.

"Well, I figured out who they were, and where they came from, but as of yet, not who sent them."

"You've been busy. Where'd they come from?"

"A small outfit out of Fayetteville, North Carolina. Three prior military buddies who worked together doing private security, obviously beyond their actual capabilities."

"I don't know, Bro," Louis said, "they seemed to have their shit together, but we held home field advantage and superior communications."

"And a player with a whole lot more experience," Nathan added. "Granted, that didn't hurt our chances."

"I copied down all kinds of intel from their office computers and found what looked to be a combination to a safe. One of the desktops had videoconference software still running; I got the address of whoever was on the other end."

"If that video conference wasn't with the Senator or his aide; I'll kiss your ass on Main Street and give you 20 minutes to draw a crowd."

Nathan laughed, "You're probably right; I just need to verify it before turning down that kiss."

"Well, let's see what you got," Louis said while rising from the chair. They walked inside to the study and Nathan laid it all out for him, in detail, and filled him in on the two satellite phones and everything else they found in the Chevy, and on the bodies. After discussing all the intel and answering Louis's questions, they decided the contents of the safe, while curious, were probably not worth the risk of investigating.

Determining who was on the other end of the video conference was decidedly more important, and that would have to wait an hour or two, as whomever it was, was probably still sleeping, given it was 5 am Central. They decided to head into town to grab some breakfast at Denny's on University drive, before returning and continuing their efforts to uncover who is behind the failed hit.

It was 6:30 am Central when they walked back in the study after their breakfast trip. Nathan placed a couple of strips of cellophane tape over the camera lens of his laptop. He configured his laptop with the IP and Mac address of the desktop computer in North Carolina and started the video conference software.

Starting a new conference, he entered the address of the other party and sent the invitation. About 30 seconds later, the connection was made and the image of a white man in a coat and tie appeared on the screen. Nathan pressed control-alt-print screen simultaneously to capture a screenshot of the image.

The man on the screen said, "I can't see you very well; your image is distorted. Is it done?"

"Yes," was all that Nathan said.

"I'll send final payment shortly," said the man on the screen before terminating the call.

Nathan opened a graphics program and pasted in the screenshot, then sent it to his color printer. Louis grabbed the printout and handed it to Nathan. "Do you recognize him?"

"Yes, that's Richland, but he looks younger than the press photos I found of him."

"Maybe he's undergone plastic surgery recently," Louis said. "A lot of the wrinkles around his eyes and mouth are gone; he probably had Botox injections. His hair has changed too; a lot of the gray on top is gone." Louis said, "Well, that kind of makes sense, he's making himself look a little younger before he announces his run for the White House."

"That must be it," Nathan replied, "and now we have the most recent photograph of him."

Louis thought for a few moments then asked, "So why would Richland risk contracting a hit himself, when his aide already did it for him?"

"Maybe he didn't trust his aide to pull it off competently?"

"Maybe he didn't know his aide already handled it?" Louis theorized.

"Maybe he did know, and used this team as a backup? He didn't ask for confirmation; he must've trusted them to take their word for it," Nathan retorted.

"Mighty damn foolish of him to talk openly on the video conference, when he couldn't see who he was speaking to."

"You're right there," Nathan replied. "He must've thought he recognized who the call came from, or he wouldn't have accepted it. We already thought he wasn't technologically savvy; he just confirmed that for us himself."

"I think it's time to go to plan B and abandon the death by natural causes approach," Louis said. "The three ghosts have provided us with the means and motive possibilities that should be easy to point at them."

"You're right about that; we can use their equipment and establish a collection of evidence pointing to them without too much effort," Nathan said. "I'll pull together the bits and pieces from their stuff to make it happen."

Louis asked, "What day is it?"

"It's Thursday, Bro," Nathan chuckled.

"They're all starting to run together on me, man. Hey, Richland's flying back to Wyoming today, isn't he?"

"His calendar indicates he leaves from BWI on his family's Gulfstream IV at 2 pm Eastern, landing at Sheridan County Airport around 4:45 Eastern, 2:45 Mountain."

"Well, I better get on the stick, if he's still planning on hunting this weekend in Ten Sleep Canyon."

"It says on his calendar hunting Saturday and Sunday, will be out of contact all day," Nathan confirmed.

"Then I better pack up and get out of here ASAP," Louis said before heading to the bedroom and retrieving his duffel bag. Out in the garage, next to his bike, he slipped into his riding pants and boots and strapped the duffel bag to the backseat.

Nathan retrieved the small Acer notebook they found in the Tahoe and removed the screws that secured the back cover, then flipped it over and unclipped the trim ring around the keyboard.

He scrutinized the circuitry located around the hinges, between the screen and the body of the netbook, and then carefully unplugged the wires connected to a micro switch, clipped off the connectors and soldered the two wires together. This bypassed the switch that made contact when the screen was closed, which would now allow the laptop to remain powered up and operating, with the screen closed over the keyboard.

After buttoning up the Acer, Nathan inserted the USB modem in one of the ports of the Acer, and a USB GPS dongle in another port and hot glued them in place. He located the car charger for the Acer, cut off the cigarette lighter attachment and stripped the wires back. He took a small propane powered soldering iron, some solder and a roll of electrical tape out to the garage to the top case on Louis' bike. The charger for Louis' old cell phone was still wired into the top case, so Nathan snipped off the end of the charger that plugged into the cell phone, stripped the wires, and soldered them to the wires of the car charger for the Acer, insulating them with the electrical tape, before heading back to the study.

Nathan came back to the garage carrying one of the satellite phones, still sealed in its plastic bag and a 9 mm pistol and its silencer in a Ziploc bag, and gave them to Louis to take with him. Nathan laid a quarter of an inch thick piece of foam rubber on top of Louis' new laptop, sitting it in the top case, sat the Acer on top of the foam rubber and plugged the charger into the power port of the Acer, opened the screen and powered it up, then closed the screen. He also gave

Louis the charger for his new cell phone that plugged into the BMW style accessory sockets on Louis' bike. He plugged the charger into the accessory outlet next to the handlebars so Louis could keep the cell phone in the tank bag while it charged.

Louis crammed the pair of desert boots into the left side case of the bike and walked out into the driveway to call Diane, to let her know he was heading out west and that he would call her later this evening. Louis fired up the GPS on the bike and punched in the destination of Buffalo, Wyoming, selecting fastest route. While it was calculating, Louis and Nathan talked, coordinating when they would check in with one another and confirming last-minute details.

When he looked back at the GPS, the route was displayed and ready, so he put on his jacket, helmet and gloves, shook Nathan's hand, fired up the bike and headed up the driveway and out to the street before rolling down the mountain. The GPS led him to University Drive, with his first turn being northwest on 53. Nathan was again in his study, clicking away on the keyboard of his high-powered laptop, connected to the Acer netbook in the top case of Louis's bike via the wireless modem. He uploaded a script to the Acer that would open a browser and connect to Google maps, enter the location from the GPS dongle and display it on the browser.

The script would then open the e-mail client on the Acer and retrieve new e-mail. The script automatically kicked off every hour to hour and a half, using a randomized timer; repeating this process all the way to Louis' destination. At Ardmore, on the Alabama-Tennessee line, Louis took the short jaunt on SR 7 to Interstate 65, heading north to Nashville, where he took 24 to where it intersected 57 in southern Illinois. Louis stopped briefly for fuel, a bio break and a couple of cold diet Dews. One went in the bottle holder and the other in the tank bag for later.

Nathan logged on to one of the desktops at Opses Limited and sent e-mail to the Acer periodically, maintaining a steady stream of communication between the office and the traveling netbook. He would then remotely log into the netbook in the top case of the bike and respond to the e-mails it received.

Louis headed north on 57, then turned west on 64 heading to St. Louis, where he navigated to 70 and headed west across Missouri, toward Kansas City. He took the loop around the north side of Kansas City to 29, heading north into Iowa and exiting just east of Nebraska City.

Nathan logged in to the aide's laptop and sent a brief e-mail to the traveling netbook.

"I need a Sit-Rep."

Nathan then deleted the sent message from the aide's e-mail client; then, logging into the traveling Acer, he responded with an e-mail containing the location and ETA to Buffalo. Northwest of Nebraska City, Louis found 75 and took it north to 34 west, to Lincoln, then on to 80 west, all the Way to Cheyenne, Wyoming, where he turned north on Interstate 25, passing through Casper and on north to Buffalo.

It took Louis 25 hours of hard riding, stopping only for fuel, something to drink and energy bars, which he always combined during a single stop–something he learned from the Iron Butt Association rides. He found a room at the Arrowhead Motel on 16, the main route between Buffalo and Ten Sleep Canyon. It was 10 am local time Friday when Louis unpacked the bike into the motel room and powered on the laptop. Putting it into secure mode he composed an e-mail to Nathan.

"I'm in Buffalo at a motel. I'm heading out to recon his ranch shortly." Then Louis sent the message. A few moments later a response came back, "I don't know how you do it, man; they should rename the Iron Butt Association in your honor. He's at his ranch now, online with his office preparing for a conference call with the DOE Secretary and a few of his buddies from the Wyoming Energy Cooperative.

Since you're going to be stopped for a while, unplug the charging wire from the Acer laptop, so it doesn't drain the bike's battery. A few updates: while you were on the road, I created the offshore accounts with respectable deposits. I found a connection between Opses Limited and the Senator. The owner, Wilson L. Banks (his original name, now Walter L. Barkley) headed Richland's security detail when he toured Iraq on his fact-finding mission. I've been e-mailing the receptionist at

Opses Limited as Banks. She believes the three of them are heading to Wyoming to go hunting with the Senator. Be safe during your recon; you're road-tired and need some rest. Contact me when you return."

Louis closed the laptop and headed into the bathroom to wash his face with cold water before heading out toward the Senator's family ranch located north of Buffalo, west of Interstate 90 between Lake DeSmet and Saddlestring, off Shell Creek Road. Louis walked out to the bike, punched the address into the GPS, and donned his jacket, helmet and gloves for the ride. The GPS led him north on French Creek Road, then right on Johnson Creek, then north on Rock Creek, and finally north on Shell Creek Road, where he stopped about 1,000 feet south of the dirt road that led on to the ranch, located on the west side of Shell Creek.

Louis parked the bike on the edge of the road and removed his riding jacket and helmet. He retrieved his binoculars from the side case and walked the hundred yards west from the road, to a small circular hill that rose maybe 60 feet above. Near the top of the hill he surveyed the ranch with the binoculars.

There were no trees, shrubs, or even fences near the road, with a winding gravel drive that led to the large farmhouse with a detached garage, located between the house and a barn. The house and garage were situated in a stand of trees on an island of manicured grass. Farther west, behind the house, the hills rolled upward, forming the eastern foothills of the Big Horn Mountains. To the east, on the other side of 90, was Lake DeSmet, the largest natural body of water in northern Wyoming, so they unnaturally enlarged it.

Nathan logged into the Acer in the top case and stopped the script that was running over the past 27 hours. He logged into the e-mail client and sent a brief message to the Senator's aide and blind-copied Banks' e-mail at Opses Limited. "Have arrived at AO." Nathan then logged into the aide's laptop and deleted the message sent from the bike.

He then logged into Banks' PC in the North Carolina office and responded to the e-mail from the bike. "Set up surveillance before getting some rest."

There were two Suburbans and a large dually pickup parked in front of the house; on the north side of the barn, under an overhang, was a camouflage-painted Ford Bronco.

That's what he uses for hunting, Louis thought. *I'll come back tonight when it's nice and dark.* Louis turned around and walked back down the hill. He put away the binoculars and donned his gear for the short ride back into Buffalo. Once back in town, he navigated over to the Bozeman Trail Steakhouse on 16. Nathan and Louis ate dinner here the last time they were in Buffalo, and the prime rib was killer.

Louis wasn't quite dressed for the occasion, as virtually everyone in the restaurant was in cowboy boots, straight leg jeans, nicely pressed button-down shirts and the required cowboy hat to complete the traditional look. They weren't dressed up for the occasion; this was just how everyone dressed. It was easy to identify the visitors to the area, as they were the ones in sneakers and sweatshirts with ball caps or no hats at all.

Louis ate a 16 ounce, medium rare prime rib, a large baked potato with all the trimmings and a garden salad, washing it down with three large glasses of unsweetened iced tea.

When he was done, it was all he could do to get up out of the chair, as the 25 hours of riding and his now-full belly caught up with him.

The brief ride back to the motel was a blessing. He took a bike cover from the side case and locked everything up before covering the bike and heading into the motel room.

He stretched out on the bed, with the laptop in front of him, and fired off a brief e-mail to Nathan indicating he was back in the motel room and planned to get some rest before heading back to the ranch later in the night.

Louis grabbed his cell phone off the nightstand and called Diane; he got her voicemail.

"Hey baby, we're somewhere out west, within striking distance of Iowa, and we checked into a motel to get some rest. I'll call you again when I get up. I love you, bye."

It was now just past 12 noon local time, and Louis set the alarm on his cell phone to wake him in nine hours. He struggled to stand up and remove his clothes, and then turned on the shower, leaning against the wall, waiting for the water to warm up. The hot shower drained what remained of the strength in his muscles and he crash-landed on the bed, passing out after a deep breath.

Nathan continued executing their plans and was able to track down the Senator's laptop that was connected through a satellite link at the ranch. He remotely enabled the laptop's camera and microphone and could hear the conference call taking place over a speakerphone, with two or three men in the room with Richland.

Although he couldn't see anyone through the camera, a blur would come and go as they passed by the laptop that was sitting open.

"How did it go in the appropriations meeting this morning? Did we get the approvals we paid for?" one of the voices in the room asked.

The voice on the phone replied, "Looks like everything worked out as prearranged."

"So will the money come through before you make your announcement?" another voice asked.

"It has to, it certainly can't happen once I announce." *That's Richland,* thought Nathan.

"Mr. Secretary, who's gonna handle the GAO and keep them out of our business?"

A voice on the phone replied, "I've got that handled; four of the seven members of their oversight committee are close friends of ours. We're all on the same team."

"This shale oil extraction facility will be the first of its kind and will pump millions into the area's economy; if it gets tied up in committee, we all stand to lose significant money."

"Especially me, since it's on the land trust controlled by my family," Richland replied.

"I think we've covered everything on the agenda, gentleman. I'll be out of touch all day tomorrow and Sunday; I'll be thinning the goat population over in the Canyon."

"Enjoy your hunting trip, Harry; we'll talk again Monday," said the voice on the phone.

"I will, Mr. Secretary; enjoy your weekend as well," Richland replied, then ended the call. Richland and the men in the room continued to talk for several more minutes before they all left the room and were out of earshot of the microphone. A few minutes later, Richland sat down in front of the laptop, still unaware of Nathan's surveillance. Richland opened his e-mail client and sent a message to his aide in Washington.

"I'm off the call now and everything went as planned. Have you heard back from Wilson?"

About four minutes later he received the reply. "Glad to hear the meeting went well. I'll hand-carry the check over to the Secretary's office before leaving this afternoon. I heard from Wilson's receptionist; she indicated he and the guys were en route to your ranch to go hunting with you. She said you invited them. I didn't argue with her, just let it slide. Enjoy the hunt and your time away from the office."

Richland replied, "I don't know what she's talking about. I didn't invite them. They're probably off in a casino blowing their payday. I'm signing off now; call me if anything comes up."

Richland got up from his computer, leaving the screen open as Nathan listened for a while before he continued with other tasks. At 4:30 pm Eastern, Nathan logged into the aide's laptop and undeleted the last message received from the bike, indicating they were at the AO, and responded to it with, "Sending first payment now."

He then deleted both messages and logged onto the Panamanian bank's website and initiated a wire transfer for $50,000 from the Senator's account to Banks' account in Fayetteville.

● ● ●

The alarm of Louis' cell phone shattered the silence in the motel room and startled him awake. He slept the entire time, flat on his back, and his throat was dry, probably from snoring, though he rarely did, except when exhausted. He grabbed his cell phone off the nightstand and fumbled around for a few seconds, trying to figure out how to cancel the alarm. A few minutes later, he was in the bathroom washing his face with cold water to bring him to alertness.

He opened the laptop and put it in secure mode, finding an e-mail from Nathan sent hours earlier.

"I spent some time monitoring a conference call at the ranch. Richland's a real piece of work, but probably no different than the rest of the politicians in Washington. The receptionist at Opses Limited has been in contact with the Senator's aide and told him that they were on the way to the ranch. The Senator didn't buy it but the aide did. Contact me before heading back out to the ranch. Hope you got some sleep."

Louis replied to the e-mail, "I'm up and getting dressed, preparing to head out to the ranch. Will contact you when I return."

Louis dressed, putting on the camouflage coveralls he purchased, along with the desert boots he took off one of the dead killers at Nathan's house. Stepping out the front door of the motel room, he removed the bike cover, stuffing it back into the pouch before storing it in the side case. He stepped back inside the motel room to get his cell phone and the laptop and put them in the top case of the bike. He locked the motel room door and donned his riding gear, cranked the bike, switched on the GPS and pulled out of the motel parking lot, heading back to the ranch.

It was approaching 10 pm local time, and the sky was dark as he made his way north out of town in the cold Wyoming air. Louis stopped about a mile south of the ranch, dug the night vision goggles out of the side case and positioned them across his forehead as he strapped his helmet down on the back seat with the bungee cords.

He pressed and held the turn signal cancel button on the handlebars for five seconds before pressing the right turn signal button, which switched off the headlight, a built-in feature of the canbus system on the BMW.

Louis slid the night vision goggles down over his eyes and powered them up to reveal a crystal-clear image of the road in front of him, illuminated by the starlight overhead. He continued down the road and again parked the bike near the small hill, close to the road where he reconned the area hours earlier.

He killed the engine and climbed off the bike, leaving his riding jacket across the seat and locking the handlebars. Louis removed the black box in the side case that held the tracking device, and connected the receiver to the GPS via the antenna connector and plugged the connector into the receiver.

He attached the transmitter to the metal frame of the bike, which activated the unit. He removed it and shook the transmitter and reattached it to the frame of the bike and watched the GPS screen. About 10 seconds later a small red crosshair appeared on screen, showing the location of the bike. It was superimposed over the green arrow on the screen, which indicated the bike's position.

Louis powered down the GPS, detached the transmitter from the bike frame, slipping it into his pocket, and climbed to the top of the small hill to survey the area before moving in.

Seeing no activity, just the lights from inside the house, he moved down the west side of the hill in the direction of the house, stopping every hundred yards or so, to scan the complete horizon. He crossed the driveway about 300 yards from the house, heading directly north to use the barn as cover as he continued his approach.

Nathan again logged into the Acer, still located in the top case, opened the browser and logged onto the banking website where Opses Limited kept their accounts. He checked the balance on the business accounts, as well as Banks' personal account, and then accessed the pending transactions, where he found the $50,000 transfer.

He logged off from the bank's site and closed the browser before logging off the Acer laptop.

Within a few minutes, Louis reached the Ford Bronco and looked around the front of the barn to ensure he was alone before he attached the tracking device on the bottom side of the spare tire mount, secured to the rear door of the bronco.

Again, he removed the tracking device and shook it vigorously, reattaching it to the tire mount in the same location. He moved back toward his motorcycle, following the same route he took across the property coming in.

Louis arrived back at the bike about five minutes later and started the GPS to verify the transmitter was working properly.

He held his jacket over the headlight of the bike and turned the key to start the engine, then reached over to the controls on the right handlebar and again canceled the headlight, before putting the jacket on and doing a U-turn, heading south away from the ranch.

He stopped at the intersection of his next turn and climbed off the bike to put the night vision goggles back in their box in the side case and put on his helmet. He climbed back on the bike and continued back into Buffalo.

The GPS showed the crosshairs locked onto the transmitter's last position before it automatically powered down to conserve battery life.

Louis stopped at a convenience store and refueled the bike before heading inside and purchasing a couple of bottles of iced tea and a diet Dew for the morning. He rode back to the motel and took his laptop and cell phone inside before locking the bike up, covering it for the night.

Louis put the earphones into the cell phone and opened one of the bottles of iced tea before walking through the parking lot of the motel to the bench he saw under a tree, in front of the motel with a view of US 16.

He sipped on his iced tea and watched the Friday night traffic a few minutes before calling Nathan.

"Hey man, how did it go?" Nathan asked.

"Easy and fast, in and out without complications. I'm back at the motel for the night."

"That's good, man, how did you sleep?"

"Like a dead man. I never even moved until the alarm went off. So what's going on in Huntsville?"

"I installed a couple of new solar powered, remote-controlled cameras with night vision out across the road, 100 feet up the street in both directions. I think I've solved my blind spot problem."

"No doubt; you may want to add some cameras inside the house as well. By the way," Louis said, "hang on to those additional weapons; they may come in handy sometime the future."

"I already have those weapons concealed in the study, and I've ordered half a dozen interior cameras that look like smoke detectors. Great minds do think alike, you know."

"Yeah, I've heard that," Louis said with a chuckle. "As soon as I'm done in the Canyon, I'm going to haul ass to Clear Lake, Iowa for some photos of the crash site before heading back."

"Got it, give me a call in the morning before you head out to the Canyon and again after the egress, okay?"

"I'll do it, Bro. Are you ready to execute your part?"

"Yep, everything is in place. I'll wait for your call in the morning before I go," Nathan said.

"Well, I'm heading in the room to catch up on the news before hitting the sack. Big day tomorrow–later."

"Later, Bro."

Louis set the alarm on his phone for 4 am and headed back into the motel room to try to get some more sleep, knowing tomorrow would be a very long day.

14

Louis managed to doze off and enjoyed an hour and a half catnap when the alarm on his cell phone broke the silence in the motel room. He quickly got out of bed and hopped in the shower, knowing it might be a couple of days before he could take another one. He stuck his face out the door of the motel room to discover it was dramatically colder outside than the night before. He turned on the Weather Channel and started digging warm clothes out of his duffel bag. Sliding into his thermal underwear, tops and bottoms, he put on a pair of athletic cotton socks and then pulled his thick wool socks over his feet, and up over his calves before putting on his blue jeans. He put on his electrically heated jacket liner and a sweatshirt over it, as the Weather Channel indicated it was 38° in Buffalo, Wyoming, with intermittent snow flurries throughout the day. *This is not good,* Louis thought, as he climbed into the insulated camouflage coveralls and fished the wire from the heated liner through the pass-through pockets of the coveralls.

Louis sat on the edge of the bed and slipped his feet into the desert boots, lacing them up snugly. He repacked the duffel bag and headed outside to uncover and load the bike. Louis cranked the engine to let it warm up and kicked his tires as if checking their pressure. The light dusting of snow on the cars and the roof was melting as it hit the ground. *This is no time to be in Wyoming on a motorcycle,* he thought as he walked back inside the motel room.

• • •

Nathan was busy at his task. He wiped a SD memory card, overwriting the contents multiple times before formatting the card, and wiping it again. He copied the simple text document he prepared to the memory card. While wearing rubber gloves designed for washing dishes, Nathan removed the memory card from the laptop and cleaned it completely with acetone and Q-tips. He tore off a small square piece of aluminum foil, and cleaned it on both sides with acetone as well. He sat the memory card on the edge of the aluminum foil and folded it over three times, wrapping the card neatly in the foil to protect it from scanners. Nathan then sealed it inside the small preaddressed envelope and used tweezers to place the postage stamps on the envelope before slipping it inside the freezer bag; he was now prepared for his morning journey.

• • •

Louis picked up his new laptop and sat it in the top case, under the Acer, placed his wallet in the top case and plugged the charging wire into the Acer before locking the top case. Again, he walked back inside and scanned the room, to ensure he left nothing there, and grabbed his cell phone and the ear buds from the nightstand. It was 4:30 am local time when he called Nathan.

"I am on my way now."

"I'll be leaving here shortly," Nathan replied. "I should arrive in less than two hours."

"Be careful, Bro, I'll call you after."

"Roger that, you be as well."

"Later."

Louis left the key to the motel room on top of the television, pulled the door closed behind him and walked up next to the bike, powered up the GPS, and put on his helmet before sliding his hands into the heavy winter gloves he pulled from the side case. The crosshairs from the tracking transmitter were yellow and stationary, indicating the vehicle had not moved from its previous position. Louis flipped the switch on the handlebars to activate the grip heaters. He stood on the left peg of the bike, still on the center stand, to make it easier to get his leg over the seat. He put the bike in first gear and rocked the bike forward vigorously, causing it to slip off the center stand as he let out the clutch and gave a little throttle, as he rode through the parking lot of the motel and headed back toward Richland's ranch.

Instead of stopping along the road where he did before, he continued on north, under the interstate overpass toward the lake, before making a U-turn and coming to a stop under the overpass. He put the bike in neutral and extended the kickstand. He again switched off the headlight and sat there with the engine idling, enjoying the warmth of the heated jacket liner. A few minutes after 5 am, the crosshairs on the GPS screen began to flash. The Bronco was now moving. Less than a minute later the crosshairs turned red, continuing to flash, which indicated the distance between the transmitter and receiver was closing. Louis could see the headlights of the Bronco in the distance, as Richland approached the main road. The Bronco turned right, heading toward Buffalo, and the crosshairs on the GPS now flashed green, indicating the distance between the transmitter and receiver was increasing. A few minutes later, the Bronco was moving through Buffalo, and shortly thereafter, the crosshairs turned solid yellow, indicating the vehicle stopped. Using the GPS controls, Louis zoomed in on the crosshairs. Zooming in even closer, it appeared the Bronco was stopped in front of Pistol Pete's restaurant, on Main Street. *The son of a bitch is going to eat breakfast,* Louis thought.

Louis raised the side stand on the bike and rode south to the entrance of Richland's ranch, stopping alongside the road and parking the bike. He removed his winter gloves, slipping his hands into a pair of burn gloves, and put on the night vision goggles, grabbing his B&E toolkit from the tank bag, and jogged down the driveway all the way to the barn, where the power meter was mounted on the pole. He cut the power company's tamper seal and opened the meter enclosure to remove the power meter, which cut the power on the ranch. Louis sat the meter on the ground and jogged over to the side of the house to locate where the telephone lines entered the house. He found them near the back corner of the house and clipped the cable with his diagonal cutters.

He located the back door, unlocked the deadbolt using his key rake tool, and did the same for the lock in the doorknob, before entering the back door into the kitchen of the dark house. Louis searched methodically from room to room before locating the Senator's laptop, sitting on a desk in a modest office on the first floor. He slid the laptop inside the protective sleeve sitting next to it, then returned to the back door and shut it as he exited. Returning to the power pole, he reinserted the meter and closed the box, hanging the tamper seal in the loop of the lock. He then jogged back to the motorcycle, stored the night vision goggles and the Senator's laptop in the side case, then slipped his winter gloves over his burn gloves.

Louis cranked the bike and proceeded toward Buffalo before again stopping on the side of the road. He put the bike in neutral and extended the side stand, and sat there with the engine idling, relishing the warmth of the heated jacket liner and the grip heaters. Louis climbed off the bike and stood next to it. Still tethered to the bike by the power wire for the heated liner, he marched in place, keeping the circulation up in his feet and legs, adding to his body heat. Louis unplugged his jacket liner and walked around to the back of the bike before opening the top case and extracting the diet Dew he stored there the night before. He again plugged in the jacket liner to maintain his warmth and sipped the Dew, keeping an eye on the GPS.

Just before 6 am, the crosshairs on the GPS again began to flash and turned green. Louis zoomed out the GPS a little so he could see the entire town of Buffalo on the screen. Richland's Bronco followed Main Street south, and then US 16 west, heading toward Ten Sleep Canyon. The position of the crosshairs updated every five seconds as the Bronco proceeded west on US 16. Several minutes later, the Bronco passed Crazy Woman Canyon Road. Louis climbed back on the bike and followed the same route through Buffalo and headed west on US 16. A few minutes later, he rode past Crazy Woman Canyon Road. Between him and Ten Sleep Canyon, US 16 climbed to 9,660 feet at Powder River Pass. It was going to be painfully cold, and more than a little dangerous, if there was any snow accumulation at all.

The light dusting of snow still falling was not sticking at this elevation, but that would soon change as the road climbed beyond 9,000 feet, just a few miles east of the pass, as the thermometer on the bike was flashing a bone-chilling 28°F. Louis slowed his pace to around 30 mph, and kept diligent watch on the road ahead of him, in case there was frozen water across the road. Louis moved his eyes back and forth between the road and the GPS screen, monitoring the location of the Bronco ahead of him, while carefully negotiating the snowy conditions over the pass. As he started down the western slope, he kept the bike in third gear, allowing the engine to slow his descent, with little to no throttle applied. He slowed to a crawl around the sharp turn on the north side of Meadowlark Lake, still 8,500 feet in elevation. Louis continued on, losing elevation as he went. Approximately five miles ahead of him, the Bronco was still heading southwest, following the sharp turn to the left and stopping near the apex of the right hand turn of the large switchback in US 16, then proceeding off the side of the road a couple of hundred feet before stopping.

Louis pulled to the side of the road and came to a stop, leaving the bike on the side stand in first gear, and climbed off the bike, unplugging the heated liner. He removed his helmet and took his binoculars from the side case, walking across the road to find he was some 500 feet above the roadway below, and located the Bronco parked in the trees. He watched through the binoculars as Richland, now out of the Bronco, removed a small backpack from the rear of the vehicle and slung it over his back. He then removed a large zippered case from the back of the Bronco, unzipped it and extracted the compound bow it carried. Richland attached the quiver to the side of the bow and again reached inside the Bronco and removed a large thermos, before shutting and locking the rear door. Louis watched as Richland hiked east for about a mile up the slope of the canyon, before turning south and disappearing over the ridge toward Leigh Creek Vee.

He returned to the motorcycle with the binoculars hanging around his neck and put on his helmet before climbing on the bike.

He started the motor and pulled back out US 16 for the short ride to where the Bronco was parked. Louis pulled 200 feet past the Bronco, off to the east of the road, parking the bike well into the trees, out of sight from the road. He locked the handlebars and removed his helmet and winter gloves. Opening the right side case, he slowly turned, scanning around 360°, verifying he was alone before he removed the 9 mm with the silencer from the side case, still in the Ziploc bag. He opened the Ziploc closure and carefully grabbed the pistol grip with two fingers, holding it while he held the silencer with the plastic bag and attached it to the barrel. Louis unzipped the front of his coveralls and slid the pistol inside the belt of his blue jeans with the bag still open, exposing the grip of the gun. He then removed the satellite phone, still in a Ziploc bag, and placed it in the rear pocket of his coveralls.

He closed and locked the side case after removing his black ski cap and placing it over his head, covering his ears. He retrieved the Nikon digital camera from the top case and stuck his head through the strap before locking the case. Louis left the bike and hiked southeast, through the trees, across old Highway 16, and started up the hill toward Leigh Creek Vee. Stopping just west of the highest point, he used the binoculars to locate Richland, now just a quarter of a mile south of him, approaching the rim of the cliff above Leigh Canyon.

Louis removed the satellite phone from his back pocket, switched on the power, and then entered the security code to unlock it, while it was still in the plastic bag. He dialed the number of the other satellite phone and waited until it went to voicemail before leaving the message, "I'm in position now; you need to deal with our buddy in Chattanooga today," and disconnected the call, returning the phone to his back pocket.

Through his binoculars, he could see several Bighorn sheep, climbing and standing on the opposite wall of the canyon. He watched Richland nock an arrow before he passed out of view near the canyon's ledge.

Louis snapped a few pictures of the Bighorn sheep before closing on Richland's position. As he approached the edge of the Canyon where Richland passed out of sight, he again took several photos of the sheep across the canyon.

There were three inches of snow on the ground, and the snow was falling harder than it was earlier. The sound of the wind moving through the Canyon was only interrupted by the clopping hooves of the sheep as they jumped and ran along the opposite canyon wall.

Louis pulled the satellite phone from his rear pocket, and pressed the power button. With it still in the bag, he entered the key code to unlock the phone and dialed the number of the other satellite phone Nathan was holding, waiting for the second call. "Hello," Nathan said.

"Hold for Richland," Louis said, and then returned the phone to his back pocket.

Holding his camera in his hands, Louis slowly walked around the ledge at the edge of the canyon wall, stopping to photograph the sheep every few yards, slowly moving closer to Richland's position. Louis noticed the smell of coffee and unzipped the coveralls, realizing he was very close now.

Just a few more steps around the bend of the cliff ledge, and there was Richland, sitting on a rock at the edge of the cliff with his bow across his lap, concealed from the sheep by the branches of the trees growing out of the canyon wall below him.

Louis held the camera to his eye, looking toward the sheep on the opposite canyon wall, and shuffled his feet to get Richland's attention.

Richland turned and looked directly at Louis, speaking softly, "Quiet, I'm hunting here."

"And I'm photographing the sheep."

Louis shifted his position, his left leg now toward Richland, his right leg away from him.

Louis was still clicking photos when Richland turned, glaring at him, then turned back toward the sheep.

Reaching with his gloved right hand, he gripped the 9 mm, the camera still in his left.

Louis drew the pistol and tucked it behind his right leg, resting the camera on his chest.

He took two steps closer, now just six feet behind Richland.

It was quiet, the wind died down and the snow was falling much harder now.

He glanced at the pistol, ensuring the safety was off, and returned his eyes to Richland.

Louis cleared his throat in an unquiet manner.

Richland stood up, holding the bow in his left hand, and turned facing Louis.

Louis presented the 9 mm, aiming directly at Richland's chest, bracing with his left hand.

Richland froze; his eyes grew wide, fixated on the business end of the silencer.

Removing the satellite phone in the bag from his back pocket, he tossed it to Richland.

"Remove your gloves and take it out of the bag."

Richland let go of the bow, removed his gloves revealing his trembling hands.

He removed the phone and dropped the bag in front of him.

"Now what?" Richland asked.

Louis smiled and said, "You have a call already in progress."

Richland lifted the phone to his ear, "This is Senator Harold Richland, who is this?"

"This is the man you just tried to kill. Obviously, it didn't work out like you planned."

"Who am I speaking to?" Richland demanded.

"That's not important. Your plan failed. The gun pointing at you is what should concern you."

"The plan is bigger than you can possibly imagine," Richland said, feigning confidence.

"You failed, Richland. You're dead," Nathan said before he hung up the call.

"He hung up on me. Who was that, who are you, and what do you want from me?"

"The only thing I want from you, I'm going to take momentarily, and that's your sorry life."

"We can reach an accommodation. I'm a wealthy man. I'll give you whatever you want; just name it."

"Hmmm, what's the life of a corrupt Senator worth at this particular moment?"

"How about a million dollars in cash, to just walk away?"

"A million dollars? One whole million to walk away, out of the roughly seven hundred million in drug, gun and government corruption money rat-holed away in your nine overseas and domestic accounts?

"How do you know about my money? Who are you? How much do you want, then?"

"Like I said, I'll take what I want. We'll take all the money as well. How does it feel to know you're leaving your family penniless after your death, all because you tried to kill my friend?"

"Ok, take it all, if that's what it costs me to stay alive. I'm going to be President."

"Well, I've only got one thing to say about that."

"What do you have to say about that?" Richland asked with arrogance.

Louis smiled, "Nathan Malone sends his coldest regards," and squeezed the trigger.

The round exited the silencer, emitting a deep thud when striking Richland's chest.

Two more rounds followed in quick succession before the first casing hit the ground.

Receiving three hits center mass, Richland was hurled backwards through the treetops.

Louis stepped forward to the cliff; peering over the edge, he heard a substantial thump.

Richland's lifeless body was 200 feet below, hanging more off than on the ledge.

He watched for a few seconds, prior to it sliding off the ledge into the deep canyon below.

Louis put the pistol back into his belt and zipped up the coveralls. He picked up the plastic bag, shoved it in his back pocket, and headed back over Leigh Creek Vee and down the other side, returning to his bike. Looking around carefully, he removed the 9 mm from his belt, placing it back in the bag, and returned it to the side case, along with his binoculars.

He walked up to the road near the parked Bronco, waiting until he was sure there were no vehicles coming, before removing the tracking device from the spare tire support and returning to his bike. He put the transmitter into his tank bag and started the bike. He stuffed his ski cap into the tank bag, plugged in his electric vest and slid his helmet over his head before riding out of the trees and up onto US 16 heading east. Louis switched on the GPS as he climbed the steep grade. The display indicated it was now 8:25, Louis took his time, carefully watching the road as he rose up and over Powder River Pass and cautiously down the other side. Arriving in Buffalo at 9:40, he stopped across the road from the Cenex Zip Trip on 16 near the interstate. Standing next to his bike, Louis placed the call to Nathan before heading east on 90 toward Gillette.

Nathan answered, "How did it go?"

"As planned, I'm about to head east. Are you in place?"

"I'm in the parking lot of the apartments now."

"Well, if you're waiting on me, you're backing up."

"Call me when you reach Rapid City. I should be back in Huntsville by then."

"Later."

The sun drove the temperature up to 44°F, and although snow was falling heavily, nothing was sticking. Louis proceeded at normal highway speeds, putting Buffalo and the Canyon's newest secret farther behind him as he went. An hour later, Louis exited the highway at Skyline Drive in Gillette, turning left on US 14 E. before stopping at a Shell Food Mart to top off the fuel, take a wiz and purchase a diet Dew for the ride east. The Saturday morning crowd at the Shell station stared in disbelief at Louis on his motorcycle.

• • •

Nathan sat in the parking lot of the apartment complex at the base of Lookout Mountain, just west of Chattanooga, where William Pritchet, the youngest of the three killers resided. He powered up Pritchet's cell phone, still in a Ziploc bag, and dialed directory assistance and asked for the number to the Memphis, Tennessee field office of the FBI. After receiving the number, he disconnected the call and dialed the number to the field office. He entered Paul Seltzer's extension and waited until his voicemail picked up. "I overheard two men I work with talking, and they mentioned killing a Senator. I didn't know what to do, so I decided to call the FBI. Please get back to me soon. I think they know I heard them." He disconnected the call and dropped the cell phone out of the bag, into the shrubs near the entrance to the apartment. Nathan then dropped the small envelope containing the memory card wrapped in aluminum foil into the mailbox next to the street.

• • •

Louis was still pumping his gas when a lifted four-wheel-drive pickup rolled up to the pump behind him. The rather fat, balding and bearded driver with what appeared to be a golf ball in his left cheek stepped down from the cab and shoved the diesel fuel nozzle into the side of his truck. "Did you ride that thing from Florida?"

No jackass, I pushed it, Louis thought, before responding, "Yep, just out for a short ride on this beautiful day."

"Ain't you cold?"

"I was before the sun came up, but I got over it."

Louis hung the hose back on the side of the pump and headed inside the store, walking directly to the men's room, where he dug through four layers of clothes mere seconds before his bladder exploded. Having successfully preserved his dryness, he resealed all layers and turned to wash his hands in the sink.

• • •

Nathan climbed back on his Goldwing and headed east toward Chattanooga, stopping alongside the highway next to the river, after making a U-turn to head west. He pulled the second satellite phone from the top case, unlocked it and waited for verification of the signal and called the voicemail number to pick up the message. He waited 10 minutes before he dialed Pritchet's cell phone. As soon as the voicemail picked up, Nathan disconnected the call and dialed the number for the second satellite phone that was somewhere in Ten Sleep Canyon. He left the message, "I'll be at our buddy's apartment in a few minutes. Don't worry, I'll handle it." He disconnected the call and stashed the satellite phone in the top case of the bike before riding back to Huntsville.

• • •

While waiting for the water to warm up, Louis came eye to eye with his image in the mirror. *You killed a United States Senator,* he thought. *That's never been done.* He studied his face. *No, the senator killed himself the moment he attempted to kill Nathan,* he thought. *It just took him several days to die.*

He washed and dried his hands before leaving the restroom, selecting a cold diet Dew from the cooler and paying his tab at the cash register. Walking back to his bike, he put the Dew into the bottle holder, donned his helmet and winter gloves, and plugged in the heated jacket liner before pulling out of station, heading back to 90 to continue rolling east. An hour and a half later, he was approaching Spearfish, South Dakota. He continued southeast to Rapid City, and then due east across the state to Mitchell, South Dakota, arriving on fumes just after 6 pm. He left the snow behind him, somewhere in the Buffalo Gap National Grassland. The temperature was holding in the high 40s when he stopped for fuel. He pulled into the Arby's on Burr Street, not really being dressed for the steakhouses in the area on a Saturday night. He choked down a couple of beef and cheddars then used the facilities before climbing back on the bike and continuing east on 90.

• • •

Back in Huntsville, Nathan logged into the aide's laptop and executed the next stage of the plan, orchestrating wire transfers from the Senator's offshore accounts to the offshore accounts Nathan created using the aide's laptop and identification days earlier, as well as wire transfers that would bounce through accounts in Europe, the Middle East, and Taiwan before trickling into his and Louis' slush fund accounts. Nathan then undeleted all of the e-mail traffic he hid from the aide and saved a local backup of all of the aide's e-mail to a .pst file on the root of the hard drive, before again deleting the e-mail traffic he created. He then removed the monitoring software he placed on the laptop and scheduled a hard disk defrag and secure overwrite of all the white space on the hard drive, following the DOD standard, to take place the next time the laptop rebooted. He deleted all traces of his footprints on the laptop and rebooted it, disconnecting the session. Nathan then performed the same operations on the PCs at Opses Limited in Fayetteville, closing out his methodical checklist.

• • •

Five hours later, Louis rolled into Albert Lea, Minnesota, turned south on 35 for the short hop to Clear Lake, Iowa, and took a room for the night at the Budget Inn, somewhere around midnight. After unloading and covering the bike, he stood in the hot shower for 30 minutes, soaking the chill out of his bones before stretching out on the bed. He called Nathan on his cell phone to check in.

"Hey Bro, where are you?"

"I'm in the motel room in Clear Lake for the night; how did it go?"

"To use your words, smooth as fresh paved asphalt."

"That's good; I'll make a field man out of you yet."

"I kept the Acer busy all day, dropping breadcrumbs. Did you unplug it?"

"Yep, did it while I was unloading the bike."

"There's nothing on the State, County or Local systems in Wyoming yet."

"It'll be a day or two before he's missed, if a hiker or hunter doesn't trip over him."

"The longer the better," Nathan replied.

"After the sun comes up, I'm going to scoot up the road to the crash site and take a wad of pictures before heading south, out of this cold weather."

"I'll keep an eye on things overnight; get some sleep and ride safe."

"Later man."

"Later."

• • •

Sunday morning, Louis stuck his head through the opening of the motel room door and received a cold blast of air, although this time there was no snow in it. He closed the door and turned on the Weather Channel, and again suited up in the several layers that had protected him during the previous day's ride. The Weather Channel indicated it was 40°F, with winds gusting out of the northwest at 35 mph, and snow on the way. Louis quickly completed dressing and loaded the bike before heading to the crash site he wanted to visit. He was a long-time fan of the pure and simple rock 'n roll Buddy Holly recorded, though it was popular long before his time. The field was just a few miles north of the motel, but could be a challenge to find.

He headed west on US 18 from the motel for just under a mile and turned on 8th street, riding north almost 5 miles. 8th Street, also known as Grouse Avenue, makes a 90° turn west. In the apex of that turn, Louis turned east on the gravel road, traveling about 1000 feet, and then north on Gull Avenue. Riding maybe a half a mile, approaching a cluster of five grain bins on the left, he continued another 200 yards to where another gravel road intersected on the right; there was a fence on the west side of the road.

Louis parked the bike and approached the trailhead marker. It was an oversized sculpture of Buddy Holly's glasses—a fitting monument that was uniquely Buddy's, larger-than-life and all alone at the end of the trail. *An appropriate metaphor,* Louis thought. He walked west, along the well-beaten trail beside the fence, for almost half a mile before arriving at the actual crash site, just a spot in the farmer's field, among the now-harvested corn crop that would be plowed under and replanted in the spring. There were many small tokens of affection left by his adoring fans. Photos, 45s, flowers with cards and letters to Buddy that adorned the site that forever enshrined the single point in time, February 3,1959, the day the music died.

Louis spent twenty minutes at the site, thinking about the crash that occurred just before 1am, on the cold and blustery night. The Beechcraft plowed into the field and balled up, ejecting the three rock-and-rollers to the ground, while the pilot remained pinned in the wreckage, with only his legs visible, sticking upward out of the wadded ball of aluminum. *Just imagine the music that would've come from them,* he was thinking, *if only the pilot was instrument rated with more experience.*

As Louis turned to walk back down the trail to the bike, he stuck his hands into the back pockets of the coveralls and found the Ziploc bag the satellite phone was in the day before, and an idea bloomed. He knelt down and scooped up a couple of double handfuls of the soil and filled the Ziploc bag before sealing the closure. *That'll make a fine souvenir,* he thought as he walked back to his motorcycle parked next to the road. He took a few photos of the glasses at the trailhead and carefully placed the bag of soil in the left side case before mounting the bike to head south, away from the cold air and the coming snow. Powering up the GPS, he selected a waypoint from the list and the GPS calculated the fastest route. The clock on the screen indicated it was almost 7:30.

The route took him east to Charles City, Iowa before turning south on US 218, which carried him all the way to Waterloo. There he took Interstate 380 through Cedar Rapids and on south to Iowa City. Louis continued on US 218, south along the west bank of the Mississippi River, passing between the birthplace of Samuel Clemens, Florida, Missouri, and his boyhood home, Hannibal. Mark Twain's stories stoked Louis' wanderlust during his youth. He rode the famous

Highway 61 to St. Louis, and I-64 east to I-57 south for the short hop to I-24 that led through Paducah, Kentucky, and south to Nashville. From there it was 65 south to Ardmore, then 53 back into Huntsville and up to Monte Sano to Nathan's home.

It was 1:30 am Monday morning.

15

Louis entered the security code to open the gates at the end of Nathan's driveway. As he slowly rolled toward the house, he noticed the center garage door opened with the light on, and Nathan standing inside.

"Man, you must be exhausted," Nathan said as Louis struggled to get his right leg over the seat of the bike.

"I feel like I've been rode hard and put up wet, but at least I'm not cold."

"Been monitoring the blotters while I prepare for tomorrow. All's still quiet in Wyoming."

"I need a hot shower, a handful of Motrin, a mouthful to eat, and a bed–in that order."

"You get on in, Bro. I'll unpack the bike for you. There's a pot of chili on the stove with your name on it."

"Thanks man, I will," Louis said as he moved stiffly through the garage door and up the hall toward the bedroom.

Nathan stood the bike up straight and heaved it up onto the center stand, walked around behind it and opened the top case. He removed the power cord from the Acer and sat it on the workbench next to the bike. Nathan opened the right side case and then the left one, where he saw the Ziploc bag filled with dirt. *What the hell is this?* he thought. *I can't wait to hear this story.* He unstrapped the duffel bag and carried it and the bag of dirt into the bedroom, where Louis was still sitting on the edge of the bed. Nathan sat the duffel bag on the floor and asked, "What's up with the dirt?" He held the bag in front of him and studied it, while Louis was bent over, struggling through exasperation to untie his boots.

"Oh yeah, that's a souvenir."

"From Ten Sleep Canyon?"

"From the cornfield."

"Why'd you get a bag of dirt from a cornfield?"

"For a souvenir."

"A souvenir of what?"

"Dirt from the cornfield."

"Why dirt?"

"Why not dirt? It wouldn't have been right taking anything else."

"Why not?"

"Cause, it would 'a been like robbing a grave or something."

"Whose grave?"

"There are no graves there."

"Where?"

"In the cornfield."

"Who's on first?"

Louis looked up from his boots at Nathan through his blood-shot eyes. "What?"

"No, what is on second."

Louis slowly sat up, looking at Nathan, then closed his eyes tight, raised his eyebrows and opened his eyes. "You lost me, Bro."

"Where, in the cornfield?"

Louis drew his head back between his shoulders while his mind caught up; Nathan stared into his eyes, looking for signs of life.

"Ah shit, man," Louis said as he began laughing, "the crash site, in Iowa."

They laughed at each other until tears and snot were flowing. The comic relief and laughter from their moment of shared confusion fractured the stress load they were carrying, washing it away as Katrina did New Orleans. Nathan, still laughing when he left the room, headed to the kitchen to reheat the pot of chili, while Louis conquered his boot strings and managed to undress himself before climbing in the shower.

Louis stood in the stream of hot water, spontaneously laughing out loud several times as he washed away the 900 miles. Climbing into a pair of sweatpants and a t-shirt, Louis took four extra strength Motrin and ate a hot bowl of chili while standing up, leaning against the kitchen counter, not wanting to sit down due to his butt muscles' throbbing protests. They talked briefly about the coming day's activities and shared status updates concerning each other's action items before Louis crawled into bed for a coma and Nathan locked up the house before retiring for the evening.

• • •

The alarm sounded at 9:30 am Monday morning, and Nathan walked down to the study to examine the Senator's laptop, where he put on a pair of rubber gloves, powered it up and made an the image of the hard drive. He set the system date and time back to the 26th, in the afternoon, and then copied the audio recording of the conference call he made to a folder on the desktop of the laptop, naming the folder "CC 11/26/10 – Me, C Bradley, W Turner, W Burkhart', which stood for Charles Henry Bradley, Secretary of Energy; and William Turner and William Burkhart, both board members of the Wyoming Energy Commission, giving the appearance that Senator Richland recorded the conference call on his laptop. Nathan then set the laptop's date and time accurately before shutting it down. Nathan again logged into one of the PCs at Opses Limited, opened a browser connecting to the Delta Airlines website and checked the availability of first-class seats to Hawaii the following day. There were eight of them available so he booked a flight for Amy Porter, round trip from Fayetteville, North Carolina to Oahu, Hawaii. Nathan then showered and shaved before dressing in slacks, a button down shirt and a sport coat. He took a pair of burn gloves from the side case of Louis's bike, along with the Senator's laptop and the remaining satellite phone, and got in his truck for the 10-hour drive to Fayetteville.

• • •

Paul Seltzer arrived at his desk, located in the FBI field office in Memphis, and began his standard morning routine of going through e-mail he received over the weekend, prior to checking his messages on his office voicemail. After responding to several e-mails, he dialed the voicemail extension and found he had three new messages. The first message was from his AIC, reminding him that his midyear review would be conducted this coming Friday, in the AIC's office at 3:30 pm. *Great,* he thought. The second message was in a muted voice that wasn't easy to understand, so he replayed it several times before saving it. The message was, "I overheard two men I work with talking, and they mentioned killing a Senator. I didn't know what to do so I decided to call the FBI. Please get back to me soon. I think they know I heard them." Seltzer dialed the number of the phone that left the voicemail. It rang six times before going to voicemail. "Hi this is Billy, can't answer the phone, you know what to do," then the beep. "This is Agent Paul Seltzer in the FBI field office in Memphis, you left me a brief message and I'm returning your call. Please call me back as soon as possible. Thank you." Seltzer went immediately to his AIC's office and knocked on the door before entering.

"Good morning, Larry, sorry about disturbing you, but I received an interesting voicemail over the weekend...."

"I know. I left it for you," AIC Church interrupted.

"I'm not talking about the message you left me about my review; it was a message that followed that you should hear."

"Why should I listen to your messages, Seltzer?"

"The caller indicated he has information about the murder of a US Senator."

"Here, call your voicemail number on my phone." He spun the phone around facing Paul, who hit the speakerphone button and dialed the number. He replayed the message for the AIC and again selected to save the message. The AIC spun the phone back around and hit the speakerphone button and dialed the five digit extension of the forensics lab.

"Forensics, Wiltshire speaking, how may I help you, sir?"

"I need a voicemail dump of one of my agents, Paul Seltzer, along with a trace of the numbers that left him messages over the weekend, and I need this yesterday."

A few minutes later the AIC's phone rang.

"AIC Church speaking."

"This is Wiltshire in Forensics, sir; I sent you the phone dump by e-mail, along with the audio of the messages as attachments."

"Thanks for jumping on that, Wiltshire," Church said before hanging up on him.

He opened his e-mail and found the message from Wiltshire, and clicked on the first recording, which was the message the AIC left. He clicked on the second message attachment, and they listened to the message repeatedly, while reading the e-mail dump that detailed the message sources and phone numbers of the caller, along with their locations.

"This may be a hoax, but I'm going to pass it up the line just in case it's not. Good work bringing this to my attention first thing, Seltzer. By the way, did you respond to the message?"

"Yes sir, I dialed the number the voicemail system indicated was the source. I didn't get an answer and I left a brief message, identifying myself, and asked him to return my call immediately. The voicemail greeting indicated the caller's name is Billy."

"Go back to your desk, fill out an action report on this, and get it back to me ASAP."

"Will do," Paul replied before heading to his desk.

• • •

While Nathan was gone to Fayetteville, completing the next stage of their plan, Louis took time to wash his motorcycle, going over it meticulously, scrubbing every bar and surface to remove the 5000 miles of road dirt, bugs and tar that caused the bike to gain a few pounds. A couple of hours later, when he completed this task, he decided to adjust the valves since the engine was cold. The work requires simple hand tools, two feeler gauges and a couple of rags to complete this two-beer job of little more than an hour in duration. Louis always adjusted the valves, believing the mechanics at the shops were too rushed to tweak them into perfection, which kept the engine running smooth and powerful; it was something he really enjoyed doing.

• • •

When Nathan stopped for gas along the way, he powered up, unlocked the satellite phone, and sent a text message to the receptionist at the office in Fayetteville.

"We're going to be out of the office most of the week, I'm sending an Army buddy to put something in the safe, and he may remove some or all of the contents for safekeeping. He should arrive around 8 pm tonight, please meet him at the office. Thanks."

A few minutes later, the text came back, "Okay, I'll be here then; where are you guys?"

Nathan sent a reply. "That's classified; will be in touch."

• • •

Louis suited up and took a ride over to the graveyard in Decatur, where his father and grandparents were buried, next to the Tennessee River. He made a point of visiting their graves at least once a year and would sit in the grass in front of the graves and talk to the headstones. He never knew his grandfather, who died just months before he was born. He spent his life working for the railroad and died from cancer. His grandmother lived until 1975, having been born in 1886, and giving birth to 11 children, Louis' father having been the youngest. Everyone called his father Pap, short for Papoose, meaning baby in Eastern Cherokee; his name was Marvin Louis Parker. He died of cancer in May of 1976, from a life of daily drinking starting at the age of 19 and smoking a couple of packs of unfiltered Pall Malls a day.

His father served in the Navy, on the *Kimberly*, a Destroyer that patrolled back and forth from Guantánamo, Cuba, up the East Coast of the United States and into the North Atlantic. After completing his tour in the Navy, he disembarked the *Kimberly* while in the Brooklyn Naval shipyard. He received his separation pay and walked out the front gate of the shipyard and across the street to the first bar he came to and drank for several hours before leaving the bar. He walked two blocks north, and in the front door of the Brooklyn Army Recruiting office, still in his Navy uniform.

He handed the recruiter his DD 214 and his Honorable Discharge from the Navy, and enlisted as a vehicle mechanic, maintaining his rank that crossed over as a Technical Sergeant, E5. He was already married three months to Louis's mother, Juanita, who was waiting for him at the apartment she shared with another Navy wife in Brooklyn. He never discussed reenlistment with her, and she was looking forward to heading back to Birmingham. When he walked in drunk, and told her he was to report to a troop ship that was leaving for England three days later, a fight broke out. It continued for 20 years, before she divorced him.

When his enlistment in the Army was up, he joined her in Birmingham and went to work for the L&N railroad as a motorcycle messenger. His job was to ride an old Harley-Davidson from the south-western switchyard, across Birmingham to the northeastern switch-yard, carrying messages back and forth in the saddlebags, no matter the weather, six days a week. He loved riding that old crap brown Army surplus Harley-Davidson the railroad issued him. After a year, they saved up enough money to buy a secondhand Packard and decided to have a baby. When she was six months pregnant, Pap left one Saturday in the Packard headed downtown, and returned three hours later on a brand-new Harley-Davidson. He traded in the Packard and still owed money on the Harley; the fight continued.

Louis' mother used to love to tell the story about his father, who spent all day Sunday washing and cleaning the messenger bike that he would park on the front porch, chained to the porch railing. When Monday morning rolled around, and it was time for him to head to work, the sky opened up and the downpour intensified every time he looked out the front door, hoping for a gap in the clouds. He suited up in his bright yellow rain slicker and WWII goggles, and rolled the brown messenger Harley down the front steps of the house into the rain, having to kick it several times before it fired over.

He headed out into the rain-slick street and turned the corner one house down, as she stood on the porch, watching the rain and listening to the sound of the old Harley as he accelerated. Then came, as she put it, "the damnedest sound of crashing metal and over-revving engine you ever heard." Five minutes later, there was Pap, pushing the motorcycle around the corner on the sidewalk, heading back to the house. As he got closer, she could see that he was covered from head to toe in horseshit, and so was the Harley he spent all day Sunday cleaning. He leaned it on the side stand in front of the stairs and looked up at her, searching for signs of sympathy. She looked back at him, his bright yellow rain slicker smeared muddy brown with scat, and burst out laughing until she peed herself. The fight continued.

Louis acquired his love for riding motorcycles naturally; it truly was in his blood. Louis had two older sisters and one younger, all four of them damaged in their own unique ways from growing up in a war zone where their Black-Dutch German mother and alcoholic Cherokee father fought daily with words, fists and flying objects. His parents divorced when he was six, and from then on, his exposure to his father was limited to an overnighter every other weekend. PTSD started early in Louis' life, between his parents and their all-night brawls, and later, when his mother married her second drunken sparring partner, who took out his frustrations with a leather belt across Louis' back, butt and legs–a more than weekly occurrence.

When Louis was 10 years old, he arrived home from school on his bicycle, and following his mother's orders, called her at work to inform her that he was now home. The step-bastard snatched the vintage one-pound handset of the tabletop phone from Louis' hand and began repeatedly flailing his head and shoulders with it, because that's what drunken step-bastards do to their unwanted step-slaves, just for the hell of it, on weekdays after school. Louis kicked him in his drunken cods and escaped his grasp, bolting out of the house and disappearing in the neighborhood until after 10 pm that night.

Louis snuck back in the house with a brand-new aluminum bat, while his mother was out combing the neighborhood looking for him. He knew from experience that the step-bastard, all 250 pounds of him, would be passed out in his bed, and that's where Louis found him. He poked him with the bat to ensure he was out cold, then drew back like John Henry swinging his hammer, and made the bat sing as he came down across the step-bastard's right cheek, nose and forehead above his left eye.

The step-bastard's head exploded like a watermelon dropped from the back of a pickup truck, with the socket above his left eye greatly enlarged and the eyeball dangling down across his cheek. Louis screamed at him, "Hit me again, I dare you."

Louis wandered through the house, walked out the front door, and sat on the front porch swing, holding the blue aluminum bat, and waited for his mother to return.

She rolled up in the driveway and jumped out of the car, hysterically screaming at Louis as she walked the sidewalk and up the stairs to the porch, over to the swing before she stopped. When she saw the two black eyes, broken nose pointing to the right, the swollen and bloody lips and the dried blood in his left ear that ran down his neck on to his school shirt that was more red than white, she said,

"What happened to you?"

"He beat me with the telephone."

"Where have you been all this time?"

"I got away from him."

"Where is he?"

"In his bed. He won't hit me again."

Louis' mother took the baseball bat from his hands and walked into the house and back to the master bedroom, where she found him unconscious and barely breathing. She called Birmingham police Detective K.O. Woods at home. They were friends since she worked for the department in the radio room when she was pregnant with Louis' little sister. She asked him to come over immediately, and explained what she knew of the situation. A half hour after hanging up the phone, Detective Woods flew up to the curb in his unmarked car and jumped out, running to the porch, where he saw Louis, still sitting in the swing, staring into space. Woods knew Louis since he was four and knew he was a good kid who just received a brutal beating and was in need of medical attention. He told Louis to stay in the swing and radioed for an ambulance.

He entered the house and walked immediately to the master bedroom and found Juanita's husband in the exact position and condition where Louis left him. He took the bat from her hand and radioed for a second ambulance, then said to her, "Nita, explain to me again what happened here." She again explained it to him, as he heard it over the phone, but this time face-to-face, so he could read her expressions and body language. Woods knew immediately that she was not involved in this, and they both returned to the front porch to check on Louis, who was still sitting calmly in the swing, but now leaning back, resting his head against the back of the swing.

Woods knelt on one knee in front of him.

"Louis, can you explain to me what happened here?"

"Yes sir, I got home from school and called Mama to tell her."

Woods looked at his mother and she nodded her head in agreement.

"Okay buddy, what happened next?"

"He yanked the phone out of my hand and hit me with it a bunch of times."

"I can see that. What happened next?"

"I kicked him hard and ran away."

"Where did you go, buddy?"

"I don't know, I ran down the alley and hid for a long time."

"Okay, what happened then?"

"My head hurt bad; I walked down Ensley Avenue a long way."

"Where did you go?"

"I went to the ball field in Hollow Park. I found the blue bat sticking in the fence."

"Okay, what did you do then?"

"I waited till the lights went out and it was dark and walked back home."

"Who was here when you got back?"

"Nobody but him. He was asleep so I hit him like he hit me."

"Do you remember how many times you hit him?"

"One time."

"Are you sure you only hit him once?"

"Yes sir."

"What happened then?"

"I came out here and sat in the swing, and Mama came home and screamed at me."

Woods glanced up at Nita, and she again nodded her head, but now she was crying.

The sound of the sirens on the ambulances grew louder as they turned up the street at the bottom of the hill on 31st street. Woods radioed to turn them off, and the dispatcher passed the message to the drivers and they silenced them before arriving in front of the house. They put Louis on a gurney in one ambulance with his mother and sped away to West End Baptist Hospital's Emergency Room. They transported her husband to the hospital downtown with what was an early version of a trauma center. Detective Woods locked the house and followed the ambulance carrying Louis and his mother, and remained in the Emergency Room with them, writing his report on a clipboard while they x-rayed Louis' head and shoulders, cleaned, stitched and bandaged his scalp, left eyelid, lips and left ear, keeping him in an upright seated position.

Louis sustained two concussions; his scalp was lacerated, requiring 22 stitches to close. Both lips were cut deeply by his teeth and the telephone receiver, requiring nine stitches to close. His left eardrum was ruptured, and the external ear was partially detached around the top and back, requiring eight stitches to close. His nose was broken, with the septum detached and internal bleeding into the sinus cavities; it was straightened and taped in place. Both eyes were swollen and severely bruised, with the left upper eyelid requiring four stitches to close. The lower left eyelid required draining to remove the blood that engorged it. His left collarbone was broken, requiring his left arm be immobilized.

Louis sustained more numerous and severe injuries in this single attack than when he and his little sister were hit by a speeding car while crossing 3rd Ave., walking home from Elyton Elementary School to Elyton Village, two years earlier. Detective Woods was chasing the speeding car and stopped at the scene immediately, before he recognized Louis and his sister. The driver of the car that hit them stopped and returned to the scene on his own, overcome by what he'd done, surrendering to Woods at the scene.

Louis never cried during or after the attack, nor after his retaliation or during the medical procedures in the emergency room, or during his stay in the hospital. He was deeply scared and in substantial pain, but never showed it; only a sedate calm about him. He recovered physically from the attack, and the wounds he received; he was permanently scarred emotionally, as well as "emotionally detached", as the doctors called it. A few months after the attack, he developed a pronounced verbal stutter and began experiencing emotional outbursts under frustration or other stress. Six months of speech therapy dramatically reduced the incidence of stuttering. Nothing helped the emotional outbursts, which continued through high school.

His mother's husband–he never called him his stepfather–sustained multiple skull fractures and severe swelling and bruising of the frontal lobe of his brain. The bones of his face, at the top of his nose, and extending over the left eye socket, were shattered into several pieces, requiring surgeries to reconstruct them as well as his nose. His left eye was not damaged, just jolted from its socket from the sharp impact of the bat. He regained consciousness a day later, in the recovery room after his first surgery and could not speak, focus his eyes or swallow for two weeks after the event. He was sentenced to just twenty-six 48-hour weekends in the Jefferson County Jail for this drunken, enraged and unprovoked attack on Louis, who was 10.

Louis' mother did not divorce the man, because they were under contract with a builder, with land and construction loans covering a new house in Pelham, Alabama.

Her priorities were clear to Louis.

A few days after his sixteenth birthday, Louis was again assaulted by his mother's now ex-husband. This time it was with a knife. Louis was badly cut on the underside of his right forearm, from his elbow to the wrist, blocking a slashing attempt at his face. Louis broke the bastard's left knee, several ribs and his jaw, and never laid eyes on him again. The PTS was now consuming Louis. Years later, Louis heard the bastard died in prison, after shooting a man outside a massage parlor in south Alabama.

16

Arriving in Fayetteville at 7:45 pm, Nathan located the office of Opses Limited, off Andover Road and Ramsey Street, a one-story shared office building–definitely not high rent. He pulled into a parking space next to a red Honda Civic and put on the burn gloves he borrowed from Louis. He slid the Senator's laptop under his coat, and held it in his left armpit as he knocked on the door marked Suite C. A twenty-something fluorescent redhead with artistically over-applied and contrasting war paint, in sprayed-on clothes, peeked through the blinds next to the door, looking around before her eyes landed on Nathan. "Who are you?" she asked from behind the window, steaming the glass.

"I'm Walter's buddy from the Army; I believe he let you know I was coming tonight."

The blinds snapped closed and the deadbolt on the office door popped as it unlocked.

"Hi, I'm Amy, Walter's office manager, come on in."

Nathan stepped inside the door and said, "Hi Amy, thanks for meeting me here after hours. I hope it's not too much of an inconvenience. I should be done in just a few minutes and I'll walk you to your car when we leave."

"It's no inconvenience. I was online with my friends; I'm always online," she said with a smile as she bounced around her desk, folding her right leg underneath as she sat in her chair, in front of the monitor and keyboard.

"If you point me in the direction of the safe, I'll get to the task at hand."

"It's the refrigerator-size box in his office, just through there," she pointed toward the closed door without looking up from the screen.

"Thanks Amy," Nathan said as he turned and opened the door, stepping inside and closing it behind him.

On the back wall of the office was a massive single-door Brown Safe, model 7228. Nathan spun the dial to the right several full rotations before stopping on 04, and completing the combination with 23, 58, 20 and 10. He then reached below the combination dial and gripped the handle, giving it a twist. He felt the smooth action of the locking mechanism disengage and he swung the door open. Standing vertically across the bottom rack were an M24, an H&K PSG-1, a Barrett 82A1 and a GALIL Galatz, four top-of-the-line military sniper rifles. On the shelf directly above were tactical boxes containing the glass for both day and night operations, along with their suppressors.

There were two pistols on the rack above that shelf, a Walther P 22 and a Browning 9 mm, both with suppressors attached. On the shelf to the right were a plastic portable file box and two large USB backup drives. On the shelf below that was a metal box about 15 inches square and 10 inches deep. Nathan sat the Senator's laptop on top of the safe and looked around the office for the cases designed for transporting the rifles. He found them in the closet, along with 12 boxes of high quality ammunition for the rifles and pistols. He laid the cases out open on the floor of the office and removed the sniper rifles from the safe, laying them carefully into their cases, closing and locking them.

He opened the door to the office and walked past Amy, carrying a rifle case in each hand out to his truck, laying them flat on the rear seat and headed back inside for the other two cases, stacking them in the rear seat as well. Nathan asked Amy, "Do you have a cardboard box or two? I have several small items to pack."

"There are two boxes of printer paper in the hall closet. You can have them if you like; just stack the paper on the floor."

Nathan unloaded the reams of paper and carried the boxes into the office, again shutting the door behind him. He loaded the rifles' scopes and the suppressors in one box and the hard drives, ammunition and pistols in the other box and carried them out to the truck, placing the box containing the rifle scopes on the passenger seat and unloading the contents of the other box to the floor under the rear seat. He locked both pistols in the glove box and placed the pair of desert boots in the cardboard box and carried them back inside the office, sitting them on the floor inside the closet. He placed the Senator's laptop on the top shelf inside the safe, removing the plastic file box and the metal box. He opened the metal box to find $80,000 in $100 bill bundles and $40,000 in $50 bill bundles. He opened the file case and found six files of varying thickness. He moved all of the $100 bundles from the metal box into the file case and closed the metal box. He looked through the desk drawers, finding an address book and a few more files with the standard office supplies.

Nathan closed the safe and spun the combination knob, then placed the address book in the file box and closed it before opening the door of the office and walking out to Amy's desk, sitting the metal box on the desk next to her monitor. "That's just about it, but I do have a few instructions for you from Walter. This metal box contains a large sum of cash and all but $5000 of it is to be deposited in the company's checking account."

"Ok," she said.

"Second, there is a round-trip first-class plane ticket waiting for you at the airport. Your flight to Hawaii leaves tomorrow morning at 10:25 am. Check in at the Delta counter and pick up your ticket and boarding pass. You are to take your company American Express card with you and charge all of your expenses, hotel, rental car, all of your meals and anything else you may need during your two-week stay."

Amy's eyes grew huge and her mouth dropped open as she shook her hands with excitement. "Ok," she almost screamed.

"Third, take the $5000 cash with you as mad money, and have a great time. Walter appreciates everything you've done around here and said you need a vacation. He said you mentioned that you've always wanted to go to Hawaii, so here's your chance, all-expenses paid. Walter and the guys are already on vacation and won't be returning for at least a month, so have a great time and enjoy yourself."

"I don't know what to say," she said as she jumped up off the seat. "I thought he never listened to me. Can I take one of my girlfriends with me?" she asked eagerly.

"Of course you can, Amy, but you need to call Delta as soon as you get home and make a reservation for her. Just charge it on the American Express card, and both of you ladies have a great time. Travel light and shop for what you need there and bring it back with you. Don't forget to take your camera."

"I just can't believe it. I need to call Rachel. I just can't believe it."

"Let me walk you to your car, and don't forget to make the deposit in the morning before you go."

Amy grabbed her cell phone, purse and keys off the desk and headed to the door, leaving the box of cash on her desk. As Nathan waited outside, she armed the alarm, closed and locked the door. They walked the short distance to the parking lot and Amy jumped into her Honda and sped away.

Nathan sat the file box on the floor behind his seat, laid his sports coat across the top of the rifle cases in the backseat, climbed inside the truck, and headed home to Huntsville. He dialed Louis on his cell phone and they discussed what he found in the safe and had with him in the truck. They decided it would be better if Nathan drove straight through, back to Huntsville, instead of getting a room for the night. It was now 8:20 pm, and Nathan estimated he would be home no later than 8 am Central time, taking his time, driving the speed limit all the way back, to minimize risks.

They decided to get Amy out of the way of the oncoming freight train that would be the FBI and Secret Service investigation teams descending on Fayetteville in the coming days. She was a civilian, an innocent bystander who would be spending some quality time with the investigators, so they sent her on the trip of her dreams that she detailed on her Facebook page with comments like "someday" and "when I hit the lottery". The dead men were paying for it, so she may as well live it up, before the credit card was canceled.

Nathan arrived home and pulled into the garage Tuesday morning, around 8:15 am. Louis, hearing the garage door opening, walked out to the garage to help unload the truck.

"How did the trip go?"

"A long drive but worth the effort. I got all kinds of goodies for you."

"That's nice; is everything in place for when the boys knock the door down?"

"Yep, and the secretary should be on her way to Hawaii, as well. Grab the cases off the backseat and I'll tote the boxes."

They unloaded the truck, taking everything into the study, laying out on the floor all the weapons and their accessories. The metal box and the plastic file case were placed on the workbench while Louis and Nathan drooled over the rifles, scopes and suppressors.

"That's a lot of sophisticated firepower for small three-man shop," Louis commented. "There's at least $90,000 worth of hardware laying there."

"Oh, at least," Nathan replied, "and there was a butt-load of cash on hand as well. I took a chunk of it and gave the rest to Amy to deposit in their account; red flags will fly like Mayday in China."

"Did she ask any questions or challenge you in any way?"

"Not a one, her eyes glazed over when she saw the cash, and the trip to Hawaii sealed the deal for her; she even asked if she could take a friend."

"Good deal. I told you I would make a field man out of you, you just graduated to spook," Louis told him with a smile.

Louis closed the rifle cases, packing everything into the corner, while Nathan opened the file box, laying the contents out to inventory. One file contained the receipts for the weapons and the accessories, as well as the federal tax stamps for the suppressors, all registered to a gun trust and held by the owner of the company. The next folder contained a US government file cover, stamped secret. Nathan opened it and found a memo with a list of 18 names, titles and reference numbers. Three of the names were scratched through with a red pen, with a date hand-written next to them. The fourth name was Nathan Malone, with the title "Operational Controller, Africa, Central America".

The 14 names listed below Nathan's included two Congressmen, one still in Congress and one retired; two State Department officials; three names he recognized from their time in the agency and seven other names he did not recognize. This memo, essentially, was a hit list. The three names above Nathan's were dated and crossed out, indicating completion. The three killers Louis dispatched arrived with the intent to scratch his name from the list. Nathan handed the document to Louis. "It looks like you never made the list."

Louis scanned the list, scrutinizing the names before saying, "Holy crap, Bro, they were on a much bigger mission than we thought. Glad we voided their birth certificates."

Nathan scanned through the rest of the documents in the secret folder, which gave brief background information on everyone named on the list. The folder, however, contained no location information for those on the list. Nathan flipped through the address book he took from the desk in the office and located a list, matching the numbers on the hit list. He flipped through several pages until he found his contact and location information on a page that was labeled with the number that matched the number next to his name. They knew his residence in Huntsville, as well as two other addresses, his mother's address in Birmingham and Louis' address in Florida.

Nathan headed toward the garage with his electronic scanning equipment and scanned his truck and his motorcycle, finding nothing out of the ordinary. He then backed the truck out of the garage, headed up toward the gate, and hopped out to rescan the vehicle. This time there was a signal, emanating from somewhere on the vehicle. After walking around it, he determined the signal was coming from the tag bracket on the front of the vehicle. He backed the truck down the driveway, retrieved a screwdriver from his tool chest, and removed the tag bracket. The bracket held in place a tag for the Original Redstone Riders and behind that was a tracking device that was wired to the running lights of the vehicle.

Using his pocketknife, he pried the adhesive loose that held the device to the bumper. Nathan opened the hood on the pickup and found where the wires tied into the right side running light, and cut them. He closed the hood, reinstalled the tag frame on the bumper, and pulled the truck back into the garage. He then backed his Goldwing out of the garage, started the engine and rode up the driveway to the gate and back down to the garage before scanning it again, finding a similar tracking device hidden inside the rear fender and wired to the taillight of the bike. He removed it as well, and headed back into the study.

"Louis, let's go check your bike real quick to see if you're bugged as well."

"What did you find?"

"I found tracking transmitters on my truck and my bike, and both are motion activated."

Louis backed his bike out of the garage, fired up the engine and rode to the gate and back, stopping in front of Nathan, with the bike in neutral and the engine idling while Nathan scanned the bike. "It looks clean Bro," Nathan told him. Louis pulled the bike back into the garage.

They walked into the house and Nathan began analyzing the tracking devices, trying to determine where they came from, and who may have planted them on the bike and the truck, without him knowing about it. Nathan accessed the FBI's online catalog that details such devices, listing their manufacturer, country of origin, operational capabilities, accuracy, and known sources for acquiring such devices. Within a few minutes, he identified the devices as ones created and used by the Israeli government and its all-encompassing intelligence and security agency known as Mossad, an abbreviation of HaMossad leModi'in uleTafkidim Meyuchadim, or Institute for Intelligence and Special Operations, in English.

These two identical devices were the type used by Mossad in desert climates to track the location and movements of persons or vehicles of interest. They were used extensively in Syria, Jordan, Iraq, Kuwait and Saudi Arabia. *Who the hell has been tracking me?* Nathan thought. *Was it the three guys that showed up?* Nathan powered up the units and found that both used the GPRS network to transmit location information by scanning the trackers' signals. After a few minutes, he identified the APN for each unit and derived the unique identifier for each.

Nathan realized the unique identifier was the same number string associated with his name on the hit list, and further realized that he held the tracking identification in hand to find everyone else on the list. He walked out to the garage and removed the GPS from Louis' motorcycle, along with the box in the right side case that contained the tracking transmitter and receiver, and headed back to his workbench in the study. He opened the receiver unit of the tracking device and removed the small memory card inside. Nathan inserted the memory card into the card reader, plugged it into the USB port of his laptop, and opened the binary file on the card. He added the unique identifiers from the hit list to the binary file on the memory card, so that the receiver would be able to identify and display the position signals from the other tracking devices. Nathan reinserted the memory card into the tracking device receiver and reset several of the micro-switches internal to the unit that modified the unit's functionality.

Since there now were 15 transmitter identifiers programmed on the memory card, the receiver was placed into multipoint tracking mode so it would receive the individual signals and plot their locations on the GPS screen simultaneously. He attached the receiver to the GPS's antenna port and the GPS's antenna to the receiver and walked out through the garage to the driveway, where the GPS could have a clear view of the sky, and powered it up. There were no tracking devices visible at the screen resolution of the GPS, which Louis tightened down to approximately 5 square miles. Nathan zoomed out the map resolution so the entire Continental United States was visible on the screen, and found there were four transmitters active, reporting their positions, being plotted on the GPS screen.

Nathan shared what he found with Louis, and they decided it was probably better to keep the tracking devices found on Nathan's truck and motorcycle active, rather than just cut them off altogether. Louis headed down the mountain to the nearest Radio Shack with a shopping list provided by Nathan, for the basic components they needed to attach these devices to a vehicle without tapping into the power supply of the vehicle.

Nathan hit the shower while Louis was gone on his errand, and returned to the study to continue digging through the information he harvested from the office in Fayetteville the night before. He restored the image he made of the Senator's hard drive to a portable hard drive that was on hand, and began combing through the Senator's e-mail history as well as all of his documents on the drive. He also restored the e-mail archives he made from the Senator's office computer systems and mail server. He set up a search job using the names found on the hit list as keywords, and after an hour, the search produced no results.

Louis came walking through the door with a bag full of goodies from the Shack and sat them on the bench next to the two tracking devices.

"Okay, what's next?" Louis asked, as he put on a pair of gloves and began wiping down all the parts he purchased, using acetone to remove his fingerprints.

"Wire the 12 volt battery containers in parallel, six containers for each tracking device."

"Got it, then what?"

"Directly connect the negative wire of the tracking device to the negative wires of the battery packs, and then the positive wire of the tracking device to the positive wires of the battery packs. Load the battery containers and bundle them all up with the wire ties and then seal them completely with the electrical tape."

"That shouldn't take too long; let me get at it."

Nathan went back to searching the e-mail archives, this time using the numbers from the hit list as keywords in the search. It took 12 minutes to complete the search, and he located one e-mail containing the numbers and the location information. They were found on the e-mail server's archive, but not on the image of the Senator's laptop. The message was deleted, or didn't originate from the laptop. In any event, he was sure there were no traces of these messages to be found on the Senator's laptop that was in the safe in Fayetteville.

Nathan then loaded the hard drive images of the machines in Fayetteville and continued to search through the data. Within minutes, he located the same e-mail on the e-mail server image from Fayetteville, as well as an eFax document, converted to a Word document and containing the names as well as the numbers from the hit list. The Senator's aide e-mailed the location information to Fayetteville and then faxed the second part of the information containing the names to the Fayetteville fax number for the company. However, Opses Limited didn't actually have a fax machine; they used the eFax service with a local Fayetteville number that would route incoming faxes to the e-mail address specified in the eFax account.

He now held in hand irrefutable evidence that the hit on him as well as everyone on that list was placed by the Senator or his aide with the company in Fayetteville. They were executing the plan to empty the bone closet, prior to the Senator announcing his run for the White House. Nathan again discussed what he found with Louis and together they decided to back-plant the evidence on the aide's laptop and mail server at the office. Nathan modified a copy of the e-mail that he found before again hacking into the mail server at the Senator's office. He replaced the original e-mail with the modified e-mail, with his name removed from the hit list, and with an attachment.

The header of the e-mail was structured to indicate the message came from the Senator to the aide, indicating to send the e-mail as well as the fax to 'the boys down south' but without the attachment. Nathan then altered the e-mail logs showing that the e-mail was sent with the attachment, before again connecting to the Web server in Fayetteville, and jumping over to the mail server and modifying the header information for the e-mail that was received, to include the attachment, which he stored on the server. The attachment was an e-mail to yet another company coordinating hits on the staff of Opses Limited, making it appear as though the aide mistakenly forwarded the entire message and attachment to them, exposing the back-story as to why they would kill the Senator.

Louis completed his task and Nathan verified that the tracking devices worked when powered up, shaking to simulate vehicle motion.

Nathan then went online to UPS and scheduled a package pickup, and did the same with FedEx for that afternoon, printing labels from the websites that indicated ground shipping to his Mother's address in Birmingham for one package and Louis' address in Florida for the other. He took two small boxes outside and filled them with gravel from the pile left over when he poured his patio. Each box weighed about a half pound when filled and sealed up for shipping.

When the UPS truck arrived at the gate that afternoon and rang the buzzer, the driver walked down the driveway to the garage to pick up the package, while Louis ran around the house and jumped the wall, mounting one of the tracking device bundles to the frame of the truck using two very large cable ties. He clipped off the long ends of the cable ties and sprayed the bundle with a can of tar sealant, made for reducing road noise, to prevent the bundle from being noticeable, before he walked across the street until the truck pulled away. They repeated this process later that afternoon when the FedEx truck showed up for the other package. Now whoever was monitoring Nathan's movement would receive tons of movement data for the next few weeks, until the batteries went dead and the data stopped.

Nathan again walked outside with the GPS, powered it up and was able to identify the two tracking devices that Louis placed on the separate trucks. They were both wandering through neighborhoods of the city. Nathan again removed the memory card from the tracking receiver, removed the unit identification strings of these two transmitters from the card, and returned the card to the receiver. There would be no need to track those two vehicles, so why have them clutter up the screen.

It was time to feed more data to Paul Seltzer, providing an opportunity for their old pal to shine.

17

Nathan tuned one of the monitors in the study to CNN, watching for any signs of a story out of Wyoming. Nothing was mentioned as of yet, so he decided to check the law enforcement systems in Buffalo, Johnson and Washakie counties as well as the Wyoming State systems for information concerning Richland. A missing person report was filed for Richland by his aide when he failed to return Saturday evening from his hunting trip in Ten Sleep Canyon. Washakie County Deputy Leon Strombeck located the Bronco parked well into the woods, off the side of US 16 Sunday morning just after sunrise. A search party was organized to comb the area, and a state helicopter was used to search the area from the air. Another Washakie County deputy, Thomas Billings, found Richland's bow, thermos and backpack at the location where he was hunting, but there was no sign of Richland. Deputy Billings found the three 9 mm shell casings while state investigators were still en route to the location Sunday afternoon, and the sheriff notified the FBI.

Agents from the FBI field office in Denver, Colorado arrived on the scene at 4 pm Sunday afternoon, and took over management of the scene while search efforts continued by Washakie County Sheriff's Department personnel, along with members of Wyoming's Division of Criminal Investigation, local ranchers and volunteers on horseback that were searching the surrounding canyons. The FBI placed a total blackout of information, to prevent the media from becoming aware of the situation until Richland was located, in case he was kidnapped and was being held for ransom. The FBI investigators harvested the evidence found at the top of the cliff, which included the shell casings, Richland's effects and the footprints found within the tight area.

Earlier Sunday morning, a team of investigators descended on Richland's ranch north of Buffalo, and determined the phone lines were cut and that someone entered through the rear door of the home and left footprints throughout the house that terminated in the Senator's office before returning to the rear door. Evidence technicians fingerprinted the rear door and the locks, as well as the desk in the Senator's office, the area around where the phone lines entered the house and the power meter and box located on the pole next to the barn, noting the power company's tamper seal was cut.

The FBI notified the Secret Service of their findings to this point; the President and Vice President were briefed on the situation before any information made its way to the press. FBI investigators went to Richland's home in Washington DC and informed his wife, Catherine, of his disappearance in Wyoming. FBI investigators went to Richland's offices and interviewed his staff and his aide, who filed the missing person report, when he could not contact Richland by Sunday morning.

The steady stream of aircraft flying into the Sheridan County and Johnson County airports, along with the police investigators passing through Buffalo heading west to Ten Sleep Canyon, drew the attention of the local press in Buffalo. Camera crews and reporters from the local news stations in Buffalo and Sheridan attempting to get information from the Johnson and Washakie Sheriff Departments were told by representatives of the FBI that a training exercise was underway in the area and was being coordinated from the Denver field office.

Early Monday morning, two FBI agents in tactical gear rappelled down the cliff from the site where Richland's gear was found. Two hundred feet below, on a small ledge, they located the satellite phone. Three hundred feet below that ledge, they found Richland's body, wedged in between the side of the steep cliff and the base of a tree, still some 400 feet above the bottom of the Canyon. Finding the three bullet holes in Richland's chest, the manhunt quickly shifted gears into a murder investigation. Another investigator rappelled down to the location where the satellite phone was found and photographed it laying on the ledge, along with the surrounding area, before placing the satellite phone in an evidence bag. The investigator then rappelled down to the location of Richard's body and photographed him from all angles before he was removed.

A harness was placed around Richland's torso and secured under his arms. Ropes were rigged to the tree and his body lowered to the canyon floor below, where he was placed in a Washakie County ambulance. Investigators continued searching and photographing the cliff face, from the top all the way to the bottom of the Canyon, looking for evidence. Richland's body was transported southwest to Worland, to the Washakie County Coroner for autopsy under the supervision of the FBI. Cause of death was determined to be coronary trauma along with massive internal bleeding, inflicted by three 9 mm gunshots at close range. The FBI field office in Denver notified the Secret Service and then Richland's wife, before announcing a press conference to be held at the Denver field office at 11 am Mountain time.

The agent in charge in Denver made a brief statement to the press that gathered. He laid out the facts he could release, along with the estimated timeline of the events, and took a few questions from the press.

"Tom Longstreet, Denver Post. Did the Senator die of natural causes, and if not, what was the cause of death?"

"The Senator did not die of natural causes. However, the cause of death will not be released at this time as the investigation is still ongoing; next question."

"Cynthia Moss Associated Press. Can you tell us the time of death?"

"It was sometime before noon on Saturday; final question."

"April Hargrove, CNN. In your statement, you indicated the Senator was hunting alone. Was this normal? And if this is a murder investigation, when will the autopsy be released?"

"Yes, Senator Richland normally hunted alone. The nature of this investigation, along with the autopsy report, will be released at a later time. That's all for now, thank you for your questions."

The AIC gave few details, as was to be expected, considering the gravity of the situation. It would be left to FBI officials in Washington to craft the official announcement to coincide with the release of the autopsy findings. However, that would be days away, once investigators were certain they harvested all available evidence from the scene in the Canyon and Richland's home.

• • •

Tuesday morning in Memphis, agent Paul Seltzer received an envelope addressed to him at the field office with no return address. He carefully opened the envelope and found a small folded piece of aluminum foil, which he unfolded to reveal a memory card. He rifled through his desk to locate a memory card reader, inserted the card in the reader and the reader into his desktop, and opened the file system on the card. He found it to contain a single text document, which he sent to the printer on his desk before removing the memory card from the computer.

The printout simply stated, 'Senator Harold Richland has been assassinated by private security mercenaries employed by Opses Limited of Fayetteville, North Carolina.'

That was the complete contents of the text file on the memory card. Agent Seltzer left the piece of aluminum foil, the envelope and the memory card sitting on his desk and took the printout to his superior, the Agent in Charge of the Memphis field office, Lawrence Church. Seltzer headed to the AIC's office and knocked on the door before entering.

"What's up, Seltzer?" Church asked, "I'm kind of busy right now."

"I received a letter this morning, here at the office. When I opened it I found a memory card wrapped in aluminum foil. I read the memory card with my computer and found a text file and printed it out." He handed the paper to Church.

AIC Church scanned the one sentence printed on the page and responded, "Holy shit.

Where is this envelope and memory card?"

"Sitting on my desk."

"Return to your desk and call forensics; have them come and retrieve the evidence."

"Will do," Seltzer replied before heading back to his desk, thinking, *First the voicemail and now this—what in the hell is going on?*

AIC Church placed a call to the director's office in Washington and waited on hold for several minutes before the call was answered.

"This is Director Marcus; I understand this is AIC Church in Memphis."

"Yes sir, this is Lawrence Church. Monday morning one of my field agents received an anonymous voicemail that was left over the weekend on his office phone number. The caller indicated he has information about the possible murder of a US Senator. The voicemail dumps and traces are in the hands of forensics now."

"Yes, that came up in this morning's briefing."

"This morning, sir, the same field agent in my office received an envelope that was mailed from Chattanooga, Tennessee over the weekend. It contained a small memory card that was wrapped in aluminum foil. There is a text file on the memory card, with a single sentence. 'Senator Harold Richland has been assassinated by private security mercenaries employed by Opses Limited of Fayetteville, North Carolina.' This evidence will be in the hands of forensics in the next few minutes, sir."

"Fax me a copy of the printout immediately. Who is the agent that's receiving this information?"

"His name is Paul Seltzer; he's been on my team for six months, since graduating the Academy."

"Put a trace on his cell phone, home phone and office phone, and all of his e-mail accounts, and have him bring in all of his personal mail he's receiving at home and open it at the office in front of you. We need to quickly get up to speed on Agent Seltzer and figure out how he's connected to this, if at all."

"Yes sir, we'll handle that immediately."

"Good work, Lawrence, stay on top of this and expect a call from the Denver AIC to coordinate."

"Yes sir, I will, and thank you."

Church walked out to Seltzer's desk just before the forensics evidence technician arrived.

"Don't open any more mail, here or at home for the time being. Bring it all to me in my office and we'll open it together, just in case you receive any more of these surprises."

"Yes sir, I'll do that."

"We're also putting traces on your phone lines here at the office and will be monitoring your e-mail account as well for the time being," Church told him, failing to mention they would also be monitoring his home phone, his personal cell phone and his personal e-mail addresses.

"I understand, sir, whatever I can do to help."

"I'm expecting a call from the Denver AIC. Stay in the office so you can join me on the call in case he needs you."

"I will," Paul replied. The evidence technician arrived from the forensics department and Seltzer indicated which pieces required bagging. The evidence tech bagged the items and gave Seltzer a receipt for them before heading back to the forensics lab.

"Add this to your file on the voicemail, along with an action report for this morning. Drop the file off on my desk as soon as you're finished."

Paul looked around the office and noticed that all the agents were watching what was transpiring at his desk. He didn't like the looks on their faces and didn't understand them.

Great, now I'm getting the stink-eye from everybody in the office,' he thought. 'I'm following procedure, I immediately reported this to my superior–what else should I do'?

Paul took a seat at his desk, logged onto the system, and created the action report concerning the letter and its contents. He printed a copy for the file and slid it, along with the receipt from the forensics tech, into the folder before walking it to the AIC's office and knocking on the door.

"Here's the file containing the action reports, sir; may I speak freely?"

"What's on your mind Seltzer?"

"What should I do about all the agents out in the pool? I'm getting this uncomfortable feeling that I'm somehow under suspicion."

"After I speak to the Denver AIC, I plan to bring everybody in the office up to speed on what's transpired. That should quell their concerns and ease your mind."

"I appreciate that, sir; I'm still the newbie here and trying to gain their and your respect."

"Don't sweat it, you're doing your job and I have no complaints on how you're handling the situation, and that's what should matter to you."

Church's phone rang; it was the Denver AIC calling. Church signaled Paul to shut his office door and take a seat. He put the phone on speaker and introduced Paul to his peer in the Denver office. Over the next 25 minutes, they discussed the voicemail and its source, as well as the envelope and the message on the memory card. The Denver AIC indicated the cell phone was found on the ground in the shrubs outside of the apartment belonging to William Pritchet of Chattanooga, one of the employees of Opses Limited of Fayetteville, North Carolina. He indicated agents in Fayetteville were searching for the owner of the company, as well as the other employees, and as of yet had not located them or the company vehicle. He also indicated they were awaiting a warrant to search the offices of the company, as well as the homes of all four employees, one of whom was in the air on the way to Hawaii, having flown out of Fayetteville early Tuesday morning. The Denver AIC asked Paul to leave the office so he could continue with conversation points above his pay grade. Paul left and shut the door behind him.

"As you know, we're ripping through Seltzer's background and all known associates, friends and relatives, as well as those in his class at the Academy."

"That's to be expected, let me know what you need from me and my team."

"I appreciate that Larry."

"Just my two cents' worth: Seltzer's not involved is my take on it. His name was picked from a hat, and I believe it could've been any of us to receive the information."

"I hope you're right, Larry. We'll figure it out. We have to–a Senator's been murdered."

With that, the conversation was over and they both hung up. Church glanced out his glass office walls and stared at Seltzer while thinking, *Kid, I hope you're righteous* before heading out into the office area where all the field agents' desks were located. He gathered all his agents into the conference room and laid out what had transpired over the last two days, and how it tied into the investigation in Wyoming. Church praised Seltzer's actions over the past two days and his cooperation in every aspect of the investigation, throwing his support behind his young agent. When the meeting broke up and everyone trailed out the conference room back to their desks, several of the agents surrounded Seltzer's desk, talking to him about what transpired and without saying so directly, acknowledged him for the first time as a member of their team.

Now, late Tuesday afternoon, every news channel around the nation and several around the world were carrying the story of the death of Senator Harold Richland. The FBI still withheld the autopsy results and the true nature of the investigation, which fueled wildfires of speculation from the talking heads and their expert consultants. There were Google maps of Ten Sleep Canyon and diagrams produced from the imaginations of the so-called expert consultants that weren't in the ballpark of reality. One television news crew out of Buffalo, Wyoming was running an interview of a local man from Ten Sleep, who told the story of the Lord from the British Parliament that died during a hunting accident in Ten Sleep Canyon, less than a half-mile from where the Senator's body was found. Speculation as to the significance of this story, and whether it was purely a coincidence, fanned the flames of international espionage in the fertile imaginations of the conspiracy theorists, which were popping up in the national news coverage.

Nathan watched the news as he prepared another memory card to be sent to Paul Seltzer. Again he performed a DOD wipe of the card's memory and created a single text file containing the tracking IDs of the 14 remaining targets that began with a single sentence.

"Future victims of Opses Limited can be found using the GPRS APN's listed here; hurry."

Wearing gloves, Nathan carefully cleaned every edge and surface of the SD card and a small square of aluminum foil with acetate before folding the card inside the foil. Nathan addressed the envelope to Agent Paul Seltzer at the Memphis field office, printing the address using his right hand, though he was left-handed, and affixed stamps to the envelope before sliding it into a fresh Ziploc bag for transport. It was Louis' turn to take a ride to Chattanooga before dropping this envelope into a general PO Box. He put on his riding gear while Nathan placed the Acer laptop with the GPS and the Verizon mobile modem in the top case of the bike and plugged in the power cord. Nathan instructed Louis to click on a specific icon once he was at the location where the letter was to be mailed, then leave the program running for several miles, then stop and shut it down, before returning to Huntsville.

Louis rode out of Huntsville heading northeast toward Chattanooga on US 72, crossing into Tennessee near South Pittsburgh and taking Interstate 24 east toward Chattanooga, and then 75 to Cleveland before exiting to 64, riding all the way to Ducktown, Tennessee on the North Carolina border. Louis stopped the bike near the corner of Main and Spruce streets in Ducktown, within sight of the post office. Still wearing his riding gloves, he walked to the mailbox on the corner and opened the Ziploc bag, dumping the small envelope into the mailbox. He walked back to his bike and opened the top case and the Acer laptop, and clicked on the icon, which automatically logged into the Verizon network and made a connection to Google maps. Louis closed the laptop lid and locked the top case, pulled out of Ducktown and headed toward Cleveland, Tennessee.

Six minutes up the road, he pulled over and climbed off the bike, opened the top case and closed the program that was running before shutting down the laptop. He closed the top case and climbed back on the bike, heading back to Huntsville in the dark. Louis arrived back at Nathan's home around midnight and packed his clothes in his duffel bag and loaded the bike for the trip home to Flatland. He'd been away from home longer than he planned, and he missed Diane.

Nathan and Louis spent about an hour talking over their next steps before Louis rolled out of Huntsville, heading toward Interstate 65 south, the first leg of the long night's journey ahead of him.

18

Louis continued south on 65, passing through Birmingham toward Montgomery just before 3 am Central. He stopped for gas just off 65 in Pelham and rolled into the truck stop near the exit that leads to Oak Mountain State Park, a place fondly remembered from his high school years where he spent many a night, camping with friends and hiking to Peavine Falls to free-climb the walls. The park was a place of refuge and peace for Louis, and just seeing the sign to the entrance made him smile.

He topped off the bike and purchased a diet Dew before getting back on the Interstate, heading south through Shelby County. As he passed by the Alabaster exit, his thoughts again turned to his high school days at Thompson, in Siluria, just a few miles away. A little farther south was the exit to Dolomite, and the rock quarry that he fondly remembered as a beautiful swimming hole, down the long gravel road in the middle of nowhere. He remembered swimming there during the long hot summer with Terri, his red-haired girlfriend at the time. Louis never kept in touch after high school with any of the friends he'd known and loved, although he would pick up tidbits of information here and there about this person or that, where they were and what they were doing.

Louis passed through Montgomery an hour and a half later and headed east on 85 toward Auburn. He turned south at Wire Road to bypass Auburn, and intersected 280 in Phenix City. He was following a small car southeast of Tuskegee when a large Whitetail Deer jumped from the side of the road, directly in the path of the Volkswagen Beetle.

The driver did not have time to react, hitting the large deer broadside, flipping the deer over the top of the car and directly into Louis's path.

Having seen the deer jump from the road and fly over the car, Louis had seconds to react before hitting the animal as well. He pressed hard on the left handlebar, causing the bike to swerve into the left lane, barely clearing the antlers of the deer lying across the road.

Louis quickly swerved back into the right lane and came to a quick stop alongside the road before making a U-turn and riding back to where the deer was laying. The driver of the Volkswagen pulled off the road to assess the damage to his car before he too did a U-turn, returning to the area where the deer lay dying.

Louis climbed off the bike and removed his helmet, leaving the engine running, powering the headlights and powerful road lights on the front of the bike, illuminating the deer, lying on its side kicking violently with broken legs, screaming in pain.

Louis removed the hunting knife he carried in the left side case, and walked around the deer, staying clear of the flying hooves, and knelt down behind the animal, grasping his antlers with his left hand, and opened the injured animal's throat wide, allowing him to bleed out quickly, releasing him from his pain.

He looked around to ensure there was no traffic coming and dragged the animal off the side of the road by his rack, to prevent anyone else from hitting it, mutilating the carcass and damaging their vehicles. Louis squatted on the side of road next to the deer with his hand resting on the deer's chest. In less than a minute, his heart stopped beating, and he was gone.

The black teenager who was driving the Volkswagen was beside himself, visibly upset, distraught over hitting the deer. He dialed 911 on his cell phone to report the incident, which took just a few minutes.

"Why did you cut the deer's throat?" he asked while crying, "Maybe he could've got up and run off."

Louis was wiping the blood from the blade of his knife, and looked at the kid a few moments before speaking. "All four of his legs are broken and he probably has organ damage from the impact. He didn't deserve to spend his last minutes alive scared and in horrible pain."

Louis stood up and walked back to his bike to put away the hunting knife, then returned to the teenager, who was now leaning against the crumpled hood of his Volkswagen and vocally crying, while streams of tears ran off his cheeks and down the sides of his face. He placed his right hand on the kid's shoulder and gently squeezed while telling him, "I saw the whole thing happen. I was right behind you and you couldn't avoid hitting him."

The teenager slid down to a seated position on the bumper of the car, holding his face in both hands, wailing painfully for the deer. "I never killed anything before; this is horrible."

"You didn't kill that deer, I did. You try to remember that. You didn't drive off the road to hit him; he jumped out in front of you. You did the right thing by stopping and coming back. Absolutely no one can hold this against you, and you shouldn't either."

While Louis was trying to comfort the distraught teenager, he saw flashing blue lights coming up the road in the distance. A minute or so later, an Alabama State Trooper arrived at the scene. Leaving his lights flashing, he climbed out of his car, placing his traditional doughboy hat securely on his head before strutting to the front of the Volkswagen. The trooper was maybe 6 feet tall in his crisp, dark uniform. His head was shaped like a cube, with wide cheekbones, a flat nose and a strong jaw protruding from his thick neck. *It's the Georgia Bulldogs' mascot,* Louis thought.

"Is anybody hurt?" the trooper asked.

"No sir, the deer took the brunt of it and the Volkswagen's damaged, but he's okay," Louis replied, gesturing toward the still sobbing teenager.

Louis spoke up again, "I was following him, heading southeast and saw the deer jump from the side the road directly in front of him. He couldn't avoid it and I barely did myself."

"You were following the Volkswagen on the motorcycle?"

"That's correct."

"That's the deer over there?"

"Yes, he's messed up pretty bad; I cut his throat and dragged him off the side of the road."

"Are you a hunter?"

"Yes I am, didn't want to watch him suffer."

The state trooper asked the young man for his driver's license and began filling out the accident report.

"Is the car drivable?" the trooper asked the kid, who was clueless and was in no shape to drive anyway.

Louis said, "You probably should call a wrecker for it; he's pretty upset and probably shouldn't drive."

Louis turned back to the teenager and asked him, "Can you call somebody to come get you?"

"Yes sir, I can call my Mama in Tuskegee, just up the road," the young man said before pulling his cell phone from his pocket to make the call.

The state trooper turned toward Louis and asked, "Is your motorcycle operable?"

"Yes sir, I managed to swerve around it before making a U-turn and stopping over there."

The trooper asked for Louis' ID and he dug his license out of his wallet and handed it to the trooper.

As the trooper copied Louis's information, he asked, "Florida? Where are you coming from?"

"I've been up in Huntsville and I'm heading home," Louis replied.

"Riding at night is dangerous, as you can see; be safe and you can continue on."

Louis got his license back from the state trooper, walked to his motorcycle, and donned his equipment before continuing toward Phenix City, leaving the teenager with the trooper. Louis continued thinking about the teenager for quite a while. *I envy his innocence,* he thought. *I can't remember ever being like that, but I must've been at some point.*

He passed through Phenix City and over the bridge to Columbus, Georgia and continued southeast toward Albany, passing through Fort Benning. Stopping south of Albany, in Pelham, Georgia for gas, he was still thinking about the teenager and his reaction at seeing that he cut the deer's throat. Louis knew the kid would get past it and let it go, and hoped he was listening to what he told him. He crossed the

Florida-Georgia line before 5 am and continued to roll south, down Flatland's Nature Coast, stopping again for fuel in Perry. He climbed back on the bike for the final leg home to Diane, who would be waking up shortly. Louis stopped alongside the road at 6:15 am and called his home number.

"Hello," Diane answered.

"Hey baby, I'm only about 150 miles north of the house and should be home before 8:30."

"I'm glad you called me. I've been worried about you, and I was hoping you were heading home."

"I left Nathan's place last night, but got hung up in Tuskegee for a while."

Louis explained what happened while Diane continued to get dressed for work. A few minutes later, they said their "I love yous'" before ending the call so Diane could head to work and he could get back on the bike heading home; he was tired.

At 8:40, Louis pulled in the driveway and waited as his garage door opened before rolling inside and shutting down the bike. He climbed off the bike and out of his gear, carried his duffel bag to the floor in front of the washing machine, and put most of the clothes from the duffel into the washer, stripping naked and adding the clothes he was wearing to the batch. He poured himself a large glass of orange juice before heading to the master bedroom for the hot shower he had been anticipating for the past two hours. Afterwards, he dressed and returned to the garage to finish unpacking the bike after transferring the wet clothes to the dryer. Louis unloaded the top case and carried his electronics into the house and returned to the right side case to remove the Walther, and began the deep cleaning process all over again. He removed the binoculars and night vision goggles from the side case, sat them on his bench and removed the batteries before he returned them to their place on the shelf in the cabinet.

Louis took a seat on the couch and stretched out his legs with the new laptop in front of him, and flipped on the television to catch up on the news. Not much had changed in the reporting, as apparently no new facts were disclosed to the media overnight. He powered up the laptop and started the e-mail client, and found an e-mail from Nathan. Nathan indicated that the FBI received the warrants and searched the offices in Fayetteville as well as the homes of the owner, one of his minions and the secretary, who was detained for questioning in Honolulu before being released to continue her vacation.

The apartment in Chattanooga was also searched. The computers from the office in Fayetteville, along with the safe and the contents of the closet, were removed and taken to the local FBI office. There was now a nationwide manhunt for the three missing employees of Opses Limited. The FBI executed a search warrant at the corporate headquarters of Verizon Wireless, to secure the cell phone and wireless modem records for the equipment owned by the employees of Opses Limited. They also served a search warrant for the satellite phone data from that provider. Nathan indicated that he received word from the scrap yard that the "cube" was transported as part of the shipment to US Steel in Birmingham, and would soon be new steel blooms headed for the Seamless Pipe Mill, to become drilling pipe for the oil industry.

Louis sent an e-mail to Nathan to let him know he was home, and shared with him the story of the accident in Tuskegee. He logged into his blog and realized he'd depleted his reserve of pre-composed posts he built up ahead of his first trip to Memphis. The system automatically posted every Monday, Wednesday and Friday morning, and it was two days since the last new post. He opened Windows Live Writer on his laptop and began detailing his trip to Memphis, Tennessee, for ribs at Rendezvous. He expounded on the details of the trip, and the road conditions and how well the bike performed, before going into detail about the delicious ribs and the friendly atmosphere in the restaurant. He published this post to his blog and sent pings to the many search engines to inform them his blog content had changed. Then he created another blog post detailing his ride from Memphis over to Natchez Trace.

He detailed the ride southwest through the Old South along with the many sites and smells he encountered on the way to Baton Rouge and into Texas. He added this blog post to the queue, ready for posting at the appropriate date and time. He created another post covering the ride to the West Houston community where the BMW group held the tech session and included all the details of the goings-on and tire kicking as well as the hot dogs and hamburgers prepared by the hosts of the event, again adding this blog post to the queue to be published in the future. He created another blog post about the ride from Houston to Biloxi with intimate detail of the road conditions and the smells of the creosote along with the rhythmic vibrations created by the expansion joints of the long bridges across the swamps. He embellished with lavish detail his experience at the Beau Rivage without divulging the actual amount of his winnings, and again placed this post in the queue to be published. One more post was needed to complete his trip home with all the details of the long ride, including the flat tire in the middle of nowhere on the nature coast of Florida, that included a step-by-step guide for repairing a puncture while on the road. He placed this post in the queue as well, before taking a break for lunch.

Digging around in the freezer of the refrigerator in the kitchen, he found a box of frozen White Castle cheeseburgers and decided it was time for some sliders. He arranged the plastic bags around the edge of the plate and poked a small hole in the center of the bags before sitting them in the microwave and nuking them, while he poured himself a large glass of peach-flavored iced tea. *It's good to be home,* he thought. *I'm tired of road food,* and he laughed aloud, watching the plate of radar-burgers spin through the window in the microwave.

He again watched the news for a few minutes while he ate lunch and quickly tired of the talking heads constantly repeating themselves, jumping from location to location around the country, to other talking heads repeating what the previous talking heads were repeating in an effort to further clarify the information they all felt was worthy of repeating.

Louis muted the squawk box and again turned his attention to his laptop and continued creating posts to load the queue for his blog. His next post was about the road trip from Flatland to Clear Lake, Iowa. Louis included anecdotes of conversations that occurred at truck stops during refueling, where there was never a shortage of questions concerning his mental state, as no one would be riding in that weather unless they were "tetched".

He added this post to the queue and began another particularly long piece detailing his visit to the crash site, along with meticulous directions to find the site. He elaborated on the sculpture of Buddy Holly's glasses and commented on how fitting a memorial they were, as they captured the essence of the image that Buddy left behind. He placed the photo he took of the glasses in the blog post as well. The final blog post he created detailed the road trip he took south along the western bank of the Mississippi River, passing between the two historic sites that marked different times in Samuel Clemens life, as well as his brief journey along the historic Highway 61.

This blog post would span a couple of days of his trip and included the deer strike incident in Tuskegee the night before. After placing this post into the queue, he again turned his attention to the talking heads.

CNN was now reporting that the FBI would be holding a press conference at the top of the hour, in Washington DC, concerning the investigation into the death of Senator Harold Richland. Louis again opened his e-mail client and sent a brief missive to Nathan, inquiring into the latest info he could access. A few minutes later, an e-mail returned from Nathan that began with a simple statement.

"You're not going to believe this, Bro."

Nathan indicated that the FBI secured the phone records from the satellite phones as well as the Verizon mobile modem. They concluded that one of the employees of Opses Limited drove around the clock from Fayetteville to Buffalo and broke into Richland's home in an attempt to assassinate him there, before tracking him down in Ten Sleep Canyon and completing the job. Then he drove around the clock back to Fayetteville, while a second employee was attempting to evade the third employee, who was trying to silence him before he could contact the FBI about the murder plot. They correlated the information as best they could, but there were still major gaps in their intelligence concerning the reasons for targeting the Senator, as well as the location of all three of the unaccounted for employees.

"Now here's the kicker," Nathan wrote, "they called me in this morning as a consultant to help examine the computer records and communication traffic. I'll be heading to DC shortly."

This can go really well or horribly wrong, Louis thought. *Nathan is a miracle worker as long as no one is looking over his shoulder or directly monitoring him.*

Nathan's message continued, "We may need to continue dropping breadcrumbs using the Acer. I know you're kind of burnt out and want to stay home a while but this really can't be helped; we need to finish what we started–actually, what they started."

Louis replied to the message with, "I'll head back up to your place after I've spent some time with Diane. I'll think of something. Be careful, you're sticking your head in the mouth of the lion, and he's hungry." Louis sent the message and refilled his glass of tea before settling in to watch the press conference.

The talking heads gathered with their remote cousins, the bobble heads, in the press room at the FBI Headquarters building in Washington. The view from the multitude of cameras in the room showed a slightly elevated podium, in front of the seal of the FBI, with American flags on each side, in front of a wall covered with dark blue curtains. A cluster of microphones was attached around the main microphone of the podium, and the room was alive with the sound of numerous conversations and the flashes from photographers adjusting their still cameras. The view of the scene at the press conference was framed in a small square to the side of the television screen while the talking heads continued to prognosticate the information to come.

They quoted unnamed sources in the Justice Department, who hinted at a conspiracy involving former military and CIA personnel. At 30 seconds before the top of the hour, a representative for the FBI, along with another representative for the Justice Department, walked onto the podium as the room fell silent, except for the sounds of cameras and the associated flashes of light. One of the well-groomed gentleman stepped to the microphone, holding a prepared statement he laid before him.

"Good afternoon, I'm Philip Hargrove, the Media Communications Coordinator for the Federal Bureau of Investigation, and this is Gordon Thomas, my peer at the Justice Department. I will read a prepared statement that will be made available to all the members of the press present at the conclusion of today's press conference." Hargrove explained the events that transpired concerning Richland in meticulous detail, connecting the subjects of the investigation through the evidence developed by the bureau and correlated into a cohesive timeline of events by Nathan. Next, the DOJ spokesman took the podium.

"Good afternoon, as Philip indicated, my name is Gordon Thomas, and I am the Communications Coordinator and Press Liaison for the Department of Justice. First, I would like to state our deepest condolences to Mrs. Richland, her family, and their friends over the tragic loss of their loved one, Senator Harold Richland. Moreover, we extend these condolences to the people of Wyoming, as well as the members of the Senate, the Congress and the White House who knew and worked closely with Senator Richland during his 11-year tenure in the Senate. This assassination of a seated US Senator has shocked the nation that mourns him, and those responsible will be tracked down, captured and brought to justice to answer for their crimes against Senator Richland, and our country. Senator Richland was a decorated veteran of the Vietnam War and served with distinction in Central Intelligence before successfully representing the people of Wyoming as their Senator. He is survived by his wife, Christine, and their two sons Harold and William, along with their wives and children. Again, our deepest condolences go out to Mrs. Richland, her family and their many friends. Senator Richland is being transported to Washington for a private family service, before he lies in state in the rotunda of the Capitol, beginning Friday evening through Wednesday, when he will be transported for burial services at Arlington National Cemetery. We will now take questions from members of the press."

Questions from the press corps continued for 30 minutes with inquiries into the number of shots, the time of death, the location in Ten Sleep Canyon where he was found, and the reaction of the President when he was notified. There were questions about the killer, what evidence was found at the scene, about the break-in at the ranch, about how the killer found the Senator in Ten Sleep Canyon, about the killer's connection to the Senator and a plethora of others.

Louis watched the entire press conference, along with the question and answer time afterward. *It's too bad they'll never know Richland's real story,* Louis thought. *The son of a bitch lined his pockets with drug money while in Vietnam, and it continued at CIA, right up until he ran for the Senate. Hell, there's no telling how many millions of drug addicts got their start on the shit he flew in from Southeast Asia.*

Louis' cell phone rang; it was Nathan.

"Did you see the press conference?"

"Touching, wasn't it?"

"About what I expected"

"Where are you?"

"I'm at the airport over in Madison, waiting to board the flight to DC."

"I thought you were done doing contract work for them."

"I was. It's been two years since they've called me for anything, but I'm back on the clock now."

"Will we be able to communicate while you're there?"

"Shouldn't be a problem, if I can't talk I'll use the phrase," Nathan said referring to a phrase he and Louis had used for years to indicate someone might be listening. "It's a good night", "it will be a good night", or "it was a good night", when casually dropped in a conversation between them, would alert the other.

"Where will you be staying?"

"Probably in the barracks apartments at Quantico—that is, unless they have me traveling."

"Don't figure it all out for them too quickly; sweat over it a while before proving you're smarter than they are."

"I'll do that. I could ring up quite a tab before this is over. My flight is starting to board now. I'll holler at you later, Bro."

"Later man, watch out for those lions."

19

ouis decided it was time to complete the cleaning process of his Walther and the suppressor, so he headed to the garage and laid out the rags before meticulously laying out the pieces that had been cleaning in the ultrasonic bath. This was a well-practiced process that resulted in a perfectly functioning weapon system that never jammed, even using the highly modified ammunition Louis preferred. While at his bench diligently caring for the metal bits before him, Louis thought through what transpired over the past week. He rode his bike almost 7500 miles, assassinated three men and killed three others in the defense of his only true friend. *A pedophile priest, a drug dealer, a corrupt Senator and three Army veterans turned mercenary,* he thought, *and a partridge in a pear tree . . .* quietly chuckling and shaking his head to dismiss it.

He returned his attention to the Walther on the bench and completed cleaning it and the suppressor, then turned his attention to reloading the Walther's clips with fresh modified ammo. He placed the Walther with the suppressor and the clips in the hiding place of the side case and retrieved the night vision goggles from the cabinet above him that he had placed there just hours before. Louis reinstalled the batteries he removed, and slid a fresh set of batteries into the case along with the goggles, after carefully cleaning the lenses. He placed the night vision goggles in the right side case along with the binoculars. After shaking out and carefully refolding his rain gear, he placed it on top of his delicate equipment in the side case and locked it.

Knowing he would again be leaving shortly, he unloaded his clothes from the dryer and folded them before returning them to the duffel bag. He located an un-opened pack of burn gloves and placed them in the side case. He then sprayed down the windshield, head-lights, road lights and the wind deflectors on the front of the bike with peroxide, to allow the bugs to dissolve into soap, so the wet and wrung-out microfiber cloth could remove the grunge buildup on the bike. He cleaned the shield on his helmet and hand guards on the bike with the rag, before draping it over the rack in the garage. He located his remaining oil change kit for the bike, which contained the last filter and four quarts of synthetic motor oil, and dragged the oil pan under the engine of the bike to once again refresh the lubricant before hitting the road.

Louis headed to the kitchen, located the two nice prime rib steaks wrapped in paper in the refrigerator, and placed them in the pre-made Jack Daniels marinade they kept on hand. He tenderized the steaks in the marinade for about an hour before lighting the grill out on the lanai, bringing it up to temperature. He dug out two large potatoes from the bin in the pantry and washed them in the sink before rolling them in a mixture of warm butter and sea salt, wrap-ping them tightly in aluminum foil and placing them on the grill to slowly cook through before perfecting the steaks. While the steaks were cooking on low, Louis opened the chilled bottle of Diane's favorite everyday wine, Beringer White Zinfandel, a sweet, inexpen-sive and readily available product of Napa Valley. There was nothing complex about the flavor of the wine, she just enjoyed it, and that's all that mattered to Louis.

The last time they were in Napa and Sonoma, Louis purchased a t-shirt at one of the vineyards with the message embroidered on the chest, "Friends don't let Friends drink White Zinfandel". Louis pur-chased Diane a shirt with the message, "Forgive Me, for I have Zinned" printed on the front. They were just simple souvenirs of their trip, but it made them laugh when either of them wore their shirt. After flip-ping the steaks, Louis sat out the plates and cutlery for dinner, poured himself a glass of iced tea, and took a seat on the lanai to keep an eye on the grill. His face settled into a contented smile, knowing Diane would be home at any moment.

When Diane came through the garage door into the house, she could smell the steaks on the grill; she dropped her purse on the kitchen table on the way to the lanai.

"Hey baby, I didn't hear you come in."

"I could smell the steaks as soon as I came in from the garage. What's the occasion?"

"It's Wednesday, and I happen to be at home for the moment. I poured you a glass of wine; it's in the fridge."

Diane walked back into the kitchen for the wine while Louis removed the steaks and baked potatoes from the grill, setting the platter on the island in the kitchen then heading back to the lanai to shut off the gas grill.

"How was your day, baby?" Louis asked while she made her plate.

"Not too bad. I got a lot done today, but I have to fly to South Florida tomorrow for an open house Friday and Saturday."

"I'm sorry to hear that."

Diane unwrapped one of the baked potatoes, releasing the steam and the smell of warm butter before cutting open the potato and loading it with butter, chives, and black pepper.

"I noticed you cleaned your bike, the oil pan is under the engine, and the clothes in the duffel bag look clean and folded; going somewhere?" she asked, already knowing the answer.

"Yeah, I need to head out again tomorrow for a few days, but you'll be in Miami anyway."

"Yes, but you didn't know that until I told you a couple of minutes ago," Diane said. "I thought that was the last trip for a while?"

"It was going to be, but things keep coming up," Louis replied while preparing his baked potato.

Diane was moving her steak from the platter to her plate and said, "We just can't seem to stay in the same place at the same time here lately; I've been missing you a lot."

"I miss you too baby, and I'm tired of the road, but that's where the stories are."

They moved their plates to the table and refilled their drinks before sitting down and enjoying the perfectly cooked beef and potatoes.

They took their time, savoring each morsel of food and the face-to-face conversation they both missed over the past week. Louis kept refilling Diane's glass with wine, just before it was empty, while they talked about the kids and Louis' trip to the crash site in Iowa. She listened intently, as he described in detail with emotion, the glasses at the trail head, and the emptiness of the harvested cornfield, the loneliness of the mementos left at the site by the fans and the bite of the cold air just before the snow was to fall on the remote location in northern Iowa. They sat together at the table talking for more than two hours, content to be there together, enjoying a meal and conversation, and each other's company for a change. Louis' cell phone rang, interrupting their island of bliss. Diane got up from the table and walked into the bedroom to begin packing for her trip to Miami, while Louis answered the phone.

"Hello?"

"Hey man, I'm in D.C. at the D.O.J. for the J.O.B.," Nathan said enthusiastically "I just sat through an hour-long briefing with two other contractors and our liaison. They gave us our IDs when we arrived at the airport and drove us directly here for the briefing."

"How does it feel to be in the Coliseum, amongst the lions?"

"Actually, it feels good; very professional and focused come to mind."

"Don't get too used to it; passing through the bowels of those lions first requires negotiating the teeth before everything turns to shit."

"I'll keep that lovely picture in mind," Nathan said. "We're heading over to Quantico in a few minutes to drop our things off before we attend yet another briefing tonight."

"I'll be heading back up to your place tomorrow morning."

"Okay Bro, got to run."

"Later."

Diane completed her packing and joined Louis in the living room, where he was watching the news. She sat down on the floor in front of him and glanced over her shoulder at him, asking for a back rub with her eyes. He slid to the edge of the couch, reached down toward her waist, grabbed her shirt, pulling it up over her head, and began massaging Diane's shoulders and neck muscles, gently at first to warm them up and increase the circulation, before applying substantial pressure to relieve the stress by forcing it out of the muscles. He walked over to the bar that separated the living room from the kitchen and found a container of lotion, and returned to his task, applying the lotion to reduce the friction so that his efforts would be focused on the muscles and not her skin. Twenty minutes of deep muscle massage from Louis' strong hands and Diane was relaxed to the point of near sleep. Louis helped her up from the floor and into the bedroom to her side of the bed, where she melted into the covers and dozed off quickly from the relaxing massage and the bottle of wine over the previous two hours. After setting Diane's alarm clock, he walked out of the bedroom and pulled the bedroom door closed behind him. He quietly cleaned up the kitchen and secured the house for the night. His lack of sleep allowed him to drift off almost as quickly as Diane.

The next morning, as Diane prepared for work, Louis completed packing his bike and installed the drain plug and new oil filter before refilling the engine with oil. The bike was ready to go in short order. Before loading his laptop into the top case, he checked his e-mail and shot a short message to Nathan. "Leaving for your house shortly, later," was all it said. Walking back in the house, he found Diane preparing a hot cup of tea in her travel mug. He carried her suitcases to the garage and placed them in the back of her car. She came through the door into the garage with her purse and laptop and put them in the car before she and Louis kissed, hugged, and said their goodbyes, wishing each other a safe trip before they went their separate ways. Within a few minutes she was heading for her office and Louis, in his gear, was headed north on US 19.

• • •

Nathan was already in his small office, outside of the FBI's forensics lab in Quantico, Virginia, along with two other contractors they brought on board to augment their staff and expand the depth of knowledge and capabilities, to ensure nothing would be missed or overlooked during this critical investigation and manhunt. The desktop PC he was assigned used biometric sensors as part of the logon procedures. Through this PC, Nathan was granted legitimate access to all of the FBI's resources as well as those of the Department of Justice, and limited access to the NSA's Echelon data retrieval system. Nathan was tasked with correlating the data from all the sources and constructing a timeline of events, overlaying the known data traffic, cell phone and satellite phone traffic with a timeline of events in Wyoming and Fayetteville. He was careful to include only the events present in their data, as well as their time codes, to ensure he didn't inadvertently introduce data unknown to them. His previously self-assured confidence was now being tempered by Louis' warnings about the lion's den, where he was now seated. Nathan constructed a simple Excel spreadsheet with columns for date, time, location, entity, action, resource and support. He began extrapolating data available to him from the investigation reports, telecom carrier data reports, satellite carrier data reports, Echelon communication transcriptions and other sources, adding these fragments of information to the spreadsheet as he went along.

At 1 pm Eastern, the team of consultants, along with their DOJ handlers, met for lunch in the conference room to discuss their progress and any new information that came to light from the field. They each in turn described their processes and the data mining techniques they were using to develop the intel for analysis. Milton Friese, one of the consultants, was tasked with the analysis of the computer systems and network equipment found in the office in Fayetteville. He received the hard drives from the different computers, after the forensic team imaged the data and fingerprinted the cases, keyboards, and mice.

Dave Packard, the other consultant, was performing a deep dive background investigation of all the employees of Opses Limited, their families, friends, known associates, friends in the Army units they belonged to, tax returns, banking records, educational records and any organizations they were affiliated with, as well as their habits, hobbies, interests, dietary preferences and outhouse schedules.

The catered pizza from the cafeteria was hot and plentiful, with all of the nutritional value and aroma of the cardboard, ketchup and Velveeta it tasted like. The gun safe from the office in Fayetteville was transported intact, and then opened in the forensics lab. There they discovered and inventoried the contents that included the laptop, which fell from the shelf to the bottom of the safe. The exterior case of the laptop was cracked and the screen destroyed. Efforts continued to image the hard drive, which was damaged as well. The AIC of the investigation team at Quantico revealed that all the weapons known to have been in the possession of Opses Limited were missing and presumed in the possession of the men that were still at large. The boxes of ammunition that were discovered in the closet of the office were analyzed and found to have the fingerprints of all three of the male employees.

A single pair of Army-issue desert boots was found in the closet of the office, and the heel and sole prints of these boots identically matched the boot prints found at the Senator's ranch, as well as the scene of the murder in Ten Sleep Canyon. The three 9 mm shell casings recovered at the scene held partial thumb and index fingerprints of one of the three missing men. The satellite phone found on the ledge below the scene held the same fingerprints as the shells, as well as the fingerprints of the Senator. No fingerprints from any of the three men were found on the power meter, the area around where the phone lines were cut, the back door locks and handle for the Senator's office desk in the home at the ranch, north of Buffalo, or on the Ford Bronco.

After the lunch meeting, everyone returned to their work areas and continued their efforts through the afternoon hours. Nathan became concerned about the efforts of Milton Friese, who was doing a deep inspection of the hard drives of the computer equipment from Fayetteville. While Nathan was certain he covered his tracks, there was always the outside chance something, no matter how minute, may have been missed.

• • •

Louis arrived in Huntsville at Nathan's home at 5:15 pm Central time. His code opened the gate and then opened the garage where he parked his bike. He removed his laptop and headed inside to the den, where he entered the archaic combination to open the hidden doorway in the bookcase. It consisted of flipping on the wall switch next to the switch for the overhead light of the ceiling fan, pulling the light chain of the ceiling fan, adjusting the digital thermostat on the den wall to 55° and then flipping the wall switch back to the off position, which would then unlock the hidden bookcase door, if completed in less than 10 seconds; Nathan was a fan of steampunk, and his elaborate access sequence was a homage. Once inside the study, Louis sat his laptop on the counter where Nathan would normally be sitting and found a CD in a jewel case in a Ziploc bag. The note sitting next to it indicated, "Find a way to get this to Seltzer in Memphis." *Okay, I wonder what's on this one?* Louis thought.

Louis decided to take a closer look at the rifles Nathan brought back from Fayetteville, so he slipped on a pair of gloves and opened the cases. Each of the cases was custom-made for its particular rifle, with cutaways for all of the accessories you could ever want or need. In the gun case of the German rifle, he found a waterproof bag that looked like a cleaning kit, but there was already a cleaning kit in the case. Louis opened the small case and inside were six more of the Israeli tracking devices with the wire splices in place, and a thin pair of needle nose pliers for crushing the wire splices. The cellophane tape, which covered the adhesive backing of the tracking devices, was imprinted with the unit's unique identification number used over the GPRS network. *How many of these damn things did they have?* Louis thought. *What does that make now, 25 of them in all?*

He returned his attention to the weapons, thinking, *Now the big toys for the big boys.* The finely precision tuned instruments that dropped into their laps could be put to good use if only they were securely transportable. *Transportable,* Louis thought. *Which of these weapons breaks down into the smallest components?* The Galil Galatz with the stock folded was only 33 inches long; with the flash suppressor removed, it was 28 inches long. *Without the magazine or the scope attached, I could easily cram this thing in a small container,* Louis thought, *but how do I camouflage the container?* That could get tricky. He removed the scope that attached to the side of the receiver and dropped the magazine to find it was fully loaded with 7.62 NATO rounds. The folding stock was ideal if you were required to carry this weapon, but for Louis' purposes it just wouldn't do, so he removed it altogether, reducing the weight and the overall size of the package. Removing the pistol grip reduced the overall height of the weapon to just over 5 inches, with a width of only three and a quarter inches.

Deciding a trip to the local hardware store was in order, Louis removed the duffel bag from the bike, headed down the mountain into Huntsville and found his way to the local "Home Freak-Show", as he called it, on Memorial Drive. Inside the store he headed for the plumbing department, where he located the PVC pipe and various PVC components from which he could assemble a watertight tube in which the transport that Galatz. He located a piece of six-inch interior diameter pipe and a pair of end caps and asked one of the store associates to cut off a 40 inch long section of the pipe and price it out for him. He found a can of PVC glue and primer and headed to the front to pay for his toys. Louis strapped the pipe across the back seat of the bike with the sack of smaller goodies in the side case, and proceeded back to Nathan's house to trim, assemble and install the latest accessory for his motorcycle. Louis spread his purchases out on the workbench in Nathan's garage and retrieved the Galatz from the study. The weapon, now substantially reduced in size, slid easily into the PVC tube.

Louis slid one end of the tube into one of the end caps, stuffed a small piece of foam rubber down into the tube, and slid the Galatz into the tube, resting on the foam rubber in the end cap to make his measurements before removing the excess length of tube. After making the final cuts and sliding the opposite end cap on, the overall length was just less than 30 inches. He removed the end caps and the weapon from inside the tube and prepped one end of the tube with the primer before applying a generous coating of the PVC glue and driving the end cap on tightly. Louis found a can of flat black spray paint underneath Nathan's bench and applied several coats to the PVC tube and caps, allowing it to dry in the air outside the garage between coats, while he figured out the best means and location to mount the tube on the bike.

Digging around in Nathan's junk drawer in the garage, he found a five-foot roll of metal pipe strapping used to suspend pipes below the floor of the house. He cut off two long sections of the strapping, wrapped it around the PVC tube and mounted it to the bottom of the right side case. The end of the tube was positioned just below the rear edge of the side case, allowing the tube to extend forward of the side case passing under the right rear passenger foot peg, and stopping about six inches behind the driver foot peg.

Louis attached the forward metal strap to the passenger foot peg mounts, and the rear metal strap he affixed to the side-case mounting block. Once completed, with both caps in place, it wasn't particularly noticeable on the large bike, which was what he was shooting for. The cap on the front of the tube was not glued in place so it could be used as the access point for sliding the weapon in and out, which he found to be convenient and easy to achieve. While riding, the heel of his right boot was directly in front of the cap, and he could ensure it remained snug by tapping backwards with the heel of his boot. The rifle scopes and the magazine easily fit in the side case along with the rest of his stuff.

He took a small piece of cardboard and put an X on it with a magic marker, grabbed Nathan's staple gun and headed toward the back edge of his property, which dropped off sharply down the side of the mountain. He climbed down about 50 feet below the edge, paced off a distance of about 400 feet, and stapled the piece of cardboard to the trunk of a tree. Louis returned to the garage, took the rifle from the tube, attached the pistol grip, and retrieved the suppressor and the rifle scope from the study, along with the magazine. He reattached the scope and screwed the suppressor in place before inserting a magazine into the well of the weapon.

He again headed to the back of the property, disappeared over the edge, down the side of the mountain, and took a prone position with the rifle's bipod extended and took aim through the scope at the small piece of cardboard 400 feet away. It was a challenge to steady the rifle without a shoulder stock, but after a few tries he found a position with his left arm interlocked under the pistol grip that would suffice. Louis chambered a round from the magazine, set the two-stage trigger, carefully took aim at the exact center of the piece of cardboard, and gently squeezed off the first round. The extremely efficient suppressor made the sniper rifle sound like a pellet gun and the bullet struck the target 1/2 inch low, but perfectly centered horizontally. *What a piece of equipment,* Louis thought. There was no need to waste another round; the setup was perfect for his uses.

He climbed the hill to Nathan's backyard and headed back to the garage, where he removed the scope, the magazine, the suppressor and the pistol grip from the Galatz. Then he ejected the spent shell from the chamber before sliding the weapon into the tube. The pistol grip fit into the tube snugly next to the weapon. Louis slid the end cap in place and knocked it on firmly with his foot. He placed the rifle scope back in its carrying case and placed the suppressor and the magazine, along with a single spent casing, in a small canvas bag in the side case of the bike. He reattached the duffel bag to the rear seat, headed back into the study, and checked his e-mail, where he found a note from Nathan asking him to call secure. Louis placed his cell phone in secure mode and called Nathan. It was now 7 pm Central time, 8 Eastern, and Nathan was walking from the cafeteria at Quantico to his barracks location, a single man room on the first floor, as were all the accommodations for the contractors.

"Hey man, been waiting for your call."

"How's it going up there?" Louis asked.

"I now remember why I didn't like this life: too many controls and too much politics."

"And too many lions."

"That too; these guys are on a mission, and taking it dead serious."

"You sound worried."

"I am, a little. One of the other contractors is scrutinizing the hard drives from the computer systems from Fayetteville. If I screwed up, he'll find it–just a matter time, I guess."

"Did you screw up?"

"I really don't believe so; however, given enough time and the enormous resources he has at hand here, if there's an oyster in the bay, he'll find it."

"Where do they have you guys working?"

"Right now we're in cube world at Quantico, but the DOJ handlers want to move us over the river to their offices; could be tomorrow or the next day before it happens."

"I'm gonna take a ride to Memphis before heading that way; try to stay ahead of him. By the way, are you keeping busy?"

"Yes, just plowing through the intel and evidence they have gathered and slowly piecing together a timeline from what they know, which still has big gaps, by the way. It could take me another week to complete extrapolating their data into a coherent timeline."

"Good, take the time, I'm going to throw some wrenches into the works and drop a few more breadcrumbs along the way."

"Be careful Bro, they're everywhere and armed to the teeth looking for the three."

"Hopefully, they're so focused on those three, little old me will go unnoticed."

"Hopefully. By the way, Seltzer and his AIC are flying in from Memphis tomorrow afternoon, on an FBI Gulfstream."

"You think he's moving from the minors to the majors?"

"He's bringing evidence and meeting with the deputy director in charge of investigations. As far as I know, we're not scheduled to meet."

"Good. I need to run. Just shoot me an e-mail whenever you need to share something, or you need me to call you. I'll be on the road a while and will check in as I can. Stay cool, man. Later."

"Later, man."

Louis shut down his laptop, picked up a small pouch with the additional tracking devices, and headed out to his bike, placing them in the top case. He then retrieved the Acer, still configured with the wireless modem and the GPS dongle, sat it on top of his laptop in the top case, and plugged in the power cord, leaving the laptop powered down. He secured Nathan's home after locking the study door, and climbed into his gear and on the bike, again heading to Chattanooga. Once he crossed the Tennessee line he turned northwest on Interstate 24, heading away from Chattanooga, and stopped in Monteagle.

Louis switched on the laptop and clicked on the icon, which started the program once again before riding a few miles to the truck stop at the top of the mountain with the giant fireworks sign you can see for miles. He rolled in next to the gas pumps and parked the bike before shutting down the program and the Acer, then proceeded to top off the fuel tank of the bike.

While still pumping the gas, Louis watched a nondescript four-door sedan with 10-ply tires come flying into the parking lot and roll past him, stopping near the front door of the truck stop. Two men in dark suits exited the vehicle; one went inside and the other proceeded walking around the lot. Louis completed fueling the bike and locked the handlebars of the motorcycle along with the side cases, and walked inside to pay for the fuel and secure his diet Dew for the overnight ride. As he approached the vehicle, he noticed the government license plates; it was two FBI agents looking closely at everyone inside the truck stop and all the vehicles in the lot. Louis made his way to the cooler then headed toward the checkout line. The young agent went back outside toward his car as Louis was paying for his purchases before exiting the building.

Louis walked directly to his motorcycle, firing it up and leaving the lot, again heading northwest on Interstate 24. *Nathan was right; they are everywhere, at least around Chattanooga, anyway. They must be monitoring the Verizon network waiting for the modem to go active, to converge on its location. I'm glad I shut it down when I did.*

Young lions are everywhere now.

20

ouis continued northwest on 24 through Manchester and Murfreesboro, arriving in Nashville two hours later, where he found his way to 40 and headed toward Memphis some four and a half hours away.

Again, Louis stopped for fuel just south of Brownsville, Tennessee, and while sitting at the pump, he entered the address for Paul Seltzer's home in the GPS. He then continued toward Memphis, turning south to Bartlett to find the home in the suburbs of Memphis.

The house was located in the cul-de-sac at the end of Marby Drive, just south of the Stage Road. Louis parked his bike in the small parking lot of the All-Stars Realty office, located on Shelby St. He removed his helmet and riding jacket and found his baseball cap in the left side case and grabbed some burn gloves, removing the CD in the jewel case from the Ziploc bag in the top box.

At 5:15 am, Louis walked quietly through the small wooded area behind the real estate office and into the backyards between two houses on Marby Drive, just two doors away from Paul Seltzer's home.

Seltzer's FBI-issued vehicle was in the driveway, and a streetlight in the cul-de-sac illuminated the car and the area around it. Louis walked down the sidewalk toward the house, slid the jewel case under the driver-side windshield wiper, and headed back to his bike.

As he was again cutting through the small wooded area behind the real estate office, a very large dog in the backyard began to bark. Louis continued the march toward his bike and stuffed the ball cap into the tank bag, quickly putting on his helmet and jacket, starting the bike and leaving the area, heading south on Shelby St..

He pulled into the parking lot of the small church on the corner of Shelby St. and Ferguson Road and parked the bike in the trees, just off Marby Road.

He removed his jacket and helmet, walked around to the right side of the bike and removed the rifle scope, suppressor and magazine for the Galatz, sitting them on top of the side case before removing the rifle from the tube.

Louis scanned the area carefully, ensuring no one was out and walking around, before screwing the suppressor to the end of the rifle and attaching the scope and pistol grip, then inserting the magazine and quietly chambering a round.

Holding the rifle tight against his side, he left the cover of the trees and walked across the street, taking a prone position in the grass strip between the sidewalk and the curb, in the front yard of the house on the corner of Marby and McCully St.

He extended the bipod under the barrel, aiming directly north up Marby Drive and locking in on the rear windshield of Seltzer's FBI vehicle, 800 feet away, using his forearms as a rear bipod with the pistol grip in his right hand.

Louis set the two-stage trigger, took a long slow deep breath, and relaxed before stopping all body motion, then gently squeezed the trigger. The rifle kicked rearward releasing a heavily muffled blast of hot gases from the suppressor.

The bullet entered the rear glass of the vehicle, passing directly over the driver's headrest, then exited the front windshield just left of the steering wheel's center-line, six inches below the top of the windshield, striking the wooden privacy fence next to the house, in front of a stand of trees.

Louis ejected the shell casing, which landed in the gutter of the street, and quickly took to his feet.

He walked briskly across the road into the shelter of the trees, disassembling the rifle components and storing them in the bike.

He donned his helmet and jacket and rode out of the parking lot of the small church, heading east on Ferguson Road, then right on Bartlett Road and south on Bartlett Boulevard.

Louis continued south to the parking lot of Christian Brothers High School on Walnut Grove Road and stopped the bike, leaning it on its side stand with the engine running.

On the north side of the high school sat the five-story tall FBI Field Office, just a few hundred yards from his location.

He walked around to the top case and opened it, opened the Acer laptop and booted it up.

Louis clicked on the icon that started the tracking program and waited till it connected to the modem and accessed Google maps to plot its location, then shut it down and climbed back on the bike, heading west on Walnut Grove Road, then taking the on-ramp of 240 north bound toward Interstate 40 east, just two miles away.

As he was approaching the on-ramp to 40 east, he could see several sets of flashing lights approaching from the south, coming up behind him on 240. As he made his way around the turn to the right on the on-ramp, the flashing lights of the string of FBI vehicles continued north toward Seltzer's home.

Louis continued northeast on 40, heading away from Memphis in the early morning commuter traffic. The sun was coming up to reveal the overcast sky. As he rode past the Colonial Country Club, he noticed the groundskeepers were already out cutting the grass on tractors with headlights.

Maintaining a steady pace, he continued northeast, passing through Nashville on 40 and stopping in Monterey, Tennessee for fuel and a bite to eat, then continuing east on 40 toward Knoxville and beyond on Interstate 81. He stopped for fuel in Wytheville, Virginia just before 4:30pm Eastern time. Continuing northeast on 81, he turned east on 64 just outside of Staunton, Virginia, heading for Charlottesville, where he took Virginia 22 to Fredericksburg, then 95 north to Triangle, Virginia. At 10 pm Eastern, Louis exited 95 at Dumfries Road and turned left, heading for the Waffle House sign.

Climbing off the bike, he was somewhat sore from the long days trek from Huntsville to Chattanooga to Memphis and now Triangle, just a few miles away from Quantico. He climbed out of his riding gear, retrieved his laptop and cell phone, and headed into the Waffle House to strap on the feedbag and warm up.

When he powered up the laptop, he saw several e-mails from Nathan. Scanning through them, oldest to newest, revealed the chronology of the events that took place in Monteagle, Bartlett and Memphis, with admonitions to call him as soon as possible.

Louis closed the laptop, ordered a huge greasy breakfast, and stepped outside the restaurant to call Nathan after putting the cell phone in secure mode.

"Hey man, where in the hell are you?"

"I'm maybe five miles northwest of your location and about to eat some breakfast."

"Damn, you've been busy today, let me walk outside where I can talk."

"Take your time; my food won't be ready for several minutes."

"That was an interesting way to deliver the CD."

"I figured I might as well get their attention while I was there."

"You got their attention, all right; the latest reports have one of the three taking the shot at their informant, though some think the target was Seltzer."

"A nice twist, don't you think? Actually, I never saw him. I egressed rapidly."

"They found the shell casing; 800 feet in the dark is impressive."

"We do what we can with what we've got," Louis said, laughing. "You could have made that shot, Bro."

"Dude just left through the back door of his house and was walking toward the privacy fence, heading toward his car, when the round struck the fence four feet to his left."

"I hope he changed his underwear before the boys arrived," Louis laughed again.

"They thought they had them at the truck stop in Monteagle, then again just outside the Field Office. Have you lost your mind?"

"Oh hell yeah, lost it a long time ago; don't know where I left the damn thing. I really should hang a bell on it."

"Man, you got more guts than a Kansas City slaughterhouse."

"Are they still planning on moving you into town?"

"First thing in the morning we're packing up and heading north to the new location."

"Any anomalies found on those hard drives yet?"

"Not yet, but he's a snapping turtle and won't let go of it till he's done."

"I need photos of the other two consultants ASAP."

"I'll get them to you shortly, along with the new location."

"The waitress sat my food on the table, got to go; I'm starving; later Bro."

"Later."

Louis walked back inside the restaurant, sat down and consumed the hot food, taking his time while enjoying the heat inside the restaurant. The temperature had been steadily dropping since he entered Virginia and was now hovering around 49°F. While still seated at the table, Louis opened his laptop and found another e-mail from Nathan, containing an address: "490 9th St. NW, Washington D.C." with a comment: "east side, above the main entrance, second window up above the doors, across from T-Mobile."

There were two photos attached to the e-mail. Louis closed his laptop and paid the check, walked out to the bike and grabbed some warm clothes from the duffel bag and headed back inside to the restroom, where he put on his insulated underwear, tops and bottoms, heavy wool socks, sweatshirt and blue jeans.

After strapping the duffel bag back to the seat of the bike, he found his insulated electric jacket liner in the side case and slipped it on over the sweatshirt, then slipped into his riding jacket and helmet. He cranked the bike and punched the address into the GPS before pulling out of the parking lot, again heading north on 95 for the 50-mile trip.

He exited 95 onto 395 across the Potomac and through the 12th St. tunnel, all the way to E St., then east to 9th St., where he turned south, and found himself in front of the J. Edgar Hoover building.

He identified the windows Nathan described, as well as the T-Mobile building across the street. Louis proceeded slowly down the street, familiarizing himself with the landmarks, then took his first left for a block then turned north on 7th, taking it all the way to I St. and heading west to the giant public parking facility on 9th St., where he parked the bike under a streetlight of the well-lit parking lot.

Louis placed the bike on the center stand and locked the handle-bars, removing his riding jacket and helmet and laying them on the seat. He took his ball cap from tank bag and locked all of the cases and put the locking cover over the bike and walked south down 9th St., past the Smithsonian American Art Museum, and another block south to the corner of the T-Mobile building.

After surveying the entrance for security cameras, Louis stopped and spoke with the elderly security guard inside the door on the north side of the building.

The security guard was dozing off at the desk when Louis opened the door. "How are you doing tonight, sir?" Louis asked the man, who looked closer to 70 than 60.

"How can I help, young man? Most of the building is closed at this time of night."

"I got a call from building maintenance saying the heat's not work-ing up on the T-Mobile floors. I was told there was a freight elevator at this end of the building that can take me to the roof to check out the heating systems."

"Yeah, the freight elevator is just down the hall, but it doesn't go all the way to the roof, just to the top floor. You'll have to take the stairs up to the roof."

"That's close enough for me. It's probably just a tripped circuit breaker, anyway; do you mind if I take a look before I drag all my tools in here?"

"I guess that'll be okay. It's the fourth elevator on the right. You need me to go up there with you?"

"No sir, I think I can find my way. I'll take a quick look and be back down directly."

With that, Louis headed down the hallway and hit the button on the freight elevator with a knuckle. Within a few seconds, the door opened and he stepped inside and pressed the button for the top floor. When the elevator doors opened, he saw a single door across the hallway that said maintenance and roof access.

He glanced out the elevator door and up and down the hallway, saw no security cameras, stepped across the hallway, and twisted the knob on the door to find it was unlocked.

He entered the maintenance room, where he found a large workbench with toolboxes and a tool belt with various tools, along with a hoop of keys and a Maintenance Personnel ID badge with no photo. He fastened the tool belt around his waist and put the badge on a belt loop, then climbed the stairs that led to a door that opened on the roof, inside a walled enclosure that encircled the giant air-conditioning and heating systems.

He walked over to the west side of the enclosure and looked through the slatted sides to find he had a good angle on the window Nathan described. He went back inside and down the stairs to the maintenance area, and back to the freight elevator for the ride down to the first floor, and headed back past the security guard behind the desk.

"I'm gonna have to go back and get my truck. I don't have what I need with me," he told the security guard. "I'll be back in an hour or so to fix the problem."

"I'll be here," the elderly guard replied.

Louis headed out the door for the walk up 9th St. to the parking area where he left his bike. It took just under nine minutes to make the walk, just enough time for him to decide what to do next, before returning to the rooftop. He removed the bike cover and stored it in the side case, along with the toolkit from the maintenance room in the building. He put on his riding gear, then opened the top case and powered up his laptop to look up another address in Georgetown. He powered on the GPS, entered the address and calculated the route before pulling out of the parking area. Ten minutes later, he was in Georgetown and killed the engine to coast in and park in the driveway of a brownstone, where all the lights were off, just down the street from the address.

Louis locked the handlebars on the bike and sat his helmet and jacket on the seat, then retrieved the 9 mm pistol from the bottom of the left side case, the same 9 mm he used on Richland; he stuck it in his belt under the sweatshirt.

He opened his cell phone and located the photo to familiarize himself with the face, and then shut off the phone. Louis walked up the street with his gloved hands in his pockets and stopped in front of the address.

The street was quiet and all the lights were off in the home. He drew the 9 mm from his belt and held it close behind his right leg after releasing the safety and cocking the trigger.

He pulled the ball cap down low over his eyes, unscrewed the bulb of the porch lamp and rang the doorbell.

About a minute later, a light came on in the townhouse and a forty-ish man in his house robe opened the front door.

Louis looked at the face of the Senator's aide before placing the tip of the silencer against his chest and squeezing the trigger.

The man fell backwards into the foyer and Louis stepped inside and switched off the light.

He placed a second shot directly next to the first, and when the hush of the silencer dissipated, the only sound was the brass tumbling around on the hardwood floor.

Louis carefully dropped the hammer and slid the 9 mm back inside the belt, covering it with the sweatshirt. He noticed the smoke detector on the wall and opened it to remove the battery before it went off from the gun smoke.

He sat the battery on the table beside the door before he slowly opened it and glanced outside, then locked the door and pulled it closed behind him.

Louis casually walked back to his motorcycle, stashing the 9 mm in the bottom of the left case.

The street was still quiet, with no traffic, so Louis removed the insulated camouflage coveralls from the left side case and slid them over his pants and up to his waist.

He removed the magazine, the suppressor and the rifle scope from the side case, sitting them on the seat of the bike in the dark driveway.

He then removed the end cap of the tube, slid the rifle and pistol grip out, and replaced the end cap.

Louis inserted the pistol grip and magazine then attached the scope and suppressor, and slid the tip of the weapon through his belt against his back, outside of his pants but inside the coveralls.

He pulled the overalls up to his shoulders and put his arms inside, then removed the tool belt from the other side case and put it around his waist to help secure the rifle in place.

Louis then put on his motorcycle jacket and helmet and quietly backed out of the driveway into the street, started the bike and rode away.

Louis rode back to the public parking area, four blocks north of the federal building, where he again parked the bike on the center stand and placed his riding gear on the seat. He retrieved his cell phone from the top case and his ball cap from the tank bag, locking everything and covering the bike. Louis took a couple of moments, looked around the parking lot to ensure no one was watching, and adjusted the position of the rifle, sliding it further down behind his butt, with the suppressor behind his left leg inside the coveralls.

He walked down 9th St. as if he owned the place, with the tool belt on his hip and the Building Maintenance ID on the belt, returning to the same entrance where he again found the elderly man, this time leaning back against the wall and snoring.

Louis eased the glass door open and stepped inside, walking quietly to the freight elevator, and pressed the button. The doors opened immediately and Louis stepped inside and again headed to the top floor.

When the doors opened, Louis again glanced up and down the hall before locating the elevator key and locking it with the doors open on this floor. He walked down the hallway of the floor in both directions, identifying additional routes down from the floor, before returning to the maintenance door across from the elevator.

He stepped inside and locked the door behind him, leaning against the maintenance bench as he dug his cell phone out of his pocket. It was 6:18 am when Louis put the cell phone into secure mode and placed a call to Nathan.

"Hey man did I wake you?"

"Nope, I've been up for about 30 minutes. I'm repacking my suitcase for the move into DC."

"What time do you think you'll arrive?"

"We're supposed to leave here at seven sharp. They moved our equipment overnight. We'll be coming straight to the building, and the handlers will be dropping our bags off wherever we'll be staying nearby."

"Do you trust me, Bro?"

"That's a strange question, man."

"It's a good question, and I need to hear your answer."

"Of course I do."

"Trust me with your life?"

"Yes, with my life."

"As soon as you get to that office, I need all three of you at that window, looking out."

"Okay."

"You need to be on the left, with both of them to your right."

"Okay."

"I want you to put your right arm over the shoulder of the guy next to you, then immediately close your eyes and your mouth."

"Okay."

"You need to fall to your left as soon as the window shatters."

"Okay."

"There will be at least two shots in rapid succession and probably two more after that."

"Okay."

"All three of you need to be as close to the window as possible. Glass is gonna fly everywhere, so don't forget to close your eyes and mouth."

"I won't forget."

"Can you call my number about five minutes before you arrive? Just let it ring a couple of times and hang up?"

"I can do that. How long of a shot will it be?"

"About 220 feet at a 45° angle downward, maybe 20° to the side."

"I trust you, Bro, make sure you get away."

"I've got it covered; I just won't be able to visit you in the hospital."

"I–I understand."

"I'll call you later in the evening."

"Sounds good, later."

"Later, keep the faith."

Okay, I've got about an hour and a half before show time, Louis thought. *Don't fuck this up.*

Louis headed to the roof behind the enclosure, near the air conditioning and heating systems, withdrew the rifle from inside the coveralls and cycled the bolt to chamber a round, then opened one of the inspection panels on the side of the giant air-conditioning system and sat the rifle inside.

He went back inside to the maintenance room and found a restroom in the back corner, where he took a much-needed bio break and washed his face before putting his gloves back on. He poured the bottle of Pine-sol sitting on the floor all over the toilet and sink when he was done.

Louis leaned against the workbench and calmed himself into a state of meditation and visualized the shots he was about to make. He mentally doped the angles, calculating the hold under for a 45° down shot, thinking through each step of aim, shoot, reload, aim, shoot, reload and so on, visualizing each step in detail and planning each breath for an event that would last no more than eight or ten seconds. He would then return to the elevator and insert the key to unlock it, head to the ground floor, and walk directly north of the building, making his way back to the motorcycle, then out of the city.

At 7:45 his phone rang; it rang once more and stopped.

Louis looked out the hallway door on this early Saturday morning to ensure the elevator doors were open and there was no one moving in the hallway.

He climbed the steps to the roof, into the air conditioner enclosure and watched through the louvered slats for Nathan to arrive.

In just over a minute, a white van pulled to the curb in front of the entrance to the building across the street, and four men emerged from the van, heading into the building; Nathan was one of them.

Louis watched them as they went through the entrance and walked around the metal detectors, heading toward the elevators.

He opened the access panel of the air-conditioning system, and removed the rifle, leaving the access panel open.

Louis slid just the tip of the suppressor through the louvers and watched the window through the scope, taking aim at the center.

A minute or so later, he saw movement in the room behind the window. He slowed his breathing, patiently waiting for his targets to appear.

He watched carefully as legs and torsos moved past the window. Nathan appeared in the window by himself, looking down at the street.

Nathan stepped away from the window, and then a few seconds later, he reappeared at the left edge of the window frame, pointing downward at the street as the other two men stepped into view beside him.

Louis stopped his breathing and aimed above the head directly to Nathan's right.

All three men leaned in close to the window, and Nathan's arm settled across the shoulders of the man next to him.

Louis squeezed off the first round and cycled the bolt, acquired aim above the second target and squeezed the trigger again, cycling the bolt.

Nathan was gone from the window frame, as was the glass when Louis fired the third shot, striking the floor in front of first man, who was falling backwards to the carpeted floor.

The fourth shot struck the wall next to the second man, who dropped to his knees before falling backwards over the first man.

Louis withdrew the rifle from the louvers and sat it back inside the access panel and shut the door, then headed toward the stairs leading down into the maintenance room.

He walked directly out of the maintenance shop, across the hall to the elevator with the key in hand, which he inserted in the lock and turned it, pressing the first floor button and holding it.

Twenty-five long seconds later, the door opened on the first floor and Louis stepped out of the elevator, turning north toward the exit, and walking past the security desk that was empty.

Louis stepped out onto the sidewalk and turned right, then walked 20 paces before turning left and crossing the street between the morning traffic.

Once on the sidewalk across the street, Louis turned left and headed back toward the corner, turning right and walking north on 9th St. with the swagger of a man late for work.

He tipped his hat as he walked past the International Spy Museum on his right.

Eight and a half minutes later, he arrived at the parking lot and pulled the cover off the bike, quickly stashing it in the side case, donned his jacket and helmet and cranked the bike.

He extended the side stand, then rolled the bike off the center stand, leaning it on the side stand and stepping over the seat, before selecting first gear and riding to the exit and out into traffic on 9th St. heading south.

He turned west on H St. and headed toward New York Ave., negotiating the maze of one way streets to his exit point, turning south on 11th then west on G St. and south on 15th St..

The sound of sirens echoed off the buildings around him; with each turn they grew louder and more numerous.

Continuing for a few blocks east on Pennsylvania Ave. NW and then taking the first right on to 14th St., he headed south toward 395.

The sirens dissipated behind him as he crossed the Potomac and continued southwest toward 95.

Three helicopters, flying no more than 500 feet above ground level and in formation, were about to cross the Potomac heading north. As they passed overhead Louis could see the FBI markings on the doors.

21

The clock on the GPS indicated it was 9:08 am when Louis selected Headline news on the satellite radio and listened while heading south on I-95. About 10 miles north of Triangle, a convoy of FBI vehicles, Humvees and FBI tactical vans was heading north at a high rate of speed toward DC.

Louis continued south of Triangle and stopped alongside the road, across the Highway from the National Marine Corps Museum, where he unfastened the tool belt and dropped it in the grass on the side of the road.

Just east of him, he saw several more helicopters leaving the tree cover and climbing out to the north. He continued south on I-95 toward Fredericksburg, where he took State Rd. 3 west before turning southwest on State Rd. 20. He turned south on US 15, intersected Interstate 64, south east of Charlottesville, and continued on until 64 turned into 81, continuing south to Marion, Virginia, where he stopped for fuel at a truck stop.

After filling the bike, he pulled to the edge of the parking lot near the phone booths and parked. He removed his helmet and jacket and headed inside the truck stop to use the facilities. When he emerged, he grabbed a cold diet Dew from the cooler and stood watching the overhead monitor tuned to CNN. The talking heads were discussing the ongoing manhunt in and around Washington, DC that began just after 9:00 am Eastern, when all of the bridge traffic and roads leading out of the city had checkpoints set up, stopping all vehicles and searching them while checking everyone's ID.

The crawl at the bottom of the screen indicated 'Washington DC under Lockdown – shots fired into the J. Edgar Hoover Federal Building.' The anchor said, "Two men were dead, one died at the scene and one died in in route to the hospital. A third man was reported to be in critical condition and was being treated at an undisclosed location."

Louis bit his lip and shook his head from side to side, looking downward. *I know I didn't shoot Nathan,* he thought. *Could a ricochet have hit him?* Louis watched the screen as news helicopters provided aerial views of the scene, and showed FBI helicopters flying below them, keeping them out of the airspace close to the federal building.

The view returned to the talking heads with a banner flashing – UPDATE - across the top of the screen. The news anchor, in his most solemn voice, stared at the camera and announced the third man died while in emergency surgery. He indicated his name would not be released pending notification of his family. Louis dropped his head, slowly walked to the cashier and paid for the Dew before walking out the door and across the parking lot, almost in shock from the news. As he reached his bike, he could hear his cell phone ringing in the top case. He opened the case and answered the phone that went immediately into secure mode. It was Nathan.

"Hey man, I thought I better call you before you saw the news."

"Son of a bitch, I just had the shit scared out of me watching CNN at the truck stop."

"The rumors of our deaths have been greatly exaggerated," Nathan said, paraphrasing Samuel Clemens.

"Where are you?"

"We got out of the emergency room about two hours ago, and they took us straight back to Quantico."

"Are you okay?"

"I'm fine. I got peppered by the glass with a couple of decent-sized pieces in my right arm that bled like hell, but I'm good to go."

"That's a relief; they had me thinking you were probably hit by a ricochet."

"They've got DC locked down tight; I don't know how you got out."

"I'll tell you about it sometime. I need to get south to warmer air and get some rest. Shoot me an update when you get a chance. I'll call you when I'm back at your place."

"Ok man; that was some scary shit, man."

"I knew it would be."

"The other two quit and headed home; the cover story of us being killed was to keep the shooter from trying again."

"Glad you're all right, man. Later."

"Later, man."

Louis climbed back on his bike with a smile on his face and continued south into Tennessee, stopping in Chattanooga to fill up the bike for the final leg down to Huntsville, where he arrived just after 10 pm Central time. He rolled through the gates into the garage, retrieved his laptop and cell phone, and headed inside. Once in the study, Louis sat his laptop on the bench, opened it and booted it up. He opened his e-mail client and found a message from Nathan.

"Don't know if you've watched the news yet so I thought I'd give you an update on the happenings in and around DC. The boys found the Galatz in the AC access panel, after finding the shell casings. Apparently, there were no video security cameras in the freight elevator or the maintenance room. The security camera on the roof didn't have a view of the inside of the enclosure around the AC and heating units."

"The security guard stationed at the north door of the building remembered a maintenance man checking the heating on the top floors sometime around 3 am, and remembered him leaving the building as well, no more than 15 minutes later. The shell casings from the Galatz matched the single shell casing found on the street in Memphis. They're now checking all small aircraft flights in and out of Memphis and the surrounding area, as well as the small airports located around DC."

"Seltzer arrived this afternoon with his AIC, along with all the evidence in their possession. The CD labeled 'Greatest Hits' really got their attention, and its method of delivery has been the source of a great deal of debate; it's now 5/2 that the target was the informant and not Seltzer. They have asked me to continue the deep dive into the hard drives of the systems from Fayetteville, as well as the Senator's laptop. I found some interesting stuff on the drives now that I have them in hand. Looks like Richland and Thomaston, the President pro tem of the Senate, have been communicating with a couple of former CIA wet boys over the last nine months."

"There is a hidden partition on the Senator's hard drive my remote tools didn't detect; now that I know what to look for, it will only take me a few minutes to update my scripts to catch them in the future. I found a similar hidden partition on the aide's laptop, and on both laptops, I found encryption software on the hidden partitions, along with message fragments I'm trying to piece together into a cohesive conversation. I'm working on getting access to Thomaston's systems, to take a peek without involving the NSA. They're up to something and it's nasty, my gut's telling me."

"Somewhere around 10 pm tonight, Richland's aide was found dead in the doorway of his home in Georgetown by his girlfriend, who went looking for him after not hearing from him all day. She was detained briefly before being allowed to return to her home. Two 9 mm shell casings were found in the foyer; they've been matched to the ones found at the scene in Ten Sleep Canyon."

"The top dogs at FBI and DOJ have been pissing themselves all afternoon, trying to explain what's going on to the White House. Give me a call when you get this message."

"Later."

Louis put his cell phone in secure mode and called Nathan.

"Hello."

"Hey Bro, got your message to call; what's up?"

"The shit is gonna hit the fan around here sometime in the morning, when I have to report my findings to this point. I know you're tired, man, but I think you ought to climb back on the bike and head home ASAP."

"What's going on; what did you find?"

"I hacked into Thomaston's computer systems and found enough information to complete the message fragments I found on the other two systems. They have been working on a plan to kill the Top Two, so Thomaston & Richland could succeed them."

"Well, that plan wandered off the trail in Ten Sleep Canyon, didn't it?"

"Richland's involvement in it did; however, Thomaston just sent a message yesterday morning indicating it was a go at first opportunity."

"Did he get a response?"

"Not that I can find yet, but I'm still trying to track down those that received the messages."

"First Opportunity is going to be a tough one to figure out; it all depends on the skill set and capabilities of the Mechanics."

"As soon as I can track them down, maybe I'll figure out who they are, and from that figure out what they know."

"Okay Bro, I'll get back on the bike and head south, should be home around sun up if not delayed."

"Ride safe, man. I'll call you in the morning, if I don't hear from you first."

"Later, man."

Louis put his things back in the bike and spent some quality time in the restroom before securing Nathan's house and again climbing back on the motorcycle and heading home to Flatland. He took the fastest route south, passing through Birmingham and Montgomery then Phenix City and Columbus, Georgia, then on to Albany, Georgia and south to the Georgia-Florida line, and onto US 19 south, arriving at his home just before 6:30 am. Louis wasted no time along the route, only stopping for fuel, energy drinks and bio-breaks. His average speed over the 650-mile route was 82 mph, and the GPS indicated his top speed was 103. He only slowed down when passing through small towns or when the radar detector alerted him to the presence of LEOs.

As he opened his garage door and rolled in to stop the bike, Diane opened the door to the garage from the laundry room, having heard the garage door open. She smiled and waited for Louis to climb out of his riding gear before approaching and wrapping her arms around him to welcome him home. Louis unfastened the straps that held the duffel to the rear seat and sat it on the floor inside the door, in front of the washing machine. He returned to the bike, retrieved his cell phone, wallet and laptop, and carried them in the house.

He took a handful of Motrin before stripping down and climbing in the shower with the hot water spraying full force on his back and shoulders, where those muscles had been screaming at him for relief over the last five hours. Diane climbed in the shower with him, soaped up the loofah and scrubbed his back as he propped himself against the wall of the shower. They bathed each other in the steam of the shower and dried each other outside the shower. Louis stretched out on top of the covers of the king-size bed, while Diane went to the laundry room and dumped the dirty clothes into the washer. Diane had just made it back to the master bedroom when the doorbell rang.

"Who the hell is at the front door this time of the morning on Sunday? If it's those damn Jehovah witnesses again, I'm going to break my foot off in somebody's ass."

Diane slipped into her house robe, headed toward the front door, and looked through the peephole. She saw two men in dark suits, unlocked the front door, and opened it wide enough to stick her head out and asked, "May I help you?"

"Yes ma'am." They both displayed their IDs. "We're with the FBI and need to speak to Louis Parker. Is he here?"

"Yes, just a minute. I'll get him for you. Would you like come in?"

"Yes ma'am, thank you." The two agents stepped inside the door and shut it.

Diane walked back to the master bedroom, where Louis was still stretched out on the bed.

"Did you run them off? I was getting ready to put foot to ass . . ." when

Diane interrupted him. "It's the FBI; there are two agents in the living room asking to speak to you. What's this about?" Diane asked, visibly upset.

"Are you kidding me, baby?"

"No, I'm not; there are two agents standing in the living room waiting on you."

"Tell them I'll be there in just a second. I need to throw some clothes on."

Diane walked out of the master bedroom back toward the living room and said, "He just got out of the shower and he's getting dressed now. He'll be here shortly. Would you like to sit down?"

"No ma'am, we're in a bit of a hurry," the older of the two agents told her.

"I'll let him know to rush," Diane replied, and then headed back to the master bedroom.

Louis slid on a clean pair of underwear and socks and one leg inside a clean pair of jeans and was stepping in with the other when Diane said, "They said they're in a hurry; what's this about?"

"I don't know baby, but we'll know in just a moment." He zipped up his jeans and buttoned them, grabbing a t-shirt from the drawer before he and Diane walked to the living room.

There are just two of them, no guns drawn; what's this about? Louis thought as he approached the living room.

"Are you Louis Parker?" the first agent asked.

"Yes."

"The Louis Parker formerly a member of the 75th Ranger Regiment, then Special Operations?"

"Yes, that would be me; what's this about?"

"Your assistance has been requested with the ongoing investigations in Washington, DC; requested at the highest level."

"Requested by whom specifically?"

"Directors of the FBI and the Department of Justice, based on the recommendation of Nathan Malone, a contract special investigator. He has indicated you have the specific knowledge, training and the skill set required to assist this investigation."

"I know Nathan; I didn't know he was back working for you guys."

"He indicated you worked together in the past, in Special Operations."

"That's right, but it is also classified."

"We need you to pack a bag and come with us now; we have a plane waiting to take you to Quantico, Virginia. You'll be briefed en route."

Diane asked, "What's this all about, Louis?"

Louis turned to Diane and told her, "At this point, I don't know, but everything is fine."

"What's this about Special Operations?" Diane asked him.

"I'm sorry, ma'am, that is classified information that cannot be disclosed," the agent told her.

"Apparently, Nathan has suggested that I could be of some help with an investigation he's working on for the FBI. I'll be home as soon as I can. Grab me a small bag while I pull some things together for the trip."

Diane headed in one direction and Louis headed to another as they quickly packed his bag with clothes and his shaving kit. Diane grabbed his hound's-tooth sports coat and laid it on the bed next to the suitcase Louis was packing.

"What is this all about?" she asked Louis again, while the agents waited in the living room.

"Nathan got called in on the investigation about the Senator that was shot, and for some reason, he mentioned to them that I could be helpful with the investigation. I don't know anything else beyond that, baby."

Louis retrieved his Glock 23, holster and spare clip from the gun safe and tossed it in before closing the suitcase, put his arms around Diane and hugged her tightly. "Everything's going to be fine and I'll be home before you know it," he whispered in her ear. "I love you, baby."

"I love you too; I'm just scared."

"There's nothing to be scared about, baby, I've just been conscripted to help with an investigation, that's all."

They again kissed and hugged and Louis grabbed the suitcase and the sport coat and headed back toward the living room. He asked Diane to grab his laptop case and cell phone from the kitchen table, along with his wallet and sunglasses.

"I need to check on something in the garage. I'll be right back."

Louis walked into the garage with his suitcase, removed the GPS from his bike, took the GPRS tracking equipment from the right side case, and stuffed them in the suitcase for the trip. *I may need the GPS while I'm there,* he thought. *You never know.*

"What's the weather like up in DC?"

"You better grab a jacket; it's kind of cool up there," the younger agent replied.

Diane went to the closet, found Louis' leather bomber jacket, and followed the men out the door to the unmarked car in the driveway, where they sat everything on the back seat.

"Call me when you get a chance," Diane told Louis and she kissed him.

"I'll call you just as soon as I can, baby," Louis said before closing the car door.

The agent drove away from the subdivision and out on US 19 heading north. A few miles up the road, he pulled into the Pasco County office complex, where a white Bell Long Ranger helicopter had landed in the parking lot, with the rotor still spinning.

"The chopper will take you to the airport where a bureau jet will fly you to Quantico."

Louis climbed out of the car with all of his gear, walked to the open rear door of the helicopter, sat his luggage inside and climbed inside taking a seat. He buckled the seatbelt and placed a set of headphones over his ears as one of the agents sitting in the back with him shut the door of the helicopter.

About 20 seconds later, the helicopter lifted off, climbed out to the north and made a 180° turn heading south. As they passed over Lake Tarpon, the helicopter banked left 45° and proceeded toward Tampa International Airport.

The agent sitting next to him in the back asked Louis to sign a confidentiality agreement, which he handed him along with a pen. Louis signed and dated the form and handed it back to the agent, who placed it in his briefcase.

"I am Special Agent Tom Hargrove and I'll be accompanying you all the way to Quantico. I'm sure you have questions about what's going on. I'll try to answer them for you."

"Okay, what the hell's going on, Tom?" Louis asked through the microphone of the avionics headset.

"As you have no doubt seen on the news, the speaker of the house, Senator Richland was assassinated in Wyoming last week. Since then, there have been more assassination attempts in Washington, DC at FBI headquarters."

"Yes, I saw that on the news," Louis said, thinking, *In person, as well.*

"As the investigation has progressed, evidence has come to light of a conspiracy to assassinate a large number of personnel, several of them US Government officials."

"How am I supposed to help with the investigation?"

"Your background and experience with the Agency may shed some light and help us prevent further assassinations. That's really all I can tell you about that; you'll receive an in-depth briefing at Quantico."

"My security clearances expired years ago."

"Actually, they've all been updated and reinstated over the past 10 hours or so."

"Wow, you guys can move fast when you actually want to," Louis said with a chuckle as the helicopter started its descent toward an open hangar, where a blue-and-white Gulfstream jet was parked, with the boarding door open.

"That's our ride," the agent told Louis as the helicopter touched down.

The door slid open. Louis and the agent climbed out, carrying his bag, and walked directly to the steps of the jet and inside.

The jet's engines went from idle to a low whistling roar as it began taxing away from the hangar toward the runways.

Agent Hargrove strapped himself in, telling Louis to do the same. In just under five minutes, the Gulfstream was airborne and heading north toward Quantico.

"We'll be landing in just about an hour."

"I haven't been to that neck of the woods in a while; this has to be the best and fastest way to get there."

Louis raised the arm table of his seat and opened his laptop, finding an e-mail from Nathan. "Don't freak out when the FBI knocks on your door. I recommended you to them. Everything will be explained during the briefing; you're not going to believe this."

I wish I'd checked my e-mail as soon as I got home, Louis thought. *Would've prevented the near heart attack and I could've prepared Diane ahead of time.*

Louis sent a response to Nathan, "I am in the air heading north; do me a favor and call Diane at home. Reassure her everything is okay. See you in an hour." Louis closed his laptop and glanced out the window for a few minutes, then looked toward the front of the cabin at a small electronic display that indicated the airspeed at .88 Mach/706 miles per hour.

He reclined the seat and laid back to try to grab a quick nap before arriving at the lion's den.

22

The phone rang as Diane was preparing to head to the gym on this most eventful Sunday morning.

"Hello?"

"Hey Diane, this is Nathan. How you doing this morning?"

"Well, hey you, we haven't spoken in a long time."

"Sorry about the early morning surprise."

"What in the heck is going on, Nathan?"

"First, let me say everything is okay; this is just one of those extraordinary times that demand action from everyone that can help."

"How can Louis help? Why is he involved?"

"Years ago, we both worked for the government; that's where we met. I'm surprised Louis never told you about it."

"He told me he met you after the Army."

"That's true, he was no longer in the Army when we met, and we were both working for the government in a capacity that required secrecy and security."

"I still don't understand why Louis is involved in this."

"Louis has some special skills and special knowledge that make him an expert concerning aspects of this investigation; beyond that I can't really say any more about it."

"What special skills are you talking about?"

"He knows quite a bit about shooting, at close and at long ranges. He is what you might call an authority on the subject."

"I know he has guns, but I've never known him to shoot them, except when he took me to the indoor gun range where we shot some pistols, and dealing with armadillos in the yard."

"Believe me when I tell you that his knowledge and skill set are needed during this investigation, to help us figure out what's going to happen and where. He'll be safe and I guarantee you he will be enjoying what he's doing."

"When this is all over, we all need to have a long talk," Diane said sternly.

"That sounds like a plan," Nathan said. "I haven't visited you all in quite a while; perhaps we can get together over Christmas."

"And I'm gonna hold you to that this time," Diane replied.

"It was good talking to you Diane. I need to run; things are getting busy around here."

"Okay, I need to head to the gym as well, bye."

"We'll talk to you soon, bye."

Diane felt a little better about the situation as she was driving to her gym for her typical Sunday morning workout. *That man finds more ways to spend time away from home,* Diane thought. *I guess I'll have to handcuff him to the bed to keep him home.* She chuckled a little thinking about the prospect.

• • •

The Gulfstream started its descent to Turner Field at Quantico, 57 minutes after it departed Tampa International, and was on the ground rolling to a stop in front of the hangar just a few minutes later. Louis gathered his things and walked down the steps of the jet to a small white van that was waiting on him and transported him to the parking lot of the barracks building where Nathan was waiting. They unloaded all of Louis's things and carried them into the barracks.

"This is my room here; you're directly across the hall," Nathan said.

"Just drop your things and grab your sport coat; we're heading to a briefing that's taking place in a few minutes."

"What the hell's going on, Nathan?"

"It's going to be good night."

"Sounds good."

"Here is your base ID and credentials; wear the ID at all times, with your credentials in your pocket."

They closed the door to the barracks and walked outside to a small sedan Nathan was issued. While standing outside, Nathan leaned against the car door, as did Louis, for a quiet conversation.

"There's a two-man team that is going to attempt to kill the President and VP."

"Who all knows about this?"

"Just me, you, Thomaston and the two-man team so far."

"So what's this briefing all about?"

"It's to bring all the investigators up to speed on all known aspects at this point."

"So what's my role in this?"

"Officially, you're to help me with the shootings. Unofficially, you're to help me figure out where and how the two-man team is going to proceed."

"I got it."

"We better get over to the auditorium; can't keep the wigs waiting," Nathan said, as he opened the car door on the driver side. Louis hopped in and they left the parking lot, heading to the briefing location, just up the road in one of the FBI buildings. Just about two minutes later, Nathan pulled into the parking lot in front of the building and drove all the way to the end of the lot before finding an open space.

"This looks like a popular hangout."

"It is today. It'll clear out this afternoon as most of these folks head back to their areas of operation around the country."

They walked to the front door of the building, where security checked their IDs before allowing them to pass. "Just take a seat here in the back and watch the show," Nathan said as he headed down to the front of the room and ascended the three stairs to the podium and took his seat. One of the other men seated on the podium stood up and walked to the microphone and tapped it to ensure he was on.

"Good afternoon, Mr. Director, gentleman and the ladies we have among us. I'm deputy director Thom Thomas. This briefing today should bring you all up to speed on the progress of the investigation into the murder of Senator Harold Richland, the manhunt for his killers, the events that took place near the Memphis field office and the events at the J. Edgar Hoover building in DC."

The Deputy Director spoke for thirty minutes and thoroughly covered all of the known events, evidence and players the bureau had developed to this point. He then introduced Nathan before taking a seat, surrendering the podium.

"Good morning, I'm Nathan Malone, and I have been a computer consultant in forensic analytics for the FBI and the Department of Justice for many years now. I was called in to help with this investigation last week, with my primary focus being that of constructing a timeline of events and evidence from the various reports, from the agents in the field, as well as the forensics analysis teams. Page three in your packet of information is a printout of what I'm about to display on the screen and will walk you through."

Louis sat in the back of the room, taking in this surreal experience, which detailed his movements and actions over the week. He sat listening, fighting back the nervous energy building in his gut, as Nathan detailed the movements of the Opses Limited vehicle, which he was able to reconstruct from the data records from Verizon Wireless. The location of every point where the wireless modem went active was mapped and tracked until it was deactivated. All these points created a giant loop out to Wyoming and back, then around Chattanooga and across Tennessee to Memphis, where they stopped.

Nathan gave details of the locations of the known satellite phones, and their movements from the records of the satellite company. Nathan also presented information that was provided by the anonymous source, thought to be one of the Opses Limited personnel, which gave detailed tracking information, manufacturer's identity and country of origin, along with the identification codes of the GPRS tracking devices. Agents tracked down all the devices, and Federal Marshals were now protecting the targets named in the list. The detailed and comprehensive timeline Nathan created specified each data point, the date and time associated with it, the geographical location the data referred to, or came from, and the information itself.

It was all laid out before the members of the FBI and the Justice Department, so that anyone could clearly see and follow this information. Across the top of the presentation was the name Nathan entered in the template they gave him, and it was now centered and bolded, across the giant screen: "A Crooked Piece of Time". *How appropriate is that!* Louis thought.

Nathan fielded questions from the agents for 20 minutes covering the data points, the sources and how the data was correlated. Nathan stood beside the podium with the microphone, answering the questions, with bandages on his arms, face and neck. Everyone knew he was the third consultant who was shot at and nearly killed at the J. Edgar Hoover building; but he didn't quit like the others. Everyone there also realized they too could find themselves in the sights of these killers. When the question-and-answer session of the presentation was completed, everyone applauded Nathan's efforts and courage in continuing with the investigation.

The next speaker was the agent in charge of the forensics lab in Washington, who detailed the evidence that was harvested from all the locations, including what was received at the Memphis field office by Paul Seltzer, who was in the audience as well.

The agent mentioned that Nathan would take over and continue the examination of all the computer equipment from Opses Limited, as well as the Senator's laptop. The agent then said, "I'd like to introduce all of you here to another consultant that will be providing insight and expertise during the investigation. Mr. Parker, could you stand up? He's seated in the back row," the agent said as everyone turned to look over their shoulders to see who was standing. Louis stood up and raised his right hand before returning it to his side, to acknowledge the agent's comments. "Mr. Parker has a particular set of skills, insight, training and experience that may prove valuable in catching the shooters. He will be assisting investigators as needed while working closely with Mr. Malone."

Louis sat down, feeling like the only lobster in the tank at Legal Sea Foods, with a starving party of diners peering through the glass at him. Nathan managed to get him on the inside of a 1000 man force looking outward, still an uncomfortable position. The briefing ended, everyone stood up and began private conversations that built to a quiet roar. Nathan left the podium, walking toward Louis, and was intercepted by Paul Seltzer. Louis watched at a distance as they shook hands like old friends who had not seen one another in several years, which was the case. They walked together back toward Louis' position.

"Louis, you remember Paul Seltzer, don't you?"

"Yes I do. It's been a few years; when did you join the FBI?"

"I graduated from the Academy about six months ago now."

"What have they got you doing?"

"Just working on staff at the field office in Memphis."

"I love the ribs at Rendezvous and the scene on Beale Street, but that's about all I can take of Memphis."

"I haven't tried those ribs yet, but I hear they're something special."

"We'll have to get together for dinner one night while we're still in town," Nathan said.

"I'm headed back to Memphis in the morning, and I've got a full schedule till then; we'll have to make it another time guys."

"That's too bad," Louis said.

"It is indeed," Nathan added.

"Well, we need to head on to the lab, Louis."

"I'm following you. I'll catch you later, Paul."

Nathan and Louis climbed back into the small sedan and headed to the base commissary for lunch. Once outside of the car Nathan said, "Well, tell me what you thought about the presentation?"

"Very informative," Louis said with a sarcastic sideways smile.

"It all came directly from their data sources, just doing what they hired me to do."

"How's the view from inside the lion's mouth?"

"I'm hanging onto his tongue so he can't bite me," Nathan answered with a smile as they headed into the mess hall.

Nathan and Louis grabbed a tray and silverware and joined the queue of Marines waiting in line. There were 80 or 90 Marines seated and in line and you would've thought it was a library. There were quiet conversations at the tables but none in the chow line, with the only noise coming from the kitchen. The food looked the same as Louis remembered it from Ft. Benning; he hoped it would taste better than he remembered it, as they walked to a table off to the side of the room, where no Marines were sitting. They both stared at the food, daring each other to go first, before Louis picked up his knife and fork and went after the meatloaf, giving it a try. While still chewing he said, "Not too bad."

"Let me tell you what I've found so far," Nathan said as they continued to eat lunch.

"The hidden partitions on the hard drives, the Senator's as well as those from Fayetteville, contained some text files as well as message encryption and decryption programs—some fairly sophisticated stuff. I was able to track down a PC used by Thomaston by decoding one of the message headers where I found the routing information for the message. I back-tracked the IP address and located the PC. The login credentials indicated it's Thomaston's, and on that hard drive, I found one of the hidden and encrypted partitions.

"From what I've been able to piece together so far, it looks like Richland and Thomaston hatched a plan almost a year ago to assassinate the President and Vice President, which would have made Richland the next in the line for succession to the Presidency. Thomaston, now President pro tempore of the Senate, would become Speaker of the House if not Vice President; that's still unclear to me. Since Richland would be the seated President, unelected, he would complete the term in office, then run for President as the incumbent."

"What lowlife sons of bitches politicians are," Louis said. "Any ideas who the wet team members are?"

"Apparently, they are a pair of mechanics that reported to Richland at CIA. I just haven't been able to identify who they are just yet. Hell, they could've been in that briefing we were just in."

"Great, I love wearing a target on my back. Can we get some flak vests?"

"I already have one; we can pick up yours from supply when we head over to the lab," Nathan replied.

"I was kind of halfway kidding, but after thinking about it for a second or two, I think I want one."

"I have found some routing information in the headers of these encrypted messages that contain IP addresses I haven't been able to find so far. These probably belong to the spooks we're looking for. My buddy Joey, over at NSA, has set up a trap in their monitoring system so we'll know as soon as they go online anywhere."

"By the way, did you call Diane for me?"

"I sure did. She's fine, and I have to be at your house for Christmas dinner."

They both laughed over the Christmas dinner comment, as Nathan had missed the last three invitations for Thanksgiving and Christmas.

"Okay, so the last message stream gave them the green light for their first opportunity; we just need to figure out when and where that will be," Louis said. "You wouldn't by chance have access to the President's and Vice President's schedules, would you?"

"Actually, that's pretty easy to come up with, as it is broadcasted every morning and afternoon to the distribution list of his staff and several others at the capital. It should be pretty easy to get on that list with the right access."

"We need it, along with all the updates, if we're going to get ahead of this. We're also gonna need a high level FBI contact that we can work with, with absolute certainty they're not involved in the plot," Louis said.

"Are there any big events coming up where the President and VP will be out in the open?" Louis openly speculated, when he and Nathan both realized at the same moment that they heard it on network television. "The funeral," they said simultaneously.

"Is that even possible?" Nathan asked.

"Anything is possible, given the right talent, the right equipment, the right location and motivation," Louis said. "Speaking of motivation, Thomaston has to pay these guys somehow; can you get into his accounts and see what's going on?"

"I've been so busy with this other stuff that I never even thought about that. I'll take a look when we're back at the lab."

"We need to find out the location of the funeral at Arlington, the actual burial plot in what section. That will shed some light on the possible shooting locations, if in fact that's where they're planning to do it." Louis said, "We've both got some research to do; we better get at it."

With that, they wrapped up their meal and returned the trays to the trash line before heading out to the sedan for the short ride to the barracks to pick up Louis' laptop and on to the forensic lab, where Nathan's computers were set up. On the way back to the barracks, they swung by the FBI supply depot, and Louis signed for his body armor and dropped it off in his barracks room when he retrieved his laptop.

"We're probably safe here on post," Nathan told him, "but we should wear it anytime we leave post, no matter where we are going."

Louis nodded his head in agreement. "There's no use catching an avoidable case of lead poisoning."

23

Nathan and Louis arrived at the FBI forensics lab at Quantico and headed inside to the small office space that the FBI assigned to Nathan, located just off the main room of the lab. There were all the comforts of home that Nathan was used to, a workbench, desk and chairs. There were also phones and a window with a view of an exercise field on the far side of the parking lot. In the main room of the forensic lab was a line of tables stacked with plastic containers bearing evidence tags. Inside the containers were the bits and pieces of evidence that have been gathered at the different sites. Around the circumference of the room were various testing equipment and apparatus used by the forensics teams in their efforts to itemize, categorize, scrutinize and classify the evidence they worked with. Louis leaned in close to Nathan's ear and asked, "What's it like in here at night?"

"No one can hear us unless the door is open; I've swept the room every day."

"That's a relief; I was beginning to feel as if they didn't trust us."

"I'm gonna try to get the Top Two's itinerary for the upcoming week; see if you can figure out where Richland's funeral plot is located at Arlington."

"Sounds like a plan," Louis said as he opened his laptop and began searching the online news agencies' websites with any mention of the funeral in their copy. Site after site produced numerous stories, all rehashing the same tidbits of information the other sites reported, while none of them knew the specifics about the funeral other than it would be Wednesday afternoon.

An hour and 20 minutes went by, while Louis dug through site after site, when Nathan said, "I got it"

"You got what?"

"Their schedules."

"So, what do they look like?"

"A list of meetings and events, along with dates and times," Nathan said with a deadpan delivery.

Louis looked up from the screen with a puzzled look and hesitated for a second. "You asshole, you know what I meant."

"I couldn't help it, Bro, you set it up perfectly."

"You got me; guess I asked for it."

"The only events on their schedules where they are together outside of the White House, are at the ceremony in the rotunda and then at Arlington, for the graveside service."

"The only thing I found so far is that every member of the Senate and the House will be attending as well. Hell, the entire US Government will be there, it looks like, including the Justices."

"I've got to get back to work on these hard drives and the message fragments; I'll be out in the main lab if you need me."

Louis decided to approach this task from a different angle. *Let's try a little Social Engineering,* Louis thought as he did a Google search for "Florist near Arlington Cemetery" that produced four pages of results. Louis checked several of the listings before finding one that was open on Sundays, and placed a call to the number that was listed.

"Good afternoon, Buckingham Florist, how may I help you?"

"Hi, I been calling around trying to schedule a delivery for Senator Richland's funeral Wednesday; can you help me with that?"

"Yes sir, you and several thousand others from around the world have us all quite busy. It's good that you called today, as we will soon hit our capacity. Have you thought about what you would like to order?"

"We were thinking of a simple wreath, something tasteful, and would you be able to deliver it Wednesday morning to the gravesite?"

"Everything has to be delivered to the maintenance entrance and searched there, before the groundskeepers take the arrangements to the designated area near the burial plot."

"That would be fine, however it's handled, and can I get your name, please?"

"Of course, I'm Martin Hoffman; we have several sizes of wreaths still available, from 12 inch to 36 inch with stands. What would be your preference, sir?"

"Let me call you back in a few minutes, Martin. I need to speak with the Senator first."

"That will be fine, sir, just don't wait too long to call us back, and thank you for choosing Buckingham Florist."

Next Louis looked up the number for the maintenance facility at Arlington national Cemetery and placed a call. "Grounds Maintenance, how can I help you?" the gruff voice of a salty, cigar-chewing older man asked.

"Hi, I'm Martin Hoffman with Buckingham Florist here in Arlington; we have several hundred arrangements to be delivered so far, for Senator Richland's funeral on Wednesday, and we're unsure how to address them so they will all go to the right place," Louis said in his most effeminate tone.

"All flower deliveries must come to the maintenance gate, located off the Columbia Pike Navy Annex exit of South Washington Boulevard, and be unloaded there so they can be inspected prior to delivery to the burial location," the gravelly voice said between breaths.

"Should they be marked or tagged in some specific way to ensure they're delivered to the correct grave site?"

"Hold on just a second while I look something up," the man said. "Just bring us a copy of your letterhead that indicates delivery to 66, 110 when you bring the flowers; the folks who inspect them will ensure they go to the right location."

"Delivery to 66, 110–is that all you need?"

"That's it; we can find it from there," the gravel voice said, then coughed.

"Thank you sir, you've been most helpful." Louis said and hung up.

66, 110 Louis thought, that has to identify the location at Arlington.

Again, Louis did a Google search for 'Map of Arlington National Cemetery' and located a link for an interactive map and clicked it to find a map displayed that was segmented into areas and labeled along with the road names inside the cemetery.

Section 66 was next to the highest section number to be found on the map, and was located on the southeast side of the cemetery, adjacent to the maintenance area. The interactive map indicated that sections 54, 60, 64 and 66 had available grave sites. *Looks like Richland will be planted in 66,* Louis thought, *and I'll bet 110 is the grave location. I need to get up there and do some scouting.*

Louis walked out into the main lab area and over to the bench where Nathan was working and stood beside him for a moment, watching as Nathan manipulated data on the screen of his laptop that was connected to several external hard drives located on the bench.

"I think I found what I was looking for."

"Oh yeah? I don't seem to be making any progress just now."

"Can you step into the office for a second?" Louis asked before heading back to his computer.

Nathan joined him there a minute later. "What's up?"

"I made some calls and I'm pretty certain where the burial site is at Arlington. I need to head up there and do some scouting; however, I need a vehicle and a few other things as well."

"You can use the vehicle I signed out of the motor pool; what else do you need?"

"A good set of field glasses, the rifle scope from an M24 and an optical laser rangefinder would be nice."

Nathan picked up the phone on the desk and punched a five-digit number. "I know a guy," Nathan said while waiting for the phone to be answered.

"Paul Biggins speaking."

"Paul, this is Nathan. I'm at the forensics lab this morning with Louis Parker, and he needs a couple of pieces of specialized equipment from the depot."

"What does he need?"

"Let me put him on the phone so he can tell you," Nathan said and handed the phone to Louis.

"This is Louis Parker."

"Hi Louis, this is Paul Biggins. I am your and Nathan's handler here at Quantico. What type of equipment do you need, specifically?"

"I need a high quality set of field glasses with integrated compass, the rifle scope from an M24 SWS and an optical laser rangefinder good to 1000 yards or better."

"That shouldn't be too much of a problem. How soon do you need them?"

"Is the next 30 minutes too soon to ask?"

"I need to make a call and get the duty officer headed to the supply depot. Just meet me there and make sure you have your ID with you."

"Thanks Paul, I'll find my way there. Well, that was easy enough," Louis said.

"If the Coyote had these guys instead of Acme, he'd eaten that Road Runner the first episode," Nathan said with a big grin.

"Is it the same supply depot where we got the vest?"

"That's the place. Don't speed on post; they lose their mind over that," Nathan said as he handed him the keys.

"Where's the office supply?"

Nathan stepped outside the office door and pointed down the hallway toward a cabinet. "In that cabinet next to the water cooler. Take what you need."

Louis closed his laptop and took it with him as he headed toward the cabinet, where he procured a writing tablet, a ruler and a couple of ballpoint pens before heading out to the car. He drove directly to the barracks and retrieved the vest he was issued, and then headed back to the supply depot, where he found the building locked. He decided to call Diane while he waited for the handler and the duty officer. Louis dialed her cell phone to find no answer and realized she was probably out shopping for groceries, as they normally did on Sundays. He left a voicemail asking her to call him back when she got a chance and told her that he loved her. Just a few minutes later, a Humvee entered the parking lot of the supply depot and a sharp looking young Marine butter-bar lieutenant exited the vehicle and unlocked the front door.

As Louis climbed out of the sedan, a blue minivan pulled into the parking lot and parked next to the sedan. A clean-cut 35-ish man dressed in slacks and a button down shirt climbed out of the car and walked around to where Louis was standing.

"You must be Louis," he said, "I'm Paul Biggins; let's find what you need inside."

Louis followed Paul through the doors to the counter where the duty officer was waiting.

"Good afternoon, Lieutenant, we need to draw a few things from supply for immediate use."

"Yes sir," the Marine responded. "I just need to know what you are looking for."

"I need a pair of 15 x 80 binoculars with integrated compass," Louis said.

"Yes sir; what else?"

"I need a10x42 Leupold Ultra M3A scope from an M24 SWS."

"Yes sir, anything else?"

"I need a pair of 10x50 LRF binoculars, and that should do it."

The Lieutenant looked at Biggins and said, "I need written authorization to release this equipment, sir."

"Once we have the equipment here, I'll get the serial numbers. I'll sign for them, then fax over the written authorization," Biggins told him.

"That will be fine, sir, thank you; it may take me a few minutes to locate this equipment," the lieutenant said before disappearing into the back room of the building.

"Why do you need these particular pieces of equipment?" Biggins asked Louis.

"I need to do some range work based on what I know about the shooter and his capabilities, to create a map overlay–that's about it," Louis told him, trying to cut the questioning short.

"Try not to lose the stuff; I can't afford to replace it."

"No problem, Paul, I'll return it to you in the same condition it's handed to me."

The Marine reappeared from the backroom carrying three cases and sat them on the counter before opening them and recording their serial and model numbers on the disposition form he filled out for the agent to sign. Louis showed a very satisfied grin on his face as he looked at the very high dollar Steiner and Leupold glass in front of him. "I'll need batteries for the LRF," Louis added.

"No problems, sir, they're in the case."

"Outstanding."

Agent Biggins signed the completed disposition form before tearing out his copy. "I'll fax the authorization over to you within the next 30 minutes," Biggins told the lieutenant before he and Louis headed out to the parking lot with the optics cases and placed them in the sedan.

"I appreciate you handling that so quickly for me, Paul. I'll hand them back to you as soon as I'm done with them."

"No problem, Louis, that's what I'm here for, to make sure you two have everything you need while assisting us in this investigation," the agent responded as he noticed the vest in the backseat of the sedan. "Make sure you put the vest on before leaving post, and keep it on until you return."

"I'm about to put it on now—not a fan of lead poisoning," Louis said as the agent climbed into his minivan before leaving the parking lot.

Louis removed his sport coat, slid the vest over his head, and adjusted the side straps, so that the vest was snug but not too tight. He climbed into the driver's seat and headed toward the main gate and out to Interstate 95 and north to Arlington.

About an hour later, he arrived at the maintenance gate of Arlington National Cemetery, just off S. Washington Blvd. across from the Pentagon. He put on his sport coat and hung the two sets of binoculars around his neck by the straps, slid the rifle scope into the inside pocket of the sports coat, and with pen and paper in hand, he walked to the maintenance gate, where he was challenged by a security guard. Louis showed the man his FBI credentials. The guard could clearly see the FBI logo on the bulletproof vest under his sport coat and allowed him into the maintenance building, where Louis located a large-scale map on the wall that detailed all the sections and plot numbers.

"Can I help you find something?" came from the same gravel-voiced man he spoke to on the phone earlier.

Louis turned around. The first thing he noticed was the cigar butt lodged between his teeth on the left side of his mouth. "Yes, you can: section 66, plot number 110, please."

"There's no one buried there yet, not until Wednesday anyway."

"I realize that, but I need to survey the area nonetheless," Louis told him as he turned to face him, displaying his credentials.

"Follow me," the cigar-chewing supervisor told him as he headed out the back door of the building and took a seat in an electric cart. Louis sat in the cart next to him as they pulled out of the enclosed parking lot, surrounded by four buildings, then turning left heading toward the cemetery, then right on Patton Drive for about 150 feet and then left on MacArthur Drive. At the intersection of MacArthur Drive and Arnold Drive, the maintenance supervisor made a 45° turn to the left and pulled into the trees at the corner of section 66, and proceeded across the section on the maintenance path, stopping near the center where a new grave location was marked out with stakes.

"This is it; can you find your way back to the maintenance building?" the supervisor asked before coughing several times and clearing his throat.

"I believe I can. I appreciate the ride."

When Louis stepped out of the golf cart, the supervisor continued straight ahead and exited the section on Eisenhower Drive, turning left heading back to the maintenance shop. Louis stood there looking at the hundreds of gravestones aligned in perfectly straight rows disappearing toward the northern edge of the section. At that moment, Louis acknowledged he was standing alone among the graves of America's fallen. It was quiet, except for the occasional sounds he could hear from the highway, but the trees around the section served to buffer the sound, adding to the sense of isolation.

Louis sketched out the area on the pad before removing the lens caps of the binoculars with the integrated compass and viewing the horizon while he slowly turned 360° to identify any potential sniper blind locations. He noted on his pad the Pentagon to the southeast of his location as well as the tall buildings on Foxcroft Heights to the southwest, next to the Air Force Memorial. Between those two locations and farther across the highway directly south of him, he could clearly see the upper sections of the tall apartment building complex that appeared to be shaped like a Y, with one leg of the Y pointed in the direction of the Pentagon and another leg pointed toward the buildings on Foxcroft Heights.

Just to the left of the building and barely visible above the tree line was the top of what appeared to be a shopping center. Rotating farther to the southwest, there was a hill located in the cemetery, which rose above the tree line. Lying due west of him, between that hilltop and the Tomb of the Unknowns, was another piece of high ground with tree cover, and then there were the buildings directly to the north, near the main entrance to the cemetery, and the tall buildings beyond that. Louis noted all these locations and observations on his tablet along with the compass directions and general descriptions before capping the binoculars and uncapping the laser range finder and taking distance readings for the locations he identified.

It was 2000 feet from this location to the center of the Pentagon wall facing him, with the left end of the wall 200 feet closer and the right end 300 feet farther, an easy and unobstructed shot from anywhere on top of that wall, he thought. It was 1600 feet from his location to the corner of the tall building on Foxcroft Heights, with a shot possible from anywhere on the eastern or northern facing walls of the building complex. He was 2750 feet from the closest corner of the Y-shaped building across the highway, and 2900 feet from anywhere along the top edge of the building that pointed toward Foxcroft Heights. *That's doable as well,* he thought as he wrote the ranges next to the locations on his tablet.

The top edge of the roof of the shopping center measured out at 2625 feet from his location, but was barely visible at the top edge of the tree canopy between them. It was exactly 1000 feet to the top of the small hill just to the west of Foxcroft Heights, and right at 2000 feet to the clear area of the hill directly to the west. The closest building to the north was more than 3000 feet away. *It would take an exceptional shot by an exceptional shooter with no wind and enough luck to draw to an inside straight to make the shot from there,* Louis thought.

Louis carefully diagrammed all the areas, as well as the numerous close-in locations around the cemetery grounds that would most certainly be crawling with Secret Service and other security details, ruling them out as viable locations. Louis completed his notes and took several photos toward the viable locations with the camera of his cell phone before walking back to the maintenance building.

He pulled out of the parking lot and turned on Columbia Pike, heading toward Foxcroft Heights and the Air Force Memorial, noting the building was five stories tall and located on a hill above the cemetery, providing an excellent angle on the grave site but a very difficult escape scenario. The Air Force buildings were enclosed by fences with guard positions. Louis made a U-turn, headed back down the hill, and turned right on S. Joyce Street, passing under the many overpasses of Interstate 395 and stopping at the corner of Army Navy Drive.

There was a clear view of the Y-shaped, 14-story tall RiverHouse building, and the eight story round tower above the Bed, Bath & Beyond on the opposite corner. The lower two stories were storefront and the four stories above appeared to be apartments or office space; however, the tower extended another two and a half stories up, with lighted letters that spelled out Pentagon Row near the top of the rounded tower.

He continued south, pulled into the parking lot of the RiverHouse building, and walked inside to locate the security office for the complex. Finding the room on the first floor, he walked inside, where three security guards were seated at different desks.

One stood up and walked to the counter and asked, "Can I help you sir?" with a bored indignation about him.

Louis showed him his credentials and said, "I hope you can. I need access to the roof of this building to complete a security survey."

The security guard turned and looked over his shoulder toward his supervisor, who stood up and walked to the desk, saying, "What's this about?"

"I'm with the FBI out of Quantico and need to take a look from the roof of this building to gauge and complete a threat assessment; it will take less than five minutes once on the roof and I'll be out your hair," Louis told him in a stern but friendly tone.

"Billy, you take him up there, I don't have time for this," the supervisor said before sitting down at his desk.

"Follow me, sir," the young security guard told Louis as he headed out the door and down the hallway toward the center of the Y-shaped building.

"We'll have to take the freight elevator," the young security guard told him as he slid his access key into the lock, which opened the elevator door. The doors opened on the roof and Louis stepped out smartly, walking north to the edge of the building facing the cemetery. He took the caps off the laser range finders and marked the spot of the burial plot to the north at 2755 feet from where he was standing, and noted it on his tablet along with an angle estimate. He then walked to the northeast corner of the building to take a closer look at the tower above the Bed, Bath & Beyond, located just 300 feet away. With the range finder, he found the distance to the Pentagon wall that faced the cemetery to be 2500 feet to the center of the wall, 2000 feet to the closest point of the wall and 3000 feet to the farthest point of the wall. Louis walked to the northwest corner of the building and noted the distance to the top edge of the building on Foxcroft Heights, which was 1500 feet to the center of the wall, 1250 feet to the closest end and 1750 feet to the furthest end.

He told the security guard he was done and then headed back to the freight elevator and back toward the security office, and Louis headed out the front door, climbing in the sedan to drive across the street to the office complex where the tower was located. After several minutes of looking, he found the management office for the complex and again explained that he needed to have access to the roof, and specifically to the tower on the corner above the Bed, Bath & Beyond location.

A maintenance man who worked for the building owners took Louis up the ladder through an access panel to the roof, and over toward the tower on the corner of the building. A built-in ladder accessed the walkway around the backside of the tower that allowed access to the signs for maintenance. Inside the tower was basically hollow except for the cross bracing which supported the weight of the signs. From the top edge of the tower, Louis did not have a clear sight of the burial position, as several trees were located between him and the plot in section 66. He sketched the details of the tower before leaving the location, thanked the maintenance man for his time, and headed back to the sedan for the hour-long drive back to Quantico.

There are several good places, with doable angles on that plot, he thought. *Surely, the Secret Service and the FBI sniper over watch details will have them covered, so how are they going to get off shots at the Top Two?* he asked himself.

Driving south on 95, he was thinking about the last time he passed this way, just over twenty-fours back, then heading south away from DC as the city was put under lockdown because of his actions. *What a strange turn of events have taken place,* he thought, *bringing me back here to prevent what I just accomplished–well, sort of.*

His cell phone rang several times as he attempted to dig it out of his jacket pocket.

"Hello?"

"Hey baby, sorry I missed your call earlier. I was shopping at the mall and you know how spotty the coverage is in there," Diane said.

"Hey sweetie, I was just calling to check in and see how you're doing and let you know I arrived."

"Where are you?"

"I just left Arlington, heading back to Quantico."

"What's going on at Arlington?"

"Well, on Wednesday they're holding the funeral for Senator Richland, the one who was killed in Wyoming."

"Yeah, I saw that on the news. Why'd you have to go there?"

"I completed a risk assessment, because the President and Vice President will be attending the funeral Wednesday."

"Don't they have people to do that already?"

"Yes, they do, but they wanted the views and opinions of an outsider, just to be sure all the bases are covered. What were you shopping for?" Louis asked, in an attempt to change the subject.

"Just finishing up the Christmas shopping for Zack, Lily, Kaydence, Wayland and Elsie Kaye, so we can wrap and ship their gifts before the last-minute rush starts. I don't understand why they needed you for this," Diane asked, returning to the topic.

"Baby, I can't really discuss this on the phone. I will explain every bit of it to you as soon as I get home. Let's just say it's what I used to do in the Army and afterwards."

"Okay, I'm sorry for being nosy. I'm just concerned."

"You're not being nosy, baby, and I'm glad you're concerned about me but really, everything is okay, I promise."

"Okay, I just pulled into the garage and need to unload the car; call me when you get a chance. I love you."

"I will. I love you too, bye."

About 20 minutes, later Louis arrived at the main gate at Quantico. After he presented his credentials to the MP, the barricade was moved and he passed through and headed back to the lab where Nathan was working. Louis parked the sedan in front of the building, carried his laptop and all the equipment into the office, and sat them on Nathan's desk. "What's going on, Bro?"

"I finally made some headway on these damned hard drives," Nathan replied. "How was the road trip?"

"Very informative. I found what I was looking for, but I'm not sure what we're going to do with the information."

Nathan said, "I deciphered several more of the message fragments and found wire transaction footprints to an offshore account on Richland's laptop, which matched some transfer activity from Thomaston's laptop to the same account. It looks like Richland and Thomaston both sent money to this account over the past 90 days, and most recently, two days before Richland was killed. They also brought me the laptop belonging to Richland's aide, which was found at his home. There's a hidden partition on this hard drive, as well, with the same encryption technology and more message fragments. It seemed Richland liked to copy his aide on everything he was doing."

"Any luck tracking down that offshore account and who has access to it?"

"Yep, there have been several transfers from that account to other offshore accounts, as well as an account here in the states. One of the transactions went to an account of an arms dealer. I've been working on cracking his systems for the last hour but they have some effective countermeasures in place. It may take me a while, but I'll work through them all."

"I'm running on empty, man. I want to head back to the barracks, take a shower and crash. Come and get me when you're ready for a late dinner," Louis told him and handed him the keys to the sedan.

"I'll do it. Get some rest, man. What's it been, three days since you slept?"

"I can't remember; must be at least that. Later, man," Louis said before heading out the door and walking to the barracks, a quarter mile away, as the sun disappeared for the night.

24

Nathan continued working his way through the layers of security, modifying his scripts at each step of the way. About two hours later, he made it through the firewalls and the countermeasures and accessed the file systems of one of the servers at the arms dealer's location in Miami. Within minutes he found an e-mail server, along with a second encrypted e-mail server, and began the process of copying all the data to the large hard drive array attached to his local machine.

Nathan scanned the encrypted e-mail folders and found about what he expected: orders for weapons by the case, with drop shipments from manufacturers to locations in Central and South America, West Africa, Egypt, Syria, Lebanon and the Baltic states. He found an order that was filled seven months prior and shipped to Opses Limited in Fayetteville, which consisted of a Heckler and Koch GMG 40 Millimeter Automatic Grenade Launcher, along with a tripod mounted three-axis controller and remotely operated fire control system. *I didn't find that son of a bitch in the safe*, Nathan thought.

The order included a case of 40 mm practice rounds and a case of 40 mm HE, or High Explosive, rounds that consist of an electronic programmable fuse, a prefragmented warhead and a propulsion system. The fuse is programmed through the fire control system of the gun and is mechanically armed at approximately 23 meters from the gun when fired. The order was delivered in pieces to various locations, including the office of Opses Limited, the Miami offices of the arms dealer, an outdoor shooting range in West Virginia and the Claude Moore Colonial Farm in Langley, Virginia.

Nathan copied this information, e-mailed it to Louis' laptop, and continued digging through the encrypted e-mail system and all of the attachments that were sent and received through that server. Nathan found one e-mail receipt from a bank in Morocco, dated more than two years earlier, acknowledging the creation of a secure account, along with the account number and a verification of transfer of €2 million from Blom Bank of Genèv.

With more digging and searching using the account number, he turned up nothing that remotely resembled a password or pass phrase for the account. After scratching his head and pacing the floor of the office for a while, he remembered the spreadsheet he found on Richland's laptop and a copy of it on his aide's laptop. He dug through his files and located the spreadsheet, and well down the list of the accounts, he found a matching account number for BMCE, a bank in Morocco, along with a password, contact number and web address. Within minutes, Nathan accessed the account at BMCE and downloaded the transaction history, beginning when the account was created.

Nathan determined that the account served as a clearinghouse for fund transfers from Richland's accounts to those he was paying for services, by transferring from this account to other BMCE accounts, one of which was the arms dealer in Miami.

There were transfers to several other accounts that Nathan spent hours mapping out and tracking down those who could access them, by tracking where the funds had been transferred, and ultimately where they landed. One such account was on Grand Cayman, where there were two names associated with the account, Robert M. Hauser and Oleg Hatalsky.

Nathan started background checks for Hauser and Hatalsky and found they were both retired civil servants, who at one time worked under Richland at CIA. Hauser served with Richland in Vietnam and Hatalsky was recruited away from STASI, the East German Intelligence Service in 1985. They were both mechanics, and both still on Richland and Thomaston's payroll. *This has to be them,* Nathan thought. *If it quacks and walks like a duck. . .'* Nathan began searching cell phone records of all the national carriers to track down the accounts these two used, as well as locating the addresses where their government retirement checks were mailed or deposited, along with vehicle registrations and tax records from which he could locate them.

Just before 10 pm, Nathan left the forensic lab and drove to the barracks. When he arrived, he knocked on Louis's door several times to wake him up so they could grab a late dinner in town somewhere and discuss his findings. Louis crawled out of bed after a five-hour nap and donned some clean clothes and his bomber jacket, and he and Nathan headed into town searching for hot food. They rolled north through Triangle and found a Cracker Barrel on the west side of 95. To their surprise, the parking lot was not packed. Within a few minutes they were seated at a booth near the window overlooking the parking lot, and both decided to have the chicken fried steak and vegetables along with copious amounts of iced tea. There were only a few tables with customers at this time of the evening and the hot food was on their table in just minutes.

"Did you see the e-mail I sent you earlier?"

"I never even opened the laptop; I hit the shower and crashed."

"I was able to find my way into the arms dealer's computer systems in Miami and found some interesting but disturbing information."

"Oh yeah, what could they be selling that would disturb you?"

"How about an H & K GMG, with the remote fire control system."

Louis stopped chewing and sat his fork on the edge of his plate, before looking up at Nathan. "Please tell me you're kidding me. That thing could rain down 40 mm grenades from 1700 yards away; with the GPS system integrated with the fire control system, they can't miss."

"Feeling properly disturbed now, are we? The documentation I found didn't indicate the shipment of the GPS system, just the remote fire control system."

"Yeah, but who in the know wouldn't go the whole nine yards and get the GPS and interface as well?"

"Pieces of the setup were drop-shipped to several different locations months ago, so they've probably assembled it and become proficient with it. Most of it went to an outdoor gun range in "West by God"

Virginia. I'll bet you a dollar to a doughnut that's where they've been test-firing it, using the practice rounds."

"That's remote country, and they could've easily zeroed it in and have it here, and if they've gotten the GPS since then, they could hide the damn thing anywhere and operate it remotely."

Nathan commented, "They can wipe out the entire government with that thing if they choose to, given just about all of them will be present at the funeral."

"No shit, you can't target two out of 1200 people standing in close proximity using 40 mm high explosive grenades, with a kill radius of 20+ feet; up to 40 feet if they use air burst."

"The order included a case of M385I Practice grenades and a case of M384 High Explosive."

"Great! They're fucked unless we find the GMG first. Did you figure out who the actors are?"

"I believe so, a couple of guys that worked with Richland at CIA named Hauser and Hatalsky."

"Hatalsky? As in Oleg Hatalsky, the STASI problem solver Hatalsky?"

"You've heard of him?"

"More than heard of him, studied his work, and adopted some of his techniques after he defected, just before the wall came down. He's an old man now, but a dangerous one. What's the story on Hauser?"

"He worked with Richland on the ground in Vietnam, a career spook, did wet work until he retired 15 years ago–that's all I know so far."

"Two retired spooks, both hands-on killers with access to modern weapons technology and backed by deep pockets with high office aspirations. Nobody's going to believe us."

"We're going to have to pass this information on so they can cancel the funeral," Nathan said.

"That won't stop them; just delay them a bit by forcing them to use another opportunity."

Nathan said, "Maybe we can convince them to not allow the Top Two to attend the funeral?"

"That may work; however, if we don't find the GMG they'll never be safe. At least with the funeral at Arlington, we know where they'll be aiming; that defines their possible shooting radius and locations," Louis said, staring out the window with his eyes fixed on the horizon, thinking through the scenarios. "What have we stepped in here?"

"But if we don't find the GMG in time to stop it, they'll lop off the heads of the government," Nathan replied.

"They already have this planned out and have picked primary, secondary and tertiary locations by now. They chose to use a remote fire control system so they didn't have to be near the weapon; this also allows them to see the results as they happen and adjust fire if necessary, as well as separation from the weapon if or when it's discovered."

"Do you think they have a backup plan?"

"Of course, they're professionals," Louis replied. "They could have several."

Louis and Nathan sat discussing the situation and finished the meal before driving back to Quantico for the night. In the parking lot of the barracks, outside of the car Louis asked, "Did you figure out how they got paid?"

"Yes, I have a fairly complete transaction history from Richland's and Thomaston's accounts, all the way to Hauser and Hatalsky's accounts in Grand Cayman, as well as transaction history from their investment accounts, with money flowing from offshore and ending up in their pockets."

Both men retired for the night in their assigned barracks rooms, and both thought long and hard on the situation, the gravity of their decisions and the consequences. Neither enjoyed a peaceful night's sleep.

• • •

Nathan continued digging through the encrypted file system of the arms dealer's mail server in Miami, while Louis began plotting the available locations around Arlington cemetery where the GMG could be placed. "I found it," Nathan exclaimed.

"Found what?"

"I found a purchase agreement for the GPS interface of the remote fire control system. It was shipped from Germany to Miami a month ago and it looks like it was forwarded to Hatalsky at a PO Box in Seven Corners three days ago."

"What kind of PO Box, post office or third-party?"

"Don't know yet. I'll have to track it down, but in any event they no longer need line of sight for the operator unless they just have to watch what happens out of curiosity."

"Given that technology, I wouldn't take the risk if it was up to me. I'd be within radio range to initiate the fire then I'd bug out and watch it on the tube. But that's just me."

"Let's hope morbid curiosity gets the best of them, so we at least have a chance at them," Nathan said as he accessed the Post Office's registration system that detailed the physical addresses associated with PO boxes.

"The PO Box it was shipped to in Seven Corners is not a physical United States post office location, probably a third-party pack and ship facility."

"Give me the address and I'll head up there and put the arm on them," Louis said.

"It's called Corner Mailbox, 6300 Seven Corners Court."

"I need the keys again," Louis said. Nathan dug them out of his pocket and sat them on the table.

Louis picked up the keys as well as the equipment that was signed out to him, along with his laptop, and headed out the door to the sedan. He opened the trunk, stashed the equipment securely, still in their protective cases, and put on the vest. Within a few minutes he was heading out of the main gate at Quantico and again back toward 95 for the drive north. Once he was on the 395 connector, he made the 270° loop to the right to get on State Road Seven that turned into Leesburg Pike heading northwest. As he stopped at the red light next to the Dar Al Hijrah Islamic Center, he saw the observant Muslims gathering in the parking lot after leaving morning prayers in the mosque, and found himself thinking, *They're the peaceful ones here, and I'm tracking down a pair of retired government assassins turned terrorists. How did all of this get reversed? Am I wearing a white hat now?*

When the light changed, he continued on to Seven Corners, just another few blocks northwest. It was 9:45 am when Louis found a parking place on Seven Corners Court and walked down the block to the small storefront operation. He walked inside and checked every corner, finding no security cameras. *No wonder they use this location,* he thought. Inside the store, there were several rows of mailboxes, from small to quite large, as well as the shipping and packing desk. He located box 121 on the bottom row. It was a box big enough for a Basset Hound to sleep comfortably. Louis waited until there were no other customers in the store before approaching the sixty-some-odd-year-old man behind the counter. "I need all the information you have on the box holder of number 121," Louis said as he showed the man his credentials.

"What's this about? We don't give out such information."

"That's FBI business and you will comply, or I'll have the Post Office put you out of business today," Louis said while staring directly into the eyes of the man behind the counter.

"I'll call my lawyer."

"Not before I close you down and arrest you for obstructing a federal investigation," Louis barked to help sell the bluff.

The steely-eyed man lowered his face to look over his reading glasses and fixed his gaze on Louis's eyes while he bit his bottom lip, thinking it over.

"Just a minute," he said as he walked to the end of the counter and grabbed the small filing box from the shelf below.

"One-twenty-one, what you need to know about it?" he asked as he found the 3 x 5 index card and withdrew it from the box.

"I need to know everything you know about it. Just set the card face up on the counter and start talking," Louis told him as he reached for his cell phone, activated the high-resolution camera and took two photos of the index card, one with flash and one without.

"He's a regular customer, been one for years, comes in once, maybe twice, every two weeks; he has a Polish or Russian accent, perhaps German; it's hard for me to say."

"When was the last time he was in here?"

"Maybe a week ago, I think, not since."

"Is there anything in his box now? If so, set it up here on the desk."

The man disappeared around the counter and Louis could hear him fumbling around behind the wall of mailboxes. He appeared with a few small envelopes and a box large enough to hold a 12 pack of tall bottle beer.

"This is all there is waiting for him."

Louis looked at the envelopes and photographed them before telling the man, "Place the box in one of those large plastic bags over there; I'll need to take it with me just to be safe. It will be returned unopened, shortly."

"What do I tell him if he comes looking for his mail?"

"Does he normally talk to you or ask you about his mail?"

"No, he just takes his mail and leaves."

"Do you call him or notify him by any means that he has mail to be picked up?"

"No, he just comes in and checks the box."

"If he comes in before I return the package, or even after, don't say anything to him."

"What if he is expecting it?"

"If he asks you, then verify you have no package for him, that's all."

"I could get in big trouble for this, lose my license or worse."

"You're not going to get in trouble for cooperating with an FBI investigation; you'll get in trouble if you don't cooperate. I'll have this back to you as quickly as possible; you have nothing to worry about."

With that, Louis picked up the sack and headed out the door to the sedan where he called Nathan.

"Hello."

"Hey man, I'm about to send you a couple of images with information about that mailbox."

"That didn't take long."

"It's amazing what a little intimidation and an FBI ID card can get you. I've also got a large box that was waiting to be picked up by the owner. I'll be back within the hour."

"Sounds good; later."

By 11:00 am, Louis made it back to Quantico and carried the plastic bag with the box into the lab.

"What have you got there?"

"Don't know; it was waiting for them to pick up. Don't know what it is, but it's bigger than a bread box."

Nathan asked one of the forensics technicians to assist him in opening the packaging without damaging it, so it could be resealed. The young technician photographed the box from all angles and analyzed the tape used to close the box before he went to the cabinet at the far end of the room and came back with a small glass container with an eyedropper. With an X-acto knife and tweezers, he slowly lifted the corner of the strip of tape before applying a couple of drops of the liquid from the bottle to the adhesive side of the tape. He manipulated the box and held it in such a manner that the liquid would run underneath the tape. After a few seconds the tape began to let go and he continued to release the tape with the liquid until the box could be opened.

"We've struck pay dirt," Nathan told Louis as he carried the contents of the box into the small office off the side of the lab and closed the door. "We've got the GPS, the interface box and the interface cables for the fire control system."

"Okay, so we got the GPS and interface–do we keep it?"

"We can keep it, or we can modify it and give it back. Let me take a look inside before we decide on how to proceed."

Louis watched on as Nathan opened the outer waterproof case of the combat-hardened GPS to examine the circuitry, doing the same to the interface box that would be mounted on the three-axis controller of the GMG's mount. The GPS is designed to be slaved to the interface box, and receive input from the remote fire control systems handheld console where the operator can punch in the coordinates of the target to be engaged.

"I know you brought your GPS with you. I saw it in the car; did you bring the rest of it?"

"As a matter of fact, I did; it's in the suitcase back in the barracks."

"Run down there and get it for me. I've got an idea percolating."

Louis went to the parking lot and climbed in the sedan for the quarter-mile ride to the barracks. Within five minutes, he was back at the lab and handed Nathan the box with the goodies.

"Will I get those back? They sure do come in handy, if you know what I mean."

"Probably not, but I can easily replace them," Nathan told him as he started to disassemble the components.

"What can I do?"

"You can fetch us some lunch here on post; I'm starving for a burger and fries."

"Okay, where do I go?"

"When you head out of the parking lot, turn left and about two miles up on the right you can find anything you want. Just don't speed . . ."

"I know I know, they lose their minds over that," Louis said as he completed Nathan's thought.

"The Quantico Café makes a mean greasy cheese burger."

"Sounds good to me; be back shortly," Louis said, walking out the door.

Nathan removed the GPRS transmitter circuitry from Louis' tracking device and managed to fit it inside the interface box of the fire control system. With diagonal cutters, some antenna co-ax, a little solder and a small soldering iron, he managed to place the GPRS receiver in line with the GPS antenna cable of the fire control systems interface box, as well as power the unit from the power supply of the interface box.

Louis returned with the burgers and watched Nathan test the transmitter and receiver to verify they were working, before they began devouring the burgers.

Nathan continued working between bites, wiping his rubber-gloved hands on the paper towels to remove the drippings. Nathan then opened the 1" x 1" square 3 inch long metal enclosure, in line with the interface cables that are used between the remote fire control system console, the GPS and the transmitter, which relays the information to the fire control interface, mounted on the weapons bipod. He took the circuit board he removed from the GPRS tracking receiver and wired it into the small enclosure using a single unused wire he found in the cable. Nathan wired the GPRS transmitter power input to the end of the cable that connects to the fire control system console, and used the end of the cable that attached to the remote fire control system transmitter to provide the ground and complete the circuit.

The pin out diagram of the interface cable indicated pins six and eight were used for ammunition programming. Nathan went to his laptop and accessed the CIA's resources for foreign-built weapons systems, where he found a cross-reference to a Jane's Information Group Manual for the GMG that contained a logic table showing the signaling used with the remote fire control systems interface. Pins six and eight work together as a pair, providing four possible logic combinations used to select and program the ammunition for the GMG.

Over the next 30 minutes, Nathan dug around in the supply cabinets, where they kept an array of integrated circuit components, and located a 7400 basic AND Gate chip. He wired the chip in so that when both pin six and pin eight wires were in the ON, or 5 volt state, the output of the AND Gate switched to 5V, which was enough to power the GPRS transmitter. Within a few minutes, the small circuit board was insulated with shrink tubing and stuffed inside the small metal enclosure of the interface cable. A few minutes later he completed testing to verify when he tied pin six and pin 8 to 5 volts, the transmitter powered up and the receiver buried in the interface box responded to the signal.

He sealed up the small box in the interface cable and sealed the interface box of the GMG's three-axis controller. He carefully placed everything back into the shipping box and the lab technician resealed the box with the original tape, using an adhesive activator, as if it was never opened.

"Louis, you're up."

"Okay, what's next?"

"Return the box to the mailbox company while I dig in on the information you sent me about the owner of the box."

"I'll be back in a couple hours. I got my cell phone if you need me," Louis said as he headed out the door with the box inside the plastic bag. An hour later, he was standing in the store, in front of the same man, and handed him the plastic bag containing the box.

"That was quick."

"We just needed to x-ray it to be sure it wasn't something danger-ous. Just put it back in the PO Box and forget about it."

"That's it, nothing else?"

"That's almost it. We appreciate your cooperation and it will be remembered," Louis told him as he picked up one of the man's busi-ness cards from the counter, wrote his phone number on the back, and handed it to the man. "When the owner of the box picks up his mail, give me a call as soon as he leaves."

"I can do that; sorry about giving you a hard time before."

"No problems, sir, we appreciate your cooperation. Have a nice day."

Louis returned to his car and began the hour-long trek back to Quantico. Along the way he placed a call to Diane at her office that went to voicemail. Louis left a message telling her that he loved her and missed her and to call him when she got a chance. After he hung up he noticed his cell phone indicated that it was 2:35pm. *A day until the funeral,* Louis thought. *Twenty-seven hours from now the shit's gonna hit the fan.*

Louis was back out on Interstate 395 heading south when his cell phone rang. It was Nathan.

"Hey Bro, what's up?"

"Where are you?"

"I'm on 395 heading south toward 95; what's up?"

"At your very next exit, turn around and head back to Seven Corners and check out the address from the index card image you sent me."

"Hang on a minute, I'll be stopped shortly."

Louis, approaching an off ramp, rolled to a stop at the bottom at the red light.

"What's the address?"

"6541 Kerns Rd. in Seven Corners is what's listed, but I can't find power, gas, telephone or cable company records for the address."

"Okay, I'll check it out and let you know what I find, later."

"Later Bro, be safe."

Louis punched the address into the GPS, which routed him back the way he came to Seven Corners, then over surface streets into a heavily wooded neighborhood, where he turned left off Sleepy Hollow Road onto Kerns Road. The GPS indicated 6541 was located on the corner; however, there was no house there, only a lot thick with oak trees. *Looks like a dead end to me,* Louis thought as he parked the car on the side street and looked around. *This is a quiet, tree-lined neighborhood of middle-class homes with attached garages and cars in the driveways, located maybe two miles from the PO Box location.*

Louis' cell phone rang. "Hello?"

"Hey baby, it's me, sorry I missed your call earlier. Been in and out of meetings all day and just got back to my office."

"Hey sweetie, I hope you're having a good day. Wish I was in the sunshine state."

"Where are you?"

"I'm in the giant metropolis of Seven Corners, Virginia tracking down a lead. How is the weather down there?"

As Diane answered, "It's a little cool, in the high 40s I guess," Louis noticed the garage door opening across the street and three doors down from his location.

"The weather here is about the same, but should be colder tomorrow," he told her as he watched an ice cream truck back out of the garage and onto the street.

"Any idea when you'll be coming back?" Diane asked in a tone of loneliness.

"Hopefully by this weekend—not sure just yet but I'm already tired of being here," Louis told her as the truck drove past him and turned right on Sleepy Hollow Road.

"I'll be leaving the office shortly; tonight is my gym night, and I need it."

"Did they make it out to the office to replace the windshield in your car?" Louis asked. "You did remember to call them, didn't you?"

"Yes baby, I called and made the appointment yesterday and they arrived here at the office around 9:30 this morning and replaced the windshield for me."

"Did they charge you anything?"

"Nope, I just signed three forms and they'll bill our insurance for it, and it came with a year warranty from the installers. I didn't know they would provide that."

"Yeah, that's a good company and they make it easy to get a windshield fixed. The year warranty is a bonus as far as I'm concerned," Louis told her.

They continued to chat about this and that, catching up on the small details and filling in the gaps since they last spoke.

"Have you been watching the news?" Diane asked.

"No, we've been really busy and I haven't actually been in front of the TV since we've been here, why do you ask?"

"Well, it's all over the news that three FBI consultants were shot at the J. Edgar Hoover federal building in Washington, and there's another story about Senator Richland's aide, who was found shot to death in his home and there may be some connection between his death and the Senator's," she told him, with a hint of curiosity, knowing he and Nathan might be working on that case.

"I haven't heard a word about it, but they're keeping us busy analyzing data they gathered. I'll have to catch up on the news when I get a chance."

"I just thought maybe you or Nathan knew the inside scoop."

"Sorry baby, nothing to report here. Maybe by the time I get back home I'll know something about it. How is Miss M's new place going?" he asked to change the subject.

"She still putting stuff away and finally received all her new appliances, and the new carpet should be installed any day now."

"I really hope she enjoys her new place; the first home you buy should be memorable."

"I think she loves it. She's making her nest and having fun doing it; that's really what it's all about."

They continued to talk for a few more minutes as Louis pulled out of the neighborhood to begin his trek back to Quantico. They were saying their goodbyes when another call came in on Louis' cell phone. "I love you, baby. I need to let you go so I can answer this other call; call me tonight when you get home from the gym. I love you, bye."

Louis didn't recognize the number displayed on the cell phone. "Hello?"

"Hello, is this the FBI man that asked me to call? You didn't leave your name."

"Yes," Louis replied.

"The man that rents box 121 just left with his mail. You said I should call you."

"Yes sir, thank you for following through; we appreciate your cooperation."

"Should I hang on to your number and call you the next time he should pick up his mail?"

"No sir, there's no need for that; you can just toss the card if you like, but don't mention this to anyone. It may impede our investigation."

"I'll just put the card in the trash then; goodbye."

Okay, so they have the GPS and interface now, Louis thought. *Surely they'll want to test it somewhere before the funeral tomorrow afternoon–that is, if we're on the right track.'*

Twenty-twenty-twenty-four hours to go . . . I want to be sedated . . . Louis thought, singing the Ramones hit to himself, *but we've got plenty to do and places to go before this nightmare concludes.*

25

Louis arrived back at the forensics lab in Quantico 20 minutes later. He removed the vest in the parking lot, storing it in the trunk of the sedan, and retrieved his laptop before entering the building and making his way to the small office, where he found Nathan with his head buried in the screen of his laptop.

"The address was a dead end, just a lot on the corner full of oak trees."

"It was worth a shot; figured it would be a bogus address, given there was no power, cable or phone records attached to it."

"I got a call from the man at the PO Box place; he told me the owner of 121 picked up his mail."

"That's good. We'll know where they are soon enough, when the tracking transmitter goes live."

"Yeah, but how can we track it since you cannibalized the receiver?"

"I have other receivers; one of them is at my house in Huntsville and feeds information to a webpage I set up."

"Oh yeah? Shoot me a link to that page."

"I have the page down at the moment while I update it to plot the transmitter's location on Google Maps; they made it easy as long as you have the longitude and latitude of the transmitter."

"That's cool, so I'll be able to track the locations on my laptop or cell phone until you build me another receiver for the GPS?"

"Exactly."

Nathan completed the modifications to the webpage and called Louis over to his laptop to show him how it worked. "I'll e-mail you the link in just a minute. Just enter the transmitter's ID number in one of these boxes and hit enter. The last known location of the transmitter will be displayed on the map."

"That's cool; you can zoom in and out as you need to for better resolution. How often does it update?"

"Same interval as the other receiver, every five seconds, but with this interface you can enter as many tracking IDs as you want; you can even color code them and add text."

"That's very cool. Too bad all the shooters covering the funeral tomorrow won't have transmitters on them; it would be really easy to identify the shooter that's mixing in."

"That's a great idea, man," Nathan said. "The FBI has tons of small battery-powered GPRS tracking devices; we just need to convince them to quietly issue one to each of the shooters covering the funeral. Let's get Paul Biggins over here and explain the advantage to him; he would be the best bet to get this implemented."

Nathan picked up the phone and entered the five-digit extension number that was automatically forwarded to Paul Biggins' cell phone.

"Agent Biggins, how can I help you?"

"Paul, this is Nathan Malone over the forensics lab; are you in the area?"

"Yes I'm down at building one. What do you need?"

"Can you come up here to the forensics lab? Louis and I need to show you something that could be of immeasurable value during the funeral tomorrow at Arlington."

"Sure, I can be there in about 10 minutes. See you shortly."

"He's on his way," Nathan told Louis. "We can't mention anything about the other tracking device I implanted in the fire control system."

"I agree, let's not open that can of worms until we have to."

Nathan sent Louis the link to the webpage and Louis placed an icon on the main screen of his phone as well as the desktop of his laptop. "Will I have to reenter the tracking IDs when I move from the laptop to my cell phone and back?"

"Nope, when you login to the page it will remember and recall the IDs you were last using."

"That's good; then you give the FBI a separate login for their people to monitor as well."

"Exactly," Nathan replied as he closed the other browser windows on his laptop that he was using to track down Hauser and Hatalsky's whereabouts.

Paul came in the door of the lab and into the small office and leaned against the desk facing Nathan. "What you got for me?"

"Well, it might be better if Louis explained this; it's drawn from his experience."

"Paul, I'm assuming that before and during the funeral tomorrow at Arlington, there'll be sniper over-watch teams in place in and around the cemetery."

"Yes, there will be several of them."

"And I'm assuming those teams will be drawn from multiple agencies?"

"Yes, at least three that I know of."

"FBI, Secret Service and County or State Police sniper teams, I'm assuming."

"You got it, what is this about?" Paul asked.

"Who in all these separate agencies will know the exact locations of each and every assigned sniper team?"

"I can't really go into it, but someone, somewhere will have a list of all the shooters and their assigned locations."

"Okay, that's good, but what if a shooter or shooters, wearing the right uniform, finds a location where an authorized team hasn't been assigned and just blends in, waiting for the opportunity to take a shot?"

"Is that how you would do it, given your background and experience with this?"

"Yes, I would. Hiding in plain sight is hard to detect, even when you're looking for them."

"So what do you recommend we do about that?"

"I'm glad you asked," Louis replied with a smile, "It's our understanding that you have access to a large number of battery-powered GPRS tracking devices such as those used to track suspects or their vehicles or equipment should the need arise."

"Yes, we have a healthy supply of those at most field offices, but using them requires a warrant."

"I don't think you would need a warrant if you issue one to each legitimate sniper team that's assigned to cover the funeral tomorrow, would you?"

"No warrant is needed for that, but what's the advantage in doing it?"

"We have a tracking system that your agents can use on their cell phones or laptops, which would show the exact location of each transponder on Google Maps. Knowing their exact locations would make it very easy to account for them, as well as identifying sniper teams without the tracking device."

Paul furled his brow and shifted his jaw to the right as he thought through what Louis just told him. "So to do this, all we need are the GPRS trackers?"

"Yes, one for every team, issued at the briefing immediately before deployment to their locations, by the supervisors who know them. That way, none of the tracking devices get out into the open and we have a fixed list of tracking IDs to put into the system."

"That's a damn good idea, guys, but my boss will have to clear it with Secret Service first," Paul told them. "I need to call my director right now and explain this; I may need you to go with me and sell the idea if he or the Secret Service has any doubts."

"No problem, that's why you flew me up here from Flat Land."

Paul stepped outside the small office and placed a call on his cell phone that lasted almost 20 minutes before he returned to the office. "Louis, I need you to come with me."

"Sure, where are we headed?"

"We're going to the supply depot, then to DC to sell this to my boss."

"Sounds good, let me get my vest and sport coat out of the car first," Louis said as they exited the building.

Louis climbed into Paul's minivan for the ride to the supply depot that took all of a minute and a half at the speed Paul was driving. As he climbed out of the minivan heading into the depot Louis commented, "I was told the MPs would lose their minds over speeding on post."

"They have to catch me first," Paul said with a serious look on his face as they approached the counter. The Marine Master Sergeant on-duty got up from behind his desk and walked to the counter. "How can I help you gentlemen?" he asked, noticing the urgency in Paul's body language and facial expression.

"I need to draw 15 Mark II tracking transponders and fresh batteries for all of them as quickly as you possibly can process them."

"Let me see where they're located. I'm not sure if we have that number on-hand," the supply sergeant told Paul as he returned to his desk to look up the devices using his inventory software. "You're in luck, I have a brand-new case of 18 back there; I'll be right back."

Paul grabbed the clipboard from the wall and began filling out the disposition form for the requisition, and everything was completed before the supply sergeant returned with the box.

"I need you to fill out a DF for . . ." the Marine began to say before seeing the form Paul slid across the counter to him. "Disregard."

As they walked out the door and climbed in the minivan, Louis said, "I find it amazing how easy it is for you guys to procure such equipment."

"Oh, that's nothing; I can sign for a jet if I need to," Paul replied as he pulled out of the parking lot and turned south, heading to the airport at a high rate of speed.

"I thought we were heading to DC?"

"We are. The chopper should be waiting for us as soon as we arrive."

"Wow, are you guys accepting applications?"

Paul pulled the minivan into a parking space beside the hangar and they walked with the box of tracking devices under Louis' arm, directly to the MD 530 already spun up on the helipad. Once seated in the rear of the helicopter and the doors locked, the pilot lifted off and turned due north, heading for DC. The fight took all of 20 minutes in this fast 'Little Bird' that headed north at 170 miles an hour. They landed at the South Capitol Street heliport and were met by a car that transported them to the J. Edgar Hoover building. Paul led the way as they entered the building, bypassing the security checkpoints and taking the elevator to the 12th floor conference room, where more than 20 suits sat waiting for Paul and Louis to arrive.

Paul walked to the podium at the head of the table as the room went quiet.

"Mr. Director, I'm Special Agent Paul Biggins out of Quantico and the gentleman I walked in with is Louis Parker, one of my special consultants. We're here to brief you on an additional security precaution for tomorrow's funeral at Arlington that we believe will add an additional layer of security and confidence concerning the multi-agency sniper teams to be deployed. Mr. Parker's credentials and experience are spot-on and pertinent to this discussion and he is available to you for questions concerning the application of this technology and its security ramifications."

Paul explained the new application of the familiar tracking devices to the audience of FBI, Secret Service and Police personnel in the room, explaining the simplicity and its enormous advantage in directly addressing the issue of sniper team identification and location. While Paul was speaking, Louis called up the website on the PC in the conference room, used for presentations on the big screen television. Louis activated two of the tracking devices and entered the identification numbers in the application. He placed one at each end of the 30-foot long, bird's-eye maple table.

Within 10 seconds, the location markers appeared on the screen and Louis zoomed in on the federal building's location, at maximum resolution for Google Maps, where both transponders' indicators were clearly visible on the screen. Louis changed the color associated with one of the indicators to demonstrate the ease of identifying sniper teams by individual or group colors. He also entered 'Team 1' and 'Team 2' for the pair of transponders being displayed.

The head of the Secret Service detail asked Louis, "How did you come up with this?"

"Nathan Malone and I were brainstorming on how to account for the sniper teams to ensure no unauthorized shooter, wearing the proper uniform, could gain access to high ground locations, where a shot could be made," he answered after standing and facing the table.

"And we can use this tomorrow, just like that?" another gentleman at the table asked.

"Yes sir, the tracking devices belong to the FBI and we have provided the secure online application that's been in development for other purposes. We can provide you as many access accounts as you could possibly need, and all I need are the transponder IDs that I have here, and the sniper team identifiers to set it up. It takes about one minute per transponder to complete setup, and your agents can use laptops or smart phones to access the application."

"That's it, that's all you need?" the gentleman asked again.

"Yes sir; however, I do have a suggestion on how to deploy these devices."

"You have the floor."

"Tomorrow morning at the final meeting before deployment of the sniper teams, a supervisor who personally knows the individual sniper team members should issue each team one transponder, with the specific instructions that the use of these devices is confidential, and that it is critical the device remains in their possession throughout the day. Agent Biggins, Mr. Malone, or I can enter the transponder IDs, team identifiers and colors for each transponder in the system ahead of time, to verify everything is functioning correctly. Again, this is not new or unproven technology; it's just a new use of existing capabilities to ensure you can specifically identify the location of each sniper team during the funeral, making it easier to identify any additional snipers by direct observation."

"Mr. Parker, would you mind stepping outside the door while we talk this over?"

"Not at all sir, I'll be just outside if you need me," Louis told the director as he walked to the double doors and stepped outside closing the doors behind him. The discussion inside the room was completed and the decision made to use this idea in under eight minutes, and Louis was invited back into the room by Paul, who asked him to take a seat at the PC and set up the application for 12 of the devices. One of the Secret Service agents sat next to Louis as he entered the data and gave him team identifiers and colors for each transponder that the agent numbered with a magic marker from 1 to 12. Everything was set up and functioning 15 minutes later and Louis removed the two units from the software that he used during the demonstration. The Secret Service agent then instructed Louis to create three accounts, one each for FBI, Secret Service and Police use.

The men at the table passed around the devices, watching the screen update as it displayed the locations for each unit. The Secret Service agent gathered all the units, switched them off to conserve the batteries, and told Paul that he would handle issuing the units at the morning briefing. After a few more minutes of conversation, Paul and Louis were on the way back to the helipad for the flight back to Quantico. "That was a great idea you and Nathan came up with today."

"Thanks Paul, I'm glad you listened and sold your bosses on the idea."

"Me too. I may get a positive letter in my jacket because of this."

"Can't have too many of those, I guess."

As the helicopter sped south toward Quantico, Louis stared out the window at the traffic below, thinking, *Man, has the worm turned. I don't recognize myself anymore, briefing the FBI and the Secret Service on how to protect the President–who'd-a-thunk-it?'* The little bird made a rapid descent and touchdown on the helipad at Quantico. Paul and Louis climbed out as the pilot applied the rotor brake, quickly stopping the high-speed rotors as a fuel truck approached. A few minutes later, Paul dropped Louis off at the lab parking lot and headed back to his office. Louis walked into the small office off the main lab, where Nathan was still seated at the desk, with his head down in the computer screen, digging through data from the hard drives while compiling a report of his findings that he would turn over to Paul after the funeral, if all went well.

"You're back; how did it go?"

"Pretty well. I think everything is set up for tomorrow morning when they implement the plan."

"You mean you've been to DC and back already?"

"Yep, it was a quick round-trip in the MD 530 with chauffeur service from the Capitol Street Helipad to the Hoover building."

"What is an MD 530?" Nathan asked.

"It's a high-speed reconnaissance and attack helicopter used by hostage rescue, they call it the little bird, and man, they are fast."

"How many people were in the meeting?"

"20 or so I guess, plus Paul and me."

"Sorry I didn't go along for the ride; sounds like a fun trip."

"It got the job done. What you working on?"

"I'm creating a summary report that ties in all the intelligence and data gathered from hard disks, the bank accounts, the arms shipment and the info on Hauser and Hatalsky."

"When do you plan on handing that in?"

"After the funeral tomorrow, if all goes well; if not, I have another report ready for them."

"Good idea. I have a good feeling about tomorrow. Let's hope my compass is pointing north," Louis said.

"So what are you going to do tomorrow?"

"I'm going to head up to Arlington, early in the morning, and walk the grounds a while."

"I need to stay here and continue working on what they hired me to do."

"It's probably best. We can communicate over the cell phones should we need to. Let me know as soon as the other tracking device goes live, in case I fail to notice it."

"I can do that; I'll probably be here all night working on this stuff anyway, so I'll be in front of the computer in the morning as well."

"You want to grab some dinner later on?" Louis asked.

"Sure, I'll take a break in an hour or two if that's soon enough for you."

"Works for me. I still need to complete the map I was working on, anyway."

They continued to chat back and forth as both worked at their individual laptops. Though both felt the nervous energy and excitement building toward tomorrow's events, neither one mentioned it to the other. There was no need to worry now; either their plan was going to work or not. Anyone could be in on it, there was just no way to tell, and if they tipped their hand too soon, Hauser and Hatalsky could disappear along with the GMG. Louis had supreme confidence in Nathan's abilities, and it went both ways. Nathan knew Louis would take extreme measures to see this through if necessary.

"What are you going to do about a gun for tomorrow?" Nathan asked.

"Got it covered; brought one with me from home."

"I've been wondering about that–not like you to walk around naked."

They both laughed and it broke the tension in the room. Louis was putting the finishing touches on the map of Arlington that noted all of the shooting positions, their ranges and angles, along with the ranges and angles between shooting positions. Though he didn't know the specific locations where the FBI, Secret Service, and police sniper teams were to be deployed, he knew all the available locations that he would choose and he based the map on that.

"Do we have access to a color printer?"

"There's one out in the main lab. The label on the faceplate has the IP address and network name, just add a printer to your laptop using that information and you should be golden."

Louis took his notepad out into the main lab, found the printer, copied down the information from the label and set up the printer. His laptop automatically downloaded the necessary drivers and he was good to go. He printed the map and the job completed before he got back to the printer to retrieve it, then he returned to his desk to review it in case it required changes.

"Take a look at this for me; I'll be giving it to Paul when it's ready."

Nathan studied the map and all the detail Louis included before handing it back to him. "Looks good to me; any details you intentionally left off that may prove useful to them?"

"I didn't include the various ballistics data on the map; the shooters will already know this, and that much detail may prove to be confusing to the trigonometrically challenged."

"You're probably right; it looks fine just like it is, then."

They continued working through their tasks and chatted to pass the time. At 6:30 pm, Paul Billings came walking through the door of the lab.

"I'm heading home for the evening, guys; you need anything before I go?"

"I'm glad you stopped by, Paul. Take a look at this map I've prepared for you. It may be helpful during the briefing in the morning," Louis said as he handed the printout to Paul.

He scanned the map while leaning against the doorjamb and after half a minute looked up at Louis and said, "Where did you get all this data?"

"I went to Arlington and surveyed the area with the equipment you signed out for me."

"You got all of this from one visit to Arlington?"

"Yes, my experience and training may have helped."

"How did you get the section and the grave number for the funeral? That hasn't been published."

"While you're correct that it hasn't been published, it's not exactly a secret, either."

"Come on now, how did you get this information?" Paul insisted.

"I simply asked for it."

"Who did you ask?"

"One of the groundskeepers at Arlington."

"And he just gave you the information?"

"I'm not sure he realized he gave me the information."

"How could he give you the information without realizing he gave you the information?"

"Easy, it's called social engineering. I'm sure you know what I'm talking about."

"Yes I'm familiar with the concept of social engineering; I'm just curious how you applied it to get this information."

"A state funeral is a big event. It's expected that individuals as well as governments will send flower arrangements, both to the capitol where Richland's been lying in state and to Arlington where he'll be buried tomorrow."

"Okay, I'm following you."

"Calls to a local florist to order arrangements for the funeral have been happening all over the city. When speaking to a florist, they willingly give you their names; they are businesspeople and being friendly on the phone is just good customer service."

"Okay, go on."

"With an individual's name and phone number, along with the name of a florist shop, it's easy to call the groundskeepers department at Arlington and ask what they need to do to deliver their truckload of arrangements for the funeral."

"I'm listening."

"Knowing these groundskeepers are going to be ridiculously busy the day of the funeral, one need only construct a question that facilitates an answer that leads to less work on the part of the groundskeeper answering the question."

"What was the question?"

"How should this truckload of arrangements be marked to ensure they're delivered to the correct location for the funeral?"

"That's it, that's the big question? What did he say?"

"Just bring us a copy of your letterhead that indicates delivery to 66, 110 when you bring the flowers; the folks who inspect them will ensure they go to the right location."

"You sneaky bastard," Paul said before laughing, "that's all it took to get the exact location where the leaders of our government will be standing tomorrow afternoon, at a specific time."

"That's it–some secret, huh?"

"Nathan, did you know about this?" Paul asked.

"I. Know. Nothing!" Nathan replied, in his best Sergeant Schultz imitation.

"I didn't tell him, and wouldn't have told you unless you asked. This isn't my first time at the square dance, Paul; I was doing this while you were still convinced girls have cooties."

"I know; your file we pulled from CIA is like a photo negative of a large piece of Swiss cheese it's so redacted," Paul said while shaking his head. "We may know 20% about you and your training and field experience. I'm just glad you're on our side and surprised that you're willing to help us."

"It surprised the hell out of me as well–not really my nature to wear a white hat. Who knew?"

"Nathan knew," Paul said. "He bent us over a barrel to bring you in on this, told me he had better things to do unless you are involved."

"For as long as we've known each other, you'd think he'd know better," Louis said with a grin as he stared at Nathan. "I guess he knew me better than I knew myself."

"Well guys, I need to get out of here. The wife's got dinner on the table and tomorrow's gonna be a big day. I'll make copies of this map for the teams. Thanks for preparing this for us; the life you save may be elected," Paul said with a wink before heading out the door.

"That's why I do this, Bro," Nathan said to Louis.

"Do what?" Louis replied.

"That feeling and sense of purpose you're experiencing right now--that's why I do this."

"The feeling and sense I'm experiencing at this moment is hunger, but I get what you're saying, I really do."

"All right, let's go strap on the feed bag," Nathan said, as he locked his laptop and picked up his keys from the desk, heading toward the door.

"What you feel like tonight?" Nathan asked.

"How about some Mexican food?" Louis replied, "I need carbs, and beer!"

"Sounds good to me, I know a place called Poncho Villa's, just down the road in Stafford; may take us 15 minutes to get there."

Nathan and Louis knew not to speak openly in the car, so they listened to the radio while heading south to the restaurant in Stafford. The talk-radio host was taking calls concerning this night's topic, which was a discussion about the ongoing investigation of Senator Richland's assassination and the killings that followed, as well as the ongoing manhunt that had produced no results to this point. The host's premise was that the FBI was dragging their feet deliberately, which allowed the killers to easily escape the country. This caused the blood of his audience to boil and his phone lines to be jammed with two camps of callers; the conspiracy theorists, for whom everything boils down to, or is based in government cover-up and conspiracy; and the apologist, who feel the need to express how overburdened and underfunded the FBI finds itself, thus excusing their supposed ineptitude.

"They really don't have a clue, do they?" Nathan said.

"They really never do, and why look for one? That may diminish the ratings bonanza they're shooting for in the first place," Louis replied. "The reality would be a much more interesting story, but would appeal to a much smaller audience."

"I guess you're right, the way they're playing this out, ping-ponging the callers from the opposite camps, trying to one-up each other is all that's keeping it going."

"Welcome to the modern world, where immediacy in the media and immediate global communications allow any idiot to express their unqualified opinion to the entire world, without having to actually think it through beforehand."

"There's the restaurant," Nathan said, pulling into the parking lot.

They entered the modest establishment and were shown to a booth. The half-populated dining room was filled with mouthwatering south of the border aromas and decorated with Christmas lights, ornate sombreros and velvet masterpieces. The hostess placed their menus on the table. "Your waiter will be with you in a moment," she told them before hurrying back to the front door to repeat the process over and over again.

"What's good here?" Louis asked as he picked up the menu and began scanning it for the carb-loaded entrées he loved.

"I've eaten here twice," Nathan said. "Both times the food was excellent and the beer is frosty cold."

A few minutes later, a thin young Mexican man dressed in black, wearing a white apron appeared at the edge of their table and asked in a quiet voice, "What for you to drink?" as he sat a basket of hot chips and salsa on the table.

Louis found the beer offerings on the menu and said, "I would like a very cold Negra Modelo and a tall glass of unsweetened iced tea."

"I'll take the same," Nathan added before the man hurried away to the bar.

"So tell me about the briefing up in DC."

"We walked into the large conference room and there were 20 or so suits seated at this beautiful Bird's-eye Maple table that must've been 30 feet long and 8 feet wide at the middle. Paul walked up to the podium, introduced himself, and went into his spiel, pretty much what I told him at the lab. I called up the app on the conference room PC and displayed it on the big screen television with a couple of the tracking devices active so they could see them working."

"Did they ask you any questions about it?"

"Yeah, one of the Secret Service bigwigs seemed very surprised at how simple to implement the whole thing was; I basically paraphrased what Paul just told them and demonstrated how easy it was to set up and they were sold on it. They did ask me to leave the room for a few minutes while they discussed it. Since it came with no price tag, it probably confused them," Louis said with his smart-ass grin.

"I wish I'd been there with you. Did you get a feel for their attitude or temperament; did they seem nervous about tomorrow?"

"They were all pretty quiet and asked pointed questions. There was an air of urgency but not what I would call nervousness. These aren't the guys that will be surrounding the Top Two tomorrow; it was their bosses, and they have to exude confidence even if they're scared shitless that someone will expose their incompetence."

The waiter brought the beers and the iced tea to the table and took their orders.

"I'll have the Grande Chicken Burrito with the rice and refried beans," Louis told him.

"I'll have the Chicken Enchiladas with rice and beans," Nathan said. "Can you bring us some of your white cheese dip as well?"

The waiter scratched the information down on his pad and disappeared into the kitchen while Nathan and Louis enjoyed the beer and continued talking.

"I didn't mean to dismiss what you said back at the lab," Louis told Nathan. "I guess I was just deflecting, but I do get what you're saying;

it's nice to be needed, and be listened to by serious people again. The corporate bullshit I tried to exist in for so long really did a number on me; made the PTS much worse the longer it went on."

"Over the past couple years, I could see the enormous stress you were under, watched it ebb and flow as you changed jobs, where it started over again. To tell you the truth, I was always worried you would snap and off yourself, or everybody in the vicinity."

"Nah, that's a postal worker thing. Thoughts of suicide have become so common to me I just let them pass on through without dwelling on it. I know my brain chemistry and wiring were permanently altered long ago. To normal healthy brains, suicidal thoughts are disturbing; at this point, they carry about the same importance as junk mail to me, so I just throw it out and see what comes tomorrow."

"I'm glad to hear that; I'd hate to have to attend your funeral, but I'd do it."

"Same goes for me, man; let's wait until we've been farting dust for 20 years before making those arrangements," Louis said with a big grin.

The waiter appeared at the table carrying a large tray of steaming hot plates and sat them in front of Nathan and Louis with the usual warning. They both reached for the hot sauce to paint their meals and dug in, while the booth filled with the wonderfully seasoned aromas of hot tortillas, beans and cheese, along with the succulent chicken in the entrées.

"Man, this is some good eating," Nathan said before flooding his throat with iced tea.

"The food is fabulous. Great suggestion; this should produce a musical ride back to the barracks," Louis said with a laugh. "You gotta love hot Mexican food."

There was little conversation at the table during the meal, except for ordering additional beer from the waiter. They took their time and enjoyed every bite, along with the chips, cheese, and beans they ate like a dip. After an hour or so in the restaurant, they paid the tab, walked out to the parking lot, and climbed in the car for the ride back to Quantico. They again listened to the talk radio show that was still in progress, with the same misguided callers expressing the same shallow opinions about the same misinformed facts of the situation.

"This is almost comical, layer after layer of conspiracy and apology with no end in sight. Just imagine the number of listeners who may be taking in this garbage, while thinking there is an air of truth in it because it's broadcasted," Nathan said with interruptions of laughter.

"If you think that's funny, you're gonna love the next one," Louis said as they approached the main gate at Quantico.

"Next one? What the hell are you talking about?" Nathan asked, noticing that Louis was holding his stomach and leaning forward in the seat with a focused look of pain on his face. "Tell me you're not about to. . ." he said before Louis let fly a Mexican Food and Beer fart that shook the front seat, drowning out the radio with a distinctive flap, flap, flap repetition that completed the barrage.

"Damn, Bro," Nathan exclaimed, laughing, "that sounded like you were shuffling bologna over there." Both burst out laughing and hit the down switches on their windows simultaneously, while Nathan rolled up to the MP standing at the main gate.

Still laughing, Nathan handed their IDs to the MP that bent over to look inside the window toward Louis, before rapidly withdrawing his head with an expression of shock and awe distorting his face. "Chemical weapons are not allowed on this facility, sir," the MP barked, then hesitated, before he too began to laugh and shake his head, then signaled the other MP to open the barrier. They laughed all the way back to the barracks and stood outside the car wiping away the tears streaming down their cheeks. "You ain't right," Nathan said, "you shot me with my mouth open back there, you sum bitch."

"I'd leave the windows down overnight if I was you," Louis said. "Crap, I gotta drive that thing in the morning."

"Crap's about right if you ask me, and the MP you ambushed!"

They stood around and laughed a few minutes, now void of the stress that had been building for days, enjoying their adolescent flashback, before heading to their rooms for the night.

26

The cell phone alarm went off at 5:00 am, Louis immediately sat up having passed the night with short catnaps and meditation to defocus his mind as the hours crawled past. After showering and shaving, he took a beta-blocker, knowing this might be an adrenaline-pumping day. He placed his hand against the window to gauge the temperature outside; it was cold to the touch. Louis put the vest over his T-shirt, and then dressed in dark-colored slacks and shirt, his shoulder holster with his 40 caliber Glock, and his heavy leather bomber jacket.

He hung his FBI credentials around his neck and collected everything he needed before locking his room. Louis stood in the hallway between his room and Nathan's for a moment, as he donned the leather gloves he kept in a pocket of the jacket, and stared at Nathan's door for several moments before knocking. When Nathan didn't open the door, he remembered that he planned to spend the night working in the lab. Louis got in the sedan and started the engine, allowing it to warm up a bit before turning on the heater. He dialed Nathan's cell phone before pulling out of the parking lot.

"Hey man."

"Have you been up there all night working?"

"Yeah, I came back up here about one o'clock; couldn't sleep anyway, and I got a lot done."

"Has the tracking device gone active?"

"Let me check, hang on a second," Nathan said as he opened the browser. "Damn, it went active just after midnight for less than a minute, but it stayed in the same location."

"Where was it when it went active?"

"It was in the parking lot at Towers Park, between the basketball and tennis courts. Just open the site on your cell phone; it's easy to find."

"I'm leaving Quantico now and should be there by 6:30 am, if traffic's not too bad and I can fly low."

"Be safe, man; call me later."

Once out on I-95 Louis flew north, maintaining close to 90 miles an hour, all the way to the I-395 connector, where he took state road 27 around the south end of Arlington, exiting on Columbia Pike and turning right on Scott, which led to Towers Park. He parked the car alongside the road and walked the couple hundred feet to the park, in case Hauser or Hatalsky were there, knowing a government motor pool vehicle would catch their attention. There were several small cars in the parking lot that separated the tennis courts from the basketball court, but no sign of a vehicle capable of carrying the GMG.

Louis walked through the park and checked all the adjacent parking lots on foot, finding nothing of the size necessary to conceal the large grenade launcher. He walked back to his car in the cold morning air, as the sun was rising to reveal the heavy, overcast sky that hung in place with no perceivable wind.

Perfect day for a funeral, Louis thought as he climbed back in the car and made his way back to Columbia Pike, heading toward the maintenance entrance of the cemetery. He parked the sedan near the exit of the parking lot and walked to the security gate that was already manned by Secret Service and FBI personnel, as well as a police dog teams. Louis approached the gate, displaying his credentials, and was stopped and questioned by the Secret Service detail.

"What's your business here this morning, sir?"

"I'm a contract special investigator assigned to the FBI security detail, reporting to Special Agent Paul Biggins out of Quantico. I'm responsible for the sniper threat assessment map in this morning's briefing."

"Wait here a moment, sir, I need to make a call before allowing you through the gate," the agent told Louis, stepping away to talk over his headset in private. Louis stood there patiently with his hands crossed in front of him, observing the security detail going through their motions with predictable repetition.

"Sir, Agent Biggins indicated the briefing will be held over at the Pentagon; why do you need access to the cemetery this morning?" the agent asked, challenging Louis.

"Just being thorough. I want to make sure I haven't missed anything, and that nothing's changed since I produced the map; I'll only be here a few minutes before heading over to the briefing."

Again, the agent communicated through his headset, talking into his left sleeve and awaiting clearance from his decision authority before allowing Louis to pass.

"Okay sir, you've been cleared." The agent leaned in close to Louis and said, "Wyoming is the password, in case you need to reenter the area after the briefing."

"I appreciate the heads-up," Louis told him, then walked through the security gate and around the metal detector that was positioned next to the concrete barriers, which were put in place overnight in the common S shaped pattern. Louis walked straight across Patton drive, into the section closest to the maintenance area, and made his way across the field among the 64 parallel rows of perfectly aligned headstones and trees.

He arrived at the other side of the section and walked through the trees that lined both sides of Arnold drive and separated the two cemetery sections, and into section 66, and continued toward plot 110, located just north of the path that cuts diagonally across the section. The only sound to be heard in the cemetery was coming from the backhoe that was making its way up Eisenhower drive, at a slow pace, on its way to remove the dirt that would create Richland's grave.

Louis turned slowly, studying the horizon, noticing the newly constructed towers in the tree lines, which would serve as camera platforms for the network coverage of the funeral. While standing quietly among the acres of three-foot tall white headstones, he was thinking, *Richland doesn't belong here; traitors shouldn't be buried among heroes, even if they were Senators.* He read the inscriptions on the tombstones on either side of what was soon to be Richland's grave and wondered what they would think if they knew who was about to be planted next to them in this hallowed ground.

Louis looked down at his feet and studied the ground and the low-cut grass, so carefully manicured and orderly, when he noticed what appeared to be a small hole near one of the headstones adjacent to the plot. *Must be were someone crammed a flower vase into the ground,* Louis thought as he stepped closer to take a look. *What's that in the hole?* He bent over to take a closer look and noticed a shiny, rounded metallic object, about 3 inches below the surface of the soft ground, when he realized what he was looking at was the projectile body of a 40 mm practice grenade, which buried itself upon impact. Louis stood next to the hole and took out his cell phone to call Nathan as the backhoe was approaching his location.

"Hey man, what's up?"

"Do me a favor; calculate the range from where the tracking device went active to the center of section 66 at Arlington."

"Hold on a minute while I adjust the map, where's section 66?"

"You see the intersection of Washington Boulevard and Columbia Pike?"

"Hang on, okay, I got it."

"There's a small group of buildings on the north side of that intersection."

"I see them."

"Just north of there is a section of the graveyard with a dirt road that cuts diagonally across from southeast to northwest; the perimeter of the section is Arnold Dr., Bradley Dr., Eisenhower Dr. and MacArthur Dr. Give me the range to the center of that section 20 feet north of the diagonal dirt road."

"Okay, let me zoom out and measure it," Nathan said, and then answered, "Best estimate is . . . about 4000 feet."

"What's 1500 m? 4900 feet or so, that's easily inside the effective range of the GMG," Louis said.

"What's going on?"

"I just found a practice grenade buried in the ground, less than 5 feet from where the grave's being dug. They must have fired it when the transponder went hot."

"It shouldn't have gone hot if they selected a practice grenade; I wired it so it would go hot when High Explosive was selected on the console."

"That could be a problem then," Louis replied, "unless. . ."

"Unless what?"

"Unless the console switch was already on HE when they powered it up."

"That would make sense," Nathan said. "The tracking device was on for only a few seconds before it shut down. If the selector switch was on HE, and then they selected a practice round before firing, that would account for the short transmitter burst and the practice round you found."

"Let's hope that's the case. What's the radio link range for the remote console on the GMG?"

"Hang on, I saved the link to the Jane's page. Just a second...it looks like 2 miles line of sight but less than that in the environment around there."

"I think we can count on the console being at an elevated position; that should help, and I bet that's how they test fired it. Damn, they must've done all this last night. I need to head over to the Pentagon for the briefing; it starts in 30 minutes. Thanks for the help, man; later."

Louis bent over, extracted the practice round from the small hole, slipped it into his jacket pocket, and watched as the backhoe operator gracefully carved out the hole inside the template they laid out on the ground. He walked down the dirt path back to the paved road along the edge of the section and proceeded back to the maintenance building with a quick step.

He exited through the same security gate where he entered, and acknowledged the Secret Service agent with a nod as he passed by on the way to the car. The short drive over to the Pentagon parking lot took six minutes in the morning traffic. He found a parking space before removing the holster and gun and locking them, and the practice round, in the glove box. Louis entered the Pentagon through the door between the Memorial and the construction area, where he encountered Paul, who just entered the building as well.

"Good morning."

"Morning Louis, you've been busy already, I hear," Paul said as they passed through the security queue.

"Yeah, I couldn't sleep. I got an early start so I could look the area over, one more time."

"Anything new to add to the map?"

"Nope, the grave is still in the same location and the place is locked down tight."

"We're in this first conference room on the left; we have a few minutes yet. I'll join you in a minute, need to hit the head first."

Louis walked into the auditorium-sized room and took a seat near the back, scanning the small groups of uniformed men that were standing and talking at various locations around the room. All of them appeared to have a copy of his map and were now discussing it. Paul came through the door, walked down front, and took a seat.

Shortly thereafter, a gray-haired man in gray fatigues walked to the microphone. "If everyone would please take seats, we can get started." He handed the microphone to another man in a dark blue suit to begin the briefing.

"Good morning, everyone, I hope you all are wearing your thermal underwear. It's going to get cold out there at your various positions. I see you all have the additional handout provided by Agent Biggins this morning. This map is a good reference for us and integrates the various nest locations with a lot of useful information, pertinent to today's mission.

"We're implementing a new procedure this morning, which for the first time will allow us to track your specific locations throughout the day. The goal of this procedure is not to track you per se, but to help us identify exactly who is where, so the observers can easily identify any potential shooters attempting to blend in. Each team will be given one of these tracking devices that will remain powered up and with you all day. These devices show up on a web-based tracking application provided by Special Agent Biggins' team of specialized consultants out of Quantico; his team produced the map as well. Handout number one details your assigned nest locations and call signs for today's mission, which of course is 'over watch.'

"I know I don't have to remind you, but I'm going to anyway—you all know the procedure. Don't watch the funeral through your scopes, continually scan your assigned fields of fire and watch the funeral on the news when you're not on the clock this evening. It's going to be a busy day, with hundreds of limousines coming and going, hundreds of potential targets on the field at Arlington. POTUS will arrive just before commencement by limousine, not in the procession from the capitol with the hearse; the decoy limousine will be in the procession. Maximum exposure is expected to be during his brief eulogy at the podium."

The briefing continued for another 15 minutes. Louis accessed the app on his smart phone, where he could clearly make out all of the assigned tracking devices that were handed out. The red indicators were Secret Service, the blue ones were FBI and the white ones were Police sharpshooters. Louis thought, *The text floating next to the indicators looks rather crowded on the screen, with all of them in one tight location; once zoomed-out to cover the entire area where the teams will be located, it'll be easier to read.*

The briefing wrapped up just before 9:00 am, and Louis headed out the door to grab a bite of breakfast, knowing the Pentagon cafeteria would be packed, and that the food served there just wouldn't cut it. He remembered the last time he ate there, and the horror stories continued to emerge to this day, though the food-service contractor had changed a few times. Louis climbed back in the sedan after slipping back into his shoulder holster with the bomber jacket over it and left the Pentagon parking lot.

He drove directly south, passing under I-395, and turned left on Army Navy Drive for the short hop to the Penta City Café and a hot breakfast, during which he took the opportunity to read the Post's morning edition. The big news of the day, besides the economy and Wall Street's efforts to kill it, was the photo exposé of Richland's coffin in the Capitol rotunda. The hundreds of visitors that streamed past which included Richland's wife, along with her sons and their families, Senators and Congressmen, the President and First Lady, the Vice President and Second Lady, lower government officials and dignitaries of every stripe, and representatives from the various embassies located in Washington.

The long-winded op-ed piece detailed Richland's life and his enormous contributions to the American people, his long years of service and dedication to this country. But they left out the millions he accumulated while laundering drug money out of Southeast Asia and Central America, and the private team of assassins that he and Thomaston were funding to pull off their own coup d'état. Of course, the balance of the information was not yet known to the press, but it would be by the end of the day.

Louis paid the check, took the paper with him, returned to the car and drove to the small park where the tracking device was previously activated. He backed into a parking space next to the basketball court and again took a walk through the park to check out the adjacent parking lots, on the lookout for a vehicle that could conceal and support the GMG. The tracking application on his smart phone indicated the sniper teams were already in their nests, and all 12 of the issued tracking devices were active and updating, marking six locations within the cemetery itself, with three positions on the Pentagon wall facing the cemetery and three nests on top the Air Force buildings on Foxcroft Heights.

While walking back to the car, and still 200 yards away, he spotted an ice cream truck that made a U-turn in the parking lot where his car was parked and headed back out toward Columbia Pike at a quick clip.

That looked like the same ice cream truck, he thought, *the one that passed me while tracking down the address.* Louis ran at full speed from the adjacent parking lot and across the park to his car, arriving there some 40 seconds later, jumped in the car and flew toward Columbia Pike in an effort to catch up to the truck which was nowhere in sight.

He turned right on Columbia Pike and slowed at each intersection, looking both ways for the truck, before proceeding to the next.

At S. Walter Reed Drive, he stopped momentarily, looking both directions for the truck, and ensured he could safely run the red light. He nailed the accelerator from his left turn lane position, proceeded across Walter Reed Drive and continued searching all the way to S. Glebe Rd., where he made a U-turn and headed back east on Columbia Pike toward the Pentagon.

He searched through the neighborhoods on the south side of Columbia Pike west of Interstate 395 and even searched the parking lots of the Army Navy Country Club directly to the south of the neighborhoods. *Ice cream trucks just don't disappear like that,* he thought, *and nobody would be buying ice cream in this weather. That has to be them; the extended top of that thing could easily be modified with a large cut out the GMG can fire through.*

Louis called Nathan to pass along the info. "Hey man, are you watching the screen, looks like the snipers are deployed already," Nathan said, conveying his excitement.

"Yeah, I saw that. I also saw the vehicle, I believe."

"Oh yeah? What kind of vehicle was it?"

"It's a white ice cream truck with multicolored balloons painted on it. I believe I saw the same truck when I was searching for the address over in Seven Corners. It pulled out of a garage and drove past me while I was on the phone the other day."

"Do you remember which house it came out of?"

"Yes, and I recall thinking how curious it was to have an ice cream truck parked in a residential garage. He came out of the third house down from the corner on the north side of the street. That's got to be Hauser or Hatalsky' home or safe house."

"I'll track it down online and let you know what I find."

"Thanks, I'm going to continue searching for the truck before checking out the sniper nest a little closer. Keep an eye on the tracking screen and call me the moment you get a blip from the tracking device of the console. Later, man."

"I'll do it; later."

Louis returned to Washington Boulevard and drove northwest past the buildings and lots that form the western edge of the cemetery, scouring each parking lot before moving to the next. *They have to stay within 1500 m of the burial site,* he was thinking, *so that limits their options somewhat.*

Finding nothing on the west side of the cemetery, he headed back south on Washington Blvd. and continued around the southern end of the cemetery to search the dozens of parking areas located around the Pentagon and the Marina at Lady Bird Johnson Park.

It was 11:00 am when he passed by the maintenance entrance to the cemetery. He noticed the line of florist delivery vans and network news trucks, already in queue, awaiting access to the grounds in order to set up, ahead of the funeral scheduled for 2 pm. *I'm glad I'm not working that security detail,* he thought. *What a pain the ass that would be.*

Louis' phone rang; it was Nathan. "What's up, man?"

"I located the address of the house you described, third house on the north side the street from the corner. It's owned by Hatalsky' ex-wife; she got it in the divorce two years before she mysteriously disappeared. The property is still in probate."

"I understand how ex-wives can mysteriously disappear; it's kind of a fantasy of mine."

"Police records indicate the report of a stolen ice cream van two months ago that has yet to be found–by the police, anyway."

"That's got to be it. I've been searching the neighborhoods around the cemetery and I'm driving through the Pentagon's northern parking lots right now, but there's no sign of it yet."

"What are you going to do if you find it?"

"I've been thinking about that. I may just ram it broadside and try to flip it over on its side."

"I'm sure that would be satisfying, but can your back take another high-speed car crash?"

"You're probably right. I didn't really consider that; guess I'll just call in the location and you can report it directly into the cop's database. Will that alert the cops on patrol?"

"It will if I enter it as a BOLO with armed and dangerous, along with an eyewitness sighting indicating the location."

"That would get the GMG and one of them, but the other would still be in play," Louis said.

"That's true, but if our original plan works, it negates the need to locate the GMG anyway."

"Good point, I just hate leaving a weapon like that in the open. I'm going to check one more location before heading back to visit the sniper nests; keep your eyes on the screen for me, later."

"Later, Bro."

Louis exited the northern parking lots of the Pentagon and continued north on Washington Blvd. exiting at Lady Bird Johnson Memorial Park on Columbia Island where he methodically checked every parking area around the marina and the park south of the Arlington Memorial Bridge.

At 12:15, Louis headed back to the cemetery. His credentials and the fact he was driving an FBI motor pool vehicle gained him access to the parking area for the maintenance buildings. He retrieved his binoculars from the trunk of the car before walking past the long line of vehicles still in queue outside the security barrier, and approached a different Secret Service agent now manning the checkpoint.

Louis walked up to the agent, displaying his credentials, and the agent asked him, "How can I help you, sir?"

"I'm a contract special investigator assigned to the FBI security detail, reporting to Special Agent Paul Biggins out of Quantico, with Wyoming," Louis told him.

"Thank you sir, you may proceed through the security gate," the agent said as he entered Louis' name on his clipboard.

Louis walked around the metal detector and through the security gate and passed the area set aside for the trucks were delivering the floral arrangements. Security personnel were going over every arrangement with metal detectors and explosives sniffers while dog handlers walked back and forth among the arrangements and inside the delivery vehicles. Network news vans were being guided into position and set up along Arnold Drive between Marshall and MacArthur. Technicians were using small carts to transport the heavy camera equipment, mounts, cables and wireless transmitters to their assigned camera positions in the towers around section 66.

Louis walked toward the first sniper nest on the third level of the first tower, located inside the corner of Arnold and Eisenhower drives. He stopped about 100 yards to the east of the position and uncapped the binoculars to look at the nest, located some 30 feet in the air and approximately 10 feet above the camera position below. As he scanned upward on the tower, stopping at the nest, he found himself looking down the barrel of the sniper, watching him through the scope.

Louis released his right hand from the binoculars and presented a short salute to the sniper, who returned the acknowledgment with his right hand from the brim of his cap. Louis lowered the binoculars, walked toward the tower, and stopped at the base, identifying himself to the police officer charged with guarding the tower. A few moments later Louis started up the ladder on the side of the tower and arrived at the top, where he took a seated position next to the spotter between him and the shooter.

"How's it going, guys? I saw you in the briefing this morning at the Pentagon."

"We're doing okay, I guess; be doing better if the sun was out," the spotter said before turning to the scope and continuing his scan. "How can we help you, sir?"

"I'm the joker that made the map that was handed out in the briefing. Just checking the positions; can I get you guys anything?"

"You made the map? Good work. It's helpful, I guess, probably more so for the outer ring of shooters."

"Must be nice knowing you're in the field of fire of the nests behind you."

"It just makes our day," the spotter said without looking up from his scope, clearly conveying his dislike of the situation.

"Okay guys, I'm outta here; you'll see me all over the place before the day is over. Go easy," Louis said as he started down the ladder, thinking, *There's another job I wouldn't want to be doing today.*

Once he reached the bottom of the tower, he walked directly west to the tree line of the hill located west of section 66. Again, he stopped and glanced at the nest with the binoculars, and again found himself being watched through the rifle scope of the shooter, as well as the spotting scope. This nest was on a platform just 6 feet off the ground, but had a clear field of fire to the area below.

"The guys in the tower 200 yards east of you asked me to remind you not to shoot them in the ass if you can avoid it," he said to the team, which responded with a laugh.

"We've got them marked on the map and the handy-dandy online site allows us all to see one another; we could've used this years ago."

"Glad you find it useful; that's why we made it available, along with the printed map."

"You're the guy who did this? I mean the map and the website?"

"Yes, my partner and I put those together; glad to see you're using them."

"Hey man, this is good stuff, thanks!"

"Thanks, I appreciate that. Got to go; more nests to visit. Go easy, guys."

Louis spent the next 30 minutes visiting all the nests inside the cemetery before heading back to the Pentagon and the three sites along the west wall with the longest shots to the grave site. Only two of the nests saw clear fields of fire to the grave; the third team was assigned to scan the road leading into the cemetery and the maintenance area.

Louis made it through the security checkpoint at Foxcroft Towers and up to the roof at 1:30 pm, spending a minute or two at each sniper team position before surveying the entire area through his binoculars.

The roads leading from the main gate at Arlington all the way back to section 66 were lined with limousines, and the area around the plot was now densely populated with those attending the funeral service who were awaiting the arrival of the motorcade with the hearse and family.

The honor guard was in place for the military honors funeral, and the network coverage was already underway. The area adjacent to the grave and behind the small speaker's podium was covered in flowers and wreaths, with the white headstones mixed in among them. Louis scanned the area with the binoculars, as well as the western Pentagon wall and the tops of the small buildings dotted here and there, looking for signs of a shooter.

He looked to the southeast at the small tower above the Bed, Bath & Beyond, seeing nothing out of place or any different than he'd seen during his site visit. He turned his attention to the tall Y-shaped RiverHouse building across the Highway and across Joyce Street from the small tower, where he spotted a white hard hat just visible above the top edge of the enclosure surrounding the air-conditioning systems on the northernmost leg of the building.

There shouldn't be anyone up there at this time, he thought. *That roof should be locked down by Secret Service.*

Louis made his way back to the stairs that accessed the roof of the building on Foxcroft Heights and ran down the five flights of stairs, exiting the building through the entrance nearest the security checkpoint, and back to his car.

He sped out of the parking lot, turning south on Columbia Pike and nailed the accelerator all the way to S. Joyce Street. He locked the brakes and again nailed the accelerator, performing a power slide through the right hand turn and quickly accelerating toward the RiverHouse parking lot entrance, where he came sliding to a stop just outside the main entrance to the building.

Louis ran through the front door and turned left down the long hallway, heading toward the center section of the building where the freight elevator was located, and where at least one Secret Service Agent should have been posted to prevent access to the elevator that led to the roof of the building.

He turned the corner to the left to find the door of the elevator unguarded and the Secret Service seal on the door broken. He pressed the button to call the elevator and placed his ear against the door to listen for sounds indicating the elevator was moving.

Louis glanced at his watch, noticed it was 1:55 pm, and realized that the funeral procession was already within the cemetery grounds, and so would be the Top Two any moment.

He waited nervously as the 20 seconds that it took for the elevator doors to open marched painfully by. He jumped through the crack in the door as soon as he could fit, reached for, pressed and held the button for roof access.

The doors to the elevator closed in slow motion it seemed, as Louis noticed the large gray trash bin on wheels in the far corner of the large freight elevator.

Still holding the button, he leaned over to look inside the bin and spotted the tip of a black leather dress shoe protruding above the cardboard in the bin.

He released the button, stepped over to the bin, and moved the cardboard away to find a Secret Service Agent, shot twice in the chest, with no pulse at his carotid artery.

He quickly searched the agent for his radio and weapon, but they were gone.

Louis removed the Glock from his shoulder holster and chambered a round before digging his cell phone from his pocket and attempting to call Paul Billings, but there was no phone service in the elevator.

The elevator came to a stop and the doors opened on the roof. Louis quickly glanced outside the elevator door, looking for the shooter he knew would be on the roof.

He exited the elevator and rapidly turned and aimed his pistol toward the roof above the elevator, in case the shooter had the high ground.

Louis backed away from the elevator and toward the north end of the building where he'd seen the white hard hat, watching for a shooter, now convinced he wasn't above him.

He proceeded down the center-line of the building, toward the air conditioner enclosure, holding his pistol in front of him in his right hand, braced with his left hand, still clutching his cell phone.

Louis crossed the 100 or so feet to the enclosure rapidly and moved to the opening on the right side of the enclosure, where he spotted a man wearing the hard hat.

He was sitting on top of the air conditioning unit and peering over the top edge of the enclosure with binoculars, with his right hand resting on the remote fire control system console.

Louis was stepping to the right on the gravel-covered roof and preparing to shoot when his cell phone rang.

The man in the hard hat quickly turned toward the sound of the phone as Louis squeezed off a shot that struck the man above his right cheekbone behind his eye, slamming him against the enclosure wall.

Louis placed the cell phone to his ear as he approached the firing console where the man had been sitting, but was now collapsed below the enclosure wall covered with his brains. It was Hauser.

"Kind of busy," Louis said as he looked at the fire control console screen that was displaying a large flashing red "8".

"The transmitter went live 30 seconds ago; where are you?"

Louis turned 180° and ran at full speed back toward the elevator, when he felt the high velocity impact against his chest.

It stopped his forward motion 60 feet from the elevator, flipping him rapidly onto his back as he noticed the rifle in the hands of the shooter on top of the elevator enclosure.

Louis instinctively sat up, raising his pistol toward the shooter, when a high explosive grenade detonated just above the fire control system console, 40 feet behind him.

In the fleeting second it took him to reacquire his target and fire, he watched his round strike the shooter's abdomen while the shooter was stumbling backward from the grenade's blast.

The shockwave disoriented Louis, as everything went silent from the enormous concussive explosion that instantly robbed him of his hearing.

A second high explosive grenade detonated above the fire control console, spraying hot shrapnel over the roof. The explosion threw Louis over on his stomach as he was attempting to stand.

The third grenade detonated, sending its fragmented shrapnel ripping through everything in range of the blast, including Louis.

Louis lay there on the gravel roof, face down and unconscious for half a minute, as the remaining five H.E. grenades arrived and detonated before he regained consciousness and gasped the air back into his lungs that the concussive explosions expelled.

He struggled to his feet, falling twice, while trying to regain his balance to make it to the elevator enclosure, before the shooter could get off another round.

Louis leaned against the enclosure wall, and slid his way toward the back side, his pistol leading the way, leaving a thick blood trail on the wall, still unable to hear and relying only on his instincts, and blurred and rapidly dimming vision.

He quick-peeked around the corner of the enclosure where he saw the shooter. It was Hatalsky, sitting flat on his butt with his legs extended wide, attempting to extract a pistol from its holster.

Louis stepped away from the edge of the enclosure with the Hatalsky in his sights.

Hatalsky managed to draw his pistol and looked up to see Louis aiming at him.

In the milliseconds it took him to think it over, he moved the pistol toward Louis.

Louis released two quick shots, striking Hatalsky on the right side of his chest below the collarbone and his abdomen.

Hatalsky lunged over toward his left side, releasing the pistol that slid across the gravel roof away from him.

Louis stood there for a few seconds, prepared to shoot again, before approaching the lifeless body to ensure he was dead.

Returning his pistol to the holster, he dropped his right arm to his side and attempted to stand up straight, to find that he couldn't do it.

He looked down at his left arm hanging at his side and realized he couldn't move it, or even feel it.

Staggering back toward the elevator enclosure, he leaned against the wall and tried to take a deep breath. That's when the sharp, crushing pain in his chest became apparent.

Louis looked down, finding the bullet hole on the left side of his chest that penetrated the bomber jacket an inch left of the zipper of the open jacket.

He pulled the left side of the jacket open and found the bullet hole in his shirt that he pried open, letting the buttons fly.

The vest below the shirt took all the energy it could absorb before the bullet tore through, penetrating Louis' chest.

Louis could feel his breathing becoming shallower with each strained gasp for air, and felt the warm blood seeping beneath the vest and across his abdomen to his groin.

He slid along the wall, then back to where he was shot, looking for his cell phone to call for help.

Louis found the phone and staggered backwards, falling against the wall of the enclosure, trying to focus his eyes on the damaged screen.

The call from Nathan was still connected, and Louis tried to talk to him but realized he couldn't hear Nathan's voice.

"I'm shot, I can't hear you. I'm on the roof of the building next to the elevator. I need help, Bro, I need help."

Louis slid down the wall and sat with his legs extended in front of him, the pain from the shrapnel in his back and legs becoming excruciatingly apparent, trying to speak to the cell phone, becoming weaker with every hard-fought breath, defeated by the sucking chest wound.

"I can't hear you, Bro, I'm shot," he said, coughing out blood, and then pulling the phone from his ear to look at the screen to find the call was disconnected.

Dialing 911 with his thumb, he watched the screen until the call connected. "I need help, I've been shot, I can't hear, I need help . . . ," was all he could say before losing consciousness.

Louis came to looking up at the blurry gray clouds overhead. He then found himself on his right side before returning to his back.

He realized the apparitions blocking the sky were medics, strapping him to a backboard, shining flashlights in his eyes and placing an oxygen mask over his mouth and nose.

Louis tried to speak, coughing blood into the oxygen mask before scraping it off his face with his right hand.

"Is he all right?" he struggled to speak.

The medic was trying to reposition the oxygen mask over his mouth when Louis grabbed his wrist and pushed it aside. "Is the President all right?" he barked, with blood flying from his mouth and nose.

The upside down face of the medic above him nodded his head repeatedly, attempting to communicate with Louis, knowing he couldn't hear him, seeing the blood flowing from both of his ruptured ears.

Louis' last vision was the removal of the oxygen mask and the hand of the medic approaching his face with a large intubation tool.

27

Nathan was still in the lab at Quantico when he heard the gunshot just before the loud explosion while on the phone with Louis.

"Louis, what happened?" he said before hearing a louder gunshot, then another explosion, then a third and a fourth, and four more in rapid succession.

"Louis, are you all right? Talk to me, man. I can't hear you; talk to me, Bro," Nathan said while dialing Paul Biggins' extension on a landline. It rang his cell phone.

"Agent Biggins."

"Paul, this is Nathan Malone at Quantico; this is an emergency. I was on the phone with Louis and heard gunshots and eight loud explosions. He was on the roof of the RiverHouse building a couple of thousand feet south of the funeral location; I'm still connected to his cell phone but can't hear anything."

"We heard the explosions from that direction, but didn't hear any gunshots. Hold while I radio this in."

"This is Special Agent Paul Biggins, I have confirmation that the explosions were from the roof of the RiverHouse building across the Highway to the south; be advised that gunfire has been exchanged on the roof and that a contract investigator is on site at that location."

"This is Agent Wilson, Secret Service; I have an agent at that location but cannot raise him on the radio," Paul heard over the radio before returning to his cell phone and telling Nathan, "I have to go Nathan, agents are on the way to the location now, I'll call you when I know something." He hung up.

Nathan was still intently listening to the cell phone for any sound he could make out. "Louis, talk to me, man, help's on the way, hang in there, Bro, they're coming."

Over the next four minutes, Nathan listened and heard nothing while aging a lifetime over the phone, pleading with Louis to speak to him.

Nathan heard two additional gunshots over the phone, pleading, "Come on, Louis, talk to me, help's on the way, man, help is on the way."

A long two minutes later, Nathan heard noise from the cell phone that sounded like gravel being kicked, then he heard Louis's voice. "I'm shot, I can't hear you. I'm on the roof of the building next to the elevator. I need help, Bro," Louis coughed. "I need help."

"Help's on the way, hang in there, don't you die on me, Bro."

"I can't hear you, Bro, I'm shot," Nathan heard while dialing 911 on his desk phone.

"911 operator, what is your emergency?"

"This is Nathan Malone calling from the FBI facility Quantico, Virginia; I just lost contact with my partner, who is located on the roof of the RiverHouse building at the corner of Army Navy Drive and Joyce Street in Arlington. I heard gunfire and explosions over the phone and my partner told me over his cell phone that he was shot."

"You're at Quantico, sir?"

"Yes, I am."

"And he's in Arlington?"

"Yes, that's correct."

"Hold one moment while I connect you to Arlington emergency services."

"911 operator, what is your emergency?"

Nathan began to speak when he heard, "This is the 911 operator in Quantico, I have an emergency call about an agent that needs medical attention. He's been shot, he's in your district; go ahead sir. I'll stay on the line."

Nathan repeated what he told the original operator and gave them the address of the building that he looked up on his laptop.

"You say he's on the roof?"

"Yes, he's on the roof; that's where the gunshots happened. He was covering the funeral at Arlington just north of his location."

"Emergency services are already on the way, sir, can I get your name and callback number please?"

Nathan told the operator his name and his cell phone number, as well as the office number in the lab before they hung up the phone and he again called out to Louis on his cell phone.

Nathan again called Paul Biggins, who answered the phone immediately.

"Agent Biggins."

"Paul, this is Nathan again, emergency services are on the way to the location."

"Yep, and the parking lot is getting crowded with Police, Secret Service and FBI responders, not to mention the SWAT teams. We're all headed to the roof now. I'll have to call you back." Then the phone went dead.

Nathan was pacing the floor before sitting down at his laptop and looking at the tracking screen. All the sniper teams were still in place, but the tracking device attached to the fire control console was offline.

The monitor in the main lab was tuned to CNN and all of the technicians were watching as the developments unfurled live on national television. News crews that couldn't make it into the funeral were already on the scene and reporting live from the curb, showing the parking lot crawling with police and federal agents.

A couple of minutes later they showed two helicopters approaching the roof, one of which was a med flight chopper; the other looked to have SWAT team personnel standing on the skids as it disappeared over the edge of the roof. Nathan was up pacing the floor, watching the screen as reporters cut to the studio for an update from Arlington.

The anchor reported that the funeral was still underway then reiterated what was known about the situation, stating that explosions occurred above the RiverHouse building in Arlington and that gunfire was heard at the same time. The RiverHouse building occupants were evacuated to the parking lot and were not being allowed to leave the area at this point.

They switched back to the on-scene reporter showing the hectic activity in the parking lot, along with the Police and Federal agents coming in and out of the building. The camera then looked skyward and watched the med flight helicopter fly away, heading northeast toward DC as the reporter listened to someone through her earpiece, then reported that the helicopter was in route to George Washington University Hospital's Trauma unit.

Nathan's cell phone rang, it was Paul. "Ok, Nathan, I have an update."

"How's Louis, is he ok?"

"He's on the way to the Trauma Unit by helicopter now. He's in bad shape; he was shot in the chest and has shrapnel in his arms, legs, butt and in the back of his head. He lost a lot of blood before they got to him."

"What can I do? I need to get to the hospital ASAP."

"He's at GWU Hospital in DC, or will be in a minute. The place is going to get crowded; call me if you can't get in. I'll make it happen. Nathan, what was Louis doing on top of this building?"

"I don't know, Paul, he was checking all the sniper nests that last time I spoke with him, before I called him and all hell broke loose."

"I saw him at Arlington, checking the snipers before he left the cemetery, but then lost track of him before the funeral."

"Let me get out of here, Paul, I got to get to the hospital. We'll talk again later. Bye."

Nathan grabbed the reports he'd completed, along with his laptop and asked one of the techs to drive him to the motor pool to get another car.

Twenty minutes later, he was on Interstate 95, barreling north as fast as the car would go. *What am I going to tell Diane?* he thought. I was supposed to be watching out for him. *I'm responsible for this, because I brought Louis in on the investigation.*

Nathan arrived at George Washington University Hospital at 3:45 pm. The heavy traffic and the security presence forced him to park several blocks away and jog to the hospital entrance, where there was a security checkpoint in place, and several news trucks set up on New Hampshire Ave. as well as I Street.

Nathan was stopped at the main entrance. He showed his credentials to the Police officer and was directed to an FBI agent standing just inside the door.

"What's your business here, Mr. Malone?"

"Louis Parker, the man they flew in to the trauma center from Arlington, is my partner and close friend. I need to get to him as soon as possible."

"I'm sorry, but I can't let you through. I have no way of knowing who is who at this point."

"You can call Special Agent Paul Biggins, the agent Louis and I work for at Quantico; he can identify me."

"Sorry, but I don't know an Agent named Paul Biggins."

"Well, hold on just a minute, I'll get him on the phone for you," Nathan said as he dialed Paul's number.

"Special Agent Biggins."

"Paul, this is Nathan, I'm at the entrance of the hospital. The FBI detail at the door won't allow me to pass; can you speak to him?"

"Of course, hand him the phone."

Nathan handed the phone to the young agent, who identified himself to Paul.

"This is Special Agent Paul Biggins; I am inside the hospital just outside the door to the trauma unit where Louis Parker is in emergency surgery. Nathan Malone, my investigator you have stopped at the door, is cleared to enter the building; direct him to the trauma unit immediately on my authority."

The young agent handed Nathan his cell phone and said, "Sorry for the delay, sir; the trauma unit is next to the emergency unit through those double doors there," as he pointed across the room. "Special Agent Biggins is already there."

Without speaking, Nathan headed for the double doors and through them, down the long hallway that led to the emergency services department, where he found Paul, along with several other FBI and Secret Service agents, talking outside the entrance to the trauma unit.

Nathan approached them with his laptop in one hand and a two-inch thick folder containing printed reports and supporting documentation intended for Paul.

"Gentlemen, this is Nathan Malone, one of my special investigators and Louis Parker's close friend," Paul said to the group of men huddled around the door.

"Paul, can I speak to you for a moment, alone?" Nathan said as politely as he could muster.

"Of course, I'll be right back," Paul said to the others.

The two stepped away from the crowd, about 10 feet down the hall, before Nathan asked, "How is he doing in there?"

"He's still in surgery. There's been no update in the last hour."

"Was anyone else hurt, anyone at the cemetery?"

"No one at the cemetery was hurt, just startled; the funeral proceeded as planned and everyone left in an orderly manner. We found two dead men on the roof and a dead Secret Service Agent in the elevator. Why? What's going on here Nathan, and don't tell me that you don't know."

Nathan looked Paul in the eyes and took a deep breath before saying, "Everything I know about this is in these reports," as he handed the folder to Paul. "We had no way of knowing who else might be involved in this plot; that's the reason I demanded Louis be brought in on this. I knew I could trust him."

"What plot are you talking about, Nathan?" Paul asked, as he stepped closer in front of him, staring at his face intently.

"We uncovered evidence that Richland and Senator Thomaston, along with an unknown number of associates, were planning the assassination of the President and Vice President before Richland's assassination. Richland would have become President and Thomaston would've become VP."

"And you have evidence to back all this up?"

"It's all in the folder I just handed you. Have you identified the two other men on the roof?"

"We've identified one of them; the other was blown to bits by what appears to have been grenades."

"I think you'll find the men's names were Oleg Hatalsky and Robert Hauser; both of them worked for Richland at the CIA. Richland and Thomaston hired them to pull off the assassinations, and I think you'll find the grenade came from a 40 mm grenade launcher that's probably still sitting in the ice cream truck where they mounted it."

"You're telling me that they planned to use a 40 mm grenade launcher to assassinate the President and the Vice President at the same time, while at the funeral at Arlington?" Paul pressed.

"Had they succeeded, there would've been many more deaths besides the President and Vice President; there could have been hundreds of deaths if the grenade launcher was allowed to rain grenades down on the crowd in the cemetery."

"What do you mean by 'if the grenade launcher was allowed to'?" Paul asked.

"We intercepted some of the key components of the remote fire control system and modified them before they were returned, prior to Hauser and Hatalsky receiving them."

"You intercepted and modified these components and allowed them back into the hands of the men who would use them to assassinate the President and Vice President of the United States?" Paul said, with his eyes wide and his jaw clenched tightly.

"Those modifications prevented them from actually launching the high explosive grenades onto the cemetery. When they set the selector switch for high explosive on the remote firing console, the tracking device we embedded in the interface transmitted the location of the remote fire control system console to the grenade launcher, which then re-aimed the launcher to fire on the remote console location. That's where the grenades came from that detonated above the building, destroying the fire control console while it was active, causing the grenade launcher to deactivate."

"This grenade launcher is still out there somewhere? How do we find it?"

"It has to be within 1500 m of the gravesite and we believe it's mounted in a white ice cream truck with multicolored balloons painted on it. I also have an address in Seven Corners where we just learned they were keeping the truck in a garage. It's all in the report that's in your hands."

Paul stood there flipping through the pages in the folder, moving his eyes from the pages up to Nathan's eyes and back to the report, trying to absorb everything Nathan was telling him.

"Stay right here; don't move from this location," Paul told him before returning to the group of agents nearby.

Nathan watched the group of men as they reacted to what Paul was telling them. They all drew in closer to Paul to hear everything he was saying and all of them at one point in the brief conversation looked over to Nathan before refocusing their attention on Paul and the documents he held in his hands.

As Paul turned to walk back toward Nathan, every one of the agents began speaking over their radios or dialing numbers on their cell phones. "Come with me," Paul told Nathan as he walked toward the double doors at the end of the hall, where no one was standing.

Paul took out his cell phone and hit a speed dial number before holding the phone to his ear and waiting a few seconds. "Hello, this Special Agent Biggins. I have a priority communication for the Director, please put him in contact with me immediately.

"Mr. Director, this Special Agent Paul Biggins. I am at the trauma unit at George Washington. Sir, I am in possession of evidence involving a plot to assassinate POTUS and V-POTUS during today's funeral." Paul listened for a moment before answering "Yes sir, Senator Thomaston." Again, Paul listened for a few moments. "Thank you sir, I can be reached at this number; we're on our way now."

"Nathan, I hope you've got your ducks in a row. The Director is taking action immediately based on what you've told me."

"I'll swear it to a judge."

Paul stepped over to the nurse's station, handed him his card with Nathan's number on it and told them to call the numbers immediately, as soon as any update was available.

"We have to go over to the Director's office now."

"Paul," Nathan said, "we had no way of knowing who else was involved in this; it's the only reason we handled it the way we did. I'm telling you the truth; it's all in those reports."

"I think I understand, Nathan; it's just one hell of a shock to find such a plan in place and being executed, without the FBI or Secret Service knowing anything about it."

"That's the thing, though, many of Richland's and Thomaston's cronies are in the FBI and Secret Service. There's a list of the ones I know of in the report, but I did not know how complete the list was or if any of them were involved. Some of the names may surprise you."

"We have to get over to the Director's office now. I'm sure we will go over this several times." Paul led Nathan out of the hospital into his car and drove the short distance to the J. Edger Hoover Federal building. They pulled into the runaround area of the building, where Paul parked the car and they proceeded inside to the elevators and to the top floor of the building.

Paul led Nathan to a small office located just down the hall from the director's office. "You will need to stay in here while I am in the Director's office."

Paul left the room and shut the door behind him. Nathan took a seat at the table and sat his laptop in front of him as he stared at the clock between the two monitors that indicated 4:20 pm.

His nervous energy got the best of him and he stood up and began pacing from the door to the opposite wall between the two tables, back and forth, trying not to look at the clock.

Nathan's mind was racing with concern over Louis' condition and jumping back and forth between Louis and the conversation in the hospital hallway with Paul.

Did I explain it clearly? he thought. *Did I make him understand what I was saying?* kept coming up in his thoughts as he paced the floor, hoping for good news about his friend's condition.

When Nathan's cell phone rang it scared the hell out of him and shook him from his thoughts, almost making him trip over his own feet. "Hello, this is Nathan Malone."

"Nathan, this is Paul. You said you included an address where that truck may be found. I can't locate it in the documents you gave me; are you sure it's here?"

"I believe it is, hold on while I check the copy on my laptop," Nathan opened his computer and found the report still open. He searched the document for Seven Corners and moved from each reference to the next until he located the address.

"Paul, it's on page 77, near the bottom in the last paragraph–do you see it?"

"Hold on," Paul said as he flipped through the pages to locate page number 77. "I found it, thanks Nathan. Any word on Louis' condition yet?"

"Not yet, Paul."

"Hang in there, Nathan, keep a good thought," Paul told him before hanging up.

Paul was just down the hall in the Director's office, with the Director and his staff going over the information that Nathan gave him at the hospital. One of the staffers was running between the office and the high-speed copier down the hall in a relay race, making 10 duplicate copies of the large report and supporting data for the men in the Director's office.

"How credible is this information, Biggins?" the Director asked. "How credible is the source of yours?"

"Nathan Malone has worked for us off and on for the last 12 years; we have never received a bad piece of information from his research."

"Where did all of this come from?"

"He and Louis Parker, the man that's in the trauma center now, have been researching all of the hard drives and telecom data that were harvested during the murder investigation of Senator Richland. They have all the hard drives in the lab that came from the private security company's computer systems that were located in Fayetteville, North Carolina, as well as Senator Richland's personal laptop and the laptop of his aide that was found shot to death in Georgetown, and the evidence that arrived anonymously at the Memphis field office."

"Why wasn't this information brought to light sooner by these men?" the Director asked. "Why did they wait until today of all days to bring it to you?"

"Nathan indicated that he and Louis believed there may be more conspirators in on this plot than they have identified. At the hospital, Nathan told me privately that he and Louis developed a list of known associates of Senators Richland and Thomaston that today work for the FBI and Secret Service."

"Where is that list? We have not seen it among these documents," the Director asked.

"Sir, I have that list, and withheld it from this report. There are names on that list that I feel should not be made common knowledge among the investigators just yet, for the same reasons that Nathan Malone and Louis Parker kept their findings from us."

The Director thought for a moment then said, "Paul, I want you and Agent Williams to remain in the room. Will the rest of you gentlemen please step outside to the hallway for a few minutes?"

"Agent Mark Williams is the senior Secret Service Agent assigned to this investigation," the director told Paul. "Special Agent Paul Biggins, the AIC of the FBI investigation team at Quantico," the director told Williams.

"Let us see the list, Paul."

Paul removed the folded printed sheet from his inside jacket pocket and handed it to the director, who read each of the 23 names aloud, along with the agency where they worked.

"Paul, there are some distinguished names on this list, with long tenures at FBI and Secret Service."

Paul thought for a moment, and then spoke. "Nathan didn't say that any of these men were directly involved, just that they were known associates of Senators Richland and Thomaston. That said, I believe it to be in all of our best interests if these men were independently interviewed and quietly investigated prior to dismissing any potential involvement."

The Director spoke up. "I believe that would be prudent as long as it was not made public knowledge within the agencies. What do we know about Nathan and Louis? What are their backgrounds?"

"Nathan was a special operations controller at CIA and has been a part-time contractor for the Justice Department and specifically the FBI ever since leaving CIA. Louis was an Army Ranger / Sniper recruited into CIA operations section with a long history of covert field operations in Africa as well as Central America. He is a mechanic; worked alone in the field. Nathan was his controller. They met on The Farm. When Richland returned from Vietnam, he was the Southeast Asia section chief. He then took over the Africa desk and Nathan was one of the controllers in that section. Richland never interacted with or possessed direct knowledge of Louis' identity; everything passed through Nathan."

Agent Williams asked, "Why was he brought in on this investigation?"

"Nathan Malone requested his assistance after the assassination attempt at this building. I believe that the information that Nathan uncovered made him feel he needed someone he could absolutely trust working with him."

The director asked, "So how did they plan on stopping this assassination attempt and how did this grenade launcher play into all of this?"

"They were researching the data found on the hard drives and apparently found highly detailed offshore banking records and purchase orders through an arms dealer in Miami, Florida. One of the weapons that was ordered and delivered was this H & K GMG, an automatic 40 mm grenade launcher. It was delivered in pieces to separate locations and reassembled by the two men who were found dead on top of the building and were working for Richland and Thomaston."

"And what happened to this grenade launcher? Why did it launch the grenades at the top of the building?" the Director asked.

"Nathan and Louis somehow managed to intercept key components of the weapons guidance system and made electronic modifications that caused the weapon to fire on the remote fire control system console. Louis figured out the location of the console on top of the RiverHouse building and arrived shortly before the grenades detonated. The exact timing of the events is still unclear; however, it is clear that Louis was shot by one of the two men with a sniper rifle, which must have been the backup plan in case the grenade launcher attack failed. Louis fatally shot the rifleman after himself being shot in the chest and considerably ripped up by the grenades."

The Director sat back in his chair and thought for about a minute without speaking. The silence filled the room before he spoke. "Agent Williams, I want you to locate Senator Thomaston and get him here to my office as soon as possible. I need to call my boss at Justice and my counterpart at Secret Service, along with the district court judge, and schedule some time for us with the President. Let's get it done, gentlemen."

Agent Williams made a call to his office for a report on Senator Thomaston's location and left the building, heading to the Senate office complex.

Nathan spent his time in the small office down the hall, wiping data from his laptop that did not pertain to the investigation. Louis had been in surgery more than two and a half hours at this point, with no update being made available to anyone.

Paul received a call from a member of his team to notify him that the ice cream truck with the grenade launcher was located at the Pentagon Maintenance facility, just southeast of the Pentagon. EOD personnel had disarmed the launcher.

"Any word on Louis yet?" Paul asked Nathan as he walked into the small office.

"I have not heard a damn thing since you left. Paul, what happened? What is going to happen?" Nathan asked.

"The Director's been apprised of all the information in your report. He wants us back in his office shortly. He is briefing Justice, the district judge and the President on your findings, and Senator Thomaston will likely be here in the next hour."

"Is he going to be arrested?"

"I am not sure how this is going to play out today, Nathan, but in the end, he will be."

"What about the list of names I gave you?"

"Every one of those men will be quietly investigated to determine if they are involved. With all of the resources you have access to, you didn't uncover any involvement by them. It is likely that we may not either."

"What about the grenade launcher and the two other men on the roof?"

"We found the grenade launcher; it was near the Pentagon, and it's now disarmed. And as for the two dead men on the roof, you were right about their identities."

"What happens next?"

"Whatever happens, Nathan, I am sure you will feel that more should be done," Paul said. "It may take 50 years for all of this to come out in an accurate, detailed accounting. They will never let it be known how close they came to assassinating the President and Vice President. That would be bad for business."

Paul was in and out of the room several times. The last time he came into the room, he left the door open so Nathan could see the hallway. A few moments later, Senator Thomaston walked past the open door, escorted by a Secret Service detail into the FBI director's office. Nathan recognized his face. "That's him."

"He didn't attend the funeral today, Nathan, the funeral of his longtime friend and colleague. He remained in his Senate office to watch it on television while every other member of the Senate and the House attended. He showed his hand, Nathan. I think you got him."

Paul's cell phone rang; it was one of the agents on security detail at the trauma center. Paul stepped outside the door to the hallway before taking the call.

"Agent Biggins," Paul answered.

"I thought you would want to know, he's out of surgery and being moved to the recovery unit."

"That's good news; anything else?"

"The surgeons removed 58 pieces of shrapnel from him. The bullet passed through the vest into his chest and through the upper lobe of his left lung, and made it through his back rib cage before stopping just below the skin on his back, against the vest."

"Damn, how do you survive that, and still be able to kill the man who just shot you? Thanks for the update. Call me as soon as you know anything else."

Paul stepped back inside the room and shut the door. "Louis is out of surgery, heading for the recovery room," he told Nathan.

Nathan could not hold back the tears of joy and excitement as the horrible stress from not knowing his friend's condition released in that moment.

He turned toward the window and looked down at the street well below, finally able to take a deep breath as the stress-driven adrenaline finally released the muscles in his throat and chest.

"I need to call Louis' wife Diane," Nathan said. "How do I explain this to her?"

"First, tell her he is alive."

The End

ABOUT THE AUTHOR

Dave Dragon is a U.S. Army Veteran, who makes his home in Palm Harbor, Florida. At the time of this publication, he is the Information Technologies Director for a major Pharmaceutical Formulation and Manufacturing corporation, which specializes in Cancer-specific formulations for Oncology patients in Clinical Trials.

An Electrical Engineer in his early civilian career, Dave made the transition into Systems Programming, Engineering and Information Infrastructure Management, with certifications as an Oracle Database Professional, Project Management Professional and others.

Dave holds advanced Black Belts in Taekwondo, Hapkido and Judo, and working on Krav Maga. He has played guitar and drums professionally, plays six-string banjo and is learning violin/fiddle for the challenge and enjoyment.

As a member of the Iron Butt Association, Dave participates in long-distance competitive riding challenges, and successfully completed the IBA 50CC Challenge by riding from the beach at Jacksonville, FL to the beach at San Diego, CA, in thirty-nine hours three minutes, earning additional awards for One Thousand miles in under twenty-four hours and Fifteen Hundred miles in under twenty-four hours, riding his customized BMW R1200GS Adventure.

Dave can be reached via email at: One.Asterisk.Publishing@gmail.com

Proof

28080041R10194

Made in the USA
Charleston, SC
28 March 2014